D0438900

H719pa APR 14 '82
HOLLAND, CECELIA
Pacific Street

Pacific Street

Also by
Cecelia Holland

FICTION

The Bear Flag (1990)
The Lords of Vaumartin (1988)
Pillar of the Sky (1985)
The Belt of Gold (1984)
The Sea Beggars (1982)
Home Ground (1981)
City of God (1979)
Two Ravens (1977)
Floating Worlds (1975)
Great Maria (1974)
The Death of Attila (1973)
The Earl (1971)
Antichrist (1970)
Until the Sun Falls (1969)
The Kings in Winter (1968)
Rakóssy (1967)
The Firedrake (1966)

FOR CHILDREN

The King's Road (1970)
Ghost on the Steppe (1969)

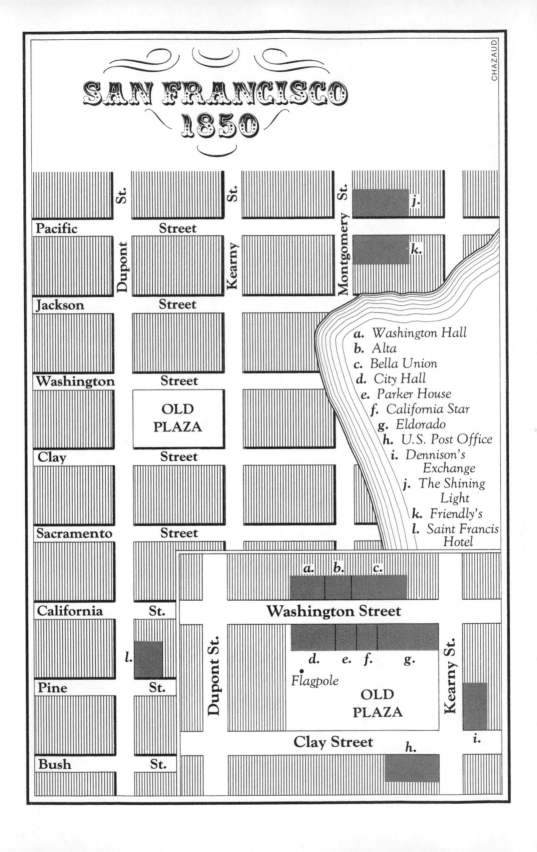

Pacific Street

Cecelia Holland

A Peter Davison Book
HOUGHTON MIFFLIN COMPANY
Boston New York London • *1992*

For information about permission to reproduce selections from
this book, write to Permissions, Houghton Mifflin Company,
215 Park Avenue South, New York, New York 10003

Library of Congress Cataloging in Publication Data

Holland, Cecelia, date.
Pacific Street / Cecelia Holland.
p.   cm.
"A Peter Davison book."
ISBN 0-395-56144-2
I. Title.
PS3558.O348P33   1992   91-27314
813'.54—dc20   CIP

Printed in the United States of America

MP 10 9 8 7 6 5 4 3 2 1

For my friend
DAVID JACKSON

Pacific Street

1

IT WAS A BRIGHT SUNNY DAY, without fog. He was walking on the cliff at Metini. It was as if he had been a long time gone. Behind him like gray bones in the grass lay the broken wooden posts of the old Russian fort. Ahead of him the curving arm of the land jutted into the sea, combing the sea's white edge.

His sister, Anna, stood on the cliff, her back to him. He rushed toward her, eager, almost running, glad to see her again. He said her name. But before he could reach her she disappeared.

He stood on the edge of the cliff enduring a grief like a hole in his chest. The grass rippled in the wind off the sea.

Anna's voice spoke. "The people join the generations together. The people grow like the grass with roots in the mothers and the fathers, with our children in our arms like seed in the grass, and when our children stand here we shall be their roots, and they shall hold their children in their arms like seed."

His sister's voice spoke, and the grass rippled in the wind off the sea. The wind grew stronger and stronger until it tore the grass up out of the soil. He saw the roots broken; he saw the blades blown away on the wind. He ran after them but they blew in all directions, and finally he ran aimlessly, his hands up, chasing whatever floating shred was closest. Catching nothing.

As he ran, the sea cliff was gone and the sky was gone, until he was running alone and in no place, around him a vast blackness like under the sea, roaring and empty and cold. And he knew if he stopped he would fall into the cold darkness, and so he went on running, but his legs were heavy, and he was getting tired.

Mitya opened his eyes. The dream still clung to him. His face was damp from the mist, from the salt spray off the bay. He lay on the deck of the lumberboat, in the prow, and now and then the boat dipped its nose into the bay and cast a sheet of water against the rail. The sun was going down.

He sat up, hunched to keep from bumping his head on the rail. His lips were dry and salty. Behind him he could hear men moving around on the boat, calling out to one another, swearing, laughing. White men. They had let him take passage across the bay because he had helped them split and load the lumber now stacked on the deck, but that did not make them his friends. He settled down with his back to the lumber, looking out over the prow of the boat, across the rough water into the fog.

The edge of his mind still held on to the dream of Metini, and he caught at it, but that drove it off entirely. Only the black void remained. He fought against the sorrow of the void.

On his left now, beyond the stacked lumber and the barge's rail, loomed the steep, lumpy peak of an island. The water here was much smoother. The lumberboat settled, and behind him a sharp voice called and the white men took in the sail and began to use oars. The boat moved forward in glides and jerks. Mitya sat still in the prow, unnoticed.

He straightened, his skin tingling, as gaunt, towering shapes appeared in the fog before him. He almost shrank down to hide from them. Then he saw they were ships at anchor.

The lumberboat nosed in past a low, flat hull with two masts, bits of rope and canvas hanging off the yards like treebeard. No men walked the deck; the railing was broken and rotting. Ahead the fog glowed in patches and points that flashed and blinked. A schooner rose against this light and slipped silently by, back into the darkness. Its bowsprit was broken off and there were holes bashed in the cabin wall. Masts and yards like stripped trees thrust up into the sky on either side and before him. In ranks the seagulls roosted on the decks and the yards.

The birds squealed and cried, and the waves slapped on the hulls of the ships; old wood groaned. Somewhere a bell clanged with the rocking of the waves. There were no sounds of men from these ships, but now a low hum reached Mitya's ears, coming from up ahead, vague as the fog made audible.

The lumberboat poked along, its oars grinding and splashing, making a crooked way through the deserted ships. A white man climbed onto the stack of lumber and called out directions to the rowers. They slowed even more, groping through fog that began at the level of the rail and climbed away into the sky, stinking of old smoke. Beneath the dense mist the air was clear and cold and still. In the glassy water a rat as long as Mitya's arm swam boldly past the lumberboat, reached the slanting hawser of an anchored hulk, and climbed up toward the deck above. As the lumberboat passed, the rat turned, and in the boat's lantern light its eyes glowed an instant, red as drops of blood.

The lumberboat slid past a sinking ship, its deck even with the surface of the bay, awash with every little wave. The hum in the air was now a roar.

Ahead, through the swaying masts, he saw more lights. The roar grew steadily louder in his ears, a heavy pelt of sound woven of thousands of smaller sounds, voices, footsteps, the clang of pots, the thump of axes, coughing and crying, snoring and laughing, things thrown and things caught, things built and things falling down. He knew this noise, he had heard it before, on the Sacramento, where also thousands of men were gathered, and all their individual doings wound together in one vast place called a city. Ahead of him, on the bayshore, was another city.

Through the fog its lights were appearing, every moment more and sharper, some dull and pale and some hot and bright, spreading out up and down from him, and ahead of him piling up into ribbons and blotches and great glowing heaps. Now he could hear the waves tumbling against the shore. The closest of the lights ranged just beyond, a line of open fires on the beach; against their fluttering orange he saw the shapes of people walking back and forth in a constant hurrying stream.

He knew its name, this place. The other men had called it San Francisco.

Now the lumberboat was butting in toward a cove like a notch in the beach. Directly ahead a crowd stood packed around a great fire, their voices like a bee swarm. The shallows and the dry sand just above the waves were littered with pieces of wrecked boats, with boxes and barrels, with scraps and rags and broken tools.

Beyond the high-tide line was a solid wall of huts, put up of branches and rocks, pieces of boxes and long flaps of cloth. Mitya sniffed, and the stink reached him of burnt meat and bad whiskey. He grunted, his fears shrinking. This was not so different; this was another place like Sutterville, on the Sacramento.

The lumberboat rocked under heavy footsteps; a man paced up past the stacked lumber into the bow and leapt down into the water. He had one of the boat's ropes over his shoulder, and turning, seeing Mitya, he shouted, "Hey! Injun! Give me a hand here."

He was pointing across the prow, to the far side, where another rope hung coiled. Mitya took it and stepped off the boat into the water, going in up to his thighs. The bottom was soft and mucky under his feet. He drove through the shallows toward the dry land, lugging the rope over his shoulder. The other men jumped into the water and pushed and heaved the lumberboat after him onto the shore.

"Let's go! Tote that wood on up here — hey! Clear a path. This here is Mr. Brannan's wood."

The lumber was stacked high on the barge's deck and lashed down tight. The workmen stood around waiting for the ropes to be untied; the boss climbed up onto the stack, feeling for the knot.

Mitya lingered only a moment. He had already gotten what he wanted from these men, the ride across the bay. The roar of the city was in his ears, and the lights dazzled him. He went away quickly into the crowd, away from the shore.

2

DAISY'S HAIR WAS FINE as milkweed fluff, the color of a dandelion, the shape of a bindweed tendril. Frances gathered it in both hands and the loose mass slid softly over her fingers, slippery and smooth.

She loved the luxury of its touch, so unlike her own hair, coarse and tight and black as soot. Winding the blond tresses around her hand, she heaped it on top of Daisy's head like a great soft crown and stuck pins in to hold it there.

"It won't nohow stay up that way," Daisy said. "I can feel it coming down already."

Frances chuckled. "That's part of the trick, dovie."

Only the thin canvas wall of the lean-to and ten feet of air separated them from the street; through the wall came a constant babble of voices and a tramp of feet that sometimes sounded as if everybody in San Francisco was walking at her. The lamp made the cramped space smoky. Daisy sat on the stool, her round white shoulders hunched a little against the night chill; she cast a sideways look at the canvas wall, at the uproar filtering in through it.

Frances picked up the loose strands of hair and twisted them around her fingers so that they dangled softly over the girl's white throat. "There now."

"Frances," Daisy said, "are you sure we're gonna get away with this?"

Frances rapped her on the shoulder with her knuckle. "Only

idea I got." She turned, reached behind her to pull back the flap of dirty canvas, and called into the foggy night air. "Gilbert! You ready over there?"

Gil Marcus stuck his head into the opening, into the yellow lamplight. His forehead was ridged with tension. "It's not going to get any readier, Mammy."

"Well then," Frances said, "let's go."

Daisy stood, turning toward her. The satin dress hissed and sighed as she moved. Carefully Frances smoothed the wide skirt, shaking out the flounces along the hem. She had worked hard on the dress, cutting open the bodice and easing the waist, and now she gave a last quick fit to it, tucking the smooth cloth around Daisy's body. Reaching in over the deep neckline she lifted the girl's breasts into the top of the bodice. The warmth of Daisy's flesh reached her like a gust of perfume.

When she bent down to straighten the hem again, Daisy took the top of the neckline and tugged at it, trying to cover herself. Frances swatted at her hands.

"Leave it. It's fine." Daisy's breasts rode halfway out of the dress like ripe peaches in a full bowl. "You look very pretty, Daisy."

"Hell," Daisy said. She turned around again, like somebody dancing, her hands loose and fluttering. "I wish I had a looking glass."

"I'll get you the best looking glass in San Francisco," Frances said, "if we get through this tonight." She stroked her hands down Daisy's shoulders and plump, fair upper arms, trying to calm her. Daisy's cheeks, pinker with rouge, were stiff with strain; the soft, sweet red-painted curve of her mouth was caught at the corners in a fitful pout; her eyes were wide and fearful.

Frances said, "Watch me, dovie. I'll be there."

Daisy reached up and gripped her hand, the pretty pale fingers closing over Frances' smaller, darker ones. "Let's go."

Frances' heart thumped. She turned and went out through the gap in the lean-to wall and held the canvas open so that Daisy could come through without having to touch anything dirty.

Outside was Gil Marcus, a lantern gripped in his hand, a bung-starter thrust through his belt. He went ahead, up onto the make-shift stage, and climbed up one of the barrels on which the plank floor rested. Facing the passing crowd in the street, he began to swing the lantern around.

"Here it is, boys — here's what you been waiting for!"

His voice was creaky with nerves. Frances shook her head to herself: this was not Gil's best line of work. Short, square-shouldered in his plaid shirt, he looked inconsequential, not worth heeding. He stopped and cleared his throat.

"Come on, fellows. Let's gather around." As he swung the lantern its light swooped in a wide circle around him, beaming on the empty little stage, catching only the edge of the street; the crowd flooding by showed up as a flutter of arms, a sleeve, a foot, a white face turned briefly toward him. Nobody stopped.

Frances went over toward the corner of the stage, where she had left the basket of flowers, and looked quickly around. They had found this place by luck, only that afternoon, on one of the trails that led up toward the hill and, farther, the lagoon. It was a little patch of gravelly sand tucked between two sprawling, flimsy buildings, half hut and half tent, where miners slept and ate and drank and gamed. A bigger tent, the light of lamps inside turning its flapping canvas peak to a dirty-yellow pyramid, stood just across the crowded street; men went in and out of it in a steady stream. The path between was a river of dirt, its pounded surface constantly churned into the air, frosting everything along it with pale dust.

The previous tenant of the patch of ground where Frances stood had obviously meant to build something here, had dragged an old longboat up from the harbor and torn off some of the wooden planks and stacked them, and then disappeared. The boat lay tilted back along the slope just behind her, half gone. The two tents where she and Daisy sheltered were built against its side. Broken planks littered the ground around it. Out of the planks Frances and Gil Marcus had put up this makeshift stage, spending a good part of the afternoon doing it, and now Gil

Marcus, sweating, hoarse, was calling out to the uncaring world for some attention.

"Now, boys, what you been waiting for, all these days, all these months, what you been looking for — "

Daisy had come up behind Frances, shy, staying in the lee of the stage. Now she said, under her breath, "That won't work." She hitched up the white satin skirts in her hands and scrambled up the barrel onto the uneven plank floor.

Frances followed her as far as the edge of the platform and bent down for the basket of flowers. She had filled it in the afternoon, picking all the blooms off the steep, sandy hillside just above the broken boat. The long white petals were curling and limp. She could not help but see it as an omen. She swallowed, feeling grim, already defeated.

Above her, Daisy straightened, standing on the stage behind Gil, and gave a twitch to her shirts. He was swinging the lantern; for a moment, as she settled herself, she was in darkness, and then the hazy glow of the lantern flashed over her.

She lifted her head. In the lantern light her white satin dress shone like pale gold. The heavy mass of her hair was already coming loose from its pins, sagging like a silk cushion. In the street, suddenly, the torrent of passing bodies slowed.

"Gil," Daisy called. "Put the lantern down. Let me do it."

Gil stopped shouting and turned toward her. His face settled, hollow-cheeked. He put the lantern down on the stage and backed away, putting one hand on the bungstarter in his belt.

Daisy stepped past him, up to the front of the stage, where the light was bright. She pressed her hands together, lifted her head like a child saying her prayers, and began to sing.

She had a thin little piping voice; Frances could not make it out well enough to recognize the song. What she was working with had nothing to do with the song. Like a rock thrown into the current, her mere presence turned the whole river. Around the front edge of the stage men were gathering, their heads tipped back, their eyes bright in the lantern glow. Behind them a rough voice shouted, "A woman, by God!"

"Nice-lookin' woman," said a bushy-haired man standing up front.

Gil Marcus had backed up as far as he could without falling off the plank platform. He glanced down at Frances, and their eyes met for a moment. Frances turned away from him, annoyed; he looked scared, or sick. She touched her lips with her tongue. Her body coursed with a rush of anticipation. The crowd was pressing closer now, all around the little stage, and a loud whistle shrilled out. Daisy's voice faltered, half drowned in the rising excitement of the men watching her.

Suddenly the stage rocked. A yard from the bushy-haired man, a lanky boy with rope suspenders was climbing up onto the apron of the platform, his eyes hot on Daisy. Seeing him, the crowd let out a wild yell. Close to Frances, another man put his hands on the stage to boost himself up; his hat fell off.

Gil shouted, "Daisy, watch out!" Pulling the bungstarter out of his belt, he started toward the boy in the rope suspenders, the closer of the attackers. But Daisy got there first. She snatched the lantern up off the stage and whacked the boy over the head with it.

The blow caught him square on the skull and stopped him flat-footed. The crowd gasped. For a moment the boy stayed up, swaying, his face frozen in an expression of wide-eyed ecstasy, and then he crashed over backward into the mass of men at the edge of the stage. Like virgins they shrank back from him, and he fell alone into the street. The rest of the men wheeled toward Daisy, rapt. The girl glared all around her.

"Quiet down!" Her singing voice was feeble, but her shouting voice carried like an overseer's. She put the lantern back down where it had been and stepped away, her hands on her hips. "Quiet down, damn you, and treat me like a lady, or I'm leavin'."

A roar of voices answered her. Onlookers filled the street, a wild, stirring mob, but they were staying off the stage. Somebody in the back yelled, "What'll you do for us if you stay, girlie?"

Daisy lifted her head. Her hair was slipping out of its pins, her cheeks were flushed, and her eyes glinted. She said, "You won't find out if you don't settle down." Her lips twitched, as if she had thought of something funny but meant to keep it to herself.

She turned and walked away with a bounce of her hips that brought a raw bellow from the men like a herd of lovesick bulls. "Give her room! Let her be!"

In front of Frances the hatless man was still halfway up onto the stage. The three miners behind him grabbed his belt and flung him bodily off into the crowd, and fought one another to take his place. One, a huge blond hulk, shouted out in a voice thick with accent, "Zing, lady! Shud up, da rest of you. Stand away, an' let da lady zing."

The quilt of faces illuminated by the lantern settled to an eager hush. Beyond the edge of the light, the packed darkness buzzed and seethed, the crowd stretching up and down the street, filling the narrow lanes between the stage and the tents on either side. Frances gripped the stage with one hand; the wood quivered like something alive. Daisy squared herself up, clasped her hands together, and lifted her uncertain voice again.

"Rock of Aaay-ges — cleft for meee — "

A low sigh rose from the faces upturned in the lantern light, and then they were silent. Gil Marcus, his forehead gleaming, paced along the rear of the stage with the bungstarter in his hand while the crowd pushed closer. Voices rose; people in the back could not hear her.

She stopped singing. Instantly a yell went up. "Sing, lady!"

"Not till you're quiet!" She tramped up to the edge of the stage. "Damn it, you wouldn't treat your sister this way!"

At the chorus of whistles and hisses that replied, Daisy put her hands over her ears. Somebody yelled, "My sister don't say damn it!" But the crowd quieted. Maybe the hymns had them in a churchy mood. With a sudden buoyant excitement, Frances watched the vast herd ease off, settling, until in the cool night air the distant clatter of something falling in the tent across the way sounded clear as a little bell.

Daisy smiled. Slow, teasing, she walked forward to the very

edge of the stage, and like an army of angels before the Lord, the men sank down before her.

Now she glanced down at Frances, in the corner, and Frances nodded and smiled and waved her on. The girl cleared her throat and faced the crowd.

"Oh — Jee-sus, Thy savin' grace — "

More confident now, she swung her arms, waved her hands, tossed her head. Every gesture brought a luxurious murmur from the crowd, but no one moved, no one called or whistled. Their docile attention made her bolder. She paced around behind the lantern, drawing their eyes after her like hooked fish. The only songs whose words she knew were hymns, but by the third tune her hips were swaying, her breasts bouncing half out of the satin, her tongue tipping between her lips; she shut her eyes and crooned through "The Old Rugged Cross" until the men shrieked and pounded on one another with their fists. Gil stood behind her, the bungstarter in his hand, but it was Daisy who held the mob back, Daisy alone. Soft with relief, Frances laughed.

It was going better even than she had hoped. Now came the most important part. Up there, wiggling and rolling her shoulders, Daisy reached the end of another song, and Frances took a handful of flowers from the basket and threw them up onto the stage.

Her first toss scattered only a couple of petals past the lantern. Her hand dipped back into the basket for more.

She needed no more. At the first shower of gifts the men howled as if their lungs were split open. Before she could draw her hand out of the basket again, the air was thick with prizes. Leather purses, coins, flasks, playing cards, hats, and scarves pelted the stage. Daisy stepped back, smiling broadly, triumphantly out at them, kissed her fingers to them, waved her hands over her head, and sang "The Twisted Tree on Which My Savior Hangs."

Two songs later she was done. Her voice was fluttering and she was tired; Frances saw it in the slump of her back, the sag of her shoulders. She cleared her throat and shook her head and said, "That's all."

The men screamed and whistled, stamped and bellowed, and flung everything they owned at her feet. "Another one! Sing another one!"

"Later," she called. "Tomorrow." She spread her arms out toward them, leaning over them like a mother. "Go home and go to bed." She turned once around, flirted her big rear end toward the crowd, and came down off the stage beside Frances, and the men sent up a cheer that left Frances' ears ringing. Daisy darted off toward the safety of the lean-to.

Gil stepped forward across the stage, into the torrent of noise, and stood there shouting and waving his arms. Frances could see his lips moving but could not hear him. With the basket she climbed up onto the stage and went quickly around picking up the prizes that littered it. The flowers and paper and hats she tossed toward the street, but the purses and other money she put into the basket. The crowd was still howling and whooping; Gil could not quiet them. Finally, throwing up his hands, he backed away, and he and Frances went down off the stage and left the crowd to yell itself out.

"There's still a lot of people out there," Gil Marcus said. "I hired a few fellows to stand watch."

The smell of perfume reached him and he swallowed. The women still made him tongue-tied and shy. He came only halfway into the little lean-to, filling the space where the flap of canvas was drawn up. It seemed like a frail defense against the turmoil in the street, especially now that the crowd knew that Daisy was here. She sat on the stool, back to him, hands in her lap.

Her face smooth with intent, lips pursed, Frances Hardhardt knelt before Daisy, wiping off the girl's face paint with a handkerchief. Without pausing in the work, Frances said, "Shut the door there, please. Did you hire colored men, as I told you to?"

Stiffly, Gil moved into the room, letting the canvas swing down over the opening. "No, I didn't. I forgot."

She gave him a single hard look. She was small, dark, female: it ruffled Gil that she should try to give him orders. When he had first met her he had assumed she was Daisy's servant. He had also assumed that she was old, a misimpression he now guessed that she worked to create. She was not old, maybe no older than Daisy. And definitely not her servant.

He let his gaze rest on Daisy.

The girl sat motionless, passive under the quick, deft hands, her head bowed. Her plump pink shoulders swelled up out of the dress. Her neck looked soft and white; her hair, still half captive in its pins and loops, was the color of champagne. Gil had not seen a woman up close for a long time, and he told himself again that that was why he liked looking at her so much, why he took this deep pleasure simply from being in the room with her. He said, "I'll be going now, Mammy." He had taken to calling her Mammy when he thought she was old.

Daisy turned to face him. "One third of that's yours." She pointed at the basket.

Gil cleared his throat. Her voice was like a feather drawn across his skin. What he had been doing with them made him deeply uneasy. He could not shake the idea that it was a lot like pimping. He said, "Look, I was just, you know, helping you out, a couple of lone women." His hands moved.

Her blue eyes wide, Daisy was gazing steadily at him, unsmiling, while Frances went behind her and began to take the pins out of her hair.

He mumbled, "I felt sorry for you, that was all. I don't want any of your money. This belongs to you."

Daisy's mouth quirked into a smile. Her cheeks dimpled. She said, "You're a good man, Gil Marcus."

"Thank you. So I'll, I'll — "

Frances said, "Sit down, Gilbert. Take your share out of the basket." She took a brush to the sleek sheen of Daisy's hair.

He could not bring himself to leave, although he still did not want any of their gold. Sharing the gold would certainly make it pimping. He sat down on the bed. Outside there was a shout and a shuffling of feet. He asked, "Are you going to perform again tomorrow?"

"Perform," Daisy said, mouthing the word, and her eyes flashed. The smile widened to a wicked grin. "Why, I think I will, won't I. We could fix the stage better." Her head swiveled, directing her bright, eager gaze toward Frances. "Do we have enough money for that?"

In the basket on the foot of the cot there were purses and sacks of gold dust, Mexican silver dollars, local banknotes; they had plenty of money. Gil lifted his head, hearing the scuffling outside, and Frances said, "We can't do it without you, Gilbert. Now you sound as if you're leaving us." She had a way of talking that ran backwards of her looks, a round Southern eloquence, as if she had been educated.

Gil said, "I told you, Mammy, I got into this because I could see you two needed my help. I don't mean to make a life's work out of it." He jerked up onto his feet, every nerve crackling, at the flat *blam* of a nearby gunshot.

Daisy said, "Oh, God." Just outside the lean-to somebody shouted, and there was a thud.

Frances came forward, past Daisy, past Gil, and pulled the flap of canvas open again. "What's going on here?"

The tent shook. In through the gap in the canvas a huge man walked, not tall, but wide and deep as a barrel. Gil moved up beside Mammy and laid his hand on her arm. "What do you want, Friendly?" He pulled on the little black woman, trying to get her behind him, but she wouldn't budge.

The fat man's face tilted toward him, wreathed in loose folds of fat, the eyelids red rimmed. "You done emptied my saloon with that damn stupid singsong, just when I was making lots of money. I come here to make sure you're moving on."

Frances said, "I think we're staying right here. Who are you?"

Friendly ignored her. His contemptuous gaze swept the little room and returned to Gil Marcus. "You get them and you out of here before tomorrah, mister, else I'll call the Regulators on you." Behind him, in the dark outside the tent, several voices sounded in support of him; he had brought a pack of men. Gil felt the fat man's presence like a weight that filled all the space around him, keeping him from breathing, from venting his rising anger. His fists were clenched at his sides. Friendly turned and pushed out of the gap in the tent wall and the tent trembled again, half uprooted.

Daisy said, "God Almighty. Who was that?" Her voice squeaked.

Frances turned toward Gil, her mouth drawn tight, the skin glossy over her cheekbones. "Who is he?"

Gil gathered in his breath. He should have foreseen this. Abruptly, like a dam bursting, a lot of other things he should have foreseen cascaded through his mind. He said, "That was Friendly — he runs the saloon across the way." He gave a single shake of his head. "This is trouble, Mammy."

Frances glanced at Daisy, perched on the stool, looking like a worried child, and then she faced Gil again. Her smooth black face was wide-eyed, the heavy lips grim. "Who are the Regulators?"

"A gang. Toughs. They wear green jackets; you must have seen them."

"Police?" Daisy asked.

Gil shook his head. "Not really. Maybe once they were. Now they just pretend to be." He sat down on the bed again and reached for the basket. Frances watched him steadily.

"What are you going to do, Gilbert?"

Swiftly he gathered up the banknotes, counted them, tossed out a few he knew to be worthless. Without a scale he could not value the gold they had collected. He took the silver dollars too, then pushed the basket toward Frances. "Take this, hide it somewhere."

"Where are you going?" Her hand closed on the handle of the basket.

He sat there, his hands full of money, and looked from her to Daisy. The girl's eyes shone with uncertainty; she was leaning forward on the stool, her shoulders hunched, her mouth half open. Everything in him strained toward her, as if he could wrap himself around her and defend her against the world. He tore his gaze away and stared at Frances.

"I'm not going anywhere. I'm going to stay here and make sure nobody bothers you the rest of the night. Then tomorrow I'm going over to see the *alcalde*. He's supposed to be in charge here, although I've never noticed him to do much. But maybe you can get some kind of title to this place. Otherwise . . ." He rubbed his nose with one forefinger, tired, getting scared. He guessed the men were long gone that he had hired to stand watch outside. He looked around at the flimsy lean-to, which shook with every breeze. Frances was smiling at him.

She said, "Gilbert, thank you."

"Don't thank me," he said. "I haven't done anything yet." Might not be able to do anything at all, he thought. He got up off the cot and moved toward the door to keep watch.

3

IN THE LIGHT OF THE MORNING SUN things did not seem so bad. Gil Marcus, looking tired and frayed, went off with the paper money. The street was still crowded, men moving steadily back and forth, stirring the dust, and half a dozen of them were sitting on the edge of the stage when Frances went out there. Little heaps of sand had already drifted against the barrels that held the stage up.

Frances knew she had to keep Daisy under cover. If they saw her for free it would lessen their interest in paying.

The men who fringed the stage watched her with an eager attention. They were all white men, whom she could not use. Frances climbed the street a little way, in the other direction from the water.

As she went, she hunched herself over, she drew her shawl up around her head, she screwed her face into a wizened pucker. Nobody noticed little old black mammies, nobody bothered with them. She crept into this figure easily now, after months of learning it; sometimes, doing it, she even felt old.

Not today. Today she felt new and young and full of expectation. The sunlight glittered down on her like gold dust. The noise and movement of the street jumped with vigorous life, a power she could take and use. The breeze in her face smelled like dirt, like sweat and rot, but like work too, work and building. She hurried up the street, not wanting to leave Daisy alone for too long, the soft dust squeezing between her bare toes, strange voices yelling in her ears.

On either side were clumps and lumps of buildings, made of whatever had come to hand, ship's sails and chunks of adobe brick, piles of wood, broken furniture, people's clothes. Nothing seemed permanent or even planned. She passed a man standing on a barrel, waving a rag over his head, and calling in a dull, overused voice, "Shirts — shirts — got some good shirts to sell." He himself was bare-chested. Other men rushed by his barrel, paying no attention.

That was how it went here. None of the men pushing up and down the street cared much about anything going on around him. Each one whirled along in his own cloud of dust, going as fast as he could, his eyes fixed ahead of him, his face set with concentration that ended where he ended.

Frances knew better than that; she kept her eyes open, looking around at everything, taking everything into account.

Under the inch of sandy dust that cushioned it, the narrow street was rutted and scored like a country track. Like the road past Fox Haven, soft under her feet; then, under the softness, hard again, uneven, a sort of warning: things weren't as easy as they seemed. She had run away down that road, from Fox Haven to the sea, and things had not been easy, but now here she was, in this city at the edge of the world, her feet moving light and quick through the dust.

She passed a lean-to that was open-sided toward the street;

within were three big wooden tanks full of water. Men sat in the water. Other men waited in line. She slowed, curious, until she saw them passing a sliver of soap around, and realized they were bathing. Then she almost laughed.

"One minute!" A boy walked along past the wooden tanks, banging on the sides with a stick. "One more minute!"

Frances lingered, hoping a few of the men would climb out of the tanks; she liked seeing men naked. They crouched in the scummy water, soaping themselves and talking, and none got out, and she grew tired of waiting and followed the street.

The street forked. The other way looked much the same as this one, a dusty, winding track through sheds and shacks and tents. She looked up its length but could not see the end, only more shanties, more dust, more people. She kept going straight, the way she had been going.

Ahead of her now the buildings were smaller, cramped close together, held up with poles and bits of rope and piles of dirt. From a narrow doorway a yellow man watched her.

At first these men with their strange skin and slitted eyes had sent cold shivers down her back, as if she were a child seeing monsters; she had thought they were black men turned off-color by some spell, some sickness, until she saw more of them and learned from Gil Marcus that they were Chinee. Celestials, Gil called them. They were as mean as the whites, and she hurried past them toward the cluster of huts and tents on the high ground.

Here a lot of people lived who had come up from South America, so that the place was called Little Chile. Flanking it was another place, a shallow gully creasing the hill, where she had seen before that some black men made camps. They built no roofs, no walls; they made fires and slept in the open. Now she walked up to four black men who were sitting on the ground around a fire.

She said, "Y'all want work?"

They looked her over, cautious, and the biggest of them stood up. He was square-faced and wore a black felt hat. "What kind of work?"

She nodded off down the street. "Building. I have some wood, have some land, want to put up something sturdy."

The big man facing her spread an easy grin over his face. "Mammy, you in the wrong place for sturdy." The other men laughed.

"We'll see," she said. "I'll feed you-all. Pay something in gold dust. It's just down the street, you can quit anytime, come back here, be no loss. Maybe, if we suit, you-all can stay on with me." She nodded at them, looking each in the face, seeing each as a separate man. "All four of you. Well?"

For a moment they did not move, each waiting for some sign from the others. Then the big one before her nodded.

"All right. I'll go." His grin had disappeared. He turned his head a little, glancing over his shoulder at the others, and moved on down toward Frances, toward the street, and one by one they got up and followed him.

The big man's name was Josh. He went once around the little sliver of land, stared at the broken boat tilted up against the hillside behind it, and nodded. "Maybe we get somethin' done, Mammy."

"First thing," she said, "is to build us some decent shelter." Friendly's invasion of the night before still raised her hackles. Along the front of the stage, in the street, little groups of white men stood watching her. She glanced at the lean-to, where Daisy slept, its walls sucking in and blowing out again with every passing wind. She faced the boat, resolute. "First let's get the wood off that."

Josh said, "You got a cat's paw?"

Her resolution sagged a little. "What?"

"Somethin' to . . ." His mouth kinked, his eyes sharp, his brows pulling down. "You got any tools at all, Mammy?"

"An ax," she said. Gil had an ax. She fought the urge to look around, into the street, for some sign of Gil Marcus. Josh was staring down at her as if she grew smaller while he watched.

"An ax. Got any nails? Hammer? Saw? Wedge, mallet, anything?"

She swallowed. She had promised also to feed them, and she had not yet begun on that. One step, then another. She said, "I'll go get the ax," and went over to the lean-to.

By noon all four of the men were working. Josh and Phineas were ripping off the planks that formed the outside of the boat, and the young one, Laban, was worrying out the nails, and Micah was hacking down the last of the scrawny brush growing around the wedge-shaped piece of land. Frances had gone down to the beach and bought fish and clams there, Indian potatoes and onions; she hired a big iron kettle from one of the fishermen and even got him to drag it up the street for her. In front of the stage she had a fire going and the kettle simmering. Phineas had told her he knew where to get some greens, and she had sent him out after them; now she was cutting the greens into the pot, and she was uncomfortably aware that from the vast, quaking mountain of canvas and wood that stood across the street from her had emerged fat Friendly.

She lowered her gaze to her hands; she hacked up the greens with a knife. Trailed by a bustle of miners, the fat man pushed through the crowded street toward her.

"I told you to get out," he said, halfway there.

Frances' arms moved in short, jerky rhythms, snip-snip through the stems of the greens. The aroma was thick around her. She faced him, the steaming pot between them, her power in the steamy fragrance, in the fire and the food. She knew the street was full of people watching.

She said, "I'm staying right here, Friendly. You can't run me out."

He stalked closer to her, round like a boulder. "This ain't your land. You're trespassing." His arm slashed out toward the work going on behind her. "You think you're going to build something? Think twice! The Regulators will dispossess you before you get two nails driven." He sneered at her. "We got laws here."

In the crowd, somebody yelled, "Friendly, you fat asshole, leave her alone!" There was a low yell of agreement. Frances tossed the last of the greens into the pot. She wondered if anybody in the crowd would try to help her if Friendly came after her.

The fat man glared from side to side and behind him. "You all drink in my place. You all got chits with me." He faced her; above his set of slumping chins his features were squeezed together into one small space, huddled around his pud of a nose. "Get out. That's all I'm warning you."

Frances straightened, the knife clutched in her hand. A noise distracted her. Off to her left at the back of the crowd there was a flurry of motion, people moving quickly out of the way. Gil Marcus was pushing through the bystanders toward Friendly and Frances. A tall, slender man in a well-fit coat and a brimmed hat came after him. Bursting clear of the crowd, Gil strode up to Frances and turned, standing in front of her. Taking over for her.

"Friendly, back off." Gil's voice rang out with a lot more weight and confidence than he'd managed in his efforts of the night before. "Get off my property."

The vast face trembled. "Your property!"

"I just bought it for unpaid taxes," Gil said, and glanced off to his left. "Mr. Rudd, will you confirm?"

The tall man who had followed him out of the crowd stepped a pace forward. "Yes. This piece of property now belongs to Mr. Gilbert Bradley Marcus."

The crowd whooped, smelling the triumph of good, and there was a spatter of handclaps. Friendly fired one brief stare at the tall man and thrust his jaw out and fixed his attention on Gil. "You just bought yourself a pine box, pilgrim."

Gil said, "You can't pick on women, Friendly. It's just too low, even for you." That brought another yell from the onlookers in the street.

Friendly's face screwed up even tighter. His gaze daggered toward Frances. His mouth contracted into a round pucker and fired a fat gout of spit toward the boiling pot; enough of it reached the pot to make a loud crackling sizzle. Turning, he barged across the street toward his saloon, his shoulders lifted up high, deeply grooved by his suspender straps. The crowd divided respectfully to let him pass, and many of them followed him.

Gil turned toward Frances, his voice lower, the note of power gone. "That's over. Everything's all right now. I put it in my name, because you — because of the way the law's written, but this place belongs to you and Daisy."

She stepped back from the pot, rubbing her hands together, staring at him: this short white man, unshaven, his plaid shirt worn cotton-pale at the elbows, who believed all these things he was saying. She said, "Gilbert, thank you again."

Behind him, Tierney Rudd said, "Well, Marcus, I've done my part, I'll be going."

Gil turned and shook his hand. "Thanks, Mr. Rudd. And thank Sam Brannan, too, for his help. Come back tonight and see the show."

Many of the crowd still lingered in the street, and now somebody called out, "Three cheers for Sam Brannan!" There was a dutiful bellow of applause for San Francisco's leading citizen. Frances turned and looked behind her, at the half-dismantled boat, the stack of salvaged wood, the four black men standing there, motionless, watching her. Her look prodded them. The boy quickest, they went back to their work, but Josh stood there a long moment, smiling at her. Then Gil called her.

She turned to face him, expecting to see the tall white man still there, Rudd. But somebody else had taken his place, short, square, with long, straight black hair and dark skin. Not black but ruddy brown.

Gil jerked a nod at him. "Do we need another hand?"

She flung a look behind her at the four men already working there. They seemed to fill the lot. "I don't — " She faced this other colored man, loath to let anybody go, even an Indian.

He was shorter than Gil. His eyes were strange, long, black as hellfire, with heavy, folded lids. When she hesitated, he said, "I build. I make house. Good hands." His voice had an odd timbre, like two notes sounding at once.

She said, "You're a carpenter?"

Gil said, "Take him. I don't know the first thing about carpentry, Mammy."

"Very well," she said. "What's your name?"

"Mitya," he said.

"Mitya," said Gil, startled. "That's Russian."

"Russian," the Indian said, and nodded. The strange long eyes slid a glance toward Gil.

Frances said, "You have to work some, first, to prove we need you, but when you do we'll feed you and pay you, and you can sleep here if you want. My name is Frances Hardhardt."

He said, "I sleep out."

"As you wish," she said. "Get to work." He went up past her toward the boat; a few minutes later he was working loose one of the big pieces of the frame.

Gil sauntered by her, his hands behind his back, his forehead clear and vague. "Where's Daisy?" he asked, without really looking at her, without really needing an answer; he went toward the lean-to, pretending not to.

Frances laughed. He had earned a little gratitude, which Daisy was better equipped than anybody else to dispense. She bent over the fish soup, inhaling the heady vapor.

4

AT METINI, THE WORK had gone the other way: tearing things down. Mitya had learned most of his carpentry pulling apart walls, working free the great silver-gray planks of Fort Ross, which the undersea people had made so well that the place took as long to come down as it had taken to go up.

Here, in San Francisco, the planks were boatskin, smaller and thinner than wall boards, and he learned fast to handle them delicately or they split.

The work made trouble in his head. He kept thinking old words, thinking old names, nearly called one of the black men Vanya, which was Mitya's brother's name. He showed the big one, Josh, how to put planks together without nails.

"Hey," Josh said. "You be good at that."

Mitya grunted at him. Hiding in the alien language he took some care not to know. With the ax he cut twice, cleaving off pieces of the end of the plank, to make a tongue, then fit the tongue neatly into the hole in the header.

He did not use these words to Josh — *tongue, header*. Useless words of the undersea people. He pointed instead. Made gestures with his hands. The other men came to watch. Somebody called the white man.

The white man came and watched. "Good," he said. "Do it that way. I can't find nails anywhere," and he went off again, in a hurry. He was always in a hurry.

So in that way they made the boat into a hut. At sundown they ate soup, stewed fish, mushy potatoes. Drank beer made of raspberries. Mitya sat with the other men, against his will enjoying the closeness, the human heat.

The little black woman spent that time moving into the new hut. She and the other woman. They kept the other woman under cover, like a girl before her wedding.

The white man's name was Gil Marcus. He had known of the undersea people, called them by the other name. He had headed Friendly off. But it was the little old black woman who gave most of the orders.

She wasn't so old, either. Mitya had seen that. Everything about her led two different ways.

He turned to Josh, the big man. "Who boss?"

"Boss." Josh blinked at him. He had big eyes that bulged a little out of his head, the whites yellow, tinged with brown.

"Old woman? White man? Boss."

The big man moved one shoulder. "Gil Marcus."

"Him boss?"

"Or Mammy." Josh sipped at the sweet, foamy beer. His forehead rumpled. "I don't get you, you got to learn to talk better."

Mitya looked away, angry. The sky overhead was dark, muffled with fog; the wind had changed, smelling of the dank tidal flats of the bay. The daylight was gone, the work over. He could go back to his own place now. Across the way Friendly's tent roared with hundreds of voices; the light of lanterns shone up through the dirty canvas and turned the fog yellow. In the street the endless crowd trudged along.

Pieces of the crowd dropped off. Gathered along the little platform in front of the hut, stood facing it, doing nothing. Mitya got another cup of the beer and sat and drank it, waiting to see what they waited for.

Gil Marcus came out of the hut and put a lantern on the platform and lit it. The waiting men called to him, and he waved and went off. More people moved in around the lit platform. Mitya began to itch to go. His place was well hidden, but at night it made him jittery not to be there. Then the hut opened and they led the white woman out.

The crowd gave a great breathy cry, like a receding ocean wave that dragged the sand back with it. Gil Marcus went ahead of the others, up onto the platform, and walked into the haze of the lantern light.

"All right, boys, here's what you come for. Now, you remember, she doesn't like roughhouse, you treat her like a lady. Here she is, the sweetest girl in San Francisco, Miss — Daisy — Duncan!"

At that the crowd roared, like the wave coming in hard. Mitya stood up. All he could see was the woman's back. She walked up and down and waved her arms and wiggled; he could not hear her voice. Friendly's emptied within a moment after she appeared on the platform, doubling the size of the crowd. In the lantern light, her clothes glimmered.

The little black woman came out of the hut and stood by the side of the platform, watching. Mitya could not figure out what the white woman was doing, and lost interest; he lowered his gaze to the black woman.

He remembered how she had faced up to Friendly, small and skinny like a spider, glowering at him across the boiling pot. He struggled to remember the name she had told him. Frances. Josh had called her something else. Mammy Hardheart. She was watching the stage, the lantern light just brushing her face. Like sunlight on the ocean, a pale color over a dark color. She turned suddenly and stared at him, and he turned away.

These women reminded him of his own women, whom he loved. Of Olga, with her round cheeks, her eyes bright and clear as rain on the grass. The merry ripple of her laughter. Prettier than any white woman. Prettier than anybody. He had no right to think about Olga now.

He thought of Anna, his sister. Not pretty. Walking toward him, the wind blowing her shawl and her hair wildly around her. Telling him in a ringing voice that he had to go, to leave Metini and his people, and never come back.

Across the street, in the flapped door of his tent, stood Friendly. He was scowling over at the stage. Behind him the saloon tent was quiet. Mitya stopped, peering past him, seeing that the great dusky space within was almost empty. Friendly was staring at him.

"You want a drink?"

Mitya said, "You let me in?" Mostly the white men kept dark people out of their places.

The fat man's face was bland. "Yeah. Sure, I need the business. I'll even stand you a free drink. Come on in." He stepped to one side, and Mitya went into the big tent.

There were only a few miners left in here, standing around the tables where they gambled. The fat man led Mitya through them toward the far side of the tent, where there was a line of wooden planks set on the tops of barrels. Friendly slapped one of these planks with a broad hand, his gaze keen on Mitya.

"Mike? Give the Indian here one on the house."

Behind the bar a white man came with a bottle and a broken cup. Mitya looked from one to the other, suspicious, but Friendly had lost interest in him, and when the other white man had poured the liquor into the cup, he and Friendly started talking. Mitya held the cup in his hand. The place was empty. Friendly had to let anybody in. Mitya wanted the whiskey, its pound in his blood, its slumber in his brain, and he took a mouthful of it.

As soon as he swallowed he knew it was bad, and he threw the cup down. But it was too late; he was already falling.

Dirt against his cheek. His hands hurt.

He opened his eyes into half darkness, smelling blood and vomit. A hand's width in front of him was another man's head, facing away from him, lying on the ground. He was a white man. His arms were twisted behind his back. Like Mitya's.

Mitya shut his eyes again. Friendly had poisoned him.

His wrists were bound and his arms were going numb. He began to work his hands around, straining at cords so tight they were cutting his skin. He got his fingers on the rope and worried it until he could get a grip on it and slide it up and down on his wrist.

Men coming. Feet, voices. He lay still, his eyes closed. His head hurt; he wanted to go to sleep.

"How many we got now?"

"Eight. No, seven, this one's dead."

"Son of a bitch."

There was the thud of something striking flesh and bone. They had kicked the dead man for dying.

"Is that gonna be enough? How many does he need?"

"I don't know. His whole crew took off for the mines, he said, he needs enough men to make it to Honolulu. It's a big ship." This man was coming closer. His voice was labored and breathy; he was doing something as he spoke. Suddenly his hands fell on Mitya, pulling at the bound wrists, pushing him roughly back and forth to see if he was awake, or dead.

"Hundred bucks a head, that's still good money," said the other one.

"Too bad we got to give Friendly so much of it."

Mitya lay still, his heart half choking him. They were selling him to a sea captain, to a sailing ship, he would never get home again. A wild panic seized him and he almost moved, almost gave himself away; he throttled that. He was not home now. He would never go home now. But he did not want to be a sailor on a ship, not a white man's ship. Not any ship.

"Come on, here comes the cart, let's load 'em up."

His mind was clearer now, in spite of the intense, sharp headache. He heard them walk past him toward the creaking and hoofbeats of a horse-drawn cart. The horse blew softly. Men grunted, lifting something heavy. Something heavy thudded into the cart. Mitya struggled with the rope on his wrists, pulling, twisting, getting nowhere, until abruptly the rope slipped and there was slack between his hands.

He lay quiet, his hands clutched together, making himself wait. They picked him up and carried him, and he landed face first on another man's body, rough cloth under him, warm flesh under that. Then another body was thrown in beside him.

"Maybe we should get just one more."

"If'n we see a drunk passed out on the way we'll pick him up."

The cart under him began to move, shaking him up and down. He worked his hands frantically, trying to get out of the rope, but in spite of the foot of slack between them his wrists were still tied together. He cocked his feet up to his hands and pulled at the rope around them. The cart was rumbling along downhill, the bodies tightly packed in it trembling and sliding against one another. Abruptly the rope around his ankles came loose. He squirmed and wiggled his way backward until his feet hit the tail of the cart.

"Hey! Look out back there!"

He lurched up onto his knees and dove sideways out of the cart into the street. A man walking down toward him dodged out of his way, and somebody yelled. His mouth full of dirt, he rolled over and over in the street, away from the cart, then got his feet under him and ran, weaving a way through the crowd ahead of him, his arms stretched awkwardly behind his back. His head pumped. His knees sagged with every step.

Heads turned as he passed. Somebody stuck out a walking stick and tried to trip him, but he dodged.

He ran back up the street to the place where he had worked all day. There were still a lot of men standing around the stage, but the girl had gone. He dashed in past the far end of the stage to the fire by the half-built hut, and stopped, panting, and looked back the way he had come.

Nobody coming. He had escaped. Like a bolt of lightning through his skull the headache pounded at him.

The white man, Gil Marcus, was standing by the fire, pouring himself a cup of coffee. Seeing Mitya, he dropped the cup and came toward him, drawing a knife. Mitya shrank back from the blade, and the white man gave him a startled look.

"Hold on. I'm just — " He waved the knife. "I'll cut you free. What happened?"

Mitya relaxed; he turned his back and felt the white man take hold of the slack of the rope. He said, "Friendly poison me."

The white man grunted, half a laugh. "It seems in character."

"He sell me, on the sea, to the sea. To a ship on the sea. He sell me one hundred dollar."

He turned to face the white man, who nodded at him. "You're lucky. People get crimped in San Francisco every day, and they don't wake up until they're halfway to Shanghai." He clapped Mitya on the shoulder. "You're very lucky, Mit."

Mitya peeled off the rope wound around his wrists. "Crimp."

"That's what it's called. It seems to be a routine occupation among a certain class of men here."

Mitya jerked his head, staring toward Friendly's. "He do it. Friendly." His gut surged with rage. He started around, and the white man caught his arm.

"Mitya, hold it. Where are you going?"

"He poison me." But the white man was right; Friendly had

power, and Mitya had none. He stopped, staring over at the tent, which glowed dirty yellow with the light of its lanterns as if the tent itself were a big lantern. His wrist was worn open and raw, and he licked it.

The white man said, "You got away, Mitya. Sometimes that's the only revenge there is."

"Stupid," Mitya said. "I know he bad. I know he not true." He clubbed his own thigh with his fist. "I hate him."

"Good. He's an evil man." The white man bent for his coffee cup. "Care for something to drink?" He squatted, reaching for the pot on the fire.

Mitya stood staring at Friendly's tent, his head seething. If he went in there now he'd be killed. If he did somehow punish Friendly, he would still be killed. He felt himself jammed face up against this injustice. There was nothing he could do. He sank down on his heels beside the white man and reached for a cup for some coffee.

In the morning, with the help of a hundred bystanders, they hauled another ship up from the bay, an old brigantine, its masts long gone. Coming up the street, the ship brushed against the tent fronts on either side; before they could move her onto their piece of land, they had to dismantle the stage. This, Frances thought, was no real loss. She liked the idea of starting from the bare ground. With Gil Marcus she walked around the wooden hulk, its sides slimy with weed and rot, rough with barnacles. The ship lay slumped to one side, its keel digging into the sand. Most of the wood looked sound.

Gil said, "Where's Mitya? I want him to see this, he obviously knows more than anybody else."

Frances rapped with her knuckles on the side of the boat. The broken railing was a good ten feet above her head. "He rubs me backwards, that one."

Gil called to Josh and sent him to find Mitya. "He's a pretty dour sort."

"Dour!" Frances laughed, startled, amused, and said the word again, mouthing it. "Dour." Gil was watching her, half a smile on his mouth under his ragged mustache. "He's a pailful of trouble, Gilbert, that's what I think."

"Shall I get rid of him?" Gil glanced away, over her shoulder, and she supposed from the way his voice changed that Mitya was coming toward her.

She said quickly, "Oh, no. Trouble has a way of making things interesting." She turned, and the Indian stood behind her.

He studied the ship with them, saying nothing; once, going up the tilted side, he reached down and gave Frances a hand, and the feel of his hand on her wrist was like a serpent coiling around her arm. They went down inside the ship, where the decks ran in layers, so close together that they had to crawl along between them, over chunks of wood and rope, piles of rat turds. The inside of the ship was like a honeycomb, made of little cells. It smelled of tar, of wet wood; it smelled like a place where wild animals had lived. They came out again and stood between the ship and the street.

Gil said, "We want to build a house out of this. How can we do it? It seems already so well made, it's a shame to pull it apart."

Mitya grunted. Frances went away down the ship, running her hand over the wood. The Indian's odd, resonant voice reached her clearly. "No pull down. Dig here. Brace. Make her stand up straight."

"All right," Gil said. "But it won't be near big enough. Can we rip out those decks without losing the side walls?"

"Brace," Mitya said. "Inside, outside. Not hard. Fast, too." He thumped the hull of the boat with his hand. "Good wood. Peel off here. Couple pieces." He put his hands one on top of each other, showing the layers of the hull.

Frances left it to them; clearly they understood this, they did not need her. Her body tingled. She felt good about this; things were going along as she wanted. Her eye caught again on a piece of wood hanging down the stern, and she stretched her arm up but could not reach it.

"Mitya," she called.

He and Gil paced toward her. Gil's face was intense, his mouth set. "We still may not have enough wood," he said.

Mitya shrugged. "Get more wood." He faced her, his long eyes unhuman. "What?"

"Get that down for me." She pointed.

He looked up, thinking it over. As if he could refuse. At once she was determined he would never refuse her anything. The long black eyes probed at her again, and he climbed up the stern of the ship like a lizard climbing a wall, gripped the dangling nameplate, and wrenched it free. Dropping to his feet beside her, he held it out — not to her. To Gil.

Gil took it, startled. Frances' gaze locked with Mitya's; between them a taut challenge formed. Gil held the wood out to her.

"That's the name of the ship," he said.

She looked down at the wooden plank, carved with letters, with a scrolled border. It had been painted; in the deep grooves of the letters some red paint remained.

" 'Shining Light,' " she said, and laughed. She lifted her face toward Gil, delighted. "That's wonderful. Let's call it that. The place. When it's done." She laughed again, vindicated. "The Shining Light."

Mitya frowned at her. "Not made yet," he said.

"Oh," she said. "That's little enough. The name is all." Light-footed, she carried the nameplate away like a captive banner to show Daisy.

5

Daisy said, "Frances keeps me penned up here like the Christmas goose. Can't you make it so I can go out for a while?"

Gil had bought a mule-drawn cart to haul wood in. He dumped out its load of redwood planks, set one crosswise in the cart's bed for a seat, rigged a piece of canvas for an awning. He and Daisy sat there, in the shade; Josh drove the mule. As they rumbled up Pacific Street, heads turned and mouths fell open and two or three boys walked along beside, peering in at Daisy. It was a beautiful day, almost hot, without much breeze; Gil sat back a little, smiling, pleased with himself.

Daisy said, "This is wonderful," and his satisfaction increased severalfold.

She bounced on the plank seat, nearly knocking it down. The awning shook. She wore a plain muslin dress, her hair tucked under a bonnet; her face shone, pink as roses. Lounging beside her in makeshift comfort, Gil got hold of her hand and held it.

"Do you like it?"

"I love it. It's practically a surrey." She wiggled on the seat again, ducking her head slightly so that she could see out from under the awning. "Where are we going? I want to see the whole of San Francisco." In his hand her fingers were cool and limp.

"The whole city," he said, amused, wondering what she expected. "All right. Josh, take us to the Plaza."

At the corner of Kearny Street there were deep ruts in the road that locked the wheels straight; Josh had to get out and lead the mule around the turn. A lean brown little man, seeing Daisy, stopped and took his hat off and stared at her as she passed. She twisted around in the seat to wave at him, as if she knew him. Her face flushed; she lowered her eyes and kicked the basket on the floor of the cart.

"What's this?"

"A picnic," Gil said. "I thought we could go out toward the Mission."

One cartwheel lurched up over a rut and crashed down again, rocking the uneven seat so hard that Gil had to catch hold of the side to keep from falling out. The awning swayed on its frail supports, buckled, and collapsed. The hot sunlight swept across the cart. Gil grabbed hold of the canvas and pushed it back up again while they banged and rattled toward the Plaza. Daisy let go of a peal of rich laughter, watching him.

His ears burned. He tried letting go of the awning, and at once it tipped over sideways; he grabbed it again. Now a small train of men was trailing after the cart, and when the awning fell they cheered and broke into a run to catch up. "Need some help there, fellah?" Gil jerked the awning hastily into place and sat there holding it in place with both hands.

Daisy said, "Let it go, Gil. It's no matter to me."

He growled something. He wanted her to himself, a big matter to him. He wanted to look good to her, able, confident. While the cart clunked along into the Plaza he worked on the wooden slats holding the canvas up and managed to get the thing stable again.

"There." He sat down carefully on the uncertain seat beside her. "Now. This is Portsmouth Square. It's named for the ship that brought the American flag here, in 'forty-six." She was hunching down to see out past the sway of the awning. Shrewdly he leaned toward her, pointing past her at the looming, raw board fronts of the buildings, streaming with red letters. "That's the Bella Union, and that's the El Dorado." Only the El Dorado's false front was of wood; the rest of the building was a vast tent, hooked on behind like a bustle. "They say thousands of dollars changes hands over their tables every night." Smooth as butter he slid his arm around her.

She laughed, her head swiveling toward him, her wide eyes, crystalline blue, only inches from his own. "I can't see," she said, and stood up and pushed the awning down on top of the picnic basket.

A roar went up from the crowd around them. Suddenly the cart was surrounded by men — Americans in plaid flannel shirts, three or four gawking pigtailed Chinamen in long blue coats, a skinny Malay like a monkey, leaping up and down, and all of them calling to her in English and Spanish and a dozen other languages. Daisy spread her arms and bowed to them. Beside her, Gil sat with his hands on his knees, telling himself to be patient and think of the picnic. She plopped down beside him. Josh clicked his tongue to the mule and the cart rolled on across the broad, dusty square. The worshipful crowd followed.

"Daisy, sing us something!"

She shook her head, waving, and pointed across the way. "What's that?"

"Post office," Gil said, his lips stiff.

"You mean, all those men are waiting to get into the post office?" As usual the line stretched the length of the Plaza. Suddenly she stood up again. "I smell popcorn!" The cart rocked and she flung out her arms to save her balance, and the crowd trailing after them gasped in delighted suspense.

Gil caught her hand and made her sit. "Do you want some popcorn? Josh."

His felt hat pulled down hard over his grin, the black man steered the mule toward the side of the Plaza. Daisy was looking all around again. "There's so many people!"

"Another ship put in just this morning," Gil said. "A lot of these men got off it. See?" He pointed. In the shelter of a doorway a dozen wretched, bewildered foreigners huddled among a pile of bundles and satchels and cases. Dressed in long black coats, in baggy black trousers, they looked like gravediggers; their black beards spread like bibs over their shirtfronts, their long black hair hung down over their ears in curls or braids. "Russians, maybe." He wasn't sure. She wouldn't know any better; he could lie like a salesman. "Maybe Germans."

"What are they doing here?" she said.

"Looking for gold, Daisy, for God's sake, what's anybody doing here?" Ahead, along the line of men waiting to get into the post office, a boy was selling popcorn in scoops made of dried husks, and Gil waved him over. Daisy was staring all around her again, ignoring the encircling upturned, adoring faces of her admirers. A man reading a letter as he walked nearly collided with the cart; tears were streaming down his face. Up at the front of the line somebody was shrilling, "Place to sell — here's a good place in the line — ten dollars! Only ten dollars." The weeping man, still rapt in his letter, banged along the side of the cart like a piece of driftwood past a boat and wandered blindly off into the crowd.

Daisy was craning her neck to see everything. "It's so new," she said. "Wasn't there anything here before?"

"Well, yes." Gil reached forward and nudged Josh, who urged the mule on again. Under the cover of his slouch-brimmed hat the big Negro was still smiling. Gil sat back beside Daisy. "You can see the old buildings in between the new ones. The little adobes are all Mexican, that little one, see, and there's one on the far side — " He bent toward her to explain all this, relieved he knew something she wanted to know, and managed to get hold of her hand again. They crossed the Plaza toward Clay Street; he pointed out to her the big brick building there, brand-new, the only brick building in San Francisco, and the new firehouse, which had a bell bigger than its water wagon. "Sam Brannan gave them the bell." Three or four men in green uniform jackets were loitering in front of the saloon beside the firehouse; Gil kept a wary eye on them, although the Regulators usually didn't bother white people.

"Is Sam Brannan rich?" Daisy asked.

"Yes."

"Where does he live?"

He felt these questions like spiked shoes walking up over his back. "I'll show you. It's on our way. Josh — "

"I'm goin'," Josh said. "Can't go no faster'n I'm goin'." Gil bent forward and fit the wreckage of the awning mostly under the seat.

The cart banged over the ruts of Kearny Street again. Most of the crowd trailing them stayed behind in the Plaza. The cart passed a grocery shop, a blacksmith's, a mercantile made of the crates its inventory had arrived in. They rolled into Mormon Town: a dozen small, trim houses with yards and gardens. A woman in a white apron stood in a doorway watching them. On the rooftop above her head a cock pulled itself up tall and ripped out a ringing salutation.

A few yards on, the street faded into brush and sand. They rattled over Mission Creek on a wooden bridge. Josh glanced back over his shoulder. "Still goin' to the Mission, Mist' Gil?"

"Yes."

Daisy twisted and looked back at the buildings they had just passed. "You mean, that's all?"

Gil cast a glance around at San Francisco. He could hear the roar of the Plaza still, dim behind them, fading into the silence of the wilderness. They had lost the last of her admirers. Around them now was sand and greasebush. "That's all."

"Where does Sam Brannan live?"

"In one of those houses. I'm not sure which one."

"Hunh." She sank down on the jury-rigged seat, frowning. "He can't be that rich."

Gil laughed, ruffled, wondering what she wanted. "A couple of years ago there wasn't anything here but a Hudson Bay Company post, a customs office, and a flagpole."

"Hunh."

There wasn't much he could say to that. After a moment he reached out and took her hand again. Silently they rode behind Josh up through the wasteland toward the Mission.

"I'm hungry," Daisy said flatly. "Let's stop and eat."

Josh heard her and glanced back over his shoulder, and Gil nodded. The road was crossing a bare, sandy flat below the brushy slope of a hill. Off to the south, Lone Mountain rose, a yellow knob. The uneven, rumpled hills to the east were old sand dunes. Josh drove the cart off the road and down behind a sand-blown ridge.

Here the high ground blocked the ceaseless wind, and some

grass grew. Josh stopped the cart. Gil helped Daisy down and got out a blanket and the picnic basket, and Josh drove on, as arranged, up toward the Mission, where he could buy vegetables for Mammy's cookpot. Daisy took off her shoes and wandered around, picking the scrawny flowers that grew among the grass stems, little purple stars, and yellow cups. Gil spread out the blanket on the ground, putting rocks on the corners to hold it against the fitful wind.

He had packed sausage and cheese and tortillas, a meal that had cost him over forty dollars, and he had two bottles of wine. The sausage was terrible but the cheese was good, and they drank all the wine. Daisy took off her bonnet.

"You'll burn," Gil said, sounding silly even to himself.

"I don't care," she said, and tossed the bonnet aside. She smiled at him, lounging on one arm, her hair all around her shoulders like a froth. "What do we do now? Didn't you bring a fiddler or two? Or a couple of acrobats?"

He grabbed her. She laughed in his face but lay back and rolled around on the blanket with him, letting him slide kisses off her cheeks and nose and forehead, her arms between them, his arms around her. She smelled sweet and wild, her flesh abundant, soft, pliant under his hands. He slid down and through the pleated muslin pressed his face between her big, soft breasts.

Her hands stroked his hair. He lifted his head, and their eyes met; she was not smiling now. She tugged lightly on his hair, and he moved up and kissed her hard on the mouth, and she lay still and yielding there under him, and kissed him back. He slid his hand up over her breast.

This time she said, "Now, now," and drew away from him. He let her go, his chest pulsing and his groin on fire. She sat up, arranging her skirts and her hair, not looking at him.

He lay down next to her, unsure. He said, "Want some more wine?"

"It's all gone," she said. She looked away, down to the south, where in the general tumble of low hills two peaks stood up like virgin's breasts against the sky. "Aren't there any trees in California?"

"In some places," he said. "California's a pretty big place. There were trees up on Lucky Bar, where I had my claim." Or there had been trees, before the miners came and cut them all down. "Were there trees where you came from?"

"Charleston," she said. "There's beautiful trees all over Charleston. Live oaks, and palm trees. Beautiful houses, you know, and shops, with all sorts of new things from Europe. Because of the harbor. We got things from Europe all the time."

"We," he said.

"Ummm," she said, and her hand rose and covered her mouth. She turned to face him, and her eyes were wicked with lies. "My sisters and me. My father was rich." She lay down next to him, on her side, her great breasts heavy against the bodice of her dress.

"How'd you acquire Mammy?"

"Mammy," she said, stupidly.

"Did your daddy just give her to you on your birthday?"

"Oh. You mean Frances." Her gaze was dreamy, unfocused, a vacuum hiding universes. "Oh, she was our cook, actually."

"Really. You and the family cook just one day up and took off for California together."

Her mouth tucked in at the corners, dimpling her cheeks; the softness of her lower lip was like a fruit he wanted to sink his teeth into. Her hand slipped the distance between them and stroked down his chest. "Well, it wasn't exactly like that." He bent over her and kissed her again, and this time she let him touch her breasts.

"Daisy," he said, "I love you."

"Oh, don't say that." She nuzzled his cheek; he had the top several buttons of her bodice open, and she twisted a little to let him get at the rest.

"No," he said. "I mean it. I love you, and always will."

"Gil, stop. You don't have to."

"Damn it, Daisy, I want to marry you."

"Gil," she said, and turned away, and sat up again. "You have a way of wrecking things."

"What?"

She looked down at her front as if she had just discovered it and began to do the buttons up. "You can't love me. It's just not going to work out like that. There can't ever be too much between us."

Gil said, "Why not?" His chest ached.

"You're a good, sweet, kind man, Gil, and I care a lot about you, but we aren't meant for each other." She had reached the top button. She straightened her head, stretching her neck, smoothing the muslin down over her sweetness. With the backs of her fingers she patted up under her chin.

"Because I'm not rich," he said.

"Now, Gil." She squirmed, her mouth curling in a grimace, as if that tasted bad, but slowly her gaze came to meet his. She shrugged. "Well, yes. But I want nice things, Gil, and a nice home. If you knew — " She bit that back, turning away from him again.

He lowered his eyes; he wished she would tell him the truth about herself, and then a moment later he wondered if he really wanted to know. She swung toward him again.

"I'd like to be happy, Gil. Is that so awful a thing? And to be happy, I need to be rich. Is that so awful? Do you really blame me?"

Gil stared at her, the beautiful curved, soft mouth saying this, the clear blue eyes believing it. There was a knot in his stomach. He said, "Yes."

She put her back to him. They said nothing more at all for the half an hour that intervened until Josh came back, the cart heaped with onions and tubers and long green stems, the awning gone entirely. Wedged in among the vegetables, they rode back toward San Francisco. Gil thought bitterly that she would have let him have his way with her if he had not said he loved her.

They rolled back down toward the Plaza. Daisy said, "Look. Is that a church?"

Gil settled himself on the seat. All along Kearny Street, there were lanterns set on poles, and the lamplighter was walking along lighting and trimming them. On the far side of the Plaza, a similar string of yellow lamps came on one by one. But something was different. A building stood on the corner where that morning there had been none.

"They were working on it when we left," he said. "They just put the steeple up."

She burst out laughing. "What a place! I love it here!" Her big, soft hands clapped together, her face swinging toward him, brilliant with high humor, her eyes agleam, her mouth jubilant. He reached out impulsively and gripped her hand and squeezed it. She laughed at him and squirmed over to sit leaning against him, and he put his arm around her. They went back to the Shining Light.

6

GIL MARCUS SAID, "I don't see why we have to do all that much digging. Can't we just pound the dirt down and go from there?"

Mitya glanced beyond him at the other workmen, watching and waiting. They had gotten the white man to ask this. They wanted to make the work easy. Mitya wanted to make the work good.

He could do nothing by himself. He said to the white man, "You boss. You no say, we no do."

The white man folded his arms over his chest. "You want to scrape all this ground level? We don't have the tools." But he hesitated, unsure. He was an unsure man. "Tell me why we should put in so much work on it."

Mitya said, "Start true, keep true. Start crooked, next thing fit bad, and next thing worse." He shrugged, suspecting this was useless. "Make it true first. Make it easy later."

The white man before him widened his eyes, turned and looked at the ship, and faced him again. Nodded. "All right. We'll do it as you say."

Mitya drew in a deep breath, pleased. He felt suddenly bigger. He looked past the white man toward the workmen and pointed. "You. You. Come with me. Others, dig."

For a moment they clung together, motionless, unwilling. Then the big man with the hat started forward after Mitya, and the others bent for the sticks and boards they were using to dig. Mitya shook his hair back. He was the boss now. With a little strut he went with his crew to dig a trench for the ship's keel.

Frances went to the big man, Josh, and said, "Do you know of any more people like us? Other than the men up by Little Chile."

"Sure," he said, and gave a deep, honeyed chuckle in his throat. "Why you ask?"

"Tell them," she said, "they can come here. From anywhere, free or slave, they can come here. I'll buy their freedom. I'll send money back to their masters. I'll give them what they need to live, if they come here."

Josh's lips pushed out, thoughtful. "Why come you do this?"

She rounded on him, angry. "Because they're our people. That's why. Do as I say."

He said, "As you say, Mammy." His lips curved in a broad smile at her. A little while later she saw him talking to Phineas and Micah, and they were all looking over their shoulders at her, and all smiling. After that, new people came, almost every day.

Josh and Micah and Mitya dug a ditch to fit the keel of the *Shining Light*, rocked her upright, and braced the back wall with timbers and rocks and chunks of sod so that she stayed upright. This would be the back of the new building. Mammy got more hands to help them. She hired black men, or brown men, no whites. Fed them from the great boiling pot, fed them all they wanted, and lots of beer. The black men sang as they worked, and although they were all strangers they all knew the same songs.

They played with the songs, one singing out words in a line, and the others twining their voices around it and against it. The singing moved the work on.

They dug up the ground before the ship, a grinding chore with the tools they had, and dragged boards back and forth over it to make it even. Then Mitya took a bowl and filled it with water. He tied bits of string and rope together into a long line. He staked out the ground where he wanted to build, and with the bowl of water he went around making sure that all the ground was level, and where it wasn't he made the other men dig the dirt down or pack more dirt higher. With the string he measured out the lines of the walls and drove stakes into the ground to mark corners.

He broke into the side of the ship, using the ax and an iron bar that Gil Marcus found. They cut through the planking of the ship until they could pick the wood out in pieces and lay it down on the fresh new ground. Gil found more tools. Mitya could feel the building around him, shaping the empty air. He stopped going away at night. Deep in the hulk of the ship he made himself a new nest. This was his place now.

Daisy woke up around noon and lay in bed wishing she could go to sleep again. Before her stretched another day of sitting here in this hovel, waiting for the night to come and the show to start.

Through the thin wall came the sounds of the men working. She thought she could smell coffee. Grimly she stared at the ceiling and called, "Frances. Frances?"

Frances wasn't there. Frances went out whenever she wanted.

Daisy thrust the blankets back and sat up. She could do whatever Frances could. For a moment she did not remember where she had put her old clothes, but some instinct steered her to a box under the bed, and there she found the pair of men's trousers and longjohns and the canvas shirt that she had worn crossing Panama and on the ship north. The hat was there too. Everything was filthy and stiff, but she refused to stay in here anymore.

The longjohns were, however, beyond any resolve. She put on the cotton drawers she wore under her dresses, got everything else on, and went out the door. She pulled the hat down hard over her head and poked her hair into it.

She had not been out all yesterday, not until after dark; she had seen nothing of the building. Now, startled, she saw how much had gone up. Before her stood the wooden skeleton of a wall, ten feet high and twenty feet long, built of uprights and cross-members. From the streetward corner another row of uprights marched away across the front of the lot; in pairs the men were lifting up the crossmembers and sliding them into notches on the posts. As she stood there watching, one of them began to sing.

"My old missus promise me — "

From all over the lot came voices shouting, "Shoo a la a day!"

"When she die she set me free."

"Shoo a la a day!"

Daisy went up closer. The Indian was working on the corner of the building, fitting a crosspiece into the cut in the upright; he stooped and picked up a dish and put it on top of the crossmember and stared at it.

He seemed more like an animal than a man, not only in his looks, his short, heavy bones and odd-shaped features, but in his movements. He put the bowl down again. His head lifted and he saw her and waved her over.

"Hold," he said, pointing at the crossmember, and then his gaze came back to her, sharp, and he reached out and flipped the hat off her head.

From all around the lot a crowing yell went up. Everybody stopped work and stared at her. Daisy stood there, her cheeks flaming. The Indian waved her off. "Go."

"No, I'll help," she said.

"Go. Go." He pushed at her. Stooping, he picked up the ax lying on the ground by the post.

"No, I want to help," she said.

"Hey, Mit," roared the big black man with the hat. "Let her give a hand."

The Indian straightened. He gave her a baleful look, lowered the ax, and took hold of her right hand. Turning it up, he ran his finger down the palm. She could feel the softness of her skin against the horny callus of his. He gave her a squeeze, like a warning, and started to let her go.

She grabbed his hand instead, and squeezed back as hard as she could.

His head rose an inch. He stared at her, and then he smiled. He said, "Strong."

"Yes," she said, pleased, and let go of him. "I want to help."

He was still smiling. He said, "Hold." And pointed to the crossmember. To reach it she had to step inside the building, where the ground was dug up, soft and crumbling underfoot like cornmeal. She bent to hold it fast while he trimmed it.

A deep black voice rang out. "Now she die an' go to hell!"

A dozen voices roared the refrain. "Shoo a la a day!"

"Hope that devil burn her well!"

Daisy stood up, listening. This was real singing, not like what she did; she loved to hear it. The Indian was watching her through the corner of his eye. She wondered if he thought she was shirking, and went hastily back to work.

He touched her arm. "Listen," he said, and smiled at her. "Good to listen." After that she stopped whenever she wanted to, and listened to the men sing.

Later, she went around the building looking for chores to do. By the end of the day many of these people were becoming real to her. The big black man in the cloth hat was named Josh, and he always sang the line of the song; he had a voice deep and smooth and sure as a river. It reminded her of her uncle's farm, although her uncle, a poor man, kept no slaves; but there were slaves in the neighbors' fields.

She didn't want to think about Carolina anymore. She refused even to think about what her uncle had done to her, once he found out she was pregnant.

She hauled water in a bucket down from the spring on the side of the hill; everybody on Pacific Street used this spring, and by midday she had to wait for ten minutes to fill the bucket. Frances was talking about digging a well, but she had no water witch. Daisy helped carry planks, held things up to be fit in place, gathered up scraps and put them in a heap by the fire. She stood a while and watched the boy, Laban, drawing with a piece of charcoal on a plank, until Josh came along and hurried him on to his work. On the plank Laban had left Josh's face, singing.

Josh said, "Boy's got a head full of dreams."

"It's nice, though," she said. "Do we have to cover it up?"

The big man took his hat off to talk to her. "I think so, miss, you want a wall there. He can make another. He does that all the time."

"Where's Frances?"

"Out finding us something to eat. Ain't easy, you know. Things cost more than gold here, miss." He put the hat back on and followed Laban toward a pile of wood. Across the way the Indian was carrying his bowl and his string toward the new work, and she trotted over to watch him.

"What use is that?"

"Make level," said the Indian. His name was Mitya, she knew, an odd name; Gil had said it was Russian. He stood on a chunk of wood, held one end of the string against the top of the post before him, and let the rest dangle. He had tied something to the other end, something smooth and white. She grabbed at it: a long pearly bead.

"No," he said, sharply. She let go, and the white bead swung in smaller and smaller circles until it hung still at the end of the string, straight down along the center of the upright. Mitya nodded at her. "See?"

"I see," she said, brightly. "Can I look at that bead now?"

"Look," he said, getting down. She picked up the bead, rubbed her fingers on it, held it against her cheek.

"This is beautiful. Is it yours?"

Mitya made a sound in his chest. With his ax he was shaping the ends of a beam.

"Is it Indian?"

He gave her a slantwise, half-angry look. She guessed he didn't like the word *Indian*.

She said, "I'm sorry. Did you make it?"

For a moment only the ax moved, brisk, precise, shaving off thick curls of the wood. Finally he said, "No. Very hard, make so. Only very good maker make so."

From the deck of the *Shining Light*, Laban cried, "Josh! Josh, look — down there, that's our little Mammy."

Daisy turned, shading her eyes; the sun was sliding down into the sky behind the ship. Laban stood there, pointing away down the street. She turned her gaze back to the glossy object in her hand. "What's it made of?"

Up on the deck of the ship, Laban shouted, "Josh, she's in trouble! They's men rousting her. Josh! I see green jackets!"

"Frances," Daisy said. She knew what green jackets meant: Gil had told her about the Regulators. She wheeled to stare down the street, filled with the busy, bobbing mass of the afternoon traffic.

Beside her, Mitya let the beam drop and walked over toward Josh, standing still, his hands at his sides, squinting down the street. Mitya called up to Laban, "What go? What go?"

Laban called, "The cart's stopped, they're rousting her, I tell you."

Josh's mouth was working. He said, low, "The Regulators, they's all got guns."

Mitya said, "Come on." He walked out through the gap between two of the wall posts and started down the street. The other men stood where they were, their hands loose; Josh looked down at his feet. Mitya turned back toward them.

"Come on!" He waved his arm.

Josh said, under his breath, "I guess we got to." He stooped to pick the iron bar up off the ground and went off down the street, with each step moving a little faster. The other men followed him. Laban came down the ladder like a squirrel and dashed after them.

Daisy went to the corner of the wall. Her heart was pounding. The men were running now, moving in a pack down the side of the street. She turned and ran toward the ladder, to go up to the deck where she could see better.

Frances had spent the whole day out searching for decent food; the cart was piled high. When she turned into the bottom of Pacific Street, the sun blazed into her eyes, and she realized how late it was. She slapped the reins on the rump of the mule and swore at it and the mule crept on a little faster.

She started up Pacific Street, but she got no farther than the first corner. There three men in green jackets stepped out into her way.

"Now, Mammy. Where you-all going?"

She gripped the reins, her mouth suddenly dry, and scanned their faces. "Let me by. I'm just an old woman."

"Ooooh," said the bushy-bearded man who stood by the wheel of the cart. "Just an old woman. But I hear you're making lots of trouble for some friends of ours. And we don't like niggers making trouble for white men."

"Get out of my way," she said, and picked up the ends of the reins and flogged at the mule with them. The mule jumped and the cart jounced forward, so that one of the green jackets had to get out of the way fast, and the bushy-bearded man stepped back.

"You ain't going nowhere, Mammy!" said the man by the cartwheel, and he took a pistol out of his belt and turned and shot the mule.

Frances screamed. The mule sagged down in the traces, stretched out its head on the dusty ground, and died. Frances wheeled toward the green jacket beside her and slashed at him with the reins.

"That mule cost me fifty dollars!"

"Well, well," he cried. He danced back, laughing at her. "It ain't no fool for work, is it. Maybe it'll draw a little better if'n we lighten the load. Hey, boys, get rid of some of that garbage in there!"

The other two men jumped up onto the cart. Frances clambered across the seat, trying to stop them, and struck at them with the reins. They whooped, red-faced, making this a game. One caught the ends of the leathers and jerked and nearly toppled her.

The other cried, "Here, Roberts — catch!" He pitched a cabbage to the bushy-bearded man.

Frances screamed again. They were throwing all her food into the street. She had spent more than five hundred dollars and they were throwing it all into the street. The bushy beard by the cartwheel stood there roaring with laughter. A crowd had gathered along the side of the street, but they kept their distance, watching. Cabbages and apples flew out of the cart and into the crowd, and some of the onlookers caught them and cheered for more. "Hey, got any peaches?"

Frances climbed into the back of the cart, sinking into the loose vegetables up to her knees, and grabbed a sack of flour out of the arms of a green jacket. "No — that's to feed my people, damn you."

"Mammy!" somebody yelled, a voice she knew. "Get down!"

The cart rocked. She dropped the sack of flour and fell into the heap of vegetables, and the man in the green jacket fell on top of her. The cart was rolling. She squirmed out from under the floundering man and sat up. Its wheels shrill, the cart was hurrying up the street at a better clip than the mule had ever mustered. Beside her the green jacket scrambled to his feet, scraps of leaf and peel clinging to his front, yelled, and bounded out.

Frances grabbed the seat and pulled herself up to the front of the cart again. Before her, in the mule's traces, Josh and Mitya, Phineas and Laban hauled the cart along at a dead gallop. They were running down the people on foot in the street ahead of them, and one of them bellowed a warning, and the crowd split to let them pass.

Frances sat down, grabbing hold of the seat to keep her place. The wild ride was tossing her up and down like a baby. She twisted to look back; but the crowd had already closed over the dead mule, and she could see nothing of the green jackets. Facing front again, she clung to the bouncing seat while the men spun her in triumph up Pacific Street and into the Shining Light.

Frances said, "Friendly set them on us, for sure."

Gil nodded. "I don't doubt it."

They sat huddled around the fire, shoulder to shoulder, drinking the last hot coffee. The sun had gone down. In a few minutes Frances had to take Daisy in to get ready for the show. She was reluctant to leave the fire; the circle of people around it felt safer than the shack.

She looked from one to the other of them. Josh's face was slack with fatigue and worry under the bent brim of his hat. Next to him Laban sat idly tracing with his finger in the dust. His shoulders slumped. Phineas stared vacantly into the fire. Even the Indian, Mitya, looked low.

Frances leaned forward, reaching for a stick, and poked the fire up, so that the flames leapt. In the sudden wash of light the men straightened, startled.

"Look," she said. "There's good about what happened today, which is that we beat them. They'd have taken all our food, wrecked the cart, maybe, but we got out of it."

Josh said, "They ain't gonna quit. They be back. And they only have to win once."

She said, "Then we won't let them win." She looked around the fire once more, wanting to blow some spark into them. Their doubts and gloom pushed her temper to the edge. "Anybody don't want this, he can go now."

There was a silence. Finally Josh said, "Nobody goin', Mammy. This place is all we got." There was a little low mutter of agreement from the men on either side of him.

Daisy turned to Gil. "Isn't there anybody we can ask for help? Isn't there a sheriff?"

Gil said, "No. There isn't, not yet. Since the United States took California, back in 'forty-six, the Congress in Washington hasn't been able to agree on even a territorial government. San Francisco has no law."

Mitya, on Frances' left, held out a little jug of whiskey. She passed it on to Gil, who poured some into his cup.

"There must be somebody," Daisy said. "Otherwise everybody would just kill each other all the time."

Gil rubbed his nose. "There's the army. But they have no money and no men, so they can't do much. There's the *alcalde*, the Mexican mayor, who was here before any of us came. That's Leavenworth, he may not sound Mexican, but he is. Nobody listens to him, since we beat up on the Mexicans, but he's still got an office and some duties."

"What about Sam Brannan?" asked Frances. "He helped you before, didn't he? About the title to the land here."

"Yes, he did. Brannan's the elder of the Mormon congregation in San Francisco. They came in 'forty-seven. The Mormons stick together, they do what Brannan tells them, and they give him considerable money, which he uses very well. But family by family they're leaving, going out to Utah, where there are a lot more Mormons than here. And I don't know what Brannan can do about the Regulators."

The fire was burning down, a great smoldering heap of coals. Frances stared at it, seeing San Francisco in it, a shapeless burning pile of power and money, not yet fallen into order. "Who are these Regulators?"

Gil said, "Most of them were part of a regiment of volunteers from New York, sent out here to fight in the war against Mexico. By the time they reached San Francisco the war was over. They more or less attached themselves to the *alcalde* as a sort of police force, but he can't control them; he's even afraid of them. They just walk around town taking what they want and doing as they please. They march on Sundays, just like real soldiers, and nobody ever says anything. A bad bunch."

"How many are there?" Daisy asked.

"Oh, dozens. Maybe a hundred. They had a parade last month with over a hundred men."

Frances pursed her lips. "Charleston suddenly seems so staid and old."

Swiftly Daisy said, "Well, we got to do something about them."

A hundred men was an army, a major force in a place like San Francisco. Frances sat staring into the fire, trying to see all this in one piece. This wasn't a city at all, just the scattered makings of one. There was no order here, no safety. Yet in disorder there were opportunities that never came again.

Mitya said, "Kill Friendly."

"What?" Gil's head swiveled toward the Indian, sitting on the far side of the fire.

"Kill Friendly. He make this trouble. He go, Regulators go, maybe."

Frances licked her lips. Gil said mildly, "Well, there are ways not so drastic."

"What ways?" Daisy asked.

"We could pay them," Gil said. "Give them a certain amount to keep from bothering us. A lot of people do that."

Daisy scowled at him. Her head jerked around, her gaze reaching for Frances for support. "No. We need all the money. Don't we, Frances."

Frances said, "I think it's time you go in and get ready for the show, so we do have some money." She had no intention of paying the Regulators anything.

"I'll see what I can do about the Regulators," Gil said.

"We should keep a watch on Friendly, anyhow," Frances said. "He might try something on the crook." Her gaze went to the Indian. "Will you watch him tonight? Then tomorrow, someone else."

"I watch," Mitya said.

Daisy said, "I say you ought to get a gun, Gil."

"I'm no hand with guns."

"Come along, dovie," Frances said, bending over her. She slid one hand under Daisy's tender white arm and helped her to her feet, and started away toward the lean-to.

Mitya sat on the deck of the half-unmade ship and kept his gaze on Friendly's, but he was thinking about Mammy Hardheart. Wondering what she was building here, side by side and within what he was building.

He already loved what he was building here. Yet it was hardly begun, it was a place of air and dreams, mostly. A bad wind could blow it away and leave him with nothing again.

At Metini he had known what to do, even when he could not do it. Here he knew only what his hands made, the truth of lines and angles, the solidity of wood. At Metini he had known the people, his kindred, as well as he knew himself. Here he knew only the outsides of people. So his hands ached for tools and his mind for the work of building.

He thought of Daisy, who had followed him around all afternoon asking questions and trying to help him. He thought he knew Daisy, a little. But thinking of her reminded him of Olga. He wrenched his mind from pretty, wicked Olga, who had betrayed him and started all this. He aimed his gaze at Friendly's again, keeping watch.

7

FOR A FEW DAYS everything was quiet, mostly. Mammy began selling whiskey in the Shining Light, and some fights broke out, and a man from Little Chile got a knife in the chest. On Sunday Gil went up to the Plaza to watch the Regulators march.

The post office was closed, but most of the other businesses were open. The Bella Union and the El Dorado overflowed with drunks and half-drunks and gamblers. In the dust below the flagpole, half a dozen Mexicans sat playing coon can. Dennison's Exchange was selling eggs for five dollars apiece and laying hens for twenty. Gil went into the Bella Union out of professional curiosity, but could not even reach the bar. He went back out to the street, bought a warm tortilla from a little brown boy in a straw hat, and sat in the sun eating it and watching the crowd. In the corner by the post office, two men who were stripped to the waist squared off for a boxing match; the onlookers cheered them in German.

Around noon the Regulators arrived, banging on drums and blowing trumpets, carrying torn regimentals on a long pole overhead.

Their appearance stilled the whole teeming Plaza. Gil backed up toward the edge of the square and found himself part of a crowd that stared and scowled and murmured but recoiled hastily out of the way as the army of green jackets swaggered through their midst.

There were dozens of the Regulators, formed into two columns. Some carried rifles proudly slung across their shoulders; most of them had pistols in their belts. As they marched they bawled out a tuneless anthem. At their head was a bushy-bearded man whose name, Gil knew, was Roberts. He tossed his arms back and forth like a drum major, his head swiveling from side to side, his jaw thrust out. The steady booming of the drums set Gil's teeth together, and the screech of the two trumpets hurt his ears. Twice the Regulators trooped all the way around the Plaza while the crowd glowered and muttered but did nothing, and then, turning crisply on his heel, Roberts marched straight toward Dennison's.

Gil and the mass of men around him blocked the way. Roberts came at them as if they were paper, his bellowing, strutting soldiers at his back. Gil braced himself, sensing all the other men around him, ready to resist, but then the men around him scrambled out of the way and he found himself moving too, hopping like a corncrake out of the path of the green jackets. His ears burned. As Roberts pranced by him he thought he saw a sardonic gleam in the Regulator chief's eye, aimed especially at Gil Marcus.

The troop pounded into Dennison's, slowed by the necessity of getting through the door. Roberts, in first, was out again almost at once, eating a red apple, two more stuffed into his pockets, a round loaf of bread under one arm. The rest of the Regulators followed in his track, into the store and out again, carrying whatever they happened to have found on the way: fruit and bread and pickles and sausages. The last few carried handfuls of eggs, which they flung into the air and into the crowd. As they marched away a clerk rushed out of the store and shouted, "Good riddance! You took it all, you bastards — don't bother comin' back, they ain't no more!"

Gil rubbed his palms on the thighs of his trousers. He looked around at the still, angry men around him, wondering why nobody stopped this, and remembered how he himself had ducked out of the way when Roberts came straight at him, and was ashamed. He went over toward the saloon to get a drink.

This time he got to the Bella Union ahead of the crowd. The air was hot and smoky, and there were sloggy puddles on the tramped earthen floor. Off in the corner was a cage of poles; Gil peered at it curiously, wondering what it was for, and then a man got between him and it, a man in a well-cut coat, a spotless collar, an air of slightly embarrassed aristocracy. He was coming straight toward Gil, smiling, and with a twitch Gil realized he knew him.

"Well, well," this man said, while Gil was still struggling to think of his name. "Marcus, isn't it?"

"That's right." Gil shook his hand, and then remembered that this was Sam Brannan's clerk, who had helped him buy the title to the land beneath the Shining Light. "Unh — Terry Rudd, right?"

"Tierney," said the tall man. "How's business?"

"Fair. Pretty fair. How's Sam Brannan's business?"

"Oh, Sam always does well," said Tierney Rudd. "What brings you up this side of town?"

Gil leaned on the counter. There was only one bartender, busy at the other end, with more men arriving all the time at the bar; it would be a while before he got his drink. He said, "Actually, I came to see the Regulators."

"Did you. Pretty disgusting, isn't it."

Gil shook his head. "It doesn't say much for San Francisco that we put up with that."

"Well," said Tierney Rudd. "That's what I'm here for. My boss wants to put a stop to it."

"Brannan?" Gil's head lifted. "If anybody can do it, he can."

"Will you come to an indignation meeting up here tonight?"

"An indignation meeting," Gil said, disappointed. "Hell, that's more like a church social." He had stopped going to indignation meetings the first week he spent in San Francisco. "Look, Rudd, what we need is some force to use against them."

"Sam wants to call a meeting. Test the temper of the people, talk things out."

"The temper of the people! Did you see what those bastards just did?"

"They've been doing that for months." The tall man had lost his smile. "We have to start somewhere. Come to the meeting to-night."

Gil looked him in the eyes. "What if I bring my crew?"

"Bring them. Bring everybody you can. The more the better."

Gil said, each word precise, "My crew is colored."

"Oh. I forgot that." Tierney Rudd scratched his nose. "Well, come by yourself, then. Mormons don't look too kindly on the Sons of Ham. We don't want trouble in the ranks."

"I thought so," Gil said. He turned to the bar. Tierney Rudd went on, moving into the crowd; a moment later he was talking to somebody else. Gil hunched his shoulders, staring at the wall, his thoughts muddled. He caught himself remembering what Mitya had said the night before: that they should simply kill Friendly. Suddenly everything in him yearned for that, for the swift, fatal stroke. The bartender was still far off; he would never get a drink here. He turned, walked out of the Bella Union, and went back down to Pacific Street.

8

LIKE ALL THE INDIGNATION MEETINGS Gil had ever been to, this was too confused even to get started. He walked along the back edge of the crowd, in the dark, Mitya half a step behind him. Josh and the other men, wisely, had stayed at the Shining Light, but the Indian suffered from a catlike curiosity and had insisted on coming. Gil kept watch around them; he had seen these things break into riots before, simply because somebody spoke with the wrong accent; and Indians were always fair game.

Mitya said, "Many, many people."

"They haven't got anything else to do," Gil said.

In the dark the crowd filled the south end of the Plaza like a churning sea, an indistinct mass of bodies, a rumble of voices and grinding feet. Out there somewhere, a gun went off, and a rough cheer answered. Somebody shouted, "Where's Brannan?"

"That's what I'd like to know," Gil muttered. He kept moving, the soles of his feet itchy. Beyond the crowd, a torch bloomed, a lick of ruddy flame. A moment later, another joined it, and another, all along the front of the firehouse.

"Brannan," the cry went up. "Brannan! Brannan!" And suddenly the whole great mass of men surged forward, roaring.

Gil reached out and grabbed Mitya by the arm. The crowd's excitement was like a sickness, communicated through the air; his temples throbbed and his mouth was dry. Another gunshot rang out, the sound zinging through him, and he jumped.

Mitya laughed. He pressed forward, toward the torches, and Gil had to follow him, trying to tow him back. Then Sam Brannan stepped up onto the top of the firehouse, in between the torches.

The roar that met him was a solid wall of sound. Gil peered up through a forest of waving arms, many holding rifles and pistols and clubs. Brannan paced up and down between the bounding flames. He was a big man, with a big, square head and an extravagant mustache bisecting his face.

He had a big man's voice. He bellowed, "Well, boys, you all know why we're here! For months we've been suffering at the mercy of the *alcalde*'s police, and now, I say, it's time to put a stop to it!"

A blast of voices answered him. Gil backed up, unnerved. He turned to Mitya and shouted, "You'd better get out of here," but by the look on the Indian's face Gil saw that not a word was reaching him. He put out one hand and clutched Mitya's arm.

Brannan was shouting again. "The Regulators have been taking what they want for months, while the honest, law-abiding men of this city stood by helpless, and the *alcalde* did nothing! Nothing! I say now let's do what we want, for once! Let's take the law into our own hands! Come on!"

He strode forward, his arm milling, urging them after him; reaching the edge of the firehouse roof, he leapt down to the ground, and the crowd howled and roared after him. The torches came down off the firehouse and sailed along above the heads of the mob.

Gil leapt back, staying to one side, his heart pounding. Brannan was racing off across the Plaza, toward the *alcalde*'s office, the mob behind him like the tail following the comet's head. Gil wheeled, looking for Mitya. The Indian was gone. Around him Gil saw only strangers, shouting and excited men who rushed by him, following Sam Brannan. Up ahead, at the *alcalde*'s little adobe, the big Mormon elder was shouting again. Gil wheeled, panting, caught up in the heat of this; he took a step after the crowd, then another, and was suddenly running fearlessly with the rest. He forgot Mitya; he felt the crowd around him like a host of other selves.

Torches flared up all around him, first one or two and then a dozen and then a hundred, driving the night back, glossing every face with light like red warpaint. Gil had no weapon; he looked wildly around him for anything he could use to fight, and somebody thrust a stick into his hand. He yelled. A bubbling desire filled him to strike with the stick, to hit and to hurt. One with the crowd, he rushed on after Sam Brannan, after the Regulators.

Brannan's Vigilantes started on the beach, at Montgomery Street. Armed with clubs and axes and guns, they came shoulder to shoulder up Washington Street, stopping everybody they found. Every door they passed they pushed open and went into, and before they had gone half a block the tents and buildings ahead of them were spewing people. Some of them joined the Vigilantes. Some turned white faces toward the advancing mob and ran away up the street.

Mitya had gotten away from the crowd when he saw what was happening. He went along ahead of the Vigilantes, staying off to the side of the street, slipping down between buildings, watching through the seams and cracks. He could see they weren't killing anybody, but they were beating some of the men they stopped, and hauling a lot of them off toward the Plaza. He did not see Gil Marcus.

He went off to the south, to Pacific Street, to the Shining Light, where Mammy's people were gathered in the unfinished room, clustered in the light of the lanterns. Josh and Laban and Phineas and the other workmen stood in the back. Daisy and Mammy Hardheart stood up front, where the door would one day be.

Mitya went past them into the hull of the ship, open like an eggshell, and climbed up the ladder inside to the deck. There he lay down by the rail to watch. Across the way, Friendly's was dark and silent.

Soon the Vigilantes came. First there was a quiet, a strange emptiness in the street. Then a rush of men running inland. Then stillness again. The level boards under Mitya began to tremble. Up from the beach flowed a tide of men that filled the street from edge to edge as far back as he could see.

In front of the Shining Light they stopped, thick as a forest. Some of them at once strode over to Friendly's and went inside. Some went into the tent-shack boarding house just east of the ship, some into the one like it west of Friendly's. Most of them stood there and waited, hardly speaking, their guns and clubs tipped against their shoulders or slung in their arms. Out of the front row of them, a tall, black-haired man walked toward the Shining Light, one hand rising to sweep off his broad-brimmed hat. He talked to Daisy.

"Miss Duncan?" he said. "I'm Tierney Rudd. I want to beg your pardon for interrupting your evening."

Daisy's back was to Mitya. Her hair hung down loose over her shoulders. She had a long coat on. Beside her Mammy was small and silent and unnoticed. Daisy said, "Mr. Rudd, you're turning the whole place upside down."

From the army in the street came a low general murmur. Tierney Rudd held his hat over his chest. "It's for your sake, Miss Duncan. Making San Francisco safe for you and others of the fair and gentle sex."

She bowed her head slightly. "Go ahead and do what you have to do, sir, and my blessings on you."

He hesitated, his gaze fixed on her, and seemed to want to say more, but the army was already moving, as if she had sent them on. The men who had gone into Friendly's came out alone and hurried on up Pacific Street. Tierney Rudd ran along beside them toward the front of the line.

Ahead, at the edge of the light, there was a sudden scurry and ripple of motion. A yell burst from the Vigilantes, and they raced into the darkness. A gun went off. Then two at once. A sobbing voice yelled, "God damn you — "

Mitya rolled onto his back. His heart was beating hard, and he put his hand over his chest there. A sudden crackle of gunshots sounded, farther away up the street, and wood broke. He could hear again the steady boom of the army's march; slowly it moved away until all he got of it was the trembling of the deck under him. That faded. In the silence he listened to the voices of the workmen, down by the lanterns, talking and joking. Daisy said something in a tired voice. Josh laughed his deep, loose laugh. Mitya sat up.

Mammy Hardheart came up onto the deck of the ship.

He knew who it was before he saw her, by the lightness and quickness of her step. He kept his back to her. She came up behind him, her breathing tight, not from the effort of climbing the ladder, and sank down behind him.

She said, "I want you to kill Friendly now."

He twitched, startled. His head turned, catching her in the edge of his gaze. The lanterns below them scattered some light over her, but he could make out nothing of her look.

She said, "Like these white men, these Vigilantes. They're making done with their enemies. We can too." Her voice was soft as night air. She said, "Nobody will know, if you do it now, with so much else going on."

He said, "Friendly has strong, deep magic."

"Are you afraid?"

He considered that; he was afraid, but it seemed right to him for an ordinary man to be afraid, sent against a magic poisoner like Friendly. He was eager for it too, for the test. He said, "No gun."

"I can't help you there. I don't have one either. Isn't there some other way?"

Mitya turned his gaze forward again, across the lantern light below, toward the dark pitch of Friendly's tent. It pulled him. He felt this work grow real and strong, pulling him into it. His hands rolled into fists. He said, "Maybe."

"Do it," she said softly. "Do it, Mitya, and I'll always be your friend."

He sat still a moment longer, nursing the hunger in him for revenge. He had power too, growing here, in this place he was building, which Friendly threatened. In his mind he saw it straight, like a string drawn taut, Friendly at one end, himself at the other. He rose and went by her to the ladder and down to the street.

Frances sat on the deck of the ship, watching the street, her eyes keen, but she did not see him go. Across the way, Friendly's looked deserted, the vast, lumpy hill of canvas only dimly lit, its creases filled with sand. The air was cold and she began to shiver. Even in summer this city had a heart of ice. After a while, restless, she went down into the hull of the ship.

The others were bedding down. The places they had made for themselves, out of pieces of canvas and wood, lined the curved wooden hull like cocoons. She walked out to the half-finished room, paced along the edge of it, touching the walls, glancing toward Friendly's, still and dark. In the doorway she paused, watching the street.

The canvas flap to Friendly's tent shivered and drew back. Silent as the fog, the Indian came out.

He had the ax in one hand. He looked around him, making sure he was unseen, and walked across the street toward her. Her breath caught short. The light from the lantern washed up over him, the broad planes of his face, the set of his lips. His strange narrow eyes. In his face she saw the sleek satisfaction of a fed cat. He stopped in front of her. She could not bring herself to speak.

He said, "Now I have a gun." He showed her the pistol in his hand.

She said, "I didn't hear any shots." Her tongue felt thick.

"No," he said. He went by her, carrying the pistol in one hand, the ax in the other. There was a bucket at the edge of the stage, and as he went by he dropped the ax headfirst into it. He walked away into the ship.

She turned, gripping her hands together, and flung her gaze at Friendly's. The wind was rising, and the great mass of canvas shook and snapped. The skin crawled all over her body. Nothing seemed different. Nothing seemed to have changed. If she had not seen the pistol she would have doubted him. If she had not seen the look in his eyes. She turned and walked back toward the ship, the way he had gone. The ax leaned up out of the bucket. The water was scummy and smelled bad with a stink that writhed every hair up on end. She carried the bucket around behind the ship, and spilled the bloody water out onto the ground, and covered the stain with dry sand.

Tierney Rudd wheeled at the window and stalked back across the room, unable to keep still; at the table Sam Brannan and his friends, the other judges, hunched on their elbows like vultures and stared at him. Brannan said again, "There's no call to hang anybody."

"These men spread terror and suffering throughout the city," Tierney said. "Attacked the wretched and the weak and the friendless, annoyed even the great and the mighty. You have managed to bring the whole city together in one tremendous effort to cleanse us, but instead of doing that you're going to let them all go!"

Young Isaac Bluxome, sitting on Brannan's left, said stiffly, "We're not letting anybody go. We're shipping them out; they'll never come back."

"They'll come back," Tierney said. "If not this particular set, another, virtually identical, when the worst that can come to them by their atrocious crimes is to be scolded and sent home."

Brannan sat back, his thumbs under his belt. "What do you want us to do, Rudd? Pick out a few of the scruffiest and crucify them? Are you suggesting we sneak by such niceties as proof and justice and laws?" The two men on either side of him started and looked down.

Tierney said, "Hang the leaders at least. Hang Sam Roberts." He was panting, his fingertips tingled, his face felt hot. The room was too small, and he could not stop moving. He looked from face to face along the table and at the two men lingering by the door. Nobody would meet his eyes.

All night long and all that morning the Vigilantes had been dragging in their prizes. Some of the prisoners walked in, some were hauled along bodily; some were untouched and some beaten half to death. Most of them probably were Regulators, and probably most of the Regulators were among the men brought in. Now, however, all these prisoners were taking up space and needing to be watched and fed. And disposed of.

Tierney grabbed once more for the power glimmering out there before him. "Hang them. Show their kind that San Francisco isn't safe for thieves and gangs. They're hanging people all over the country, damn it; they hanged a woman down in Dry Diggings, didn't they? We'll look like a free ride."

Brannan said, "Rudd, you've been a big help all through it, but you're letting it get in the saddle on you. Go home and go to bed." Isaac Bluxome cleared his throat, lifted his eyes to Tierney's, and nodded.

Tierney wiped his hand over his forehead again. He was exhausted, too tired to sustain his indignation. He saw the opportunity fluttering away from him like a piece of thistledown, lost before he even knew what it was.

"No," he said. "I've been here from the beginning. I'll stick it out." He went around the table and sat down again, slumping in the chair, a dull throb of pain now banging at the roots of his skull. Brannan nodded to the guards, and they brought in the next of their prisoners.

9

JOSH SAID, "I'm telling you, she got something strong. I knew an old woman like her, back in Mississip'. Lived in the swamp. No bigger'n a mosquito. She could heal any wound, any sickness. Heal black man, heal white man. Make love charms, take away babies." His voice sank. "Kill anybody she want to. With a word and a sign. You see Friendly gone."

Mitya laughed. He didn't want to say anything about Friendly.

They were sitting on the deck of the ship, looking out over the frame of the Shining Light's new roof, eating corncakes and apples. In a few minutes they would start working again. From here Mitya could see across Pacific Street up toward the Plaza, where the high false fronts of the gambling houses rose like a wooden cliff.

Just across the street below him, Friendly's tent was already disappearing. People took away parts to use other places. The front was just bare sticks. While Mitya watched, two little yellow boys rolled up a big piece of canvas from the sagging roof and toted it away up Pacific Street toward Chinatown.

He thought: This place grows, that place dies. The idea satisfied him. Better than Josh's talk about Mammy.

Josh said, "Mostly, you know, the power in the world, it goes to the men. But now and again a woman gets hold of some, and then she's got more power than you can think about." He patted Mitya on the shoulder. "I telling you this 'cause you just an ignorant Indian." He got up hastily, nimble for a big man, pretending to dodge. His smile flashed white in his broad black face.

Mitya said, "Maybe. But you an ingrant nigger." He reached for the apple core that Josh had left on the deck.

Josh gave a last chuckle, like a leftover. He settled down again at the rail. Mitya ate the apple core, crunching the seeds between his teeth, and gestured out over the open room before him. "We put on the roof next, before rain."

"Rain. Hell, it don't rain here."

Mitya turned toward him, startled, and smiled. "Tell me more about ingrant." He laughed into Josh's face. "Get roof on next, sure. Come on." He started up onto his feet, and Josh followed him.

"I ain't seen it rain here, not once."

"How long you here?"

"Six months."

Mitya laughed again. They went down the ladder on the side of the ship into the building.

He had brushed off what Josh said about Mammy, but he had already thought about it himself. Mitya's own people believed in such powers — the poisoners, men who lived in the woods, who dug holes and put charms in them, who killed with their looks, and the dreamers, women who lived among the people, saw the deepest truth, sucked the evil out of the sick, kept the names and fates of everybody gathered in the caul of their dreams. But Mammy told no dreams, and she was not a poisoner.

He had beaten the poisoner. Far from his homeland, alone, he had come on Friendly face to face and killed him. He carried that in him now like a fire in his gut. He thought the power here lay not in Mammy but in the place itself, in the Shining Light. As long as he was here, he drew on that power. With Josh behind him, he walked out into his building and called the rest of his men up, to work on the roof.

Now and then, in the stream of wealth that flowed through the Shining Light, Gil saw a Mexican dollar or a gold piece from the Atlantic states or even English money, but there was very little coin in San Francisco. Everything bought was paid for in gold dust, weighed out on tray scales, packed away in deerskin pokes, in tobacco tins, in the hollow shafts of goose quills. Some of the banks springing up — in a safety box, on the back of a mule — began to write out scrip, but the banks went up and down like miners' hopes, and most businesses would not accept the scrip at face value.

Still, there was a lot of money around, in many forms. Gil had never had so much of it and could not resist spending it as fast as it came. Finding things to buy was the hard part. He went to auctions and bought up whole lots of goods on the waterfront, parts of the cargoes off ships whose crews had deserted, household effects of men desperate for a stake. Half of these goods he turned around and sold within a few hours, to other men with handfuls of money and a desperate urge to spend it.

One lot he brought home included sacks of lime and linseed oil and boxes of red and yellow ochre and bluing. Once they had raised the inside walls of the Shining Light, he went to Mitya and said, "We could mix up some paint to cover these walls."

Mitya had his bowl of water and his string and was laying out the bar. He said, "Later."

"I'll do it," Laban said. He had been watching from one side with the other men. He stepped over the stack of wood between him and the wall and went out.

Mitya measured a distance out from the back wall, picked up his ax and pounded a stake into the ground and hooked his string around it, payed out an arm's length, and marked the ground there. Gil went to watch him, fascinated. With the string and his stakes Mitya laid out the two corners of one end of the bar, and walked down twenty feet and laid out the other two corners, as precise as a surveyor. Gil had never seen him measure anything twice and had never seen any of his measurements turn out wrong. He wrote nothing down; yet he remembered it all.

Laban appeared out of the back storeroom carrying a bucket and an old stick broom. The tang of wet lime spread through the air. Gil waved him away.

"It stinks. Start at that end." He pointed toward the finished wall, as far from the rest of them as possible. Laban lugged the bucket off. Mammy had hired some Mexicans to play the fiddle and the guitar before Daisy's show, and they came out on the stage and began to practice.

Mitya stood back and gave orders, and the other men went to work setting posts in the corners and down the length of the bar. The Indian got his bowl of water and leveled every post himself. On the stage the Mexicans played dance music. Mammy came into the room.

She went up to see the bar first and stood by Gil a moment, watching the men shovel pebbles into the hole around a post; her gaze rose and traveled over the ceiling. Her gaze sharpened and she turned completely around, toward the front of the building. "What's that, now?"

Gil turned. "Laban's just painting the walls." But then he looked more closely.

The door cut the front wall in half. Laban had covered nearly all of the left half of it with whitewash, lightening up that whole corner of the room. It was nearly noon, and the day's first customers were leaking in the door; they had stopped and gathered around to look at what else Laban was putting on the wall. Mammy went down there to look, and Gil followed.

Laban turned toward them, a piece of charcoal in his hand. Across the wall in front of him, spreading upward as if flowing forth like a river from his hand, was the reclining figure of a woman sketched in black lines. The figure was eight feet long, bold and full and rich, one arm lifted up around the head, cradling a mass of hair. The face was blank, but still there was no mistaking her identity. It was Daisy.

Gil let out a laugh. "God damn!" It came to him, offhand, that a darkie shouldn't make pictures of white women naked, but before him, on the wall, the bold black lines made something so real and true it seemed to have been there all along.

Mammy said, amused, "Now, now, Laban, you gon' put clothes on her?"

Behind Gil there was a low whistle. The music cut abruptly off; everybody else in the room was coming down to look.

Josh said, "What you doin', boy?"

Laban was standing there, his eyes darting back and forth, between Gil and Mammy. "Can I keep it?"

"Daisy's got to see it," Gil said. He stretched one hand out toward the wall, where she lay like a great white bird about to wing away.

Mammy said, "That's pretty, Laban. But I think you're supposed just to paint the wall."

Laban's head twisted; his gaze poked at her and then slid toward Gil. "You gonna make me cover it up?"

Daisy walked up behind the crowd gathered before the picture. She gasped, "That's me!" and pushed in past Gil, thrust her head forward, and peered into the blank face on the wall.

Laban was still staring up at Gil. Mammy was smiling now, looking wizened and ancient and kind. "It's all right with me," she said.

Gil said, "It's up to Daisy, isn't it?" His eye followed the elegant curve of the charcoal haunch and then shifted to the fleshly Daisy.

The girl's face shone. "Oh, I love it. Yes, leave it. Finish it." She nodded to the young man before her. "Thank you, Laban."

Laban swelled visibly, smiling. He lowered his eyes and stooped for the piece of charcoal, and then wheeled back to Gil. "I can paint other things?"

Gil shrugged. "I don't see you have much talent as a carpenter, Laban. Do what you're good at."

Laban's smile widened an inch on either side. He went back to his work. Mammy folded her arms over her chest, her gaze resting on Gil a moment.

"We're going to need more whiskey tonight, for sure."

"I bought all Friendly's stock," Gil said. "The drover came by this morning and says he'll deliver it this afternoon."

Mammy cocked her eyebrows. "All right. Guess you got it well in hand, Gilbert." She looked past him at Laban. "Don't you be putting me up on no wall, boy." She leaned down and swatted Laban on the arm, making her point, and went away.

10

TIERNEY RUDD SAID, "Congratulations, Gil. This place is starting to look like something." He brushed off the top of the new bar and leaned his elbow on it, and smiled. "Not exactly the El Dorado, but it has its charms."

Behind the bar, Phineas came up quietly with a bottle of whiskey and two glasses. Gil said, "It's a start."

Around them stood the solid, well-framed walls of a building that would last; the floor was still trampled earth, but Mitya had plans for that, as soon as Gil could find him more wood. The stage was a solid, steady floor, smooth and waxed. The extravagant drapery of the backdrop disguised its origin as several mainsails.

The rest of the room was well lit and well crowded. The miners whose ready supply of gold fueled all this got what they paid for: good whiskey in real glasses, which the men behind the bar kept filled and clean — Phineas stood only a few feet away from Gil and Tierney, washing and drying the stock. The four big lanterns that had once lit Daisy's stage now hung at cardinal points from the ceiling beams. The first of what Gil hoped would be eight or ten gaming tables stood directly beneath the eastern lantern; he could not see it because of the crowd around it, watching a solid ring of men play three-card monte. He was still looking for an honest faro dealer. Another crowd fronted the far wall, where Laban had finished the picture of Daisy and was filling up the space behind and around her with red and yellow ochre.

Off behind the bar, a sheet of canvas painted white covered the hole into the hull of the ship. The space beyond quartered the growing number of people who lived in the Shining Light. As Gil watched, the canvas swayed back a little and Mitya came out, dark and squat and massive as a block of wood, his long black hair lank over his shoulders.

Tierney said, "You got a lot of coloreds here."

Gil shrugged. "It's Mammy's place." He liked the variety, the flavor of this crowd, with its Indians and Chinese and Negroes mixed in with white men from all around the world. From where he stood he could hear voices speaking Spanish, German, Chinese. He felt himself a bigger man for being here. "All the Regulators were Americans, weren't they."

Tierney cleared his throat. His smooth-shaven face stiffened into a grimace. "They were all New Yorkers, to be precise. We got rid of them."

"Shipped them out of town. That seemed mild enough. I'm surprised you didn't hang a few."

Above the impeccable collar, the perfectly fitted coat, Tierney's face was bland again; he lifted his glass to his lips. "I tried, but the other judges got cold feet." His skin looked polished over the arches of his cheekbones. His eyes flicked toward the stage. "When does she come on?"

"Later," Gil said.

"I'm wondering — " Again something held in check ruffled the glassy surface of Tierney Rudd's expression. His mouth performed an excellent smile, which drew everything straight. Over the rim of his glass he said, "I'm wondering if you would care to introduce her to me."

Gil's head jerked back; a knot formed in his belly. He said, "She's a good woman. Just because she sings and dances doesn't make her up for sale."

Tierney sipped the pale whiskey. "Are you her . . . protector?"

Gil stared into the other man's eyes and said, "No, I'm not. But I am her friend."

"And I can see," Tierney said, "that the subject disturbs you. I withdraw the request." He shifted his elbow on the bar a little, changing the subject. "You've heard about the new strike in the Sierra?"

Gil had been in the Plaza when the news came that they were raking up nuggets by the flour sackful in a place called Downieville; he had seen the huge square empty like a holed boat, every man there footing it at coat-flapping speed for the waterfront and the steamer to Oakland. "Half of San Francisco was across the bay in two hours."

"But not you. Had your fill of mining?"

"I did some mining," Gil said. What he remembered most acutely about his time in the placers was the peculiar, gut-twisting suspense of panning the dirt, sloshing away mud and sand, peering into the gravel in the bottom of the pan. Sometimes, suddenly, the dull grit bloomed with a few flecks of gold dust, glinting, brilliant, never enough.

"Easier ways to make a living," said Tierney. "Easier ways to get rich. Look at Sam Brannan — he's the richest man in San Francisco, maybe in California. And he's never dipped a pan into a stream."

Gil said, "Cheers to Sam Brannan." He had seen the renegade

Mormon elder only a few times, mostly during the business with the Regulators, when Brannan with his tremendous voice and endless vigor had led the mob in pursuit of justice.

"Getting richer, too." Tierney rubbed his nose. His voice was velvety, too mild, concealing a gravel of envy in his craw. "Brannan makes money off everything — like the assault on the Regulators. You know he already owns half of San Francisco. Pretty soon he's going to own a whole lot more."

"Is he." Gil made a quick mental survey of the land around the city. "There isn't too much more to own, is there? Aside from the hills and the dunes."

"Well, this land isn't exactly terra firma." Tierney laughed, raw, more of his deep feeling breaking through. "He's a clever, clever man, Brannan. We could all learn a little from him. You know when the tide goes out, how it leaves those mud flats along the waterfront?"

"God," Gil said. "That's not land."

"No. It's not. Unless the town council of San Francisco votes to call it land and allow building on it."

Gil said slowly, "Is Brannan on the council? Yes."

"Yes. Oh, yes. But so also is the *alcalde*, of course, and the *alcalde* has blocked this particular scheme of Brannan's for months." Tierney rolled the foot of the glass on the bar top, his eyes glittering. "However, the Regulators were the *alcalde*'s men."

"Not really," Gil said. He had wondered a few times since that wild night why Brannan had suddenly taken up the cause against the Regulators. Now he saw something colder, harder in it.

Tierney went on, "In the eyes of nearly everybody, they were the *alcalde*'s police force. And now, of course, with the Regulators dumped, the feeling is, the *alcalde*'s been dumped too. So to speak. He won't dare stand in Brannan's way, anyway."

"You mean," Gil said, "that Brannan will be able to buy that land cheap because nobody else will know that the council is going to rezone it?" He felt like a fool suddenly, Brannan's dupe, as if he had been hanging in the air all this time and had fallen only now.

"Oh, yes. Look for our friend Sam to resign from the council somewhere in the proceedings. Before the auction's called." Tierney set the glass down with a clink. When Phineas turned from washing glasses and picked up the bottle, the tall man waved him off. "Actually, if you want my opinion, he's playing this one too close to the edge. The gold in the Sierra will peter out soon enough, and when it does, San Francisco will fold like a busted flush. Those lots won't be worth a handful of sand." He smiled, showing no teeth. "My regards to Miss Duncan." He put one hand to his hat brim and sauntered away across the room.

Gil stayed where he was. Bitterly he thought that Daisy would have accepted those regards. He chewed over the other thing, that what had looked to him like justice had looked to other men like money. Some part of his understanding felt painfully enlarged. He was still leaning against the bar, mulling the whole thing over, when a yell brought his mind back up to the surface.

"Get this darkie offen me!"

Gil hurried forward, toward the disturbance spreading through the crowd halfway down the bar. A man in a sailor's canvas pants and short-cut blue jacket backed in a rush away from the bar, shouting, while the people all around him scattered back, giving him room, and giving room to Mitya, who stalked after him.

Mitya roared, "Crimp. Crimp. No crimp here."

The word spread around the room, and everybody turned. The men around the card table even left their game a moment, and all along the bar the heads swiveled. The man in the blue jacket stopped in the middle of the room.

"I ain't no crimp. You fuckin' Injun, I'm gonna kill you!" He pulled a long knife out of his belt.

Gil bounded forward, one hand out toward the wide blade. "Hold it. What's going on here?" He put himself in between the sailor with his knife and Mitya.

The Indian's strange eyes blazed. "Crimp," he said. "Crimp!"

The crowd seethed with whispers and hisses, the men pushing in close enough to see, smelling a fight.

Now the crowd's voice doubled to a roar. Gil turned to the sailor. "Get out. I won't have men like you in the Shining Light."

"I ain't no crimp," the other man said. His face was bright red. The nicked blade of the knife glinted in the light of the overhead lanterns. "You gonna take the word of a fuckin' Injun? It's his liquor! He's the crimp!"

Somebody yelled, "Throw 'em both out!" Gil, wary of the knife, wiped his hands on his pant legs, his stomach churning. His mind was frozen and he could not think what to do. The notched blade seemed more dangerous than a clean edge.

He realized the whole mob was watching him; he had to take charge here. He said, "Get out of the Shining Light."

The sailor ignored him, looking from side to side for help. "Come on, boys — you gonna let this Injun hit a white man?" He cocked his knife arm and plunged past Gil, straight at Mitya.

The crowd screeched. Gil wheeled, knowing he should be stopping this, unable to see how to do that. The sailor flung himself on Mitya and the two men staggered back, locked together in a grotesque dance, the packed onlookers giving way behind them. They crashed down onto the ground, Mitya underneath. His legs wrapped around the other man's, his arms coiled around the blue jacket. The knife caught the light an instant. The locked bodies rolled over and over, the roaring crowd making room.

The knife clattered down. A scream cut through the howling of the crowd. Mitya sprang to his feet and leapt back into the middle of the room, his arms spread. His head turned; he spat something onto the floor. There was blood all over his mouth. The sailor lay curled up on the floor, moaning.

Gil's legs unlocked and he went up beside the Indian and took hold of his arm. Mitya jumped. Under Gil's palm the muscle of the other man's arm was hot and hard like a gun just fired.

The sailor still writhed on the floor. His hands covered his face. The people closest bent over him, keeping a fastidious distance. He rolled onto his back, his hands to his face, blood streaming

down over his cheek. Somebody let out a shriek almost volup-
tuous with horror. "Bit his nose off, by God."

Gil's stomach heaved. The crowd gave a collective gasp that
seemed to suck all the noise out of the room. Gil cast a single quick
look into Mitya's face, the square, dark cheeks slick with sweat,
the narrow eyes unyielding as an animal's.

Mitya said, "No crimp." He walked away toward the bar,
through a mass of men who shrank from him but could not look
away. Vaulting up onto the bar the Indian walked its length to the
opening into the back and disappeared.

Gil swallowed down the sulfurous taste in his throat. He lowered his gaze to the man slumped on the ground before him,
sobbing with pain, the thick blood oozing down his face. One
hand covered his nose, or what was left of it.

From the crowd a curious boy darted quickly out and picked
something off the ground. "Here it is."

Gil stooped and got the man by the collar and hoisted him
toward his feet. "Get out."

The crimp had no resistance left in him. Limp as a stepped-on
snake he hung in Gil's grasp, and Gil had to muscle him toward
the door while the onlookers buzzed and murmured and craned
their necks to watch. Gil flung the crimp out into the street and
turned.

In the middle of the room the boy was saying, "I got it, I got it,
it's mine." Men packed thick around him, peering into what he
held in his hand.

Behind him, by the bar, a towheaded man uncorked a pint
bottle and sniffed it and ran his tongue over the rim. "Crimp juice,
for sure."

Gil's knees quaked. He went over to the bar and leaned on it.
Phineas brought him a glass and a bottle. "Have a drink, boss."
Gil reached for the glass.

"A land auction," Frances said meditatively.

Phineas had come to her in the half-finished cookhouse, which
they were building separate from the saloon, wary of the risk of

fire. "You can ask Mr. Gil about that. I didn't really get all of that."

"Mr. Gil has no business head," said Frances. She leaned over the soup. She had acquired a reliable source of greens and herbs now, down the peninsula, and the broth, thickened with beans, gave up an aroma of sweet corn and hot peppers. "Very good, Phineas. I'll keep it to your credit."

"For sure he wants Miss Daisy," Phineas said.

"Yes. Unoriginal of him." Frances dipped up a cupful of the soup and held it out. "Eat. I want you back behind the bar while Daisy's on the stage. And go find Mitya for me."

"Yes, Mam." Phineas took the cup and moved over toward the cool of the yard, and Frances rang the bell that summoned in the others to their supper.

Mitya walked along the back of the stage to the little doorway cut through the curved hull of the ship. He had been waiting to talk to Mammy alone. Waiting until she wanted something more from him.

He went down through the Shining Light, along the boards laid over its keel. On either side, boxed off by walls of wood and canvas, were the nooks and ledges and dens where the rest of the people here lived. A lamp hung amidships; the beams and walls of the hull cut the light into shafts and spots. In the stern, two little steps led up to Mammy's room.

He knocked on the door and she let him in. He knew the room perfectly; he had made it, walling over one corner of the old captain's cabin. Standing in the middle of it he had to bend his head to keep from bumping the deck above. She sat in the captain's little cave of a bed, tucked under the slant of the transom of the ship.

She said, "Mitya, I need you to do some work for me."

Stooping made his neck hurt. He sat down on his heels and looked her over.

In here she did not try to seem like an old woman. She sat straight on the edge of the bed, her head high, her chin out, looking proud. He said, "I do work already." Thinking of Friendly, not the walls around them.

She smiled at him, and he wondered whether she thought of Friendly too. She said, "Yes. Now I need something more."

He put his hand up over his mouth, going slow with this, making sure he got where he wanted to be. She made him think of his sister, Anna. She had the same certainty, as if she saw more than anybody else. He said, "What work?"

She said, "There's a white man I need to know something about. I want you to find out what you can about him."

He shook his head at her. "I hate white men."

"You like Gil Marcus."

"I hate white men," he said again.

"Just find out about him. I don't like them either." Her voice quivered. "I have suffered quite as much from whites as you have."

He said, "Then I want something back."

Her face smoothed out, bland as an egg. Ready to bargain with him. She said, "What? Money?"

"You," he said. He reached out and took hold of her wrist.

Her eyes went white. She fell still as a quail in the grass, her arm in his grip; he could feel her muscles locked and tight and frightened.

He said, "I want you." He let go of her; she could go nowhere anyway, he blocked the whole little room.

She said, "No." She crouched on the bed, pressed against the incurving wall. He moved in a little closer and put his hands on her.

"No hurt you," he said. He touched the buttons on the front of her dress. She put her hands on his hands, and he stopped.

She said, "This can't happen."

"Yes," he said. "Let me."

"Please. I'll give you money. There are other women."

He smiled at her. "Oh. Other men, too. Why you ask for me, then?"

Her face changed. The still fear eased and something else looked out; she stopped thinking of herself and thought of him. She looked into his face and he saw what moved in her, what came toward him, what wanted him too.

He said, "You have another man?"

"No," she said, and drew back again. "Only whites. When I was little. Forced me." Her voice tightened.

"Then you start," he said. "Kiss me."

Her lips parted. Her eyes grew big and bright; her nostrils flared. He sat there waiting for her, his hands on his knees. She leaned forward and put her mouth against his. Her lips were smooth and dry and then she opened her mouth and he put his tongue into her.

She pulled away from him, turning off. She said, "I don't want this."

"You want it." He took hold of her with one hand and with the other unbuttoned her down to the waist, and she did not stop him.

"Nobody else can know." She faced him again, certain again. Through the opening in her clothes her skin showed dark and sleek.

He drew his hands back. "Nobody know but us."

Her lips parted, and the tip of her tongue showed. Her eyes were hot. "All right." Her voice got a raspy tone in it. "All right then."

He reached out and pulled her dress down over her arms, baring her to the waist, a young woman's body, lily-shaped, with breasts like suns. He touched her nipple and it squeezed hard and erect. Gently he began to take the rest of her clothes off, and she leaned back, her eyes closing. He went slowly, slowly, to keep her ahead of him until she could not say no anymore.

11

MITYA'S GRANDFATHER had been an Aleut, a hunter of sea otters and seals for the Russian American Company. At Fort Ross he was a great man, who spoke face to face with the commandant himself. Sometimes he took Mitya in his boat with him. The boat was a two-man *baidarka*, light as a leaf, a tube of stretched hide with holes in the top for the hunters.

His grandfather wore a *kamleika*, a long coat made of seabird skins. Mitya still remembered the touch of the thin leather, so soft and fine, smelling of fish oil. His grandfather put Mitya under the *kamleika* with him so that his head stuck up through the opening in front.

Then his grandfather paddled the *baidarka* out onto the surging water of the ocean and swooped up and down the waves. A few strokes of his paddle sent the boat shooting through the sea, the green water curling around them. They climbed a wave and skidded down the far side, and Mitya looked up and saw the vast white-topped breaker rising above them, its shadow over them, while his grandfather roared and laughed and spun his paddle in his hands, a force as vast as the sea.

With his back pressed to his grandfather's chest he felt the old man around him as if nothing could ever separate them; he would be safe forever in his grandfather's love. Everybody said he had the old man's eyes. He did not want to remember when his grandfather left Metini, along with the rest of the undersea people, sailing away over the ocean, never coming back.

So he had lost the knowledge of swift and effortless movement, the dizzying free glide of the *baidarka*. Trapped in the drudgery of walking, he stumped over to the Plaza near the end of the day, looking for the man Mammy wanted to know about.

He already knew that Tierney Rudd worked for Sam Brannan,

and he went there first, to the newspaper office on the corner of the square. Three ships had put in on the afternoon tide, and the square was full of people who looked strange and lost. Slouched against the wall in the alley, Mitya watched a man in a round hat taking things out of the pockets of people as the endless crowd streamed by; it reminded him of a bear taking salmon. The man stood by the side of the square until he saw something, plunged into the crowd, dipped his hand quickly into a coat or a pouch, and swam back out to the side again. Nobody in the crowd stayed in one place long enough to notice, except Mitya.

Then from the newspaper office came Tierney Rudd, and Mitya followed him across the sandy square and down Clay Street to a boarding house.

Tierney Rudd went into the boarding house, nodding to a man coming out. On either side of the older house white men were putting up buildings of timber, and Mitya walked around looking at them. One was only half framed. The other had walls and a roof; the doors were unhung and the windows gaping holes. The white men built differently from him. Through the corner of his eye he watched the men who went in and out of the boarding house like wasps around a mud hole. Night was coming. In one of the new buildings the workmen put down their tools and went away, and he went in and studied their tools and the way they fit timbers together.

A window on the side of the boarding house opened, and Tierney Rudd leaned out and emptied a basin of water onto the ground. Mitya kept his head down, staying shy behind a corner.

After a little while longer the tall man came out of the door. Now Mitya was sitting on the ground in front of the half-done house. Tierney Rudd looked the same as when he had gone in, but as he passed by, Mitya could smell soap on him, could see the red mark of the razor on his cheek. He watched the tall man saunter away down the street, his stride neat and rhythmic, until in the constant swarm of traffic he was only one more thing moving.

Getting up, Mitya went to the window on the side wall. It was made in squares for glass, but only one of the holes had glass in it.

He looked into the room beyond, which was almost as small as Mitya's den at the Shining Light. The window was latched, but all he had to do was reach his hand in through an empty square, and he pushed the latch aside and climbed through.

Disappointed, he went around the room touching everything, but there was nothing to see, nothing to steal, nothing to tell Mammy about. Tierney Rudd with his neat clothes and smooth, well-kept face and hands looked rich, but his room had less in it than Mitya's. The bed was made of planks and rope and laid with a straw mattress. The covers were folded carefully over the end of it. A wooden box against the wall had a bowl on it, a pitcher, a piece of a candle. On shelves on the wall there were two white shirts and a set of short pants of thin white fabric, and a book.

He went out again. The night had come. Along this street and in the Plaza there were lanterns hung up on the fronts of the buildings; swarms of insects coated them, and bats swooped and dove in the air around them. The air was cold and still.

In the Plaza he went to a store near the post office that sold to anybody with money, and bought himself a bottle of whiskey. When he came out, somebody recognized him.

"Look. That's the Indian from the Shining Light."

He ignored the murmur, the heads turning. Pulling the cork out of the bottle he put three swallows of the whiskey down his throat.

The Shining Light did its best business around midnight and boomed until well past two or three in the morning. Then the place calmed and slowly emptied until around four or four-thirty, when the door closed. While Mammy and Josh and the rest cleaned up and counted the money, Gil had the habit of going out back to the empty cookhouse, where the morning coffee already simmered in the pot, and drinking a cup of it.

After the constant uproar of the saloon he craved the silence, the freedom of being unwatched and at ease. It never lasted. Other people knew his ways, and before he had poured his second cup of coffee there was a tap on the door.

He answered; on the threshold stood a man wrapped only in a

blanket, his hair and beard wild as matted brambles. His head was bowed and his gaze pointed straight downward. Without looking up, he mumbled, "Got a little bite of somethin', gov?" and Gil went and cut a chunk off one of the loaves waiting in a stack for breakfast, poured a cup of black coffee, and brought it to him. Without much of a thanks the beggar shambled out to the yard with it. Gil shut the door.

A moment later the door opened again, letting Mitya in. The Indian looked sick and very bad-tempered. He trudged to the fire and picked up the pot of coffee.

"Are you all right?" Gil said.

The Indian growled at him. His eyes were bloodshot. He ran one hand up over his face and sat down heavily on the bench with his coffee.

There was another knock on the door. Gil got up and answered it, found another beggar, and fed that one too. The first beggar came back with his cup, which Gil dumped into a pile of dirty dishes on the table.

To Mitya he said, "Do you want some breakfast?"

Mitya looked the other way. He slurped at the coffee, grimacing over the bitter taste. Another of Gil's regular customers came to the door, like them all dirty and half naked, with a shrunken look of exhaustion.

This time when Gil came back into the kitchen the Indian was staring at him. Mitya said, "You feed everybody."

Gil said, "They're hungry." He stood by the chopping block, sawing off another slice of the warm bread; he loved how the soft pale brown inside, when he cut into it, gave up a moist, delicious cloud of steam. "Do you want something?"

The Indian rubbed his hand over his face again. "I get," he said, and rose. Gil sat down again. A few minutes later he was back at the door, taking in dirty cups and handing out others; every morning a few more people came here and knocked.

Mitya said, "They eat here, they come back, they eat more, come back more."

"Yes. Mammy and I have discussed this."

"Mammy unlike it."

"Mammy cares only for people she has a use for," Gil said, and felt at once he had said more than necessary.

But Mitya laughed, a thin, thready laugh that seemed to hurt his head. He said, "My people, we feed only us. No good, feed people not us. So Mammy."

Gil thought Mammy's charity rather more Calvinist than that: she expected a return, even sevenfold. He asked, "Where did you come from?"

The Indian's face closed up. He lowered his head down over his cup, and Gil expected no more from him, but suddenly Mitya said, "My people live by the sea. Out from here. That way." He nodded toward the north.

"Really." Gil had a sudden feeling of the world opening up toward the north, becoming real. "What's up there?"

"Trees," said Mitya. He drank more coffee, and absently he took the slice of bread from Gil. "High tree. You know — redwoods."

"Any grazing land? Is it desert? Farmland, like San Jose?"

Mitya ate the bread. His gaze slid away from Gil's, finding some window of memory. "Grasses, the sea comes up, and then the land rises, steep, high — " His hand shaped a cliff in the air. "Little river run down, the sea come in on sand and rock."

Another knock interrupted them; Gil cut slices off another loaf and poured more coffee and while he was at the door retrieved several dirty cups. The sun was up now, and the cookhouse was full of the dingy dawn light; he trimmed the lantern down and opened the two windows in the back.

He said, "Did you have a family? A wife, children?"

Josh came in, massive, slow, solid, and Gil thought Mitya would say nothing more. But the Indian said quietly, "A wife, once." His jaws milled steadily through the bread. "You wife?"

"No. Not here, not back in Baltimore."

"But Daisy, maybe."

"Daisy!" Gil snorted. He glanced at Josh, pouring himself coffee; the big man turned and smiled at him.

"Mornin' there, Mist' Gil!"

Gil raised one hand to him. Facing Mitya again, he said, "I'm not rich enough for Daisy."

Mitya's face cracked into a smile; his eyelids drooped. He looked tired. He said, "Women all trouble." His gaze rested on Gil, amused. "So sad being men."

Josh gave a harsh guffaw. "That kind of trouble I wish I had some of."

Phineas and Laban came in, arguing; Phineas said, "You could stand behind the bar for a while. Anything."

"I'm busy," Laban said. "I don't have all that much paint, Phin. I got to paint when I got colors."

Phineas said, "I think you ought to work for what you get, boy, whether you got colors or not."

Gil sat back. The cookhouse was getting crowded now, and the knocking on the door had stopped; Mammy would be here in a moment, and Mammy gave no handouts. Mitya got up and stood washing his cup in the basin of grimy water.

Josh reached out and tugged on his shirt. "Where you was all night? We could of used you."

Mitya grunted. Yawning, wrapped like a Christmas present in bright Chinese silk, Daisy sauntered in through the little side door. "Good morning, everybody."

Several voices, all at once: "Hey, Daisy! Mornin', Daisy!" Like a song for her. Gil tried to ignore her but could not; wherever she was was the center. She spoke to everybody, she hugged Laban and patted Phineas' hand, she saw at once that Mitya was sick, and touched him and said something, and the Indian responded, softer toward her than he was toward the men, more trusting. Like them all he loved her. Gil lowered his eyes, one of the herd.

Josh was saying, "Had people fightin' all night long over by'm monte tables. You be here, nobody fight, Mit, you know that. You don't get to goin' off."

Gil said, "That's true, Mitya. You're the resident demon, you've got to be here and be obvious."

"I sent him out," Mammy said, coming up behind him. Gil had not seen her enter the room, and he jumped. She laid one hand on his shoulder. "Your heart is too good, Gilbert, and now there is a shortage of bread for breakfast."

"I've eaten," Gil said. He glanced up and down the table, where now the people of the Shining Light sat shoulder to shoulder, waiting to be fed. "I'm sorry."

Mitya said, "I eat too." He stood up, turning away. "Feed you own, Gil," he said, and went down toward the door and out.

Josh said, "He oughtn't drink, that man. Hits him bad." Mammy brought the loaves of bread on the platter and sent Laban for the coffee.

Gil was tired and not hungry, but he liked being here. He sat back and watched them plow into the simple, homey breakfast. In spite of what Mammy had said, there was bread enough; she must have baked extra, because he had given away six loaves. Laban and Phineas got into it again, the boy lazy and resisting, the man nagging him on. The others began to chime in, mostly on Laban's side. "Let him paint. He can and we can't."

Phineas said, "Everybody's got to work."

"That's his work," Daisy said.

Phineas growled at her. He sat hunched forward as if to protect his food from the others. He said, "Work ain't what you want to do. Work's what you got to do."

"Now, now," Mammy said.

Gil lifted his gaze and caught Daisy watching him. She looked away, but her cheek went red. Since the picnic they had not said much to each other. She stared down at the tabletop, littered with bits of bread and dirty cups, and would not even meet his eyes. Gil swallowed.

"Well. I'm going off to bed. Morning, everybody." He started up, lifting one knee up and across the bench, and all down the table the others also rose and stretched and said good nights. Daisy stayed at the table, looking loftily into space. Gil went away to his room.

Mammy said, "Then Tierney Rudd is not rich."

Mitya laughed; his head hurt, and he leaned it on his hand. "Not rich."

She was rubbing her hands together, palm against palm. She gave him a glassy stare, her outside eye seeing him, her inside eye seeing something else. "But he wants to be rich."

Mitya saw no argument in that. Everybody in San Francisco wanted his hands full of something, even Gil Marcus, who gave everything away. He said, "I sleep."

"Yes, I can see you need to recover," she said. Her hands were still sliding together, her inside eye was still fixed on something not there. Mitya went away, into the hold of the Shining Light, to his den, and curled up there and slept.

Frances sat for a long while on her bed, letting things settle in her mind. One problem was out of the way; to her relief, Mitya was keeping his promise. The sex between them had meant nothing more than a few moments' pleasure. When other people were around he paid no more heed to her than necessary, maintaining an indifference as cool as spring water.

She remembered the hard thrust of his body, the tenderness of his hands. She wanted him again, if she could keep it like this, with no consequences.

Tierney Rudd was now uppermost in her mind. She had asked some questions to go with what Mitya brought her, and she thought Tierney Rudd was a man she could use. He was clever, handsome, ambitious but thwarted, and no more honest than anybody else. The only problem was Daisy, who might not go along.

Daisy had done everything that Frances had asked of her. From the moment they had met, in the kitchen of the Charleston brothel, there had been something strong between the two women — the frightened country girl, her belly round with child, and the runaway black cook. Almost from that meeting Frances had seen that they could go on together.

The baby was born dead. Before the next Sunday, Frances and Daisy had talked their way onto a ship bound for Panama.

"Do what I tell you," Frances had said, over and over. "Do as I say and it will all work out." And it had, so far. Now they had something else to do, centering on Tierney Rudd, and on what Tierney Rudd had let slip about the sale of the tidal flats. Frances thought through it again, feeling for weaknesses, for dangers. It certainly had its dangers. But thinking of it excited her, a deep tremor of her nerves, a tightening of her belly. Maybe this was how men felt as they went off to war.

She lay down on her bed, but she could not sleep. She went over the plan again and again as the day wheeled by toward night, and toward the next beginning.

12

IT HAD RAINED OVERNIGHT, and Washington Street lay under steaming sheets and puddles of water, under a thin, damp goo of mud that clung to anything that touched it. Part of a crowd of people on foot and horseback, the cart bumped and slid along toward the Plaza, splattering up gouts of red silt that Daisy fended off with one gloved hand, protecting herself and her dress. Beside her, Frances sat rigid as a little doll.

"I got to see him," Daisy said, under her breath. "I can't just . . . you know."

"You'll see him," Frances said.

They skated around the corner into the Plaza, where for once the crowd was motionless and mostly quiet. In the middle of the square was a raised stand, fenced off, where several men sat, and one was speaking. The speaker's arm jerked in the air, pulling up words by the roots. Frances said something to Josh, who was driving, and pointed, and the cart rolled up toward the back of the crowd. The wheel cast up a fine spray of grit. Daisy brushed dirt off her dress.

Her heart jumped again. She wondered why she was so edgy. Surely this was nothing new; they had planned something like this since Charleston. She kept thinking about Gil, wishing she could talk this out with him, knowing if she did he would hate her.

She missed him. She saw him every day, but they hardly spoke anymore. He was just an ordinary man, and he would never be rich; he had a sheepish, plowboy look that would never take her to balls and parties. She did not understand why she was searching for him in the crowd even now. She sat up straight, eyes forward, and pulled herself together.

As they came into the crowd the men turned and noticed her, there was a low murmur of interest, and a lot of people moved to give them better space. Somebody called her name, and she waved.

At that, the whole back part of the crowd turned toward her, and a cheer rose. "Daisy! Daisy!" On the platform, the speaker stopped, pulling a kerchief out of his pocket, and glared at her.

"Be still," Frances said. "You're holding things up."

Daisy settled down again. They had brought some cushions into the cart and she fussed with them, getting more comfortable. Up on the platform somebody said, "With this new constitution, California will take her place in the forefront of the several states!"

There was a ragged, bored cheer. Up near the front a man bawled, "Depends on which way you're facing, don't it? Either we're way in front or way behind." The crowd laughed, louder than the cheer.

Somebody else yelled, "When do we get a governor?"

"Elections coming up," said the speaker. "Can I go on?"

Under a volley of jeers and catcalls he decided to sit down. Frances said quietly, "Here comes Mr. Rudd."

Daisy lifted her head, feeling a jolt under her ribs, her blood racing. Another man stood up on the platform, and she kept her eyes on him as if she were watching the priest elevate the Host, while all her other senses strained in another direction.

"Let's have a voice vote," called the man on the platform. "All in favor say aye!"

"Aye," a thousand people roared.

Closer, quieter, she heard someone approach the side of the cart.

"Miss Duncan?"

She turned her head, her throat dry. I won't know what to say, she had told Frances. What should I say?

She said, "Mr. Rudd, I have not had the chance before to thank you for your very kind conduct on the night of the Vigilantes." She smiled at him, looking him in the face, and a shock of pleasure went through her. He was wonderfully handsome. His black hair capped his head, smooth and close, and he dressed very well, his chin smooth, his collar trim and clean. His eyes were gray, direct, hard, which she liked at once, that hard interest. "You made me feel much better. After speaking with you, I knew all would come right in the end."

The man on the platform called, "Everybody against, say nay!"

"Nay!" Just as loud.

"I'm very flattered you would say that, Miss Duncan," said Tierney Rudd.

He put his hand out, and she took it, noticing her glove splattered with the mud, which almost made her laugh. She resisted laughing. Tierney Rudd, she saw, was a very serious man. She wanted him too, just from looking at him, touching him. This would not be so bad after all. She looked into his eyes and smiled. "Maybe you'd come over tonight, after the show," she said, "and have supper with me."

He swelled; his eyes bored at her, and his tongue got going at the gallop. "I would be delighted — very much, very delighted, overwhelmed — "

"The ayes have it," said the man on the platform, and a yell of outrage went up.

"No! Nay, damn you, nay!"

"They're fighting now," said Frances. "The idiots, they can't agree on anything."

Daisy jerked her gaze from Tierney Rudd and peered up toward the platform; the speaker was shouting, waving his arms, trying to calm the crowd, while in front of them several men beat and kicked and leapt on one another. The fighting was spreading. The horse snorted, throwing its head up, as a man in front of the cart wheeled and swung a fist at the man beside him. On either side of her, people stood foot to foot, their arms milling, their faces twisted into grimaces of rage. The horse's rump bunched, the beast squatted back, half rearing, and the cart backed up a round of the wheel.

Tierney Rudd clung still to her hand. "Miss Duncan," he shouted, over the din, "you should leave before harm comes to you." He lifted her hand and pressed his lips to it so fervently that there was a damp spot on the glove when she drew it back. Josh whistled to the horse. "Tonight," said Tierney Rudd, and lifted his hand, and the cart turned and spun rapidly away, the wheels throwing up sheets of mud.

Frances twisted on the seat, looking back at the mob. "So this is law and order." She brought her gaze back to Daisy. "What do you think?" The cart bounced her in a rapid jitter that set the edge of her shawl dancing.

Daisy laughed. "He'll do."

"Good." Frances nodded, her eyes bright, her mouth tightening into a smile. "This will be good, Daisy. I promise, this will all work out nicely." Josh drove them splashing and jolting down Kearny Street.

Mitya had torn down the shack that was the first thing built of the Shining Light and in its place raised up two new rooms for Daisy, square and trim like everything he made, with a short corridor leading down to the stage door and a longer corridor running off at right angles to the cookhouse. Gil Marcus had bought up whole lots of furniture, now stored in the hull of the ship. In there Daisy found a table and two broken chairs, which Josh fixed, and a carpet. One end of the carpet was moldy and they cut it off. Laban painted things on the walls — quickly; she could see he ached to be back at his real work, the great picture now spreading down the wall of the saloon.

She sat in the midst of this splendor, her heart in her throat, waiting for Tierney Rudd.

Frances moved softly around the room, setting the table.

"You got something good?" Daisy asked her. "I don't think he'll like fish stew."

Frances laughed. She wore an apron tucked around her. Her quick, dark hands moved across the table, placing glasses right, folding linen. The table pleased Daisy very much, with its quiet luxury of cloth and silver tools, and she reached out and laid her fingertips on Frances' arm.

"Thank you, Frances."

Her friend turned toward her and took Daisy's face between her palms. "No thanking me, dovie. This is us, this is both of us, no thanking yourself, is there." She bent, and her cool, smooth cheek pressed briefly against Daisy's temple. Then there was a knock on the door.

Frances wheeled, straight as a pin. "There, now." She gave Daisy one quick glinting look, smoothed the apron, and went to the door to answer it, and Tierney Rudd came in.

"Miss Duncan," he said. He gave his hat to Frances and looked around the room. Surprise softened his face. "My God," he said. "It's like a New Haven drawing room."

Frances took his coat and went to hang it up. Daisy smiled at him; she felt enormous, ungainly, packed into this space, and at the same time hidden small and far away at the center of herself; she fought the urge to shout across the distance to him. "Are you from New Haven, Mr. Rudd?" She wondered where New Haven was.

"I attended school there." He stood uncertainly on the middle of the carpet. Frances, brisk, silent, turned a chair for him to sit in.

"Please make yourself comfortable," Daisy said. "Frances will bring us something to drink. Tell me how you came to California."

He settled himself, their chairs nearly side by side under the window. Now, close up, she saw the threadbare cuffs of his immaculate shirt, the patch on his waistcoat; she imagined him alone at night with a needle, struggling to keep up appearances, and leaned slightly toward him, tender with motherly sympathy. He sat primly upright, his feet together, his hands in his lap.

He said, "You should know, Miss Duncan, not to ask questions like that of anybody in San Francisco." His eyes poked at her; no smile softened the rebuff. He said, "How did you get to San Francisco?" in a voice of mild accusation.

She laughed, amused; a sudden rush of confidence made her easier about this. She lived here, belonged here, here she was in control. Also what he had said gave him away. "I understand what you mean," she said, and Frances came in with a bottle of champagne.

"In California nobody has any history," he said. He took one of the slim glasses from Frances and held it while she poured the amber liquor into it. "We're cut off from everything — as if this were Eden, we have nowhere to go but forward, certainly no shackles binding us to anything gone before." He put his nose over the edge of the glass, into the little circus of bubbles popping off the top of the wine. "Excellent champagne."

"Thank you," Daisy said. "I believe we bought it through Mr. Brannan."

"Probably did," said Tierney Rudd. He leaned forward, his arm on his knee, staring at her. "Brannan's a good example, too, you know — failed at everything he did, back in the States, and now look at him." He himself was busy looking hard at the front of Daisy's dress. She shifted a little to give him a better view, arching her back so that her breasts plumped above her lowcut neckline. At the table on the other side of the room, Frances was pretending to fold a napkin; she gave Daisy a look like a thrown lance.

Daisy looked away. Frances was in too much of a hurry. Brannan's name had come up, but the timing was wrong. If they rushed it Tierney Rudd might get suspicious. She said, "I've never met Mr. Brannan — all the Mormons seem so churchy and stiff. Shall we eat?"

"At your service, Miss Duncan." He got up, bowing, reaching one hand out to her. "May I call you Daisy?" His gaze caressed the abundant flesh revealed above her dress.

"Actually," she said, "I've been enjoying 'Miss Duncan.' " She did not take his hand; she went to the dinner table a free woman, while Frances seethed in the shadows, and Tierney Rudd stood staring at her from the middle of the room, his face suffused with new color. Sitting, Daisy picked up her fork and pointed at the other chair.

"Sit down, Mr. Rudd."

Stiff as a Mormon he took the other place. Frances came forward and served them; as she ladled the gravy over Daisy's meat one bony elbow gave the girl a whack. Daisy covered her smile with her napkin. This was turning into a game of fun.

Frances poured more champagne. Tierney arranged himself, prissy as a cat, avoiding Daisy's eyes. When he tasted the beef a murmur of approval left him.

"This is excellent."

"Frances is a splendid cook," said Daisy. "Among her other talents."

Now for the first time the white man turned and looked at Frances, but he said nothing to her; he faced Daisy again. "Excellent," he said, and gave himself full-hearted to the joys of eating.

Daisy ate little. The champagne was buzzing around the edges of her mind; she felt warm and soft, ready to be petted. "Did you enjoy the show tonight?"

He patted his mouth with his napkin. There was a spot of gravy on his mustache. "To be frank, I saw only the end. The dancers have more enthusiasm than skill, I fear."

"Do you." Daisy took her napkin and leaned across the table. "Hold still." She dabbed away the gravy from his face; at her touch his eyes blazed, and he gave off a sort of wave of excitement, like a burst of heat. She settled back in her chair and smiled at him. "On the other hand, as long as they do it with their clothes off, it's the enthusiasm that carries the day, doesn't it." Under the table, she worked one foot out of its shoe.

"To a miner starved just for the look of a woman, I suppose it is." Tierney was done eating; Frances came forward for his plate and poured him another glass of the champagne. "A man should have better things to do, though, building the world."

"Building the world!" She nudged his shin with her bare foot. "How wonderful that sounds. How I envy you, going where you wish, making your dreams come true." His lips parted. Her foot stroked gently up toward his knee. "How I wish I were a man. Sometimes."

"Oh, Miss Duncan." His voice was coming apart. "Believe me, no one else could wish such a thing. No one." His hands slipped under the table, and abruptly her ankle was caught tight in an eager grip and his fingers caressed her instep.

She said, "Men can do so much more than women." She pressed her toes against his sleeve. She had slid down somewhat in her chair, to stretch her leg under the table; she coiled her arms up behind her head in a luxurious stretch and wiggled a little closer to him.

"Men will do them for you," he said. "I will do them for you." He drew her foot toward him, up between his thighs, and pressed her sole to his crotch. "Only request something of me, sweet Miss Duncan."

She laughed. Off in the corner Frances was a taut black fury cased in calico and bolted to the floor. Daisy said, "There is something." Her toes fondled broadcloth and buttons straining

over a hard rod. "May I tell you?" She pulled back against his hold
on her.

His hand tightened on her ankle. Half lying on the chair, her
hands stroking through her hair, her body displayed before him,
she fixed him with as sweet a smile as she knew, and did not fight.
After a moment he let her go, and she sat up.

She said, "I understand some of the waterfront lots are to be
auctioned off. I'd like to put in a bid."

That startled him. His hands reappeared above the tabletop and
reached for the napkin; he busied himself mopping his lips again.
"You could do that yourself, I suppose," he said. "The new
constitution, you know, approves women's property rights."

"I heard that," she said. "I'm not sure how much California
approves the new constitution, day to day."

His eyebrows moved up and down. His face had sharpened,
fighting the laxity of the champagne, and he folded the napkin
before he put it down. He said, "No, I can see your point perfectly. You need a man to do business for you with other men. I
thought Mr. Marcus stood in that capacity."

She lowered her gaze. "Mr. Marcus and I . . ." What she had to
say would not come through her lips; she raised her eyes to
Tierney Rudd's, and said, "Gil is a sweet, kind, noble man in
many ways, but this is not something he's good at."

"Perhaps wise of him. I must tell you, sweet Miss Duncan, that
I consider the investment unwise. The price of land in San Francisco is monstrously inflated now, and will surely plunge when
there's no more gold."

"There will be gold forever," she said.

"Such is the common belief." He shrugged. "I do not agree.
But — if you wish it — I shall stand in for you. Have you gotten
the bid ready? Do you know which lot you want, for instance, and
what you want to offer?"

Daisy glanced at Frances, who came out of the corner like a
panther, and put the envelope on the table at his elbow. Tierney
Rudd picked it up. Watching him, Daisy gathered up her hair in

both hands and drew the tresses around under her chin; she did not look again at Frances, who withdrew to her corner. Tierney lifted the envelope in his hands and turned it over but did not open it.

"Well," he said, "I suppose no harm's done, if you lose a little money." He slid the envelope inside his waistcoat.

"Good," she said. "Thank you." She smiled at him over the frame of her hair. Under the table her toes walked slowly up his calf, bringing him back out of his business frame of mind. He ran his tongue over his lower lip; the tongue retreated, but his mouth stayed a little open. She said, "Would you like to see the rest of my place?"

"Is there more?"

"Well," she said, "the bedroom's rather nice." She stroked her chin with the locks of her hair, soft and fragrant, caressing herself with herself. "Frances, you may go."

13

IN THE MORNING Tierney Rudd went discreetly out a side door of the Shining Light and made his way up Pacific Street toward Kearny. He felt charged with new energy, although he had hardly slept; he felt like a man chosen out from all the others and set upon the road to glory. In the Plaza, he remembered the envelope she had given him, and took it by the *alcalde*'s office, where he signed the outside and dropped it on a desk.

The envelope was an afterthought to him; he had not read it or even opened it. Nor did he think about it again at all until three or four days later, when Sam Brannan walked up to him in the office of the *Californian* and thrust the envelope into his face.

"What the hell is this?"

Tierney had to draw his head back slightly to see what it was that poked him in the nose. The sight of the long brown envelope startled him into a sudden rush of guilt. His signature glared at him from its front. He gathered himself, wary.

He said, "Mr. Brannan, I consider that matter confidential."

Brannan gripped him by the arm. "Come with me."

Tierney twisted out of the other man's grasp. He glanced around and saw the men by the presses watching, their faces vivid with interest. Brannan was scowling at him, the envelope clenched in his fist. Tierney nodded to him.

"Lead on, sir, then." He steadied his voice, kept his eyes level, squared his shoulders.

Brannan grunted, a dark rumble of displeasure, and strode away across the newspaper office toward his private room in the back. Tierney went after him; the pack of onlookers followed with the eagerness of dogs called to the hunt. At the door Brannan turned and swept them with a glare that drove them all back a step. "Stay out of this. Rudd — "

Tierney went past him into the private office. His nerves were jumpy. Facing the wall of the next building, a few feet away, the only windows let in no sun, and he crossed the room, cluttered with stacks of paper and piles of books, and pulled down the ceiling lamp and lit it. Brannan slammed the door.

"What the hell is this?" he said again.

Tierney wheeled. He could not at once fathom why the man glowering at him was taking on such a temper over a single piece of land, and that under water, but he meant to say as little as possible until he found out. He folded his arms over his chest. "You've read it, obviously."

"Look, Rudd. I'm not stupid." Brannan crossed the room in two strides, swept paper and a half-full bottle off the desk, and sat down. The bottle, uncorked, lay quietly at his feet leaking onto the floor. "I know who you are. I checked up on you when I hired you. I know who your family is, and why they don't want to see you back in Connecticut anymore, and why you had to work your way out here even though they're all rich as Croesus. I know you don't have any money. So tell me how you can support a bid for one hundred twenty thousand dollars for all those lots on the cove!"

Tierney stared back at him, cold, his past laid open and his present suddenly a nest of snakes. He wished he had read the bid. He should never have trusted Daisy Duncan. He had assumed she wanted only one lot. Even she, with the resources of the Shining Light behind her, could not raise one hundred twenty thousand dollars, and why would she want the whole damn cove anyway? He felt cooked, under his coat, as if his heart were a furnace, now turned up full blast. Having nothing to say, he stared at Brannan and said nothing.

Brannan's broad face was red. His neck swelled against his collar and his eyes blazed. The spilled bottle at his feet was yielding up a perfume of Scotch whiskey; abruptly he bent down and picked it up and set it upright on the desk, although it was empty now.

He said, "You've got a backer, Rudd. Who is it?"

Tierney said mildly, "I'm sorry, I can't reveal that."

"You know those lots are under water half the time. They're useless. We only put them on the list to — to fill up the plat."

Tierney smiled, which raised Brannan's color even higher. The Mormon thrust his head forward at him.

"Go to your backer, tell him you've made a mistake, and withdraw that bid!"

"No, sir."

"You're fired," Brannan roared.

"Yes, sir." In spite of his panicky confusion Tierney began to enjoy the other man's rage. He had never liked Brannan. There were plenty of other jobs.

"I want to know who it is!" Brannan shouted.

"No, sir, I can't tell you."

"Damn you." Brannan stood up off the desk and prowled around the room, kicking at the piles of trash that filled it. He took off his hat and flung it down on the floor. "I want those lots." He faced Tierney again. "But I'm not paying one hundred twenty thousand dollars for them."

"They're useless," Tierney said mildly. "Under water."

"Damn you, Rudd, I'll have you run out of San Francisco."

"I don't think so, sir." Tierney reached out and flicked his forefinger at the envelope. "In any case, the bid's already been recorded, hasn't it." The *alcalde*, of course, would have accepted this bid with delight.

They faced each other a moment in silence, their gazes locked. Somehow Tierney felt in command of this, even if he didn't know what was going on, and he waited, watching Brannan's high temper crack and dissolve away, leaving behind a baffled frustration. Finally the Mormon lifted his head.

"All right. I'll make you one offer, and one only. Twenty thousand dollars cash. Take that, withdraw the bid, I'll forget the incident."

Startled, Tierney almost blurted out an oath; he fought himself to a cool calm, trying to look as if he had expected this to happen. He shook his head. "I don't know, sir."

"Get out. Go talk to whoever's behind this, tell him, damn him, whoever he is, he'd better take the twenty thousand or he'll wind up with nothing! Nothing at all. You understand me?"

"I hear you," Tierney said. "I can't promise anything." He reached out and plucked the envelope from Brannan's fingers and walked out of the office.

He opened the door on a buzz of excited talk, but at his appearance the packed front room fell into an electric silence. Every eye followed him to the door. He ignored them, sliding the envelope away inside his coat, and went down the steps to the Plaza.

The sunshine was brilliant, the great square teemed with men and wagons; Tierney saw none of it. He needed quiet and time to think, to figure out some way of acquiring that twenty thousand dollars for himself.

The bid itself stuck sideways in his craw. Daisy had given it to him, but there had to be somebody else, or something more, behind it. He knew Daisy now, and this was too bold and big for her. She had a certain guile, but it was womanish guile, a way of managing people, a way of managing him. Just thinking about her churned up a physical eagerness, a rippling of desire. He had to find some way of keeping the money and Daisy too.

He had crossed the Plaza, blind to the crowd and the dust and the sun; his feet took him off toward his boarding house. If Daisy herself wasn't behind this, then who? He thought of Gil Marcus, and knew immediately why the man from Baltimore had been sidestepped. Not Gil's way of going, this. One hundred twenty thousand dollars! The idea of so much money quickened him as much as the memory of Daisy Duncan, soft and pink and naked in his arms.

Twenty thousand seemed like poorhouse fees by comparison. But still.

He wanted Daisy too. There were few women in San Francisco, and none other like her. Having her would make him a prince in this place. There had to be some way of having both the money and the woman.

He went to his room, bare as a monk's, and sat down on the bed and got out the envelope. Maybe she had merely misunderstood, had written a smaller bid for one lot but somehow managed to get it construed as a bid per lot for all of them. But when he looked through the document he saw that it was very clear, and in fact whoever had written it had used his name, Tierney Rudd, in the body of the paper. Even before he had agreed to it he had been part of this, willy-nilly.

Who? His mind went questing after the hidden partner. He had been to the Shining Light a number of times; he knew nearly everybody connected with it, mostly blacks and other coloreds. Impossible for it to be any of them. He went over what Daisy had said, asking him to take the bid in; nobody else had been there at all except the little black mammy in the corner. He thought over Gil Marcus, who maybe was more complicated and underhanded than he seemed.

If so, he was a genius at dissimulation. Gil had a name throughout San Francisco for openness and honesty, for being the easiest touch in town.

He folded the bid and put it back in the envelope. The first thing to do was to get the twenty thousand dollars before Brannan changed his mind or went broke or dropped dead. He walked back across the city to the *Californian.*

Brannan was in his office with several other men; layers of blue segar smoke hung in the air. Seeing Tierney, the Mormon gave a grunt, cast a sideways look at his company, and said, "What is it now, Rudd?"

Tierney said, "I've come to conclude our agreement."

The broad red face before him settled slightly, like something left out in the rain. Brannan was relieved. That surprised Tierney, who had thought this man too powerful, too confident, to have doubts. Brannan went behind the desk and opened a drawer.

"I can write you a draft on the Bank of California," he said. The other men in the room were watching, curious. He gave them a look, and in unison all three of them turned toward the windows and inspected the wall of the next building.

"I'd prefer cash," said Tierney, admiring his own coolness.

"Naturally." Brannan brought out a cashbox, set it on the desk with a thud, and opened it. "I assume you'll take notes?" He began to count banknotes into a stack.

Tierney watched his hands moving, watched the pile of paper grow. He would have liked to have gold, but twenty thousand dollars in gold would be a staggering weight. The heap of banknotes was growing to an impressive size. They would all be notes on the Bank of California, which was sound enough. Watching the pile grow seemed to swell him up as well; he felt lighter, buoyant, too tall for the ceiling. Finally Brannan stood, decked the money together like playing cards, and held it out.

"If you're smart you'll leave San Francisco."

Tierney ruffled the edges of the bills, most of them brand-new, stiff and smelling of ink. He said, "I'll go to the *alcalde*'s office right away and withdraw the bid."

"Good. You do that." Brannan put the cashbox back in the drawer and slammed it shut. His hard stare pushed Tierney out of the room.

Tierney crossed the busy Plaza again, to the *alcalde*'s office, and withdrew the bid; it came to him belatedly that he could protest the fact that Brannan had gotten hold of it, since all the bids were supposed to be confidential and inviolate. By the look on the clerk's face when he took the bid back, he guessed that everybody in the whole office knew what was going on. He left, his steps bouncy, energetic with a new haste, a vague sense of urgency. Maybe he could bluff it out, say nothing at all to Daisy, let the hidden partner draw his own conclusions.

He could say, of course, that he had read the bid and decided against placing it.

Like a door opening, that idea spread new light over the whole issue. He could just take the bid back to her, tell her he knew she had no such money, tell her to rethink it. Light-footed, he went back to his boarding house to hide the money.

When he opened the door there was somebody else in the room.

He stopped. A sizzle of foreboding ran up his back and out along his arms.

"Come in, please," said the little black mammy. She was sitting there on his bed, her hands in her lap, a shawl around her. At the foot of the bed stood the Indian from the Shining Light, with a double-barreled cap-and-ball pistol in his hand.

Tierney was still holding the door open; the narrow corridor behind him was empty, a straight run down to the door, to escape, and for a moment everything in him yearned to do just that. The two dark faces before him seemed to fade into the shadows. He swallowed once; the Indian held the gun at his side, aimed at the floor, but what Tierney remembered, what swam upward in his memory like some horrible fish in a dream, was the sight of him biting off the nose of the crimp. Tierney stepped into the room and shut the door.

"Very good," said the mammy. "Mitya." She glanced at the Indian, who put the gun into the waistband of his pants and went silently around behind Tierney to stand by the door.

"What are you doing in my room?" Tierney said hoarsely.

The small, dark, shapeless creature perched on his bed turned her wide black eyes on him. "My name is Frances Hardhardt. I don't believe you know that."

Tierney cleared his throat. The Indian behind him felt like a pressure he had to resist constantly in order to keep standing upright. "I know who you are. You're Daisy's maid. I don't understand what you're doing here." He tried to work some righteous indignation into his voice. "Did she send you here?"

She said, "You had a talk with Brannan today, came back here, went back to Brannan, went to the *alcalde*'s office. All that has to do with the bid we placed on the cove lots. I want to know what you said to Brannan and what he said to you."

Tierney hesitated, struggling to cobble up some temporizing answer, and she glanced behind him. "Mitya."

"No," Tierney said, before the Indian even moved. "Very well, the bid is after all your bid — Brannan was furious, fired me, and told me to withdraw the bid or he'd run me out of San Francisco."

To his astonishment the woman laughed, a clear, bright sound like glass breaking. She glanced past him at the Indian as if sharing her mirth with him. Her gaze returned to Tierney's face. "And you told him — "

"I told him nothing," Tierney said. "I don't know anything." He was beginning to see this from a wholly new perspective, as if he stood in the corner watching; he saw himself as a tool, masterfully used.

She said, "That's true. And that's all Brannan said?"

"Yes."

"He made no mention of money?" Her voice was sleek as cat's fur.

Tierney stared into her face, every inch of him aching to say no, there was no money; in his memory jingled the sound of her voice telling him every step he had taken that morning. She knew everything. The new Tierney, watching from the corner, bowed his head in growing admiration. He said, "Yes, he gave me twenty thousand dollars." Reaching into his coat, he took the money out and held it out to her.

"Mitya," she said, and the Indian came around Tierney's side, took the wad of bills, and carried them to her. He went back to the door, his face impassive.

Frances Hardhardt counted the money on her knee into two piles. She said, "Very good, Mr. Rudd. You did exactly as I wished of you." She took one of the stacks of bills and held it out to him. "This is your share."

Startled, he blinked; his mouth fell open. He had thought himself done out of this completely. He reached out and took the money from her, ten thousand dollars, a deck of power in his hand.

She said, "Daisy is very fond of you. She'll see you tonight, after the show." Her gaze traveled around his room, her face bland, and returned to him. "You should use this money to set yourself up in a more suitable establishment. You cannot entertain her here."

He said, "No, I suppose not."

"She's fond of gifts, too. Did you know that?"

"No," he said. "I don't know very much of anything, do I."

Her mouth curved with amusement. "Don't be bitter, Mr. Rudd. You made a profit." She took a little box out of her shawl. "Give her this. It's only a bauble, something lost at the tables in the Shining Light, but she will enjoy it, and you, all the more." Rising from the bed, she brought the box to him and set it in his hand. "Thank you, Mr. Rudd." She went by him, no taller than his shoulder, and the Indian opened the door for her and followed her out.

Tierney stood where he was for a long moment. He had been a fool, been used for a fool, when he had thought himself cleverest; he felt as if his mind had cracked around him like a carapace and let him out into the real world. In one hand he now held ten thousand dollars. He opened the box that he held in the other.

Inside was a gold ring, shaped like two hands clasping, not costly but pretty enough: a lover's gift. He closed the box again and put it in his pocket, next to the money.

14

MAMMY SAID, "Keep that gun out of sight."

Mitya gave her an irritated glance, but he pulled the tail of his shirt out to hide the gun. They went down the street from Tierney Rudd's boarding house toward the Plaza. A wagon rumbled past them, throwing a sheet of dust into the air. In the alley between two buildings a man stood pissing against the wall.

He had to walk slow, short-stepping, to keep from leaving her behind. Being out in the town with her made him uneasy; he thought everybody they passed was looking at them, but when he tried to take hold of her arm, to protect her, she shook him off.

He grunted at her. "Why you bring me?"

"Because I needed you. And you did very well."

"I do nothing."

Her voice was round with amusement. "Yes, but you did it perfectly."

"Why you give him money?"

"Because he needs money," she said.

That brought a bark of laughter from him, and he turned to stare at her. "So?"

She said, "He'll need more money, and he'll come back to me looking for help."

"Stupid," he said.

She struck his arm with the back of her hand. "You don't follow me. You don't know white people. I grew up in a white man's house, waiting on the daughters. That's how I talk so pretty when I want to, I learned it from them. Pretty talk will get you anything you want."

"I no like him."

She gave a throaty laugh. They had reached the edge of the Plaza; ahead was a great crowd of men, all yelling, and he walked closer to her, one arm out to defend her. She pushed him off again. He moved away, annoyed with her.

"Can you shoot that gun?"

He shrugged. "Guns easy. Point, shoot." He had never fired the gun, or any gun.

They were sliding and weaving through the edge of the crowd, which heaved and rolled back and forth in a vast, restless surge, their backs to Mammy and Mitya. A shrill whistle carried over the general uproar.

She said, "Do you want some of this money? You can have it, you earned it."

"No need money."

The crowd gave a howl and lurched forward. Mitya craned his neck and stood on his toes to see what was happening, and past a shifting wall of heads and shoulders he saw two men fighting. At first he saw only flailing arms, and then a knife blade flashed.

Beside him, paying no attention at all to the crowd, Mammy said, "White men have everything. Only way to get what I want is to use a white man to get it for me."

"What you want? Money?"

He glanced at her as he spoke, expecting another of her quick, clever answers. Instead he saw her face tighten a little, frowning. She made no answer. She looked away. A howl rose from the crowd behind them.

They went by the corner of the Plaza, where a boy stood waving a newspaper over his head. "Get the *Californian*! Get the news true for once! Get the *Californian*." As they passed, Mitya smelled the greasy odor of the ink. They walked down the side of Kearny Street, stepping over the deep ruts.

She said, "Where are your people, Mit?"

He blurted out, "Gone." And bit his lips together.

She said, "Because of white men?"

He said nothing.

She said, "There's a war between us and them, you know. Whites on one side. All colored folk on the other. Don't you forget that. There's no choice. Either we fight back or we go under."

In the stream of people walking toward them were faces colored sand-pale to black as old leather. He was thinking of Metini and the white men there, giving orders to his people, taking away what they had. He remembered Anna saying, Do not fight. He gathered the air into his lungs as if his chest had been bound tight.

He said, "I want to fight." It came out without his meaning to say it aloud.

"Good." She smiled at him; she put out her hand as if to touch him and then clenched her fist and tucked it against her front again. "I knew you were a warrior, Mit. The first time I saw you."

He lowered his eyes, his lips pressed together, thinking he had let out too much. He put his hand against his shirt and felt the gun underneath. Thinking of the flash of the knife blade in the fight going on behind him. He saw a use in being able to kill from a distance. The gun rubbed against his stomach, hard and cold. They had reached the corner of Pacific Street. A light rain was starting to fall.

Every few weeks new people arrived, most of them black or brown. Mammy took them all in, gave them shelter, found them work, either in the Shining Light or elsewhere around the city. When Sam Brannan's big new house was done, she got jobs in it for several of her people, and other men building big new houses came to her for help in staffing them.

Others of the newcomers, especially families, went off to work on their own, to build farms and stores. She gave them money; she gave them letters of referral, and advice, and the promise that if they failed the first time she would stake them again.

Most of them succeeded. All of them kept in touch with her, especially the people who worked in the big new houses of the rich white men.

In September, just after the first elections, two more women moved into the Shining Light, an octaroon girl named Theresa, whom Mammy bought from her owner, and a white woman named Peggy, one of the last of the Mormons, whose husband had deserted her to go to the mines. Peggy could sing, in fact she sang very well, and soon took over from Daisy, who was bored with the work now that she had Tierney Rudd. Theresa had only one talent, for the exercise of which Mammy provided her with a room just behind the bar and a cashbox.

Gil went over to Daisy's apartment early one evening, when he knew Mammy would be there. The two women had eaten dinner together, as they often did, and were sitting side by side on the sofa drinking champagne and laughing. When Gil opened the door, Daisy swiftly made room for him next to her.

"Come sit down and have some bubbly!" She waved the champagne glass at him. Her face was rosy. Her Chinese dressing gown, of red and gold silk, enhanced the high color of her cheeks. He knew that in a few hours she would be leaving to spend the night at Tierney Rudd's suite at the new Saint Francis Hotel.

Even knowing that, he stood a moment, relishing the look of her, warm and ripe, her abundance of flesh overflowing the confines of her corset and peeping through the front of her dressing gown. Her hair tumbled around her shoulders in a froth of buttery curls, and her eyes sparkled, and the cascade of her irresistible laughter made him smile even while he wished he could spit in her face.

He went into the room but did not sit on the sofa. He took the other chair and sat facing them, Daisy white and gold in a flurry of embroidered silk, and Mammy like a little dark button in the middle of it all.

Mammy said, "Gilbert, you look very serious. Is something wrong?"

"Well, Mam." He fingered the front of his coat. "This is hard to say." Around him he felt the Shining Light like a living thing, a creature he had nurtured, that he loved. "I know you have your ideas about things, Mam, but I have mine."

Something in his tone sent his meaning on well ahead of his

words. The mirth faded from Daisy's face; she cast a quick look at the little black woman impassive beside her, and leaned forward toward Gil, both hands out. "What are you saying, Gil?"

"I'm saying I've got to go," Gil said.

"Oh, Gil. Why? Don't you love us anymore?"

Mammy put her hand on Daisy's. "Hush now. Gilbert, what is it?"

He shook his head. "I've about decided, Mam. You have your ideas about things — "

"Is it Theresa?" Mammy said. She looked around for the bottle of champagne and filled her glass and Daisy's.

"I'm not a whoremonger," Gil said.

Daisy blurted out, "We'll send her away." Her eyes danced with tears. The sight amazed him.

Mammy said softly, "Now, now." She put one hand on Daisy's arm. "Is that all, Gilbert?"

"No," he said. "There's you and Tierney Rudd, too, and that you won't change, will you."

He glanced at Daisy as he spoke, but he was aiming his words at Mammy, and she understood him. Her hand drew back from Daisy's arm. She sipped the champagne and put the glass down and leaned back into the cushiony deeps of the sofa.

"No. That we won't change."

"Gil," Daisy cried. "You've been with us from the beginning. You made the Shining Light."

"We all made it," he said. "And you can keep on making it without me, there's nothing you really need me for, anymore."

Mammy said, "Gilbert, half this place is yours. You're due a lot of money."

"I don't want any money. I lived here, and I had the — " He swallowed, fighting a rush of feelings; he had known this would be hard. "I had some good times here, building this place. Taking money would tarnish that."

"Gil." Daisy wheeled on the woman sitting small and dark and neat beside her. "Make him take it."

Mammy was smiling at Gil. "You constantly surprise me, Gilbert. No, Daisy, honey, he won't take it. Listen to me, Gilbert. Anything you need, ever, you can have from us. Anything."

Gil said, "I know that, Mam." He stood up, the thing done, the split working its way down between him and them. He said, "I have to find a job. That shouldn't be too hard."

Mammy said, "In San Francisco, with your standards, it might."

Daisy sat stiffly looking down at her hands. Her cheeks were sunken. She looked older. Gil bent down, reaching his hand out to her, and said, "Good-bye, Daisy."

"You've always got to make me look bad," she said, and abruptly she recoiled, her arm wheeling up, and struck at him.

"Daisy," Mammy said. Gil stepped back. Daisy twisted away, her back to Gil, her shoulders hunched up like bat's wings. Mammy leaned toward her, crooning something. Gil went out.

He walked through the front room, where the early customers were lining up along the bar and gathering around the gaming tables. Laban sat perched on top of a stool, painting a clipper ship on the wall. In the doorway Gil paused and looked out into the street.

The twilight was deepening. The rain had stopped, but no stars showed in the high black sooty sky. Across the way a man in a plug hat was lighting the lamp over the door of the boarding house that stood where Friendly's had been. Gil took a step out of the Shining Light. Down the street, beyond the crowd rumbling through the darkness, he could see the edge of the bay; they were raising new buildings down there, and soon the harbor would be hidden from this view.

He went two more steps out, toward the street. Going up, away from the bay, the street rose like a set of giant steps between ungainly buildings, some lit and some dark, gambling halls and sailors' rests, dens full of thieves and crimps and whores, where the new sheriff with his shiny revolvers and his strutting deputies dared not go. As he watched, more lights came on up there, picking out the line of the street, gleaming on the puddles.

Someone came out behind him, murmured, "'Scuse, boss," and lit the lantern over the door of the Shining Light. Gil moved aside to let the increasing flow of customers pass by him into the bright room within; voices rose, laughter, the first screech of fiddle music. He had made this place and now he was leaving it. Like a hand around his heart, it held him there a moment longer, and then he put one foot in front of the other, walking away. As he went, the rain began again.

15

IT WAS A LESSON IN LIFE, Tierney thought, how money changed a man. He had a fancy place to live now, and a beautiful woman, and fine new clothes. He took Daisy to the new Melodeon and sat in a box and heard a European diva sing Italian operas, and suddenly he had a lot of friends, men who wore clothes as fine as his, who went to the opera. Men with money.

Unfortunately, in elevating his circumstances he had spent nearly all the ten thousand dollars he had made in the deal over the water lots. He paid his bills, he smoked his segars, he kept a poker face, but under his silk brocade waistcoat his heart quaked: in less than a month he would be broke again.

He did, however, have all these new friends, and in San Francisco, friends were opportunities. One morning when he brought Daisy home to the Shining Light, he sent her off to find Mammy Hardheart.

She went, leaving him in her sitting room, with its faint smell of perfume; the rain was beating overhead. He had memorized what he wanted to say, and while he waited for Mammy he rehearsed it all again in his mind. The uproar from the saloon reached him, a throb like a distant engine. She had money, he knew she had a lot of money. Finally the door opened, and Daisy came in with the little old black woman wrapped in her shawl, like a doll his sister had once had.

Her look froze him. He mumbled a greeting. Daisy brought them all champagne, chattering away about the play they had seen and how filthy the streets were. Mammy sat in a chair opposite Tierney, and her eyes never left him. He felt as if she were looking into his mind.

Abruptly she turned to Daisy and said, "Go on, dovie, get ready for bed. You're tired."

Meekly Daisy went into the back room, and Mammy settled herself in the chair again, her gaze fixing Tierney before her like a spitted fish. She said, "Yes?"

He had the feeling she already knew what he was about to say, that she had already made her mind up. He recited his arguments, searching her face for signs of her intentions.

She said, "Borax. What's borax?"

"It's a mineral," he said. "I could explain it in detail, but what matters is that it's very useful in industry, and there isn't a lot of it immediately available." He sat with his legs crossed, one foot swinging furiously back and forth through the air; he could not keep himself still. "You use it in glassmaking. Other things. Cleaning solutions."

"And this friend of yours — "

"Thomas Blake."

" — has found a rich supply of it."

"Apparently. Blake was a chemist, back east. He came out to California overland, through the basin, and he says he saw deposits of borax there that staggered the mind."

She said, "You have confidence in him?"

"Blake?" He snorted. "Blake's an idiot. I'll have to carry him on my back to get him there — he had a run-in with some Indians that scared the scalp right off him. But I'm sure what he saw was borax." He clasped his hands together on his knees. His foot beat a mad tempo in the air. "But he has no money, and I have no money."

Her face was smooth as glass. In her eyes the lamp reflected a double point of light like an inverted image. She said, "How much?"

His heart bounded in his chest; she was going to give it to him. He sat up straighter, eager, pressing. "Ten thousand dollars, Mammy. For six months. I'll pay you fifteen percent interest."

She grunted at him. Rimmed by the dark shawl her small, round face hardened. "Half," she said. "I want one half of everything you make."

He startled. With the thing almost in his grasp he felt it jerked away from him again. "That's impossible," he said tightly.

"You'll need more than ten thousand, I think, anyway," she said. "You need to hire men, buy supplies, you have to maintain yourself. Twenty thousand, cash, now. No need to tell your friend Mr. Blake where you got it. Half of the profits for you, half for me."

"I won't do it," he said.

She shrugged. "Very well then. Good day, Mr. Rudd."

Behind her the bedroom door opened, and Daisy came a little way into the room; she had changed into a long silk gown the color of poppies.

Tierney lifted his head to look at her. She was combing her hair through her fingers, her head to one side. She had taken off her make-up, and her face had the nude look it wore when he laid her down on his bed. She said, "Are you-all talking still? I'll get some coffee or something." She gave him a twitch of her lips like a smile and headed for the door. Going by Mammy she stooped and put her arms briefly around the little black woman, and went out.

Tierney's hands were clenched on his knee. He unlocked his fingers, uncrossed his legs, and faced Mammy Hardheart, and for a long moment neither of them said anything. They both knew he was going to take her offer.

"I want Daisy to come live with me," he said.

Mammy's eyebrows rose. For a moment he thought she was

smiling. He could not remember ever seeing her smile. She said, "Very well. Here she comes." The door opened, and Daisy came in; behind her was the Indian.

Tierney jerked; he was on his feet before he realized it. The Indian was carrying a tray with an old coffee service, ornately turned of gleaming silver. He put it down on the table and went back to the door. On the way his gaze raked Tierney. The door shut behind him.

"I'll pour," Daisy said, and sat down by the coffeepot.

"Dovie," Mammy said, "you know, you got that dress all ruined, coming back here in the mud."

Daisy giggled. "We damn nearly drowned, Frances." She lifted her blue eyes to Tierney's. "Remember?"

"It's certainly an adventure walking down here when it's raining."

"I think," Mammy said, and reached for the filled cup, "it would be best if you stayed up at the Saint Francis with Mr. Rudd."

Daisy was pouring another cup full; she put the pot down with a clatter. "You mean — leave the Shining Light?"

"You can always come back to the Shining Light," Mammy said. "But, you know, the kind of life you have now, it's real different, isn't it. And you don't want to get your dresses dirty."

Daisy licked her lips. She looked quickly at Tierney and then at the little black woman, and some intelligence passed between them, like a flicker of heat lightning. Finally Daisy looked down at the cup of coffee before her, picked it up, and held it out to Tierney, but her gaze returned to Mammy.

"I can come visit," she said.

"Of course," Mammy said. She reached out and her hand slid over Daisy's arm in a touch soft as a lover's. "Now go and bring me some paper. I have to write a bank draft for Mr. Rudd."

Daisy's head swung toward him again, her eyes wide and blank. She said, "Oh." She got up and went across the room, brisk.

"What about a contract?" Tierney asked.

"No need for that," said Mammy. "I know our arrangement."

Daisy brought her a sheaf of paper and a steel pen and inkwell. Mammy bent over it; Tierney saw she could write, and wondered how anything she did could still amaze him. Daisy was looking at him again with that same wide, blank, innocent look.

He thought: They planned this all along. The *scree-scree* of the steel pen on the paper sent a shiver down his spine. He said, "It's better this way, Daisy."

Mammy gave a sound that could have been a muffled laugh. Daisy gave her a long look and then leaned toward him, intent.

"I want a carriage," she said.

"What?" He glanced past her at Mammy, looking for a translation.

"I want a carriage," Daisy said. "With horses."

"Daisy." He laughed, sat back, one arm draped across the chair. Mammy held out a piece of paper to him and he took it. "There's no streets here fit to drive a carriage on."

"I want one anyway," she said. "And a driver."

"All right," Tierney said. He glanced at the paper; the figure leapt at him. Twenty thousand dollars. Quickly he folded the paper and tucked it away, before the words and the money could fly off the page and escape. "I'll buy you a carriage. Are you ready to go?"

Daisy said, "I'll need my things," and went away into the bedroom.

Mammy sat with her hands in her lap, her eyes bright. "She loves to get presents. Always has."

Tierney said, "I'll get her whatever she wants."

He kept his attention aimed at the curtain that had now swung closed between him and Daisy. Mammy had meant this all along; she had planned this. The urge struck him to get up and walk out, tear up the paper and leave Daisy behind and walk away, a free man.

He stayed where he was. He had to have the money, and he needed his woman. The conviction formed in him, like an iron soul, that sometime in the future he would get rid of Mammy Hardheart.

He did not look her in the eyes again, lest she read his mind. His heart gave a little gallop. Cunning as she was, he had to be patient, he had to be smart. Wait for his moment. He thrust the whole notion away into the back of his mind, to think over later, and watched the curtain for Daisy.

16

MITYA BUILT ROOMS for the people of the Shining Light, a whole layer of them, up over the old ship, but he still lived in his den under the bow. In the dark he curled up like an old bear and listened to the rain falling and thought about Metini and drank until he fell asleep. Sometimes Josh came and drank with him. When Josh got drunk he sang. He had lost his people too, somewhere back beyond the Snows. But his songs didn't mean much to Mitya.

He had gotten caps and bullets for Friendly's pistol, and Josh showed him how to load it. There were rats everywhere, black ship rats. Josh took a lantern and Mitya took Friendly's pistol and they hunted the rats through the belly of the old ship. When Mitya fired, the shots thundered like drumbeats. Even Mammy left then. She bolted out of her nest at the far end of the ship, her hands over her ears, and made for Daisy's old room. Mitya liked shooting the rats, and he killed off every one.

The rain went on. Mammy got them all out to do something about the street.

The street: deep, sticky red ooze. People threw things in to walk on — boxes, logs, clothes — but the ooze swallowed it all. Across the way two white men had begun building on the empty ground next to the old Friendly's, until the rain made them quit. They left piles of building wood, and Mammy bought away all their wood, and she put Josh and Phineas and Mitya to laying down a walkway along Pacific Street past the Shining Light.

They made this, working in the steady cold rain. Mammy helped them. She and Mitya got in an argument about setting in the walk from the street to the door of the Shining Light.

"Drive some posts into the ground," Mammy said. "Go deep enough, you'll hit something solid."

Josh and Phineas went in under the eaves of the building, out of the rain. They had leveled the two lengths of ground for the walk, but the rain made it mucky.

"Nowhere solid," Mitya told her. He stooped and ran his hand along, level with the ground. "Build broad, flat, long, so's float."

"Float, you fool, this isn't a ship anymore, is it? I — " Her head twitched around toward the street.

Mitya straightened. A white man with a tall black hat picked his way up the wooden path, being careful for his shoes. It was still morning. Not many people were out. This one was smiling. In one hand he held a flat black thing.

Mammy stopped to meet him, her hands on her hips. The white man put out one hand to her.

"I do believe you're Frances Hardhardt?"

"Yes, I am," she said. Her voice was still harsh from the talk with Mitya. Behind her, Mitya backed up into the doorway, where it was dry.

The white man touched the brim of his black hat. The flat black thing in his other hand was a case. He said, "My name is McGowan, Mammy. I represent the Democratic Party of California, the party with the interests of the honest hardworking ordinary people of this community at heart."

He said that so fast, like a prayer or a song, that Mitya understood none of it.

"You may not know," the white man went on, "that there's an election coming up, but there is, and we're hoping to get Mr. David Broderick elected to the state senate, where he'll do all of

San Francisco a lot of good. And we're giving you the chance of a lifetime to help us, starting right at the git-go."

Mammy folded her arms over her breast. "What you want?" she said.

"We're considering putting a poll here in your place. You may not know it, Mammy, but this place has a reputation all over — everybody knows the Shining Light. The Democratic Party would like to set up a poll here on Election Day." He cocked his knee and lifted the flat case on it, getting ready to open it, and then Mammy slammed her hand down on it.

"Don't bother," she said. "You ain't puttin' no poll in here."

The white man went on smiling. He had fluffy pale whiskers spread around his chin. His eyes were wide apart like a baby's. His face looked wide and open and cheerful. A gambler's face, Mitya thought. The white man held his flat black case by the edges, as if he could open it and out would come every answer in the world.

He said, "The Democratic Party has plans for San Francisco, Mammy. Once we get our boys in, we'll be running this town, with me myself, Ned McGowan, as justice of the peace." He began to nod, a little deeper each time, bobbing above his caseful of answers. "You want to stay in good with the Judge, don't you, Mammy."

The wheedle in the white man's voice was like grit in Mitya's ears. This sounded like poisoners' talk to him, and he shifted and cleared his throat. In front of him Mammy reared up straight and her hands clenched before her and her voice came out black as tar.

"You look around, mistah! You see anybody here can vote?"

As she spoke one arm swung wildly off toward the Shining Light; Ned McGowan ducked, his eyes popping. The case slid off his knee, and he gripped it up under his arm. Mammy lunged after him, spitting words at him.

"You see anybody here gonna care who's senator in San Jose? You white folks! You one little island in a whole big sea of people, why you think it matters to the rest of us what you be doin' allatime?''

The white man was moving fast. Not so careful of his shoes, he skipped and slid back down to the boardwalk. "You'll regret this." One foot slipped. He wobbled over the streaming red slop and his voice squeaked. "You'll regret this good, Mammy!"

She bent down and scooped a handful of mud into her palm. "Then I'll do it whole hog, Judge!" Her arm swung back, awkward, slime trickling down into her sleeve. Lugging his case, the white man took off down the boardwalk, his free hand on his hat.

Mammy dropped the handful of mud. "That case got one piece of paper in it," she said. "And all it says is 'Keep running.'"

Mitya could not help smiling; when she turned toward him their eyes met a moment, and she began to smile too. She looked like a girl then. She came up past him into the shelter of the doorway.

"All right, do it your way," she said. She went by him into the barroom and set to yelling at Laban.

Josh and Phineas were still standing under the lee of the roof. The rain came down past them, silver like fish scales. Josh said, "Mammy gon' get us all in trouble."

Phineas grunted. "We be in trouble always." He had the shovel in his hands. He came out through the glitter of rain, looking around at Mitya. "What I do now?" Mitya went out to build the walk.

Frances did not see Mitya the rest of the morning, but when she went up to her room in the afternoon to sleep a little, he came in after her.

He said nothing, did no courting, but straight off took hold of her and pulled off her clothes. At first she could not accept him. She never could, but lay stiff and cold in his embrace, fought against his touch, muscles clenched and teeth bit together. Holding her fast, he slid his hands over her breasts and down between her legs, one by one he turned the keys to her body. He unlocked her. He set fire to her, hot coals like fiery blossoms in her flesh, burning lava in her veins. She thrashed and trembled in his arms, glutted. When she was satisfied he laid her down on her back and rode her. He let his whole weight down on her; crushed under him, she braced herself against his thrusts, possessed.

He moved away from her, rolling onto his side. Her hand followed him, her fingers against his chest, and she drew her arm back, not wanting to give him any more than he already had. The only light in the room came from the little lamp above the door, which was behind him, so that shadows covered his face.

She said, "You could knock."

He said, "You no let me in." In the odd music of his voice there was a throb of amusement. "I steal you, every time."

She moved away from him, annoyed, unsettled. "I want you. But you move too fast, you get me all rattled over it." Her voice rang false even to her. The sex had left her open, vulnerable; she rushed to cover up the tenderness, to get back on top. "You be doing too damn rough, anyway, I ain't one of your Chinee whores."

He said nothing for a moment. At first she wondered if he'd thought she didn't know about the yellow girls. Then he said, "You talk black to the Judge. You chase him good."

"The Judge."

"He come back?"

"If he wins, he will."

"I go after him?"

She shook her head. On her body she still felt something of his imprint, but the loose, dangerous excitement was gone. She felt easier. She could touch him now, stroke her fingertips along his shoulder, without the feeling of falling away into him.

When her hand barely pressed on the corded muscle of his upper arm he winced. She cupped her palm over the hurt spot. "What happened?" Against her hand the rough heat of injury. She thought of it healing, growing strong and smooth again.

"Not much. I get the Judge?"

"No. Men like that, you can't just kill them, they have too

many other people behind them. The law. Those men in San Jose." She let her fingers travel down the length of his arm to his hand and gripped it. "You could find out about him. But if the election goes the wrong way for him, you know, it will be another bunch."

He shook his head. He did not understand the white men's way of power. He was holding her hand, but he was already going, his head turned, his body shifting slowly around. He said, "You need me, say." His fingers, hard as claws, tightened on hers for a moment and then let go, and he rolled out of the bed and began to put on his clothes.

Frances stretched out across the bed. Where he had lain the mattress was warm and packed. On her side, under her cheek her hand smelling of his body, she watched him pull his shirt on.

"Where are you going?" she asked.

His back was to her; he turned slightly, looking down at her over his shoulder. "Yellow girl."

"Damn you." She kicked out at him, and he turned and caught her ankle and they struggled a moment, and then he pushed her leg down and pounced on her, and they kissed. She wrapped her arms around his neck.

He said, "You best. You only real one." He nuzzled her cheek, his hair all over her face. He pushed up and away from her, blocking out the light, and went to the door.

"Be careful," she said. The door swung closed. The light filled the room.

In the new little silence of the room the sound of the saloon filtered through the walls to her, the rumble of voices and the shuffling of feet. It was still too early for the show to begin. Peggy would sing, and there was a fiddler whose dog danced. Frances stretched out along the bed, filling all the space, thinking of Mitya.

She wondered why he came to her. Not just for sex; there were women now all along Pacific Street who gave him whatever he asked for. She thought something in her connected him to whatever lay behind him.

He had done it this time, she knew, because she had chased off the white Judge. That pleased her. It was homage, then, an offering. She spread herself across the bed, justified.

17

THE CRIMPS STILL WORKED on Pacific Street, but after Mitya bit the one man's nose off they stayed out of the Shining Light. So when a crimp named Rudy came in twice one night, Mitya knew the hunt was up.

He had his knife. He went up to his den and got the gun and hid it under his shirt, stuck in the waistband of his pants.

When he went back to the saloon the crimp was still there. Mitya started across the room toward him, and Rudy faded away toward the door.

Rain was falling. Along Pacific Street some people hung lanterns in front of their doors. The slants of light gleamed on the streaming puddles of the street, bounced on the slick bodies moving in a thick braid down the walkways and paths. Like strings of stars the lights dotted the course of the street on up the hill.

He loved this street. The houses crowded along it gave off bursts of noise, shouting, songs, people laughing. He could go into any of these places, no one kept him out. Even the white men here gave way to him. On a big shelf above one door, inside a rail, sat three girls; two had only pants on and one had on only a top. They knew him and shouted to him, and one jiggled her bare breast at him. He followed the crimp close enough to let Rudy know he was there.

Rudy saw him. Mitya could tell by the way he walked, stiff, his head back.

They went up Pacific Street past Kearny, to the place called Sydneytown. Here even the street ran crooked. All the little buildings had grown any way they could, alongside and overside and underside one another, some with tent roofs, some with teetery walkways and stairs. A lot of the yellow people lived here. He could hear their music now, mixed in with white men's music. In the doorway of a place a man stood calling, "Free whiskey! First drink's on the house!" This man too knew Mitya and called to him.

He went along after Rudy until the crimp came to a saloon called Big Jim's and turned into the alley.

Knowing Mitya came after him, Rudy would never go into an alley unless he knew help waited. Mitya did not follow him down the alley. The rain was falling hard, dripping and splashing off the eaves of Big Jim's. White men wouldn't wait around in the rain. At the far end of the alley, he knew, was a covered walk, and he guessed they would be waiting there. He went on around the other side of the saloon.

The space there, between the saloon wall and the next, was piled up with garbage, now half liquid in the rain. Mitya crept down over it, feeling his way along in the dark, to the corner.

A broken board in the wall let him through to the covered walk beyond. It was so dark he could see nothing. He crouched down with his back to the wall, smelling rotted wood and mud and shit and stale food, hearing the low mutter of voices from the saloon behind him. Then, up ahead of him, he heard a whispering.

"He was right behind me! Keep quiet — he's coming."

Like a picture in his mind he saw them, waiting at the far end of the walk, peering out into the alley and the rain.

He took the knife in his right hand. In the wet sometimes the gun did not work. And there were a lot of them. He could not count them, not with his ears, but even through the clatter of the rain on the roof over his head, he could hear the overlap of breathing, the brushing together of bodies, the shifting of feet. He moved down through the dark. At the far end now he saw a shadow of light and, briefly, a head black against it.

Now he could smell them, sweat and liquor and old tobacco smoke. He could feel their warmth against his cheek. Gliding another step closer he drew back his right arm and plunged it forward.

The knife pierced cloth and air and then yielding flesh; he yanked it out and jumped forward into the close press of bodies and rammed the knife in again, and this man screamed. The others whirled. "Damn! Damn!" The mass of men packing the alley exploded into a tangle of thrashing bodies.

Mitya crouched down; somebody stumbled over him and fell. Somebody screamed, "Get out!" He aimed the gun into the uproarious dark and fired twice.

The stink of the powder flooded his nose. They were running, howling as they ran; the dim oblong of light at the end of the alley fluttered and wavered with their headlong passage through, and then the quiet came back. Somebody was breathing hard and bubbly, almost in front of Mitya. He put his hand out and touched a body that jerked, and picking up the knife again he drove the blade down and down and down until the body stopped jerking.

His heart was pounding. The crash of the rain on the roof packed the alley with its sound, like some kind of shield. For a while he crouched there, breathing the stench of blood and gunpowder, his hair on end, his heart drumming in his chest. Finally he moved up into the light from the open alley, got out the pouch with powder and bullets and caps, and did the little ceremony of reloading the gun.

It had fired both times. The force and roar of the shots stayed with him. Stronger than the knife. Somewhere out there people who had not even been near this place knew that Mitya had killed.

He went out again the way he had come in, but turned the other way, at the back of the saloon, and crawled over a roof and down a rickety stair to a lane that led him into the next street.

Yellow people lived there. A yellow man with a long pigtail watched him walk out into the street. Mitya ignored him. The rain was slackening a little. Mitya pushed his hair back off his face with one hand. He jammed the gun down into the waistband of his pants, in full view now, so that everybody would see that he went armed. He walked away down the street in the rain.

In a drenching downpour Gil voted for state senator, going to three different polls before he found one that would let him vote Whig. The Democrats, mostly New Yorkers, seemed in control of San Francisco. After that he went to the post office, bought a place near the head of the line for fifteen dollars, and sent a letter to his mother in Baltimore. There was no letter for him, but as he went away across the Plaza in the rain, he realized somebody was walking along beside him and looked over and saw Mitya, topped by a broad-brimmed hat.

"Well," Gil said. "What are you doing over here, and in the daylight, too?"

Mitya pulled the hat down with one hand; the other held a bundle to his chest. "Come see if you drown."

Gil laughed, glad to see him, and gestured across the square. "Come on, my room's real close."

The Indian followed him down the alley to the back of the rambling building that housed Dennison's Exchange. "You vote?"

"Certainly did. Not to any effect, I think."

"You know McGowan?" Mitya mangled the name almost past recognition.

"I think we're all about to know McGowan very well," Gil said.

He unlocked the door in the back wall of the store and let Mitya into the room beyond. The table that filled most of the space was covered with paper; he spent most of his free time writing.

Mitya went in, threw down his big hat, opened the shutter on the window and let some light in. Looking around, he said, "Good place."

"It isn't bad," Gil said. "It isn't like the Shining Light." He had a job selling dry goods in Dennison's Exchange, for which he received the use of the room and some money; the job was tedious and the room lonely. "Sit down." There was a little old stove in the corner; he lit the charcoal and put on a pot of coffee. He had bought a pail of water that morning from the street vendor and there was still plenty left; he even rinsed the pot. "What about McGowan?"

"He win?" Mitya pushed away the papers on the table and set the bundle down.

"One of the polls I went to had a whole set of ballot boxes waiting in the corner, already stuffed. This is Tammany, transplanted. Where these boys grew up, God is a Democrat, and they're bringing His church to San Francisco."

Mitya opened the bundle, unwrapping a loaf of bread. "I bring you food," he said.

Gil sat down on the far side of the table; the aroma of the bread floated to him, and he groaned. "Mammy's enchanted loaf." He broke a big chunk off and bit into it, the rich, tangy bread of the Shining Light, which fed all lost and lonely men. Mitya leaned his elbows on the table, watching. His face settled into a frown.

"Why you give Daisy away? Why you let cold bastard take her?"

"It was her choice," Gil said, startled. "I don't see it's any business of yours, anyway." He rubbed his hand over his mouth. "You don't understand, Mitya, maybe your people do it differently. Here the woman has her choice, and she chose him." He went over to the stove and took two cups off the shelf beside it. It still hurt him to think of Daisy with Tierney Rudd.

"You bleed water," Mitya said. "How you give her up?"

Gil set the cups on the table and poured coffee into them. "There is nothing I can do." He put the pot back on the stove. "Besides, the person you ought to talk to is Mammy. Mammy's the one who threw her at Tierney in the first place."

Mitya said, "Mammy no big part."

"God, Mit." Gil gulped the coffee; he reached out for more of the warm and nutty bread. "She's the whole of it. Everything that happens, she hustles for her own ends."

At once he knew he had said the wrong thing. Across the table the Indian swelled up, his eyes glinting. "You no talk so, you black."

"No, maybe I wouldn't." He lifted the coffee cup again and then set it down, leaning over the table toward Mitya, trying to make him see this. "But it's true. She's just using you, all of you."

Mitya's hand slammed down on the table. "You no talk so. You white, everything there in front of you, you choose and choose and choose." His voice was so low it came out a hiss, like wet wood burning. "Color no choose, do what she can, what must, you goddamn judge, damn you!" His hand came down hard again; the table rocked, the cups jumped and splashed. His voice jerked out of him, raw-edged. "How you give her up? My wife, she go with white man, I no stand and watch her go, I kill her."

Gil said stupidly, "You mean, if she had, you would have wanted to kill her."

"No," Mitya said, showing his teeth like an animal. "She go. And I kill her. I hit her till she die."

Gil blinked at him, overcome by sudden understanding. He said, "That's why you left."

"Yes." Mitya had calmed. His eyes glittered. "I want to kill white man too. My people send me away."

Gil swallowed. The Indian was steady again, but in the gleam of his eyes, in the set of his shoulders, Gil now saw clearly the hot rage in him that had always been there, packed into him like his blood and bones. Suddenly Gil was aware of his own skin as if an electric current prickled through it. His guts writhed. A sharp, momentary sympathy struck him, for the Indian woman ground to nothing in that rage.

"My people send me away," Mitya said again. "Mammy not. I kill Friendly, I kill crimp. They do bad, I kill them. All white men. I kill them." Carried off in little words, his temper was fading, his eyes half shut, and he looked away. "Not you," he said.

"Thank you," Gil said. He thought: I should have known that, about Friendly.

The Indian would not meet his eyes. He seemed impossibly far away, knee to knee with Gil inside the little room. Gil remembered him fighting the crimp, and realized that Mammy had seen that fury in him all along. As he thought that, he recalled what had set all this off.

He said, "Tell me what's happened with McGowan." He wanted to build up something common between them again.

Mitya described McGowan's visit to the Shining Light; he faced Gil again, and seemed easier. He said, "This make trouble?"

"Probably," Gil said. "Mammy's likely a match for it. Don't kill McGowan."

"That she say." Mitya was getting up. He reached down behind him for the broad-brimmed hat. "You come back sometime?"

"Yes."

"Sure," Mitya said. His hands rolled the floppy hatbrim. "I no say too much."

Gil reached out and gripped the other man's arm. "No. We're friends, you can say what you want to me, Mit." For the first time he saw the gun stuck in the waistband of the Indian's pants. That chilled him; he felt the impotence of all his words, his good intentions. "We are friends still, aren't we?"

Mitya stared at him a moment, his face impassive. At last he said, "Yes. Friends." He put his hand out, and Gil shook it.

"Thanks for coming, Mit. Thanks for the bread."

The Indian crammed his hat down on his head. He threw a look around them, at the little room, and nodded to Gil. "Come home," he said, and went out the door into the thrashing rain.

18

"EAT, DRINK, AND BE MERRY," Tierney said, "for tomorrow we go to Nevada."

Thomas Blake laughed. He always looked a little undone, his neckcloth limp, his trousers rumpled. He stood rocking back and forth on his heels, his thumbs hooked into his belt, like a fat farmer. "How can you leave this, Rudd? This is right handsome, here."

Tierney said, "Daisy did it."

"A pretty job, too."

Tierney was inclined to agree with him. They were in the front room of his suite at the Saint Francis, which Daisy had spent weeks putting together. Now that it was finally fit to live in, he was leaving.

In this room there was still no furniture except for a sideboard. The emptiness made the space larger. The thick carpets on the floor and the heavy wall coverings, washed in the glow of the dozen wall lamps, drew the eye onward, the space stretching away like a gallery into an indefinite golden haze. The walls were varnished yellow pine, and on them hung a big landscape with lion and unicorns, mirrors in gilt frames, silkwork from China, all smooth surfaces that the flickering mellow light caught on and enriched. Along the sideboard were candles in branched sticks, a deep, mysterious pile of some green stuff with a few flowers tucked in, and the wine and the glittering crystal.

Tierney's other guests strayed through this space, their voices hushed, their footsteps muffled in the carpets, and peered and gaped at the artwork. One of Mammy's blacks took a silver tray among them, offering them glasses of wine. Tierney swelled, pleased, and fought off the urge to tell Blake what it had all cost.

The door behind them opened and Daisy came out, with the woman that Blake had brought with him. Emitting a shrill cry, this woman draped herself sinuously along Blake's side. "Honey, ain't it beautiful? Daisy, I'm so jealous!" She wore yellow satin with a skirt that was flounced and gathered over whalebone hoops, so that when she leaned on Blake half her dress swayed out to one side with an audible hiss. Tierney thought he had seen her before, but he could not remember where. She was dark, maybe part Indian, with a pretty, snub-nosed, round face, tilted eyes. Leaning on Blake's shoulder, she fluttered her eyelids at Tierney and said, "Mr. Rudd, your place is just beautiful."

Tierney murmured something, turning away from her. Blake annoyed him, with his coarse manners and his bad clothes, his garish whore. Daisy, on the other hand, belonged here. She stood by the sideboard, smiling, looking around at the party, her hair done up in long ringlets and a crown of little curls. She wore a gown of several layers of silk crepe, without hoops. She disliked hoops. Tierney wished she paid more heed to fashion; it annoyed him that she did as she pleased. But nonetheless she was beautiful. Looking at her, he felt a rush of pleasure and pride, and he went over to her and slid his arm around her waist.

"Very nice, Daisy. Everybody loves it."

She laughed, not interested in that. "Naturally." She looked him quickly over, head to toe, and fussed with his neckcloth. "Dinner will be ready in an hour. Frances is bringing everything in now, up the back stair."

"It had better be good." He had not wanted to use Mammy Hardheart's resources for this, but he had very few other choices.

"It's wonderful," she said. She patted his neckcloth into place. "Phineas, over here." The darkie with the tray brought Tierney a glass of whiskey.

Tierney felt a start of triumph. His family back home thought he was scum, a disgrace to the name; and maybe this wasn't an Eastern drawing room, and maybe these weren't the Shipleys and the Madisons, but it was close, and for San Francisco, damn good. He hadn't fallen into the gutter, as they'd all predicted. The world wasn't Yale or nothing. He sipped his whiskey. When Daisy started off he reached out and gripped her arm. "Where are you going?"

"Just to talk."

"Stay here with me. Damn it, I'm leaving in twelve hours."

Blake lumbered toward him again. "That's right, Rudd! Live it up. Once we're out in the desert there's nothing but sagebrush and sand." His voice boomed; he was drunk. Suddenly he flung his arm around Daisy and hugged her. "Live it up, girl!" He pushed his glass toward her face.

Daisy recoiled from the liquor. Tierney lunged forward between her and Blake and thrust his partner away. "Get your hands off her."

Everybody in the room wheeled to look. Blake staggered back a few steps and fell. His mouth dropped open; sitting on the floor, his glass beside him and a dark puddle spreading over the expensive carpet, he goggled up at Tierney. Daisy gave a soft cry. She snatched up a napkin from the sideboard and knelt down and mopped at the spilled wine.

"Damn you!" Tierney bent, got her by the shoulder, and pulled her roughly up onto her feet again. "You're not a servant, don't act like one." Instantly the darkie was where she had been, taking over from her, cleaning up the wine.

Startled, Daisy said, "I just — I love the rug." Tierney pushed her back, making her stand up straight, and snatched the damp napkin out of her hand. Everybody was staring at them.

"Go and see about the dinner," he said, between his teeth, and shoved her toward the door.

Blake was trying to get up. "Sorry, Rudd," he said, stiffly. "Theresa, help me." His woman took his arm and hauled him onto his feet.

Tierney swallowed; he knew he was making a scene, and he throttled his temper. He said, "Have another drink." A quick glance around deflected the pointed, curious stares aimed at him from every side. Slowly the guests went back to their drinking and talking. Blake's round-faced woman gave off a bleat of laughter and leaned on him again, the hoop kicking out. Tierney went through the side door into the next room.

There more of Mammy's people were laying out linen and silver along the table; the light was softer, candles instead of lamps. Daisy stood in a corner, her hands gripped together. When Tierney came in she wheeled toward him. "I didn't mean anything."

He strode up to her, clutched her arm, turned her back to the room. "What are you trying to do to me? If you can't actually be a lady, at least act like one!"

She flinched at that; he saw that he had struck a weakness. His mouth inches from her face, he whispered, "I'll be gone for months, but I'll know everything you do while I'm away. Don't you dare whore around." She was pouting at him, her lower lip out, but her eyes were wide and dark with worry. He stepped back, looked her over, reached out and shook her skirt straight. She had gotten a little wine onto the silk. "See? You've wrecked the dress."

She wrenched away from him. "I have guests," she said, and went back out to the front room.

Tierney stayed where he was a moment. His armpits were damp. It was Blake's fault, all Blake's fault, the fool. Glancing over his shoulder, he saw one of the darkies leaning over the table, putting white flowers into a vase; another brought in a tray full of covered dishes. Nobody was watching him. Everything looked as it should — looked elegant and in order.

It looked that way, but it was all dream gold. If he failed, if Blake let him down, if any of a thousand small details went wrong, everything would disappear. His head swam, from the heat, the smoke, the champagne, the sudden sense of impermanence and chaos that swept over him like a wave. The whole room seemed too small, the golden haze a suffocating miasma. His blood thrilled with a sense of urgency, the panicky feeling that even as he grasped for what he wanted, it was all slipping away from him. He glanced back over his shoulder and saw, at the far end of the room,

Mammy Hardheart watching him. He went back into the next room, to the gusty laughter of the party.

Frances said, "It went well." Tierney was off seeing the last of their guests out the door.

"The food was delicious," Daisy said, and laughed, remembering; the dinner had delighted her, a constant stream of talk and good things to eat, admiring looks from all the men. And she had seen old friends, all the people from the Shining Light, sliding like shadows through the gilded elegance of the party. "Laban looked so funny in his monkey suit."

She sat down in front of the little dressing table in her bedroom, and Frances came up behind her. The small, dark hands began to take down Daisy's hair. Under the delicate, caressing touch a dreamy lassitude crept through her, and she smiled at herself in the mirror.

"You're happy," Frances said.

"This is what I've always wanted," Daisy said. "To be rich, and to be loved. But I miss the Shining Light."

Frances laid handfuls of her glistening hair down on her shoulders. "You have to stay away, at least for now. He's very bent on respectability. You saw that."

Daisy sighed; she turned her head, trapping one of the other woman's hands between her shoulder and her cheek. "Then let's have more parties, so I can see everybody. Bring Mitya next time."

"Mitya. Here?" Frances laughed. Gently she drew her hand free, and undid the buttons down the back of the dress. "Such a pretty gown this is. I love the feel of the cloth."

"But I got wine on it."

"I'll get that out." Frances undressed her, stroking her shoulders, and bent quickly to kiss the back of her neck. "I don't like Blake. We'll have to find someone else for Theresa."

"He has lots of other friends," she said. "Here he comes."

Frances stepped back. The door opened and Tierney walked in, walked past Frances without noticing her, and stood watching Daisy in the mirror. He looked tired and half drunk; Daisy knew he was worried about the expedition to Nevada. Come back rich or not at all. She smiled at him in the mirror, her dress down around her waist, her corsets half open. He came up behind her and slid his hands down over her shoulders and cupped her breasts, and she leaned her head back against him and shut her eyes.

"There it is," said the wagonmaker. "I don't know what you're going to do with it."

"Oh," Daisy said. "Oh, it's beautiful."

She walked once around the carriage, which stood in the middle of the warehouse floor; all around were ordinary wagons, carts, and parts of wagons and carts, wheels hanging on the walls, yokes and whiffletrees in piles in the corners. In the center of this the carriage stood like a swan among the geese, its body lacquered shining black, trimmed all the way around with a line of gold.

The wheels stood high and narrow, with spokes of red and more gold trim. The front seat was perched up in front on a box that curved gracefully forward to balance the heavy passenger section behind. On either side of the driver's seat a thin curved sconce held a lantern with glass lights; the whip already stood in its boot by the seat, the lash curled neatly around it.

An iron step hung down off the side. She put her foot on the step and reached up, and there was a handrail right where she needed it to pull herself up. As she went up, the carriage dipped just slightly under her weight. The seat was covered in wine-colored plush velvet.

The wagonmaker had followed her, stood there by the iron step looking up at her. "I don't know where you're going to drive it, but he paid me already, and it's done."

"Yes," she said. "It's beautiful. It's everything I wanted." She stroked the cushioned seat beside her. "Thank you. We'll leave it here for now; I just want to sit in it a while."

"Glad you like it, ma'am." The wagonmaker backed off, put his hat on, and went away.

She sat in the carriage, looking straight ahead. She could smell the newness of it, the tang of paint, the mellower flavors of the wood and cloth and leather. The brass gleamed on the lanterns and the lacquers. She would have two big black horses, with plumes. She would have a red harness with gold medals. When it rolled out into public view everybody would look; she and Tierney would ride along like the king and queen of San Francisco.

Now there were no roads to drive it on. Certainly there would be roads, someday. She could wait. And anyway, what mattered was that he had gotten it for her, even without the roads; he had given her what she wanted, he would give her anything she wanted. She sat there in the carriage, in the dusty warehouse, and waited to become happy.

19

RAIN FELL. The city council sent crews to cut brush on the hills, haul the branches in, and throw them into the streets, and the heaps of twigs and old leaves like everything else vanished into the red mud. A mule drowned in a puddle in Montgomery Street. On Washington a house fell in, the ground beneath it washed away. Two days later the house next to it went down too. An old man crept up and down the boardwalk past the Shining Light, leaning down into the muck, panning the rivulets for gold.

Mitya walked around the streets looking at the new buildings, which were going up everywhere in spite of the rain. Outside the Bella Union a white man unloading a crate from a wagon offered him a drink to horse the crate into the saloon.

He had never been in this place before; the doormen kept out dark people. The room was big, with stairs up. The floor creaked, the boards rocking, not tight and flat like the floor he had laid down in the Shining Light. They broke open the crate with iron bars and took out a huge glittery thing, made of wire and curved shiny metal and hung all over with bits of glass. On a rope they hauled it up to the ceiling, where it swung gently, jingling and sparkling.

In the back of the room was a cage. There was a man in the cage.

Mitya helped pull the rope that raised the shimmering thing up to the ceiling. He kept looking over at the cage. The man inside was naked and hairy; he sat on the floor, drinking from a clay jug and chewing on bones. When the glittery thing was strung up right, the boss brought Mitya a cup of whiskey.

The man in the cage went up to the bars and leaned on them. "Oofty goofty!" He banged his head against the bars.

Around the room the other men turned, and several of them laughed. The boss said, "Too early, Oof," and waved.

The naked man yanked on the bars and banged his head against them again. "Oofty goofty! Oofty goofty!"

The rest of the men in the room were all watching him now. Many were laughing. Somebody called, "Hugh, feed him."

"Damn," said the boss. "He eats like a horse." He went into the back of the place and came out with a pail full of bones.

The naked man in the cage saw the bones and began to jump up and down. "Oofty goofty! Oofty goofty!" The boss took a bone from the pail and threw it through the bars, and the naked man jumped on it.

The people outside the cage all roared and laughed and clapped their hands. They moved in a crowd toward the cage and stood there watching the naked man chew the bone. He growled. Slaver dripped from his mouth.

The boss came up to Mitya and took the cup from him. "All right. Thanks for your help, now clear out."

Mitya moved toward the door. He kept watching the man in the cage. It knotted his guts to see a man gnawing on bones like a dog. This man's skin was white, but he was in a cage, and the men outside it jeered at him and laughed, splashed whiskey on him, poked him through the bars. His voice rang out again. "Oofty goofty! Oofty goofty!"

Mitya did not leave; he hung back, staying by the wall, and drifted around behind the cage, where there were shadows. Gradually the crowd got tired of watching and moved off. The naked man sat on the floor of the cage chewing meat from the bones. Mitya waited until nobody else was paying attention to him.

He saw a door at the back of the cage, fastened with string. Quietly he went to it and undid the string and pulled the door open. "Tsssst."

The naked man sat there chewing. He paid no heed to Mitya.

"Tssst!" Mitya gestured to him, and the man looked up.

Mitya pushed the door open, pointed to it, pointed out. He beckoned, and the naked man jumped to his feet.

He did not run out the door; he did not take the escape Mitya had made for him. Instead he began to yell, "Hey! There's a damned Indian in here — get this damned Indian away from me!"

Mitya stepped back, astonished. The door hung open, but the naked man now backed up as far from it as he could, his back pressed against the bars, and screamed, "Get this Indian out of here!"

Then from all around the saloon the white men ran at him, and they got him by the arms, and they threw him out into the street. The door slammed behind him. Through them he could hear, like a war cry, the voice calling, "Oofty goofty! Oofty goofty!" He picked himself up, ashamed, and went back to the Shining Light.

He talked to Mammy about it later. She shrugged. "Keep out of places like that."

She had taken over Daisy's old rooms. She had changed nothing of it. The same furniture stood in the same places, the walls were still bare wood. It smelled different, sweeter, wilder.

He said, "Why stay? Why eat bones?"

"Easier than working," said Mammy. "Don't you have any work to do?"

He wanted to talk to her, he wanted her to explain it to him. He wanted to touch her and laugh and make jokes and play with her, as he had played with his wife long ago. She held him off. She liked sex with him but nothing else. He felt stripped to his skin, to his bones, the bone of his penis. He got up and went out of the room, and found Josh and took him up to the roof, to show him what he meant to build next.

Gil woke up before dawn, coughing; his nose hurt, and when he drew in a deep breath, all he took in was smoke.

He yelled, coming wide awake, every hair on end. A thick, stinking heat pressed at him from the wall beside his bed. Throwing back the blankets, he stood up into a dense fog of smoke; the air was hot and gritty. He grabbed his clothes and his boots and stumbled toward the door, choking and gagging. As he opened the door, the wall behind his bed suddenly burst into flames.

He rushed out into the cool darkness, clean air flowing into his throat and lungs like a holy liquor, and his bare feet sank into mud up to his ankles. Panicked, he struggled to run; the muck gripped his feet like manacles. A wave of heat struck him from behind. He tore one foot free and then the other, staggered out into the street, and turned and saw flames shooting out the doorway like a tongue thrusting out of an open mouth.

"Fire," somebody howled, out in the street. "Fire!"

Gil's feet were sinking into the mud again. He yanked them free and slogged backward away from the heat, his eyes still fixed on the fire. For a moment longer the two-story wall before him was dark, only the red tongue leaping from the doorway, and then up from the roof there rose a sheet of snapping, fluttering amber, and the wall below dissolved into flames. Gil recoiled from the heat's blast.

Somebody caught his arm. "Are you all right?"

"Yes — yes." Dazed, he wiped his arm over his face, and only then realized he was still holding his clothes. He dropped his boots and stuck his legs down into his pants and pulled his shirt on. A bell was ringing somewhere, and the street was filling with people,

mostly standing there and staring up. He turned in a circle, looking around, wondering what he should do, and the building next
to Dennison's erupted like a volcano, shooting up a tower of flame
forty feet into the air. Gil shrank back, gasping, his eyeballs hot.
He flung one arm up before his face, but he could not turn away.

"Here!" Somebody thrust a bucket into his hand. "Carry water. Come on, everybody — "

Gil gripped the wire handle of the bucket; he backed up again
from the heat. His mouth was dry. His nose still itched and
burned from the smoke. Where five minutes before he had been
sleeping there was now a howling blaze, everything he owned
converted into heat and red light and rolling black smoke. He
sobbed, grateful to be alive.

"Come on, damn it — help us!" Somebody struck him. Along
the street now, a chain of bodies moved, indefinite in the gaudy
light of the fire, passing buckets along. The water in the buckets
smelled of muck and seaweed; the end of this line reached the
harbor. Gil swallowed. His feet were cold. He pulled them up out
of the ooze of the street and pushed into the line, passed his bucket
down, and took the full one coming up, a pitiful drop of water
against the roaring blaze.

The firebells and then the wild news and rumors reached the
Shining Light just after breakfast, and Frances went up on the roof
to watch the fire.

Mitya had left a walkway along the deck of the ship, between the
old railing and the wall of the new building where her people slept.
She stood at one end of this walk, with the long downward pitch of
the front roof falling off before her. The air was rough with smoke.
A faint low roar lay like a carpet under all other sounds. Across the
rooftops, the great swelling patch of flames was spreading like an
eruption of light out of the heart of the city. Just as she stood there
the fire bounded upward, abruptly much brighter, its lashing peak
higher than anything else in San Francisco, burning many buildings
at once out there, burning more every moment.

The wind rose suddenly; a glowing ember drifted down past

Frances' shoulder. As she turned to call for someone to bring water, she saw the men gathered on the ship deck behind her.

The ruddy glow shone over them. Josh was already turning toward the hatch, going down again. Phineas followed, his face grim. By the rail stood Laban, open-mouthed, staring, motionless, glazed in the flickering color. Frances nodded to Josh. "Go back to the well and draw some water. In case we have to wet down the roof."

The big man turned, spoke a few words, and went off below with Phineas and Laban. Some of the women came up as they went down, Peggy the singer, Theresa, two others; they stood close together, their arms around one another, and one of them began to cry.

Frances put her back to them. They were cowards, they shrank from anything wild. She herself stepped forward toward the edge of the roof, into the unsteady gleam, and stretched her hands out as if to warm herself. Out there in the distance, through the dull, resounding voice of the fire, came thin shouts and screams, and now and then a gun went off. Peggy said, "Where is it? Can you tell?" Behind them the men were lugging buckets of water up onto the roof.

"Near the Plaza," Frances said. Phineas sloshed a bucket of water down over the rooftop past her feet, and she wheeled toward him, impatient. "What you doin'? It still blocks away. Just be careful, is all. Save the water."

Phineas straightened. He said, "Hear that?"

Against the mat of other noise a long dull boom rolled out, like summer thunder. At the sound Frances' skin frizzled, every hair turning. Behind her, the women all gave shrill little mouselike screams. "What was that?"

"Sounds like dynamite," Phineas said.

The daylight was whitening the sky. Below it, the fire licked across half the city's roofline, purifying San Francisco, and carrying it away to heaven. Frances began to murmur, and to step from one foot to the other. As if her motion pulled at him, Laban, still off by himself, swayed slightly from side to side. Phineas brought up two full buckets of water and stood them by the edge of the roof, and Josh came up, and some of the other men. Peggy stood softly singing a hymn.

Another peal of thunder rumbled through the air. Josh said, "They blowin' up the buildin's. I seen 'em do it before. Time the fire gets there, ain't nothin' there left to burn." A crackle of gunfire came like birdsong over the rooftops. Or maybe that was only the fire spitting.

Mitya came up onto the roof. He made a quick circle of it, seeing the water in buckets waiting, and came over to Frances and stood beside her. He almost touched her; she could see he wanted to, and she moved away from him.

Laban said, "Maybe we should go help."

"No." Mitya was staring out at the fire, his hands at his sides. "They shoot. People steal, under the fire, break houses, they shoot everybody. Stay here."

Theresa went up beside him, taking shelter from him, what Frances would not take. "Where is it? What about Daisy?"

"Daisy far off," Mitya said. He waved west, away from the fire. "Gil burn."

"No," Josh said.

Phineas murmured, "Maybe us, next."

"Not us," Mitya said. He turned and looked at Frances and said, "Wind blow wrong."

Frances looked away from him. He thought he was reassuring her. He thought he had some power over her, but he did not. She hugged her arms around herself. The fire did not frighten her. She watched it with excitement, almost exaltation. She felt again the tides of this place, the fury that built and the fury that destroyed, so strong here the ground itself sometimes shook from the tension. She began to sway back and forth again. Around her all her people took the step from her, gathered close, arms around one another, and their voices rose, and they danced, in honor of the fire.

20

GIL STOOD IN THE MIDDLE of Montgomery Street and looked west, straight across the Plaza to the storefronts on Kearny, and nothing obstructed his view except a single charred timber. From Clay Street to Jackson, all that was left was smoking ruin.

He rubbed his hand over his face. He had nothing left to his name except the clothes he was wearing, which he had worn now for three days straight, fighting the fire and then sleeping in the back of the Monumental Engine Company's firehouse. That reminded him of his boots, and he looked around at the trampled mud without much hope of finding them, and did not.

He was broke and homeless, but he had been broke and homeless before. And he knew where to go to start over.

He walked along Montgomery Street, his feet sinking into the mud and sucking back out again. Two Chinese passed him, carrying a handtruck loaded with debris. Out there in the wreckage, a dozen more workers stooped and shoveled at the mess and stacked timbers in a heap.

The ruin was still smoking, but already they were starting to build again. A surge of pride straightened him. Somebody yelled his name, and he waved, striding out, barefoot, with a new optimism.

His city. No mere fire could end his city.

The fire had actually attacked only one chunk of it, anyway. The flames had met their match at Jackson Street, where the firefighters had blown up two boarding houses to stall its course. The dish-shaped craters were half full of red water and floating bits of char. Just beyond, the buildings rose up again, untouched, tight-packed, many still with canvas roofs and walls.

When he turned into Pacific Street he could pick out the Shining Light at once, halfway up the block, with its distinctive sloping roof like the bill of a cap. He caught himself hurrying, spry as a goat along the broken pathway of boxes and brush and wooden walks that threaded through the mud of the street. But when he got there the front door was shut and bolted.

He went around through the alley between the saloon and the boarding house next door. The rear of the building was utterly changed; two new walls stretched from the back of the cookhouse to the corner and then down toward the street again. The cookhouse door was open. He went through the empty kitchen and opened the door into the corridor.

This too was different; the roof was gone, and the walls had been raised a full story on either side. A row of glassed windows stood tilted against the foot of the west wall. In one corner was a bowl of water and a coil of string. He went on up to the front, where the corridor branched off, going right to Daisy's old room and left to the saloon. He went left.

He came into the big, open room, into a silence that seemed electrically charged. A mass of people filled the front part of the room, between the door and the faro tables. Gil stood by the end of the bar; above him, Laban was perched on a scaffold, a paintbrush in his hand, but he was gawking off into the center of the room, not painting. Gil went forward a few steps.

As he did, Mammy's voice rang out. "What do you think you're arresting me for?"

Gil stopped by the front of the stage. Now he saw it all clearly. The pack of men by the front door, armed with pistols and shotguns, were spread out to cover the room. Josh and Phineas and Mitya stood halfway down the bar, their hands at their sides, and as Gil watched, Mitya shifted his weight from one foot to the other and three guns swiveled toward him. Beyond him, in the shadows of the far end of the bar, was another group of people, mostly women, none Daisy; he saw Daisy nowhere.

Mammy stood in the middle of the room, under the only lit ceiling lamp.

Opposite her was a man in a fine gray coat, carrying a briefcase, a man with a wide, empty, meaninglessly friendly face. Gil had never met him, but he had seen him often: this was Ned McGowan, justice of the peace of San Francisco.

McGowan said, "Mammy, you're running a disorderly house here. I can't have that going on." His voice was soft and edgeless as running water.

From the rear, by the bar, a woman's voice called out, "It wasn't disorderly until you got here, Judge."

"You're not going to arrest me," Mammy said. "What do you really want?"

McGowan was looking around, appraising the place. Slowly he brought his gaze back to her. "You got to keep the law, Mammy."

"Certainly," she said. "Tell me how much it will cost me to keep the law with you, then, and get out and let me get back to my work."

McGowan's smile looked soldered on. His eyes never stopped moving. He said, "Well, one thousand dollars would put you right, I think. For now."

"Forever," Mammy said.

He blinked at her. "Until you run afoul of the law again, Mammy."

Mammy said, "Bring me the cashbox, Phineas."

The woman by the bar called out, "Mammy, don't do it." Nobody else said anything. Phineas, slow and stooped, went around behind the bar and came back with a strongbox, and Mammy nodded to him to put it on the edge of the stage. There was no lock. She flipped the lid of the box open and began to count out scrip. When she had a stack of paper money two inches high, she set it down on the stage and backed away.

"Take it," she said, and McGowan himself went over and picked up the wad of bills and fingered the edges.

"Excellent," he said. He slid the stack of money away inside the front of his expensive gray coat. "I'm glad to see you've got some common sense, Mammy. Good day to you." He turned and walked out through his pack of deputies, and they filed out after him. They left the door open behind them; at once the day's customers began to trickle in from the street.

Gil sighed. Mammy turned, shutting the lid of the strongbox, and saw him, and her head rose. "Gilbert. Alive and well." Mitya came up behind her.

"Mammy," Gil said. "That was very unedifying."

She snorted at him. "We'll see what happens next. We thought you'd been burnt up, Gil. Are you coming back to us?"

Gil said, "I'd like to, for a while. Maybe I could help you with McGowan. Damn it, that was pretty brutal."

She smiled at him. She wore a dumpy dress, a rag around her head, but she smiled like a girl. She said, "Gilbert, you expect too much of people." She lifted her head and nodded to someone else, down the room, and handed the strongbox over to Phineas.

Gil said, "There ought to be something you can do."

Mitya came up toward them, one hand sliding across the top of the bar; he gave Gil a sideways look, almost shy. "You no burn up."

"A little singed at the edges." Gil put his hand out.

The Indian took it slowly, and his face eased; he said, "You come live here now? We got many new rooms."

"Show me."

He went off, and Gil followed him to the door by the stage and out to the corridor; one branch of it went on down to where the little old room had stood that was the first room they had ever made here, and he looked that way and said, "Where's Daisy?" in as casual a voice as he could compose.

Mitya swung toward him. "Gone. Now she live with Rudd. You lose." He showed his teeth in a smile, but he looked angry. "Come on." He led Gil away down the corridor into the heart of the Shining Light.

Mitya had found out where Judge McGowan's woman lived, in a little wooden house on Post Street. Mitya went up there in the evening.

The rain had stopped. In the cool dusk, the fog was drifting in off the bay. The house where McGowan kept his woman had two floors. The light from the bottom-floor window turned the fog to a gold mist, but the upstairs window was dark. Mitya went around to the back of the house.

A couple of saddlehorses filled up the little yard, dozing. From inside, Mitya heard voices now, a shout of laughter. He tried the back door, which was open, and slipped through into an unlit hall.

At the far end of the hall was a doorway. Light slanted from it, and shadows worked back and forth through the light: people moving in the room beyond. Another yell of laughter. Mitya eased down the hall a little way, trying to see in, and someone tramped out and down the hall toward him; he ducked into the corner. The man walked right past him, opened the door and went out to the back yard, came in again a moment later with an armload of wood, and went back to the front room, never seeing Mitya.

Mitya edged down the hall again. He could make out several voices — a woman's, McGowan's, other men's. He got to the bottom of the stairs and went up. At the top he looked down, through the rail.

Below, McGowan came out into the hall; he still wore the soft gray coat he had put Mammy's money away into. He stopped, lit a segar, and turned to face the big man who had come after him. This man carried a revolver in his belt. He and McGowan stood talking a moment. Mitya backed up from the stairs and looked around him.

In front of him now was a door. As soon as he opened it he knew a woman lived here. The air stank of old flowers. The dark room was crowded with fluffy furniture. It was hot. In the dark, Mitya followed the heat in the air to the far side of the room, where there was a little fireplace built into the wall.

A screen covered it. He pulled that away and put his head into the fireplace, into a rush of hot air, and looked down through a grate toward the fire roaring in the hearth below. As he watched, white hands laid more wood on that fire.

From that room below, the woman's voice cried out, "Oh — Judge! So clever you are!"

Mitya sat back on his heels. He wanted to shoot McGowan, but Gil and Mammy were right: everybody would suffer for that. He got up and went around the room to the big fluffy bed and dragged off the pillows and comforters and jammed them into the fireplace, packing it full.

That muffled the laughter and the high voice of the woman. He went back onto the stairs, crept down halfway, and waited.

From here he could see the door to the front room, the light gushing from it, the busy patterns of shadows. He could hear the gurgle of their voices. The voices did not change much for a moment, but Mitya saw a tendril of smoke curling out by the top of the doorframe.

In the lit room, somebody coughed. Somebody else said, "Hey."

Then somebody else yelled, "Fire! Fire — " and the woman screamed.

They thundered toward the door. Billows of smoke rolled out through it, while the crush of people scrambled and fought to escape. They filled the hall, yanked open the front door. McGowan shouted, "Marie!" He dashed out into the hall, dragging the woman after him, and Mitya sprang down off the stairs.

The hall was still full of people, screaming and yelling, shoving at each other as they fought to get out. The smoke, thick and gray, rolled through the top half of the space. Mitya clawed past two burly men to reach McGowan, wrapped one arm around him from behind, and plunged his other hand inside McGowan's coat.

The people around McGowan banged into him, and somebody stepped on his foot. McGowan howled. With one arm wrapped tightly around the man's chest, Mitya wrenched him around off balance. Inside the front of the coat Mitya's fingers closed on a wad of money. McGowan roared, "Help, help, I'm being — " Mitya jammed his knee up into the Judge's backside, dropped him hard, and fled down the hall to the back door.

"Stop," somebody yelled. "Who's that? Stop!" Mitya ran out the back door into the cool, damp darkness.

At the Shining Light, he did not go in through the door like a customer. He went to the side and climbed in through a hidden opening in the wall, which he had put in so that he could get into Mammy's room whenever he wanted to.

She was not there. In the dark he waited. He took the wad of money out of his shirt and felt it, thinking how pleased she would be. Then he heard her coming into the next room.

Not alone: Theresa was with her. He liked Theresa, who had shown him new ways to make love; he went to the door and heard them talking.

Mammy said, "This one is rather good-looking, I think. You'll like him better."

"Do I have to go live with him?" Theresa asked.

"Don't you want to?"

"I don't want to do what Daisy did. I like it here," Theresa said. Mitya stood by the door and held his breath to hear it. Every word grew bigger in his thinking, like a flower blooming. Theresa's voice went on. "I can still find out what you want to know, Mammy. I can snoop out a lot of them, then, like that miner the other night. I like having a lot of men."

"If that's what you want. I have other girls who'll do what Daisy did."

Mitya laid his hand on the door. He felt cold all over. He remembered what Gil had said to him. He had not believed it then, but now he had to believe it. He saw Theresa as a key that Mammy used, opening up men to be plundered. He saw Daisy like that too.

His heart clenched. He wanted to tear up the money he had brought like a trophy to her. He saw himself in her hands, turned and turned like a key in a lock.

He left the money on the bed. She would know who had left it. He went out his secret way and shut it behind him. He fastened it well. He did not intend to use it again, not ever. He went instead up through the back of the Shining Light to his den, where he had a bottle of whiskey.

Laban sat on a stool, his back bowed, a little tub of yellow paint in his hand; he dipped in his brush and daubed off the excess on the rim of the paintpot. Gil stood behind him, a cup of coffee in his hand. "You haven't done Mammy yet," he said.

The young man only laughed. He had covered this whole wall with images of the Shining Light. He seemed to use only one color at a time: he was painting in the yellow, here and there, wherever it belonged, working up and down the wall. Gil stopped to admire a portrait of Josh, singing. Laban had no skill at perspective, or maybe no interest, but he could catch people, and he had caught Josh, the broad black face swelling with his song, one arm, the only other piece of Josh included in the portrait, curled around the shoulders of Laban himself.

"You see you?" Laban asked, and pointed with his brush.

"Where?"

"Daisy singing." The young man did not look up from his work. Gil went down the wall a little, to a big picture of Daisy in full voice, her arms extended. Other pictures filled the space around her, faces of the miners, heaps of gold, a mule drowning in the muddy street, a Chinese dragon, the steam ferry to Oakland, but he did not see himself, not for a long while, until he looked at Daisy's outstretched hands. On either palm was a head of Gil Marcus.

He felt himself go hot, his mind a rumble of confusion. He started to say, "I don't love her anymore," and clamped his mouth shut.

Laban said, "You be here now for good, Mist' Gil?"

"Don't call me that," Gil said, surprising himself.

The young man did him the ultimate compliment, turned from the painting, and smiled at him. "All right." Their eyes met.

"Yes, I told Mammy I'd tend bar."

"Good," said Laban. "Now maybe we'll get Daisy back."

"I don't think so. Where's Mitya?"

"In the gallery."

Gil went on down to the stage door and through it, and into the long corridor back to the cookhouse. Mitya and Josh were at the far end, banging away with hammers at something on the ground; when he went up he saw that they were building a ladder. Mitya hardly looked at Gil, only said, "Help," and put him to work steadying the ladder while Mitya climbed and Josh handed him up a beam of wood.

They laid the wood like a rafter across the roofless top of the corridor, and hung a rope over. With this rope they hoisted up the first of the windows that leaned against the foot of the wall and set it in place on the top.

Theresa came in carrying a jug and a basket. "Come eat," she said. "Don't work so hard."

The men sat down on the ground and ate bread and cheese. Josh and Gil and Theresa drank beer, but Mitya drank from a bottle of whiskey. Gil looked up at the one window they had put in.

"What are you going to do?"

Mitya's cheeks bulged, full of bread. "Windows all along. That side, this side. Light come in."

Gil laughed. "That's called a clerestory."

Mitya grunted at him, gave him a sideways amused look. Reaching out one hand suddenly he grabbed Gil's arm. "You say it. I do it." He smiled, wide, amused, and let go of Gil and took his bottle instead.

Theresa sat on her heels between them. She wore only a thin shift that clung to her breasts and her hips. She glanced shyly at Gil, but she grabbed Mitya's bare foot. "You come fix my door?"

"Sure." He ate bread.

Josh said, "Gil, you see that fire?"

"That fire damn near killed me," Gil said.

"Hey, hey." The big man grinned at him. "Brought you back to us, it can't be all bad."

"He come back for Daisy," Mitya said.

"No, I didn't," Gil said. He knew he was flushing; his ears stung.

Josh stared at him, not blinking. "Daisy gone uptown, she's real fancy now, she don't even come around here no more."

Theresa said, "She'd like to, but she can't," and covered her mouth with her hand.

"She no care," Mitya said. He brushed the crumbs off his hands. His long black hair hung down his back; he wore only a shirt and a filthy pair of canvas pants. He said, "You stay, Gil?"

"Yes," Gil said. "I'm staying. I like it here." He looked up at the wall, where soon a string of windows would let in sheets of daylight.

Theresa said, "I need my door on again. That man last night tore it right off."

"I bang his head off, he break my building," Mitya said.

"Oh, yes," the girl said, and tossed her thick hair back. "He can do whatever he want with me, but touch your place, why, hell will rise." She got to her feet, and Mitya caught hold of her skirt.

"Anybody hurt you, I shoot." He lifted the bunched skirt in his fist and kissed the hem. His free hand slid up under the cloth, and the girl bounded away with a little squeal.

"Hunh!" She strutted off, waggling her hips. "What do you think I am — cheap? Come fix my door first." Josh and Mitya crowed after her, ebullient. She went out.

Josh said, "You do the door, or me?" He looked oddly eager for the work.

Mitya said, "You go." He got up, setting the whiskey bottle carefully in the shelter of the wall. "Gil help me."

Josh said, "All right," and went briskly off. Gil and Mitya spent the rest of the day putting in windows.

21

LABAN PAINTED THE FIRE, using the last of his red and yellow mixed with egg, which made it stick better to the wall. Next he got some blue and finished painting Daisy walking out the door with Tierney Rudd.

He thought he would paint Gil Marcus coming back, bigger, with all the people laughing. Laban especially was glad to see Gil, and not just because Gil helped him get paint.

The fire reached into the corner of the side wall, where he had started with the huge figure of Daisy lying on her side and everything streaming out from her — the first cookfires by the old boat, the building of the Shining Light, the dog that danced, the miners and the mud, Mitya and his bowl of water and his string, Josh singing, Phineas and Josh arguing and working. The spaces between he would fill with other people, the miners and the gamblers and the drunks. In the corner he colored the fire up into the peak of the ceiling and onto the next wall, behind the bar.

This wall was different because it was part of the old ship. The wood curved out into the room, and scars and bolt ends broke up the surface. He fit the bulges and knobs into the pictures. He worked all the time on the painting. Mammy sometimes asked him to do something, but she had lots of other hands now, so he worked all day on the painting. Usually people stood watching him, which didn't bother him anymore. Sometimes people came up and tried to pay him to paint them in.

When three men in dusters walked in and tried to rob the Shining Light, Laban was painting, and he painted right through that, the crash of the shotgun blast, the sudden hush, the yell demanding money. He painted the three men as he saw them, enormous, from floor to ceiling, covered with their pale dusters, their faces only dark slits between collar and hatbrim. Their shotguns stretched halfway down the wall, and at the end, much smaller, he painted the end of the bar, and Mitya leaning over it, the pistol in his hands. At the muzzle of the pistol he put the red flash he had seen when it went off, and across the back of one of the dusters he painted a broad red blotch.

Then just past the first Mitya he painted another, this one wheeling to shoot the man way down the wall, and at the far end of the wall he painted the men with dusters really small, two down and dying and one running out the door.

People came and found themselves painted onto the wall and brought in crowds of their friends to see.

He painted the second big fire, in the spring, which destroyed half the waterfront. He painted the crews of workmen going up the street in the summer, digging the street up and raking it smooth, as smooth as ever Mitya made them dig the ground when he built the Shining Light. Then they came with planks of wood and laid down the planks on the smoothed-out streets, and now the streets were fine and hard in all weather, and carts and wagons could go easier on them, and so the new planked streets were crowded with wagons and not just people walking.

In every open space he put San Francisco's faces, black and brown and yellow and white with black hair, and white with blond. And he put in heaps of gold; whenever he had yellow paint, he painted big piles of dusty gold.

But mostly he painted the Shining Light. He painted the stage and the people on it, singers and dancers, the juggler who was so bad he juggled only once. Laban put him on the wall, where he juggled that one time forever.

People came in and out of the doors of the Shining Light, and Laban himself went out often enough. He went down to the Clay Street wharf with Mammy when she went to buy vegetables, and saw barges of redwood lumber wallowing in the shallows, saw ships unloading bricks from Boston and coal from up in the Columbia River country. Saw ships going out — the mail steamers, the ferries to Oakland, to Sacramento, the clipper ships, frail as dragonflies, setting out to China, carrying gold and dirty laundry.

He saw men working everywhere — the bent-backed stevedores, the carpenters banging new buildings together, the brick-
layers raising up walls, the pipelayers putting down pipes for the
new water company, to bring water down from the lagoon right
into the houses. With Mammy he drove out toward the Mission
on the new planked road; the sound the wheels made, and the
evenness and smoothness of the ride, stayed with him like a charm
for hours.

When he went back to the Shining Light he painted the Mission
onto the wall, and made it real. Because Laban knew that what lay
outside the boundary of the work was only dust and air and light,
until he put it onto the wall. What that meant about Laban himself
was not something he thought about very much.

22

BREEZE-WHIPPED, LEAPING, the brisk water of the bay caught
the sun in a million glittering facets; the sky was bright as a new dollar. All up and down the wharf, the waiting crowd clambered and
yelled and leaned over the railing, peering toward the rolling plume
of smoke that marked the oncoming steamship from Sacramento.

One of the horses snorted. Phineas got down out of the seat of
the carriage and went up to hold the team's heads.

Daisy was jittery all over. The touch of the wild wind was like
nettles on her cheek. She could not sit still; her legs quivered and
her heart was drumming tattoos in her chest. She had Tierney's
letter clutched in her hand — laconic, commanding, the first word
she had had from him in months, since he left San Francisco to
make his fortune in the desert. Now he was coming back, on the
white steamboat that butted up the channel through the harbor,
and the terror almost overwhelmed her that she would not know
him when she saw him.

The steamer wallowed down along the side of the wharf. Its railings and the upper deck were packed with passengers; she could make out no one face among them, they were all strangers. The boat's side hit the wharf with a crunch, and its gangplank swung out; before the wharf end was safely down, the passengers were rushing off. As the steep gangplank clogged with bodies, men began to vault over the railings of the steamer down onto the dock.

Daisy's horses stirred, restless, as people hurried by them. Daisy swallowed, her gaze searching the churning mass of strangers that swept past, her hands fisted in her lap, and then suddenly coming down the crowded wharf toward her was a man with a ragged black beard, in battered boots and a buffalo jacket, a man who stared straight back at her, and the eyes were the same: it was Tierney.

She jerked a smile onto her face, but her heart stopped. He looked poor. He looked as if he had failed.

He reached the carriage and stepped up into the seat. "Well," he said, "here I am."

"Yes," she said, afraid to ask him what had happened. She turned forward. "Phineas, take us home, please."

Tierney said, "I'm sorry. I should have cleaned up in Sacramento, but I was in a hurry to get back." The carriage moved off at a smart clip down Montgomery Street, the wheels clicking over the seams in the road planking. She felt him next to her like a sack of hot coals. His arm slid around her, and she stiffened. He said, "Do I smell bad?"

"Yes," she said. She could not look him in the face. She knew he had failed.

"Well," he said, and reached into his coat, "this ought to make me smell better." He took out a deck of paper money as thick as her wrist.

She let out a squawk. "Tierney!" Twisting on the seat, she flung her arms around him and kissed him, the beard like fur against her face. "You did it."

"Yes, I did." He slid the money away into the coat again.

Rough and hairy, he stank like an animal, but his voice was smooth with satisfaction. "And that's just the beginning, Daisy." He kissed her again, longer, slower, and drew back to gaze down into her face. "This company will buy three shipments a year. There are other buyers too, just waiting in line. I have to talk to Mammy about reinvesting her share — I want to build a refinery in Oakland. We'll move out there eventually." Above the ragged fringe of beard his eyes blazed; his arms tightened around her. "We're going to have everything."

"Good," she said. "Where's Blake?"

"Blake," he said scornfully. He drew off a little, sitting frontward on the seat again, and reached into the coat and got out a segar. "That son of a bitch. He ran out on me." He laughed, bit off the end of the segar, and spat it into the street. "Just before we struck it."

"Good," she said. "I hated him. Do you like the carriage?"

"Yes. And the roads; that's an improvement." He was staring out of the carriage now, at the new buildings going up on Montgomery; turning abruptly, he looked the other way, his face furrowed. "Where the hell did all this come from? I don't remember any of it."

She laughed, one hand on his arm, keeping hold of him. "I suppose a lot has changed since you left. Do you want to go for a drive and see it all?"

"No." He swung toward her. There was a quickness in his moves, an urgency, an eagerness; she wondered if it had always been there, if she had missed it before. "No," he said. His eyes burned. "I want to go to bed."

She slid her hand up his arm to his shoulder and leaned toward him. "Phineas, go faster." She lifted her face up for another kiss.

Frances said, "You see this? You see what this is?" She waved the paper at Mitya.

The Indian grunted at her, unimpressed. He was half drunk, as he always was lately, his shirt open all down the front; he smelled of whiskey and sweat and wood. She had dragged him down off

the roof to show him Judge McGowan's paper, in which he took
no interest, and now she got up from the chair and went up in
front of him and shoved the paper into his face.

"If you was a civilized man and could read, you'd see this is a
judgment against me, you fool, to the tune of ten thousand dollars." She slapped him with the paper. "That's what you got me,
stuffing up his chimney and stealing back that money. That's what
you got me!"

Mitya's eyes were almost shut. Under the heavy lids she
thought she saw a glitter of malicious amusement. He said, "I
shoot him now?"

"No," she said. "Damn you, get out of here. And don't do
anything more, do you understand me? I'll handle him my own
way."

She swatted him again. He ignored it. She thought he liked
making her angry. He baffled her. She had thought she owned
him. Maybe it was the liquor. He never came near her anymore.
She supposed his other women satisfied his animal nature. Or else
he wasn't a man anymore, because he drank so much. She told
herself again she didn't need any man, especially not this one, who
had let her down.

She said, "Get out."

His lips twisted; maybe he was smiling. She wished she could
order him away from the Shining Light, but it would be like telling
the boards and the rafters to get up and leave. Even now he defied
her; he drifted toward the door, in no hurry, looking around the
room as he always did, like some farmer in his garden wondering
where to plant more turnips. There was a knock on the door. She
flung the paper down.

"I got off the first time with just one thousand," she said, between her teeth. "But thanks to you and your stupidity, now it's
costing me ten times as much. Come in!" The door opened, letting
Theresa in with her arms full of flowers, and Mitya went out.

The barber had good, soft hands. Tierney relaxed and stretched
back in the chair, chin up, yielding his beard to the deft stroke

of the razor. He shut his eyes. The smell of rose soap and bay rum tingled in his nose; around him, like a warm envelope of satisfaction, he felt his rediscovered cleanliness, his skin sweet from the bath, his body sleeked into clean cotton and a well-made suit.

For six months he had lived in hell, in the desert, digging and arguing and fighting and eating hardtack and drinking cold coffee and sleeping on the ground, but that was over now.

Now he had money again, and lots of it. Now he had Daisy again.

That was the real prize. She had waited for him, she had had her doubts, they hadn't always gotten along so well, but she had waited for him. Kept the door open for him. That was the picture he saw in his mind: Daisy standing in a doorway, bright lights and laughter behind her, good food and drink and people to admire him, while he toiled up through the darkness toward her. Real life behind her, through the door that she held open.

The barber said, "New to San Francisco?"

"I've been away," Tierney said.

"Up to the mines?"

Tierney said nothing. The placers would have been better than the desert with its sour water and heat and grit. He did not intend to supply the barber with any of this insight.

"Fellah come in here the other day," said the barber, his voice as smooth as the glide of his razor, "telling me about some beach up north that's half black sand and half gold dust."

Tierney still said nothing. Borax cast no haloes.

"I always figured," the barber said, "why go up to the Sierra when sooner or later all the gold in the Sierra's got to come to San Francisco." He took Tierney delicately by the nose, and the blade whisked away the hair from his upper lip. The door opened, admitting another customer and a gush of sound from the Plaza just outside.

"Take a seat," the barber called. "I'll be a few more minutes."

"Take your time," said the newcomer.

Outside there was a roar from the crowd that beat through even the shut door of the barbershop. Tierney said, "What the hell is going on out there?"

"Indignation meeting," said the barber. "Happens all the time. How long you been gone?"

"A while," said Tierney.

"Notice much different about the place?"

Tierney laughed, careful of the razor skimming the flare of his throat. "I left a city of mud, came back to a city of marble. Or brick, anyway."

The barber gave a dutiful chuckle, not catching the allusion. The other customer said, "Aren't you Tierney Rudd?"

His head immobile under the knife, Tierney rolled his eyes around to see this man's face. "Who are you?"

"Isaac Bluxome." The man got up and came two steps across the narrow shop to shake Tierney's hand. "We fought the Regulators together, remember?"

"Yes. Of course. Still here, are you?"

"Oh, yes." Bluxome moved toward the door again so that Tierney could see him more easily as they talked. "I have my own business now — I buy and sell."

"Oh, really. How's trade?"

"Terrible. Supply is high, demand is low, the city's in debt to its armpits."

Tierney laughed. "Sounds like a bad situation."

"It ought to get better," said Bluxome. "It always does. But it will never be like 'forty-nine, never again." His voice sang with regret.

"There you go," said the barber. He wiped Tierney's cheeks and chin with a soft cloth, brushed at the shoulders of his suit, and handed him a looking glass. Tierney pushed the glass away and got out of the chair.

"Those were the days," Bluxome said. He moved over and took Tierney's place in the chair. "I'll tell you, Rudd, things were a lot easier then. And safer, too. I think, my God, men walked around with fortunes in gold dust in their pockets and nobody bothered them. Now you can get knocked over in the street for a twenty-dollar IOU."

Tierney laughed, his interest piqued by this outburst. "Were you robbed?" He fingered a ten-dollar gold piece out of the coin pocket of his vest and dropped it into the barber's tray.

"Much obliged," said the barber. He shook his towel with a dextrous snap.

Bluxome said, "Everybody's been robbed. Or burned down. God, it's awful, it's like London, or New York." He shook his head. "If this was 'forty-nine, we'd just hang a few of the bad apples, as we did with the Regulators."

Outside, the crowd gave another yell, pierced by whistles. What Tierney remembered best about the matter of the Regulators was that none of the judges would let him hang anybody. He said, "Is it a gang, or just some free lances?"

The barber was folding the towel around Bluxome's skinny neck. He said, "The worst are the Sydney Ducks. Australians, ticket-of-leave men from the penal colony there. They're coming into town in droves. They're all crooks, and they all stick together. If one of them gets in trouble with the law, they pony up a warchest and buy him off."

"The Ducks are just the little men," Bluxome said. "The real crooks are these damn Democratic judges who have no respect for the law." He eased himself in the chair; the barber stood by his hip, paddling a cup of soap to a thick froth. "Crooked law makes crooks."

Tierney said, "Where's Sam Brannan? Why isn't he doing something about it?"

The barber began to plaster thick suds onto Bluxome's cheeks. "Brannan's too busy making money."

"That's not fair," said Bluxome hotly. His breath blew dollops of soap into his lap. "Sam's suffering — we all suffered in that last fire — but things have changed since the Regulators. It's just not that easy anymore."

Tierney's coat hung on the rack by the door; he reached for it, turning away from Bluxome. "I don't remember that things were so easy in 'forty-nine."

"Oh? Well — hey. Don't go." Bluxome pushed the barber's

hand away, the razor gleaming in the empty air, and sat up. "Wait a minute, Rudd, until I'm done here. I'm going up to a meeting with Sam and a couple of the others, to talk about all this — come with me."

"I have to go to the bank," Tierney said. He settled the coat on his shoulders. Made before he went into the desert, it fit poorly, too snug across the back, too loose along the waist. This pleased him. He meant anyway to go out and have clothes made, everything new, everything the best. He, at least, was in a mood to spend money.

Bluxome said, "Then go to the bank, and meet me over at Brannan's office. Where the *Californian* used to be. Come on now, Rudd, we need all the help we can get, or we're just going to lose this town completely."

Tierney faced him. "What are you planning to do?"

"We don't know, damn it. We've talked of forming a Vigilance Committee, but nobody knows how. It's like — " Bluxome flung his hands up. "We don't know. But we have to do something."

"All right." Tierney nodded to him, keeping his face straight, hiding the visceral excitement stirring in his gut somewhere. They didn't know, they hadn't known what to do, back in the days of the Regulators, but Tierney had known. Tierney still knew what to do. He said, "I'll see you at Brannan's office, then. Half an hour?"

"Half an hour," said Bluxome, and lay back under the razor.

23

"YOU CAN'T DO THIS," Jenkins said again; his voice was an off-key Cockney twang. He was a burly man, bearded, stinking, drunk when they caught him, hardly sober even now. It took three or four men to keep hold of him, to keep him moving.

Tierney walked along behind him, Isaac Bluxome on one elbow, a squat little man named James King on the other. With one hand gripping the butt of his pistol, Tierney stayed on the edge of the crowd and watched for trouble.

The firebell was still ringing, two strokes, a minute's empty air, two more strokes, as it had been ringing for hours. Stepping off the boat from Oakland that afternoon, he had heard it, and a thrill had gone through him, even before Bluxome came running up to him, red-faced with excitement, and said, "We've got a prisoner."

Jenkins had robbed a store in broad daylight, knocked the old man behind the counter over the head and hauled off the iron safe. When people chased him he got into a rowboat and rowed off into the harbor and dropped the safe overboard, but they had caught him anyway. Then it got interesting, because instead of taking him to jail, the men who had caught him handed him over to Tierney's new Vigilance Committee.

Up ahead, Jenkins shouted, "You can't do this," and braced himself for a brief, savage struggle, and Tierney with the others closed on him and heaved him on, up dusty Clay Street, into the Plaza.

Bluxome trotted across to Tierney's elbow. "So far, so good." His face was pulled lean with tension; he had a pistol in his belt, and he kept grasping the curved butt and then letting go as if it bit him. His eyes darted back and forth. "Everybody came, I think."

"There will be a lot more after this."

After months of recruiting they had upward of twenty-five or thirty Vigilantes, but only a dozen of them had answered the first ringing of the bell. The small number had actually been an advantage, since they could agree on something, which was that Jenkins was guilty and should hang. On rumors and the ringing of the bell, a mob had gathered in the street outside the Committee's headquarters, and when they brought Jenkins out, suddenly there were three hundred more Vigilantes ready to carry out justice.

Now with every step more joined them, curious, bored, angry men all wanting to be on the right side. Tierney swallowed down the surging excitement in his throat. Everything was going as he had planned it.

The lamps of the big saloons on the north and east sides of the Plaza cast even the dark end, by the post office, into a deep, flickering twilight. Knots of men stood here and there in the open square, and the white-painted porch of the new Parker House swarmed with onlookers. When the Vigilantes with their struggling, complaining prisoner marched out into the Plaza, a ragged cheer went up.

"There's the sheriff," someone said.

Tierney rubbed one hand quickly over his face. His jittering nerves would not let him stand still. Before him, before them all, Jack Hayes, the sheriff of San Francisco, was riding pompously into their path, a row of armed deputies behind him.

Sam Brannan, as usual, walked at the front of the crowd. He strode out to argue with the sheriff, and the other Vigilantes stood hesitant a moment.

Jenkins called, "Sheriff! Sheriff, get me out of this!"

Tierney's skin felt hot. He scanned the Plaza in a single wide glance and turned to Bluxome beside him. "Where are we going to do it?"

"The flagpole," someone called, hoarse-voiced, and pointed.

The crowd yelled. Those who before had been only lingering to watch were joining the Vigilantes, raising their voices, louder than the little band of men at the center who had started it all and done everything, and who now moved abruptly forward, toward the flagpole. Sheriff Hayes and Brannan were still standing face to face, shouting at each other, but nobody was paying them any heed except the prisoner, who gave another frantic call.

Striding along with the others, Tierney rubbed his shaking, sweating hands together. "Who's got the rope?"

"Hey, wait," Bluxome said. "We can't hang somebody off the flagpole. That's the liberty stick, damn it. The Stars and Stripes flies there, not crooks."

Tierney felt as if he was going to blow up. He flung one arm out, pointing at an adobe building on the corner. "Over there." With

Bluxome beside him, he turned to the men holding Jenkins and waved, and they towed Jenkins forward.

The mob rushed along with them, splitting to pass by the sheriff and Brannan and the deputies in the middle of the Plaza. Brannan and the sheriff were still arguing, but now they were left behind. Jenkins gave another desperate, almost seductive cry, and the men around him took him by the arms and hauled him bodily across the square to the adobe, with its projecting roofbeams.

Tierney rushed along with them, looking around him for the rope; a wild urgency drove him, as if he would die if he could not get his hands on the rope. This side of the Plaza was dark, and the crowd was churning, boisterous, confused. He could not find the rope, his stomach hurt; then, to his shock, a deep voice roared, "Pull!" and he turned, and over the tossing heads of the crowd he saw Jenkins rising into the air.

He yelled, his voice lost in the howl that went up from the rest of the mob. The legs of the hanging man jerked and thrashed in odd, mechanical angles, like a jointed doll's, so that he swung violently back and forth, hitting the wall of the building, careening off to dangle over the heads of the crowd. Tierney shoved and clawed his way through the packed bodies toward the wall of the adobe.

He had to get his hands on the rope. Jenkins gurgled as he swung; his tongue stuck out. He gave off a sudden stench of shit. Tierney reached the rope. Twenty other men were lined up along it, leaning back, braced against the gyrating body on the other end. Tierney had to push and fight to get hold of it. The tension in the rope seemed to match some vibrating tension in his gut. He leaned against the weight, and Jenkins' struggles quivered down through the rope and through Tierney Rudd, shivering and shaking all through Tierney Rudd, like a transfer of the life force.

At last the body dangled motionless. The crowd stood around it all night; as the men holding the rope tired, others came up and took their places. Sheriff Hayes left, promising inquiries and inquests and further investigation. Sam Brannan and Isaac Bluxome and Jim King eventually went also, but Tierney Rudd stayed there until the sun came up, and was the last man home.

On the stage the three girls kicked their legs up, once, twice, three times, and then spun around and tossed up their skirts. Since they were only rehearsing they were wearing long, ordinary dresses, and the effect was mild. Frances debated telling them not to wear underthings. Beside her, Tierney Rudd leaned on the bar and watched the bartender, a runaway slave named Ink, pour whiskey into his glass.

He tasted it, looking wary, and then his eyebrows rose. "Very good," he said.

Frances nodded to the boy behind the bar. "Go on now, we need to talk." The boy slid away, down toward where Gil Marcus was bent over the bar counter scribbling something. Frances turned to Tierney Rudd.

"Don't insult me in front of my people. Do you expect my liquor to be bad?"

His face flattened, and for a moment he looked angry; then a mask slipped over his features and he looked suddenly like a stranger. "My apologies. You constantly surprise me." He saluted her with the glass. "Your health, Mam."

She accepted that, grudging, pleased. He looked as beautiful as a racehorse, tall, slim, his clothes perfectly fit to him, every hair polished. She said, "Everything's going well?"

"Very well. The refinery is already working nearly at full capacity, I've got orders waiting, people are paying me to just listen to them."

"Good," she said. At the other end of the bar, Gil had finished writing for the moment. He straightened, tucked away his bit of paper, and went back to washing glasses. He was always writing something down. Laban came out of the stage door carrying paint and brushes. The girls on the stage kicked again. She was determined that they should not wear underthings.

To Tierney Rudd she said, "I hear you have other business as well, stretching ropes."

He smiled at her. For an instant she saw something in his face that chilled even her. But then it was gone. She had imagined it. He said, "There are four hundred men in the Vigilance Committee now. We mean to keep the peace in spite of the law."

"How? Besides stringing up the unlucky."

He sipped the whiskey. "We're starting night patrols to watch for arsonists and housebreakers, that sort of thing."

"The problem," she said, "is judges like McGowan."

He smiled again. "You too? Our boy Ned has stepped on a lot of sore toes."

"It seems to me, if this Vigilance Committee is any good, it could handle white men in clean collars." Laban had come in behind her and was working on the wall there, using black this time; on blank patches of pale brown, faces appeared, all watching her. She turned her shoulder to them. "Get McGowan," she said to Tierney Rudd.

He finished the whiskey. "Be patient. The circumstances have to be right." His voice dropped to a murmur; she had to lean closer to hear him. "We're recruiting more men constantly. It's just a question of time."

"Hunh." She waggled her fingers in the air, dispelling nonsense. "It's just a question of one of you suffering directly." Josh was standing down at the other end of the bar, waving to her: the charcoal man had come. She stepped back. "Tell Daisy I'll come by, see her, maybe next week." She looked him up and down, pleased again with his fineness, this man she had made, who knew his place and played his part so well. "Good day, Mr. Rudd." Dismissing him, she went off toward Josh, to settle accounts with the charcoal vendor.

The summer passed. There were no more strikes in the Sierra; the gold seemed to be running out, as Tierney Rudd had always predicted. The great warehouses along Montgomery Street bulged with goods that nobody had the money to buy. Still the city grew, sprouting new buildings, new streets, now climbing up the sides of the hills; with steam engines the workmen blasted off pieces of

Telegraph Hill and Russian Hill, and little railroad cars trundled the rubble down to the bay and dumped it into the shallows, and houses rose on top of that. The state capitol moved from San Jose to Sacramento; nobody cared, as long as the politicians stayed out of San Francisco.

In the fall there was another great fire, which consumed warehouses and gambling halls and ate its way into Pacific Street. The planking that made the streets easy for wagons now made it easy for the fire, too. The flames ate up the dry wood and shot through the covered ditches underneath, where the sewers ran, and followed the laterals up into the buildings, which exploded into balls of fire, and it looked as if all of San Francisco would die.

Mitya drove the people of the Shining Light to its defense. With axes he and Josh tore away the planking in the street while the fire crisped their hair and blistered their hands; they stuffed rocks and mud and rags into the sewer ditches, lined everybody up with buckets and tubs and hats full of water to wet the building down. When they ran out of water, Mitya dragged crates of French champagne out of the storehouse, and they soaked the roof with that.

And that was enough. The fire singed off their eyebrows, blackened the road, burned down the boarding house where once Friendly's had stood, but when the flames died and the smoke blew away, the Shining Light remained.

24

TENDING THE BAR at the Shining Light, Gil listened to everybody, and everybody told him stories. When he knew so many he began to forget them, he wrote them down, and a friend of his who was trying to start a literary magazine published two of them.

"I'll take more," the friend said, "but you have to pick your style up, Gil. You write like a schoolmarm. Make it a little wilder, you know, grab people by the throat."

One morning after breakfast, when everybody else was asleep, he sat in the kitchen trying to grab people by the throat, without doing much except use up expensive paper. It was raining, a constant chatter on the roof overhead, but the kitchen was warm and dry, smelled of bread and coffee. Mammy came in, yawning.

"What you writing about?"

"Being snowbound in the Sierra."

She folded her arms over her front, looking at the papers scattered over the table. "I saw that magazine. Sometimes you write just about us. Like that bit about Laban."

"Why should I not write about Laban?" He went over to the fire and reached for the coffeepot, pulling the cuff of his shirt down over his hand against the heat. She stood in the middle of the room, her arms folded under her breasts, her eyes snapping.

"I don't want you ever writing about me," she said.

He poured the coffee into his cup, brought it back to his place at the table, and sat down, studying her the whole while. She allowed this, although he knew she resented it, as she hated and feared and resented any attention from men. He said, "Mammy, nobody would believe me. I'd be laughed out of San Francisco."

At that her face softened; she was amused, gratified. Seeing a victory where it mattered most to her: in people's minds. "Gilbert, you know there are a few who would." She laughed, slapped the door frame, turned to go. "They're the ones who would hate you worst for it."

"Sit down and drink a cup of coffee with me."

"What, and tell you everything I'm thinking?" She snapped her fingers at him. "I'm off to bed, and you would be, too, if you were an honest working man." She went out, and Gil turned back to writing.

The building around him fell slowly still, in the deep hours before dawn, but never really still. The rain rattled down, slacked off, beat harder again, like a fall of stones: maybe a hailstorm. He heard someone call, once, off in the warren of rooms where Mammy's people lived. Somebody laughed, once.

The rain stopped. The room slowly filled with daylight and he turned out the lamp, and there was a knock on the outside door.

He put down the pen in his hand. "Come in."

The door remained shut. The knock came again. He went over and opened the door himself, and there stood a Chinese boy.

Seeing Gil, the boy began to nod vigorously, and gestured to him to follow, and turned away down the narrow cluttered alley toward Pacific Street. Gil said, "Hey. Wait, what is this?"

The boy came back. Under his shabby shirt he was small and thin, his hair braided, his face so unlike a white face that Gil could not read his expression. A rush of fear crawled up the man's back. The boy gestured at him again to come, and when Gil still hesitated the boy came up to him and took hold of his sleeve and pulled.

He said something now, twice, and the second time Gil understood. The boy said, "Mitya."

Gil gave out a long, shuddering sigh. "Just a minute." Pulling off the apron, he went back to the table, put his paper and pen away, and got his coat off the wall. The boy waited in the alley. When Gil came out, the boy turned and made off like a rabbit.

Out on Pacific Street, damp and gray in the dawn fog, they turned up the hill. The boy scurried along the slick wooden sidewalk, sliding past the few people on the street at this hour. Gil followed him more slowly, mindful of the slippery planks underfoot.

The clammy air soaked the outside of his coat almost at once. He passed two blocks of boarding houses and saloons, the boy getting farther ahead of him with every step. Across the street, out of sight, somebody was having a loud argument; he smelled bread baking, heard the long cry of the coal vendors. When he was well past where he had heard the argument, suddenly a shot banged out from that building, and the shouting abruptly stopped.

The boy had doubled back for him and was waiting just ahead. They were coming into Little China.

Gil wondered what this was about. He knew Mitya came up here, but he had no guess as to why the Indian would send for him. He kept close to the boy, edgy about being here.

The planking on Pacific Street ended abruptly in a two-foot drop to the dirt. The night's rain had puddled the street, but after the long dry season the earth was still packed hard as cement. The corner of a buried crate protruded from it like a dinosaur bone, woven around with ruts. The street itself twisted and broke into a maze of tracks threaded among rickety buildings piled up like nests one on the other. Their crooked rooflines shut out the rising sun, and the air was dank.

Here the people were already awake and busy. He went by a row of stalls where little wizened yellow people were hanging up pots and cloth to sell. In one stall a row of hooks held fowl dipped in honey, the bird and the hook sealed in one vast gilded drop bleeding slowly to a pond below. The street was steep, uneven, pooled with slops. On the tent-shaped buildings were painted signs and symbols. He passed a temple that smelled of incense, its roof facings carved into scrolls. With the boy one step before him he toiled up and up the street, drawing looks from every passer-by.

In a room behind veils of hanging garlic and mushrooms and onions he saw two robed men sitting knee to knee with a board between them. His curious lingering glance drew a cold black stare in reply, and he turned hastily forward. He smelled hot starch and hot metal. In the street people turned to watch him walk by. The boy led him past the theater with its streamers of colored silk hanging from the eaves. They turned into a shadowy alley where two fighting dogs abruptly broke away and ran at the sight of them. Down another alley; at the end of this lane was a small crowd of Chinese.

When they saw Gil they all began to talk; they sounded like a flock of strange birds. He went into their midst. At the back of the alley someone was holding up a lantern, and beyond that two people stood with sticks raised, threatening something on the ground.

Gil saw what it was. He burst on past them, pushing down the sticks. "Don't — be careful! Get back, get back." He shoved them back down the alley, even the man with the lantern, which dimmed the light shining into the blind end of the alley.

There in the mud, backed against a slatted fence, Mitya huddled, doubled up. He was filthy, his hair hung in his eyes, his head wavered with the effort of lifting it, and his eyes glittered, wild, unseeing, reflecting the lantern. In one hand he had his gun, and its aim traveled back and forth over the crowd. A low, raspy growl sounded from him. He stank.

His arms stretched out, Gil got between him and the Chinese. "Mit. It's me. Come on. Put down the gun." He went up a little closer, and the gun swung toward him. Above it were two eyes like blind flames. Gil said, "Mit. Please. Please." He crouched down, making himself small and harmless, waddled forward on his toes. "Mit." The Indian's head wobbled; he was past drunk, he was half dissolved. The gun pointed straight at Gil, and the eyes behind it pointed at him; Gil held those empty black eyes with his gaze and reached out slowly and took the gun.

"Gil," Mitya said.

"You have to get out of here, Mit, somebody's going to find you like this and do an end for you." Gil struggled to move him. Mitya gave off a sweet stench of alcoholic corruption. He lay like slack iron in Gil's grip. "Help me, Mit, come on, please."

The Chinese still packed the alley, watching, keeping their distance. Gil got one arm around Mitya and pulled, and the Indian gave a feeble effort and they staggered up out of the end of the alley, and the Chinese moved before them in a tide, backing away, intent. Gil dragged the Indian out to the street. It was a long way home; his strength flagged when he thought of it. But it was all downhill. He gathered Mitya up over his back a little, one arm slung down over his shoulder, and tottered off toward the Shining Light.

Laban was painting blue and purple on the inside front wall of the saloon, using the early morning light streaming through the open door, when Gil staggered in carrying Mitya.

The white man had used all his strength getting here. As soon as he crossed the threshold he was falling, letting Mitya's bulk slide down off his back to the floor. Laban leapt up and went to roll Mitya over.

"Is he all right?"

Gil sat up, breathing hard. "He's just drunk."

Mitya was moving on hands and knees, crawling; he went off into the dark of the saloon and stood up. Turning, he faced Laban and Gil and said a long string of gibberish, or maybe it was his own language, and with great majestic strides he started for the door.

"No." Gil flung himself forward. "I just damn near killed myself getting you down here." He leaned on Mitya, trying to hold him back.

The Indian, knocked off-balance, reeled away sideways. He rattled off some more babble, glaring at Gil, and his hand went to the waistband of his pants.

Laban's hackles rose. He looked quickly around him and picked up a bungstarter lying on the edge of the stage.

Gil was still standing between Mitya and the door. He said, "You're not going anywhere, Mit."

The Indian stood with his head down and snarled something. He was keeping his balance, just barely, by swaying back and forth through vertical. He was darker than the wall behind him.

Gil said, "Come on, you have to go to bed."

The Indian roared something and charged him. Gil stood his ground, blocking the door, and Mitya swiped at him with one arm, the other cocked back to strike. Laban stepped up behind him and laid him out cold with the bungstarter.

Gil had caught Mitya's first blow square on the side and gone sprawling. He looked up from the floor and said, "Thanks."

"Well," said Laban, dropping the bungstarter, "he'd kill you like that, and never even remember it when he was sober. Come on, we got to get him out of here."

Gil got Mitya's feet and Laban took his shoulders, and they lugged the Indian down the corridor to the cookhouse and up the staircase to the upstairs rooms.

Everybody here was still sleeping. Mitya usually slept with one of the girls, but there was an empty room two turns down the corridor, and they put him there, on the floor. Laban went and came back with a blanket, and they folded it around him.

Laban reached out and stroked the Indian's long black hair back. He was thinking uneasily of the Mitya on the walls of the Shining Light, who shot and drank and fought and roared, invulnerable. "He gets like this, once, twice a week now."

"What happens when he comes to?" Gil asked.

"He be back together then, nearly. Stay so, as close as doesn't matter, for a while, you think he be all right, then he go like this again." Laban shook his head. "He shouldn't drink."

"You can say that twice," said Gil. Like an afterthought he took the gun out of the inside pocket of his coat and put it on the window ledge above Mitya's head.

Laban twitched. He remembered Mitya pawing at his belt, and said, "That's what he was going back for." He reached out again and touched the Indian's head. In there something terrible was going on.

Gil watched with a slumped exhaustion on his face. Slowly his gaze rose, traveling over the pine walls of the room. "He built this place," he said plaintively. He passed one hand over his face as if wiping something away.

Laban wondered what he meant. Gil baffled him. To Laban Gil seemed unfinished, as if he struggled toward something else to be, something bigger and beyond him. Mitya was asleep and would sleep now until he was sober. Laban went away into the saloon again, and on the wall, below where he had been working before, he painted Mitya's face stretched up and down the trunk of a redwood tree.

25

"I DON'T CARE WHAT YOU SAY," Tierney said between his teeth. "I care what other people think." He glanced up at Phineas, on the driver's seat of the buggy, to see if he was listening. Behind them somebody shouted.

"I'm bored." Daisy's face was bright red. "I want something to do. You have the refinery, you go out there all day long — "

"Have another party," Tierney said.

"I'm tired of parties, the same people all the time, and they're dull. I want to put on a play."

Tierney throttled his temper; he wanted no scene in the public street to match the one they had just had at the hotel. Somebody behind them was shouting again. "Respectable women don't act, Daisy. Have another party."

"Those people are boring."

His self-mastery slipped. The people who bored her were the best people in San Francisco. He sneered at her. "Steady, steady, my dear, your complexion's quite out of color with your gown."

At that her eyes blazed, and she bit her lips together; she jerked her gaze forward and sat there in an arctic silence. Behind them there was another angry yell. "Hey, up there, move on or move over!"

On the high perch of the driver's seat Phineas sat straight and paid no attention, either to his passengers or the traffic he was holding up, keeping the horse to a sedate walk to preserve the arrangement of Daisy's hair. The new French maid had piled her hair so high on her head that Phineas had been forced to remove the top just so she could get into the buggy. Tierney, beside her, tipped his head a little to admire it again. The glistening curls rose like sea waves, wound through with ropes of pearls, and peaked by an egret plume tipped in rose pink, to match her gown.

Over all of this, hair, pearls, feather, gown, they had showered fine gold dust, so that Daisy glittered; as the buggy rolled from streetlamp to streetlamp, she seemed to bloom and fade and bloom again with a fragile, glorious radiance. Maybe that was why most of the people caught behind them were keeping quiet about it.

Beneath her towering headdress Daisy sat still and straight. Gold dust clung to her throat like a loose powder. Tierney had to hold himself back from pressing his lips to that throat. Instead he sat with one arm stretched casually along the back of the seat, not touching her, just surrounding her.

They turned the corner into California Street, into a blaze of lights and a roar of noise. Ahead of them a line of other carriages waited to let their passengers off at the door of the Opera House. The street was full of people, the crowd spilling off the sidewalks and lapping up the theater steps. Almost all of them were men; there were still few women in San Francisco. Above the crowd rose the clifflike face of the new theater, lit white with gas lights, a square-cornered lump of imported marble sculpted with ribbons and medallions and ridged around with cornices.

"He must have bought the carving by the yard," Tierney said. "Phineas, take your time and get as close as you can. I don't want her to have to walk in the mud."

"Yes, boss."

Daisy said, "It's nice. I like the sculpture." She was still pouting. He raised his arm from where it rested along the back of the seat and with his fingertips flicked at one of her dangling earbobs.

He said, "It looks like a big pile of money."

"Nothing ever impresses you, does it, Tierney." Angrily she reached up and plucked the earbob out of his teasing fingers.

"I'll be impressed the first time somebody builds something in San Francisco whose first purpose isn't to show off how much money it cost." The big rig in front of them was rolling off, and Phineas drove them up to the broad, shallow sweep of steps.

The crowd had seen Daisy. When she stepped down from the buggy and the blaze of lights caught her, a hundred throats called her name. She stopped on the foot of the steps and waved all around her, the egret feather waggling on her head, and the crowd roared, lovesick. Tierney came after her, carrying her opera cloak over his arm.

She had no right to argue with him, when he loved her so much. When he took such good care of her. She was his woman and she had no right to argue. She moved ahead of him through the swimming shadowy light like a golden fish, her plump rear end sleekly, tightly gripped in pale satin. When she walked, she undulated.

The banker who had built this place had a Medicean appetite for antique statuary. Griffins with raised paws stood beside the stairs. Venus waited like a ticket-taker between the two front doors; on a boxy pedestal in the lobby, above the noisy, milling San Franciscans, a bronze Mercury stood, frowning, one arm stretched forward, as if he was ordering them all out. There was no room, and Tierney and Daisy had to wait a moment to present their tickets. The air smelled of rose and gardenia. Daisy at once was waving, calling, standing on her toes to see over heads and shoulders. The men around them were gaping at her. Somebody screamed, "Daisy! Your hair!" Tierney bought a shot of whiskey from a peddler in a braided jacket.

He knew most of the men here, either from business or the Vigilance Committee; the businessmen called out to him loudly, reaching over other men to shake his hand, but the other Vigilantes only met his eyes and nodded. He drank the shot, and the peddler was there at once for the glass. Judge McGowan was coming through the door with his French whore on his arm. He had grown a sweeping set of mustaches that hid the corners of his constant smile. Tierney nudged Daisy on ahead of him, up toward the doors to the upstairs and the boxes.

The broad mezzanine corridor, still empty, swung in a crescent around behind the private boxes. The carpet was dark red with gold stitching, and the curtains covering the entries to the boxes were dark red velvet with gold braid and swag ropes. An usher took them to their box. On the way they passed a doorway, curtain flung back, spilling forth a rush of laughter and ebullient talk. Through the gap in the curtains Tierney saw Sam Brannan himself there, a bottle of champagne in one hand and two girls in his lap.

The great man saw Tierney; he smiled, waved, drunk as an earl, innocent as a baby. Tierney lifted one hand and went quickly on after Daisy to their box.

When he pulled the curtain back, the noise from the theater rushed up to meet him. Daisy was already in the box, already leaning out over the gilded railing, screaming to her friends, the same people who bored her at parties. Tierney dumped the opera cloak over the rail and gave the usher a twenty-dollar slug.

"Thank you, Mr. Rudd. Much obliged."

"Bring us some champagne and a tray of oysters. On the top shells."

"Yes, Mr. Rudd." The boy bounded away. Tierney swelled a little. He liked deference. Sitting down, he took a segar from his coat pocket and felt around for the little knife he used to trim the end.

The crowd was streaming into the vast room below. In the orchestra the fiddle players were tuning up; the drummer was bent over his bass drum. A horn blared. The curtain, painted with naked nymphs and hairy-legged satyrs, hung closed, but while Tierney looked, one side twitched back and a head poked out briefly. Two waiters came quietly into the box behind him, one with a bottle and an ice bucket on a stand, the other with a covered tray. Daisy was leaning over the railing to talk to the woman in the next box. When the two servants had gone Tierney reached out and smacked his palm on the broad expanse of creamy satin that covered her backside.

With a screech she popped upright. He sat back, smiling at her. "Careful, your hair will fall off."

She glared at him, but now she was having too much fun to fight. She plopped down in a chair and reached for one of the champagne flutes. "Everybody's here. Isn't this wonderful? Look at Belle's dress, she says it cost six thousand dollars. Isn't that incredible? Look, there's Marshal Richardson! Oh, look at that hat!" She surged up again, rushing to the railing, the tower of her hair swaying.

Tierney glanced to his right. Richardson, who was a federal marshal, his wife, and another couple were moving into the next box. Richardson wore his top hat; there was a running joke in town that he never took it off because his head was shaped that way. His wife wore a plain gown, her hair neatly rolled under a bonnet. She fussed over her chair, her head down, her shoulders hunched; Tierney saw her sneak a glance at Daisy. Her mouth worked; he wondered if she was shocked or just jealous. She caught him watching her and turned hastily away.

He leaned back, smoking his segar and eating oysters. The lines of seats below were filling rapidly, the noise level rising. He wondered if he would even bother coming to the opera if he had to buy seats like that. The oysters were delicious; he liked the feel of them going down his throat.

Daisy sat down again, glowing. "Isn't everybody beautiful? Aren't we all beautiful?"

Looking into her face, Tierney felt his heart jump; he put his hand over hers. "You are, darling."

She smiled on him, gilded, happy, and he kissed her. For a moment there was nothing between them but love.

The lights went down. The opera was in Italian. Crowds of people stood around on the stage shrieking at each other to shut up. At the end of the first act there was a sword fight. In the intermission Belle Cora came rushing out of her box and into theirs.

"Oh, your hair, Daisy. Who did it?"

Daisy sang, "Oh, la, la — maybe I'll tell. I love your gown. What's this underskirt?" She reached down and began to hike up Belle's hem.

Belle's keeper, the gambler Charley Cora, took the chair next to Tierney. "What d'you think of it?"

"Of what?" Tierney asked. "The opera? The Opera House? Daisy's hair? Belle's dress?" The Coras were friends of Daisy's, not his; their flavor of disrepute put him off.

Cora seemed to know this and enjoy it. He sat by the rail, one arm on the front wall of the box, a sleepy smile on his face. "Rudd, do you ever have a good time? How's the trade in borax?"

"Constant," Tierney said. "How's the gambling business?"

"Very difficult." Cora turned, looking away; his hand covered his mouth. Perhaps the question bothered him. His gaze sharpened. "Isn't that Gil Marcus?"

Tierney hitched himself forward. Down in the mass of people swarming around the cheap seats, he saw nobody he knew.

Charley Cora leaned past him, pointing. "Over there. In the brown jacket."

Daisy turned. "Who are you looking for?"

"Gil Marcus," Tierney said. To Cora he said, "He and Daisy are friends, from the old days at the Shining Light." Now he saw Gil, sitting on the aisle below them. He was balding on the crown of his head; his jacket was out at the elbows.

Daisy seemed to hover a moment, staring down at him. She wheeled, her cheeks suddenly bright. "He's not my friend." On her far side, Belle's face grew keen with curiosity.

"Oh," said Cora. "That's rather too bad, I was hoping you'd introduce me. I'm a passionate admirer of his work."

"Really," Tierney said. He was staring at Daisy, whose reaction had startled him.

"Yes, you know, he's quite a good writer. He does some very clever things for the *Argonaut*, observations, sketches."

"I can introduce you," Tierney said. "Actually, you know, you could introduce yourself — there isn't a man in San Francisco more open than Gil Marcus."

Daisy had turned her back on this entire discussion and planted all her attention on the next box; she engaged Belle in a giggling appraisal of the frumpy little Mrs. Richardson. The marshal's wife had noticed. She tugged angrily at her husband's arm and spoke to him, and he flung a glare at Daisy and Belle, which set the two women laughing all the more.

The lights were going down; the next act was beginning. Daisy quieted at once. Tierney sat back to watch.

In the last act everybody died, at length and at top volume. The audience gave the diva three curtain calls — more, Tierney thought, to celebrate themselves than the singer. Afterward, when they left the box, Marshal Richardson was standing there waiting for them. He let Charley Cora and Belle go by and then launched himself at Tierney.

"Now see here, Rudd — "

Tierney brushed past him, ignoring him. He got Daisy's arm and tucked it firmly in his own and started down the mezzanine. Daisy resisted, looking back; she wanted to fight.

Richardson scooted along beside them. "How dare you bring women like this here — my wife was deeply insulted, sir! Deeply insulted!"

Ahead of them Cora stopped and spun around. "Get off my back, Marshal."

Tierney shoved Daisy on ahead of him and got Cora by the arm. "Not here, Charley. Let's go." He pulled, and the gambler yielded, and they went on down the mezzanine, past clumps of staring onlookers.

Behind them the sheriff bellowed, "I won't have you insulting my wife!"

Daisy and Belle were hurrying on one stride ahead of the men. Daisy said, "Damn him, I'll go to the opera any time I want!"

Tierney said, "Forget about it. Richardson's a drunken fool." But he knew he and Daisy ought not to be seen with the likes of Cora and his whore. San Francisco was changing; all men weren't equal anymore. Beside him Cora was walking along, away from trouble, but now he twisted his head to look back again, grim-faced. "What's the matter with you, Charley?" Tierney asked him.

"He's been on me lately." Cora straightened. His hand slipped down the front of his jacket; Tierney knew he was making sure his gun was there.

"He'll be gone in the next election," Tierney said. Certainly, he thought, he would avoid Cora henceforth. They went down the stairs after the women.

"They run this town on gambling taxes," Cora said. "But they want us to stay down out of sight on Pacific Street." That reminded him of something else. As they joined the two women at the Opera House door, he turned and scanned the crowd streaming out past them. "Help me find Gil Marcus."

Daisy said, "I don't want to see Gil." Her voice trembled with the intensity of her conviction. Tierney put her cloak around her shoulders.

"Another time," he said to Cora.

"All right. Good night." The gambler and Belle went off in another direction. One arm around Daisy, Tierney piloted her through the herds of ordinary people and down the steps to the street, where Phineas had the buggy waiting.

"I thought you liked Gil," Tierney said. He handed her up into the back seat.

"He thinks I'm a whore," she said, and her voice was still trembling. She pulled the edges of the cloak together. Gold dust clung to the creases of her eyelids. "And he's right," she said. "He's right." She plopped down on the seat of the carriage, and Tierney saw, to his amazement, that she was crying.

26

THREE DAYS LATER Charley Cora shot the U.S. marshal in the street outside the Blue Wing Saloon. Before nightfall he was in jail, and every newspaper in San Francisco began to scream for a hanging.

Daisy said, "Wasn't it self-defense?" She folded up the copy of the *Bulletin* and laid it on her lap. "How can they hang him for defending himself?"

Tierney said, "Keep away from Belle Cora."

He sat beside Daisy in the carriage; Phineas was driving them down to the Jackson Street wharf, where he would catch the morning steamer to Oakland. It had rained all night, but now the sky was clear and the sun shone. They had bought the *Bulletin* on the way. Tierney took it from her and folded it under his arm. He knew the editor of it, one of his friends on the Vigilance Committee, who wanted not merely Cora hanged, but also the keeper of the jail, the sheriff, and the judge. Jim King was not a man for half measures.

"Wasn't it self-defense?" she asked again.

"It doesn't matter," Tierney said. "I don't want to have anything to do with those people, I've told you that."

The note in his voice warned her; if she pressed him he would lose his temper, and they were in the middle of Montgomery Street, rattling past the busy waterfront, surrounded by half-naked stevedores and crowds of people waiting for the ferry. She collected herself. As if he understood that, he reached out and gripped her hand.

Then he said, softer, "Have you done anything about — what I talked to you about yesterday?"

She twitched. She had hoped he would forget that. "No."

She tried to get her hand free, but he held it tight. "Do it," he said. The carriage had slowed to a creep, moving along through streams of people hurrying toward the ferry; the whistle blew its shrill warning. Phineas stopped the carriage and Tierney got off, the newspaper under his arm, his papercase in the other hand. "Do what I tell you, Daisy." He gave her a sharp look full of intent and walked off, a tall man in dark clothes striding faster than the crowd, as if he had to get there ahead of everybody else.

Daisy sat back. "All right, Phin."

Phineas clucked to the horses. She wondered if he liked this work. She hoped not, because that was what Tierney wanted her to do: find another driver and send Phineas back to the Shining Light.

The carriage spun along the waterfront. A sea gull skimmed by her on cupped wings. On the right, the high, blank walls of warehouses rose like a cliff of paintless boards; on her left, the wooden wharfs with their fringe of boats and houses on pilings hid her view of the water, except for quick flashes between buildings and masts. Her fingers wound together. She did not want to let Phineas go. She did not want to turn away Belle Cora. She felt as if Tierney were cutting off pieces of her, removing whatever he did not want of her, trimming her to nothing. The day stretched endlessly ahead of her, a narrowing road, with nothing to do except wait for him to come home. The carriage slowed at the foot of Clay Street and turned west.

Phineas turned his head sideways to her. "Goin' back to the hotel now, missy?"

She bounced once on the seat, resisting the idea. In her mind the suite at the hotel shrank to the size of a bandbox. "You know that nice new shop on Dupont Street?"

"Yes, ma'am."

"I'll buy a new hat. That will make me feel better."

Phineas' voice vibrated with pent amusement. "What you say, missy." He clicked his tongue to the horses. They strutted off, their plumed heads bobbing. On the sidewalk, people turned to watch her drive by, and a long whistle rose. Daisy settled back, pleased.

She had almost everything she wanted, after all. She could be content with that.

Halfway up Clay, she saw Mitya crossing the street.

Without even thinking, she let out a yell to him; she had last seen him months before, when he had come to help her move the new furniture into her parlor. At the sound of her voice he swung around, a short brown stock of a man, his long black hair hanging down his back. Tierney would not like her talking to him either, but she thrust that aside.

"Phin," she said, "pull over." She could talk to Mitya, just for a little while.

Phineas reined the horses over to the side of the street. The Indian came toward her, solemn at first, his face dark and set, but as he drew closer his mouth stretched into a smile.

"Daisy. Long time." His hand rested on the brass railing beside her. His slanted dark eyes snapped.

"It certainly has been. What are you doing over here?"

"Look at things," he said. His head jerked, pointing up toward the intersection, where two high-sided wagons clogged the street; rows of men unloaded bricks from them, and she could see other people digging in an empty corner lot.

"Oh," she said. She wondered what interest he took in other people's work, and shrugged that off. "How's Frances?"

"Good," he said. "Everybody good."

"I saw — I read something that Gil Marcus wrote about you-all." She stared down the street at the workmen with the bricks, trying to seem unconcerned. "You people are all famous." She wanted to be cool, to be cautious, but a strange pressure was forcing up through her throat, pushing that name out again. "How is Gil?" She raised her eyes to his and found Mitya smiling at her.

"Gil good," he said. "He come back, make him good. You come back soon too, Daisy."

The pressure in her now was like a scream about to erupt. She swallowed hard, shutting it down again. "It's too late. I can't. I'm not like that anymore, Mit." Then, on the sidewalk, someone called her name.

Mitya stepped back; Daisy tensed, flushing with a sudden panic. She should not have stopped. She should have gone straight home, gone inside, where she was safe. She said, "Phineas, let's go."

"Daisy," Belle Cora cried, much closer. She was running up the sidewalk toward them, clutching her ruffled skirts in one hand, reaching out with the other. "Daisy, I have to talk to you." She launched herself across the space between them and gripped the railing of the carriage. Her striped silk dress was as rumpled and stained as if she had not been out of it in days. Her face was red and her eyes glistened inside rings of smeared black paint. "Daisy, I need some money."

"Not now," Daisy said. "I have to go. Phineas — "

"Please, Daisy! They'll hang him!"

Daisy's will bent; one arm still reached forward, to send Phineas on, but her head turned toward Belle, toward the pain and pleading in Belle's voice. "They won't hang him," she said. "It was self-defense."

"He's a gambler," Belle said. "He shot a U.S. marshal. And the newspapers — I need money, Daisy. I can bribe some of the men on the jury. They'll let him off for enough money."

At that Daisy snapped forward, a knot in her belly, a sizzle of alarm in every nerve. "Phin, go."

"Daisy!"

"Phineas, go!"

The carriage rolled briskly away from the sidewalk, cut in front of a big dray full of barrels, and clipped off up Clay Street. Daisy sat rigid, staring straight ahead. Suddenly, desperately, she longed for Frances, who had always known what to do.

Frances would have sent her back to the hotel. Her eyes burned. It was Belle Cora and her lover she should have been crying for, but the face that rose again and again before her mind's eye was that of Gil Marcus. She wondered how this had happened to her, how she had come to be so unhappy.

Phineas said, "Missy, which way?"

"Home," she said. "The hotel."

"No new hat?"

"No," she said; the tears were leaking out of her eyes. She had to get inside before she fell apart in public. "Just take me home." She clutched the rail; the outside world faded into an unfocused mist of grief.

Mitya wondered what Daisy was scared of. He stood on the sidewalk and watched her horse-box rattle away up the wooden street. He remembered how she had been once, a big, soft, glowing spark of a girl, but she was different now; fear made her smaller. Through him went a rush of hatred for Tierney Rudd, who had done this to her.

His head hurt; he needed a drink. He knew how to handle this now. He had to drink a little whiskey all the time, just a little: too much and he went someplace else, a black howling pit, a dead space, that terrified him; too little and he got sick, hurt all over, could not keep steady enough even to work, and that terrified him too. But if he drank a little whiskey all the time, he could do anything he wanted.

That seemed easy enough. He could live that way forever. He went off to find a store that would sell him whiskey and then went back to watch the men building on Clay Street.

Mammy said, "Phineas was unsatisfactory?"

Tierney shrugged. "He lacks a certain polish."

"I'll find you someone else." She went around the room once more, restless, and sat down in the stuffed chair by the table. It annoyed her to have her arrangements tampered with.

"I have another driver," Tierney said. "I'm sorry, I suppose I should have asked you first." His voice was smooth as cream. "I'll be building a new house, out in Oakland. I'll need your help finding staff."

She watched him through narrowed eyes, suspicious. Phineas had always kept an eye on Daisy and Tierney for her, and now she felt disconnected. But the notion of a big house intrigued her. She could put twenty people into it, and Tierney would have to pay them; she could feed a lot of people on one white man. This enticed her. She straightened, pushing at the heap of papers on her table, and asked, "What does Daisy say about moving out of San Francisco?"

"She'll like Oakland," he said. "It's very pretty and quiet. I'm considering putting a small theater in the house, to give her something to do."

"A theater. Good. She'll like that." She fiddled with the papers again; the top one was a letter from a man in the East, wanting money to arm the slaves of Virginia and start a rebellion. But he was a white man. She had her doubts that a white man could do much. She said, "What about this murder trial? I heard that Cora's fancy woman is buying every juror in the box."

"Belle is not exactly keeping it under her bonnet, no," Tierney said. He rolled the ash off his segar into the saucer of his coffee cup.

"Well, what are your Vigilantes going to do about it?"

The man across the table from her adjusted himself on the hard chair, picked a shred of tobacco off his tongue, crossed his legs one over the other. "Nothing, actually."

"Hunh. Don't see much use in it, then. You told me you'd go after McGowan and his pack of crooks. Are you scared?"

"No. But we can't do much over this case." His fingers tapped busily on his knee. "Cora shot Richardson when the marshal had him backed up to a wall with a drawn gun. Richardson was drunk and sought him out. There are twenty killings a month in San Francisco that are justifiable self-defense, and this was one of them."

"And he's a friend of yours."

"He's no friend of mine. Be patient, Mammy. There's a lot at stake here. You're happy with your investment with me, aren't you?"

She got up again, prowling around the room, rubbing her hands together. "Yes." The borax business was making her rich, she had to admit that. Of all her arrangements, this one was the steadiest, the most fruitful. Out of the last check he had sent her, she could pay McGowan's tribute money, she could send this man Brown thirty thousand dollars for his Virginia slave rebellion, and she would still have enough to stuff the couch pillows full. But the Cora case disturbed her. She glanced across the room at Tierney Rudd. "All right. I'll settle for that. You can go. Tell Daisy I'll come see her one of these days, we'll have a nice long talk."

"I'll tell her," he said, and obediently he rose to leave.

27

TIERNEY LAID HIS HAT and gloves to one side of the table and sat down; the waiter held the chair opposite for Daisy, who arranged herself on it, fussing with her skirts. He had come back earlier than usual to take her out to dinner, but she still looked fretful. He wondered if she were ill, or maybe drinking too much when he wasn't looking. He would have to find her a companion, someone who could keep a watch on her when he could not.

He said, "Would you like some champagne, darling?"

They were sitting in the dinner room of the new Parker House, rebuilt from the ground up after the last fire. He remembered the old Parker House as rough-hewn, with sawdust on the floor, tables made of redwood stumps. He lifted his gaze again to the chandelier hanging from the ceiling, broadened his view to sweep the whole of the room, with its flock of white-clothed tables, its glitter of silver and crystal. The walls were painted pale yellow, the tall windows and the ceiling were framed with carved moldings. Clumps of green ferns fountained from the corners. A colored servant swept briskly by, carrying a tray of dishes; he wore fancy red livery, like the rest of the staff. The room was full and the other diners kept up a steady, agreeable music of low laughter and murmuring voices, the chime of glasses, the gurgle of wine.

She said, "I'm tired of champagne." Her voice was plaintive as a child's. She sat with her shoulders hunched together, her hands in her lap, her face drawn into a sulk. "I'm tired of San Francisco. Let's go somewhere."

Her whining rasped him, the irritation familiar, something that happened often, more often all the time. Tierney forced himself to be patient. The waiter came back with glasses, an ice bucket, a magnum of wine. He was colored; perhaps he belonged to Mammy Hardheart.

Tierney said, "We'll have lobster en brochette. Do you still have the black Beluga?"

"Yes, sir." The waiter poured wine for him, keeping his eyes lowered, proper deference in every expert move.

"We'll have that for starters. Onion, boiled egg, very lightly done toast, a double portion of the caviar."

"Very good, sir." The waiter screwed the big green bottle down into the ice in the bucket and marched away.

Tierney lifted his gaze to Daisy again, who drove him crazy sometimes but never bored him. "They have a wonderful dessert here, a marrons glacés, you'll love it, darling."

She said, "We could go to Europe. Brannan took his wife to Europe."

Tierney said, "Someday soon we'll go to Europe." Then, through the tail of his eye, he caught sight of Isaac Bluxome hurrying into the room.

He sat back, surprised; his path and Bluxome's seldom crossed outside of the Committee. The younger man was coming straight toward them, his face lit like a lantern. Reaching the table, he said, "Rudd, it's — " and then looked at Daisy as if he had only then noticed her there.

Tierney said, "Sit down, Isaac. What's going on?" The waiter was coming with a covered silver tray, and Tierney held his hand up to Bluxome. "Wait."

Bluxome swung around a chair from a nearby table and perched on the edge, leaning forward, so tense he seemed to vibrate. The waiter set out the crystal dish of caviar, the triangles of toast, the little heaps of chopped onion and hard-cooked egg, a whitecap of soured cream. Daisy sighed; she began to smile at last, and her hands rose above the table. The waiter filled Tierney's glass again.

"A glass for the gentleman, sir?"

"Yes," Tierney said.

"No," said Bluxome. "I can stay only a moment, Twenty-two."

Tierney startled at the use of his Committee number. He waved the waiter off and faced Bluxome with new interest. "All right. What is it?"

"Jim King's been shot."

"King! Who shot him? When? Is he dead?"

Bluxome's voice dropped to a murmur. "Well, you know he's been running editorials in the *Bulletin* about one of the Democratic supervisors."

"Casey," Tierney said. King had just recently published the choice news that San Francisco's third district supervisor had spent two years in Sing Sing prison in upper New York state. Tierney crumpled up his napkin and put it on the table in front of him and turned square to Bluxome. "He shot him?"

"Right in front of the *Bulletin* office. Dozens of witnesses. Jim's not dead yet, but he's close."

Tierney kept still a moment, tasting this. Yet he knew, as obviously Bluxome knew, that this was their opening; a giddy excitement was expanding through him, a crackle in his brain, a knotting in his belly. He turned to Daisy. "I have to go. I'll leave the carriage so that you can get home. Enjoy the lobster."

"You're going?" In one hand she held a piece of toast heaped with fish eggs; she put it down and stared at him. "What are you going to do?"

"I'll talk to you about it later. Go home, stay home. Understand?" He rose to his feet. His knees were shaky with anticipation. Gripping Bluxome by the arm, he urged the younger man on ahead of him out of the dining room.

* * *

Mammy said, "I miss Daisy. I wonder if she'll come around and see me one of these days."

Josh said, "I can take you up to see her."

"Fancy place like that. She doesn't need me up there."

She sat small and old on the seat of the cart, staring straight ahead. A bandanna covered her hair and she had her shawl around her as a turtle has its shell. Josh knew she had told Daisy not to come to the Shining Light; he thought she was just complaining to make noise. He swung wide into Montgomery Street and waited while the omnibus swung by, a rolling room, the windows dotted with the heads of the passengers. He slapped the reins on the mule's flank, and it trudged along head down after the bus.

"Remind me this here was once the shore," Josh said.

Mammy laughed. Her laugh always sounded too young. She lifted her head, looking toward the rows of warehouses and stores that lined Montgomery Street's lower edge and the streets beyond, where the cove had once been. "Can't even see the water from here," she said, and laughed again. "Go on, we still have places to stop and it's already late."

Josh lifted his hands with the reins, and then, low in the corner of his hearing, something caught his attention. He lowered his hands. "What's that?"

She said impatiently, "Go on, will you? Can't you keep your mind on what you're doing?"

He whistled to the mule, and the cart rolled forward. The boardwalks on either side swarmed with busy people, and before him was the omnibus and behind him other wagons, yet below their noise he heard it again now, two low strokes of a bell. He turned to Mammy again, and started, "Don't you hear — "

She had heard it. She reached out and laid her hand on his arm, her face intent. Someone cut directly in front of the mule and crossed the street running, and Josh reined in. Now he heard nothing. He turned to Mammy again.

"That the firebell," he said, "but it ain't ringin' right." Firebells rang steadily, not like this, stopping and then starting up again. He turned to Mammy, who always knew.

She knew this time too. She sat there rigid, her lips pressed together. She said, "It's the Monumental Bell. Come on, let's get home." Her face shone with a sudden fierceness.

Josh urged the mule on, keeping to the right of the street so that faster traffic could get by. He could see that other people were noticing the odd firebell; at the foot of Washington Street a little crowd had gathered, talking with their heads together, and just beyond a man strode purposefully out of a shop and stood with one hand behind his ear.

The deep double stroke sounded again, like a shiver in the air, and the man on the sidewalk wheeled and plunged back into the shop, was out again in a moment, a key in his hand. Drew his door to, locked it, and ran off.

Josh said, "I done heard this afore."

"It's the Vigilante bell," Mammy said smoothly. She smiled at him. There was a fine, hot fire in her eyes, a gleam like the shine on new money. She said, "It's all right, Josh. Let's go home." Her lips curved into a slick, sweet grin. He hunched his shoulders, not so sure, and drove the mule toward Pacific Street.

28

THE STREET IN FRONT of the jail was so full of people that wagons and carts coming up from Montgomery were stopping and turning around. The rooftops all around were massed with onlookers, many of them armed. Gil stood on the sidewalk opposite, watching half a dozen men in front of him who were burning a pile of copies of the latest edition of the *Herald*, whose main headline denounced the Vigilance Committee.

Pieces of burning paper floated up into the twilight air. Two more men rushed up, their arms loaded with newspapers, and began to feed the flames. Gil moved off a step, his head sinking down between his shoulders. This was a bad thing, and only the beginning of it.

Across the way, in a little knot of other people, a burly man cupped one hand beside his mouth. "Hey, Tom — any word about Jim King?"

One of the people burning the newspaper backed up a step, squinted toward the burly man, and shook his head. "Ain't dead yet."

"Well," the burly man said, "there's always hope." The people around him gave off a splattering of laughter.

Gil went on down the street. Night was falling; the air smelled like rain, and fog drifted by the square rooflines of the buildings on either side, the cocked roofline of the jail. He went up to Sacramento Street, past dark shops and businesses, to the head quarters of the Vigilance Committee.

What he saw there drove a cold alarm through him like a dagger. The Vigilantes had taken over a two-story brick warehouse, and now it seethed with men, all carrying rifles, most of the rifles equipped with bayonets. There had been rumors all day that the Committee had broken into the National Guard Armory; obviously it was true. They had gotten more than rifles. The yard between the front of the warehouse and the street was walled off in a four-foot-high barricade of sandbags, and worked into this fortress wall were two small cannon, their muzzles pointed at the street.

While Gil stood there gaping, a friend of his drifted up to him, looking casual, hands in his pants pockets. "What's going on?"

Gil said, "Nothing good."

"King isn't gonna die, is he?"

"I don't know."

The other man shook his head, looking away. "Ain't much room in this for an honest man, you know?" He walked off, whistling.

Gil stood wrapped in a gray fog of foreboding. He knew most of the men at the center of the Committee, commission merchants and traders, bankers and businessmen. Sam Brannan was in

Europe with his wife, but the other Vigilantes were all cut from his pattern: money men, arrangers, power-jealous and self-righteous. They saw themselves as pillars of society. That was how they had gotten into the armory: many of them were National Guardsmen. None of them were Democrats.

Maybe they were right. This was San Francisco, the phoenix, the edge, cauldron of invention: maybe they had cooked up a new way to deal with corruption. Part of him saw the point here. When the crooks controlled the law, anyone who fought against them naturally became an outlaw.

As he stood there nagged with doubt, the front door of the Vigilantes' fortress opened, and several men came out.

Not armed. Too important to carry their own guns. Gil crossed the street, moving up to the sandbag wall; in the midst of the group he recognized the governor of California, Neely Johnson, side by side with Isaac Bluxome and Tierney Rudd. Behind them was a man in a uniform, maybe the militia commander, whose name was Sherman. At the sight of them, the mass of armed men inside the sandbag wall wheeled around expectantly.

The governor stopped on the bottom step, below the door. "Men," he called, in a voice that boomed like an empty barrel, "I'm here to tell you that we share your concerns, and we've made an arrangement."

Gil swallowed. He glanced up above the governor, at the roof of the warehouse, where three or four men were struggling with a large object.

The governor raised his arms. He was very young, with a splendid set of whiskers and a good speaking voice. "We'll try the man who murdered Jim King, fair and square, and when he's found guilty, we'll hang him — all inside the law. Your Committee here has chosen the judge, and they'll preside over the selection of the jury. Meanwhile, the sheriff has agreed to allow twenty of your men inside the jail to guarantee that these bloody murderers do not escape."

The roar that went up from the Vigilantes drowned whatever he said next. Gil doubted if any of it mattered. If twenty armed

Vigilantes got inside the jail, the matter would be out of the hands of the authorities very quickly. His gaze was drawn again to the men on top of the building, who swung their burden over the front edge of the roof and lowered it halfway down the wall on ropes.

It was a piece of board, big enough to cover several windows. On it was painted a huge eye.

The crowd saw it and bellowed. Governor Johnson stopped trying to talk; behind him, the militia commander leaned forward and said something, frowning, and the governor waved him off. Still smiling inside his flourish of beard, Johnson turned and shook Tierney Rudd's hand. Shook the hand of Isaac Bluxome. For some reason, maybe just habit, he shook the militiaman's hand and every other hand he could reach. Then, with a pompous strut, he walked out to the street, where a covered coach waited for him. He was going off and leaving this to Tierney Rudd and his Committee.

Gil clenched his jaw tight. The huge Eye on the building was a warning: the Committee was looking at a lot more than one murderer, and they meant to be doing that looking for a while. He backed up, studying the warehouse.

He stayed there the rest of the night, one of a growing, milling throng of people. Rumor played over them like a butterfly in a field of flowers: King was dead, King was alive and getting well, King was dying; Casey had escaped, Casey had been murdered in his cell; the army was marching on San Francisco, San Francisco was taking over the army. Gradually Charley Cora's name began to appear in the constant circulation of talk. He had killed a marshal, and was to get off through bribery: another of the vultures feeding on the livers and lights of the law-abiding.

Gil went around the building several times, but there was no way in except through the front door, behind the two little cannon, the wall of sandbags, the lines of men whose rifles ended in the spikes of bayonets.

He was tired but he could not rest, could not even stand still for very long before a nervous, fretful energy sent him on again. All night he wandered around in the street, part of the steadily growing throng. Nothing happened. At dawn, word came that Jim King was still alive.

That news arrived at the same time as the first edition of the *Chronicle*, the morning paper. Gil came back to Sacramento Street from one of his restless, useless prowls to find a boy in a cloth cap selling copies of the newspaper as fast as he could hand them out. Gil had no need to buy one to learn what it said. The headline shouted at him from the stack on the ground by the boy's feet: JUSTICE AT LAST.

Gil turned his back on the paper and the eager men buying it. His mouth tasted like gunpowder. There on the building before him the great wooden Eye stared out across San Francisco. His hands tingled. He was exhausted, and from the shouts and whistles of the crowd around him, he guessed that he was the only man here who hated what was going on.

But he did hate it. That fixed him, pulled him upright, like a steel spine. He hated this, and he was going to do something about it. He turned and walked off along Sacramento Street, back toward the Shining Light.

Tierney left Fort Vigilance after midnight. Having made the deal with the governor, the Committee had nothing to do until Jim King died, which gave Tierney several hours to tend to his own business.

He went down Montgomery to Pacific Street. The dank, cold air of the waterfront rolled up over the lowland, pebbling every surface with dew. The sky was charcoal black behind a shroud of high fog. The streetlamps on Montgomery shone in little feeble cups of light. There was no one on the street but Tierney — no sign even of the hundreds of cats that usually prowled these alleys and wharfs.

At Pacific Street the lamps stopped. He looked up the long, rising roadway, like a ladder to hell, with its dives and stews and sinks, and wondered if it really was quieter tonight or if he just imagined it.

It seemed quiet. The street was all but empty: a brewery wagon rumbled slowly down toward him, its load of barrels banging and booming together like some strange orchestra. Heaps of rags, or maybe bodies, lay on the sidewalk in front of the brothel next to the Shining Light.

Even Mammy Hardheart's place was closed and still. He tried the door, found it unlocked, and went inside.

A single lantern lit the empty front room. He stopped a moment, pulled his coat sleeves down, took his hat off. The painting on the wall was like a watching crowd surrounding him; he had to shrug off the sensation of being stared at. He went around to the stage door and through, into the corridor beyond.

Still he met no one. He tried to walk softly, but it seemed to him that his footsteps thundered on the floor. At Mammy's door he stopped and knocked.

She answered. "Well," she said. "I thought you'd be busy, Mr. Rudd. Come in."

He said, "We're just waiting now." He went by her into the little parlor. There was a fire in the grate and the room was stuffy. His hands were trembling. He put his hat down on the table and faced her.

Small, swathed in her shawl, she smiled at him in triumph. "Everything goes well?"

"Exactly as we planned it," he said. "We've enlisted over a thousand men, and more all the time."

She nodded. Going by him toward the fireplace, she bent to take a kettle from the heat. "I was just going to brew some tea." She stooped, her back to him, and he reached into his coat and took out his pistol.

He said, "Stand up, Mammy." He cocked the pistol.

She wheeled around, her smile gone. Her eyes went big as cue balls. He aimed the gun at her face.

"You dog," she said.

He chuckled. The gun felt heavy, a bolt of lightning in his hand. He said, "Did you really think I'd take all that guff from you, Mammy, all these years, and never even try to escape? I've been planning this all along. From now on, I'm in control, and you're going to do as I say."

She straightened, which did not make her all that much taller. "If you shoot me you'll never get out of this building alive."

"Oh, I'm not going to shoot you," he said. "I'm taking you in. You're under arrest."

Her lips drew back from her teeth; she glared at him, fierce as a little brown bat, wrapped in the folds of her shawl. "You wouldn't dare try me! I'll tell everybody — "

"You won't tell anybody anything, Mammy. Come on now. Start walking." He backed to the door and opened it. A broad smile spread across his face; he had waited a long time for this, he feasted on her rage, delighted. "Come on now. Let's go."

She braced herself. "I'm not moving."

"I'll carry you if I have to. You want that?"

She stayed where she was, her chin up, her teeth still bared at him, but when he moved toward her a step, she broke. "Don't touch me," she said. "I'll go." Her fists clenched on the edges of her shawl. She went forward, out the door.

He followed her, the gun leveled at her back; he did not want to shoot her, not out of any feeling for her, but because this building teemed with savages like her who would tear him to pieces, and a shot would bring them down on him. Then, at the end of the corridor, another door opened.

"Josh," she said, "get back."

Tierney lifted the gun. Mammy paced steadily down the dark corridor toward the saloon, while the big black man standing there in the doorway stared at her, flicked a glance past her at Tierney, and then shrank back against the wall. Mammy walked by him, not even looking at him. Behind her, Tierney aimed the gun at the big man's middle, and the nigger shivered and pressed himself against the wall as if he could pass right through it. Mammy opened the door. Tierney went after her, out to the street, and took her away to Fort Vigilance.

Josh leaned against the wall a moment, his eyes shut, listening to their footsteps fade. Then he went back into the heart of the Shining Light and began waking people up.

The excitement in the city had shut them down early, and everybody was in bed. He went from room to room knocking, calling, rousing them out.

"Mammy's gone. The Vigilantes took her. Mammy's gone."

Theresa wailed. Standing there in her long cotton gown she lifted her arms up like a preacher and let out a cry of despair and terror.

Josh pushed her. "Go, damn you — we got to get out of here, in case they come back." He went on, wakening the other women one by one, and they dressed and grabbed their shoes and hurried out.

"Where?" Theresa cried, padding after him in her bare feet. "Where we gonna go?"

Josh seized her arm and shook her. "Calm down. Gonna go up the street. There's that burnt-up place. Ain't nobody there now but rats and drunks. Go there."

Her voice went up again like a steam whistle, but she turned and ran off; he heard her clattering down the stairs. He went to waken the men.

"Get up, get out of here. Mammy done gone, the Vigilantes took Mammy. We got to clear out before they come back."

Most of the other men, yawning, dazed, obeyed him. He could not find Mitya, and Laban would not go. "I ain't leavin', Josh. My picture's here."

"Damn you, boy, maybe they come back." Josh hushed his voice. "They won't try no niggers. They'll just kill us where we stand."

Laban's face tightened. "I ain't goin'. I belong here. They can come kill me, if they want, but I ain't leavin'."

"You're a fool. Where's Mitya?"

"I ain't seen him."

"You're a fool. Get out. You can paint another picture."

"Ain't no other Shining Light," said Laban.

"Damn you. Where's Mitya?" Josh went back toward the kitchen, calling the Indian's name. There was no answer. In the kitchen Theresa was packing up loaves of bread, stuffing them into flour sacks, pushing the flour sacks into Phineas' arms. When he was loaded up too full to carry more she started piling things on Ink. Her cheeks were moist with tears. "What's gonna happen to us? What'll they do to poor Mammy?" She stuck a coffeepot and a sack of coffee on top of Ink.

"Get out," Josh said. "Just get out of here. Have you seen Mitya?"

Nobody had seen Mitya. Josh went at a trot back down the corridor to the front of the Shining Light, looked into Mammy's rooms, looked into the saloon. In the saloon Laban was sitting up on his stool, a pot of paint in one hand and a brush in the other, the lantern at his feet. Josh stood in the middle of the room and called Mitya's name but got no answer. Finally he went out the door and ran away up the street, toward the burnt place.

29

GIL REACHED THE SHINING LIGHT just after dawn, a time when everybody there was usually asleep; he was not surprised to find the place utterly quiet. He went in through the kitchen door, at the back.

The fire was cold and there was no coffee. He stirred up the fire and lit it, and then looked for the coffeepot and could not find that, nor could he find any bread or bacon left over from break-fast. At that he stopped worrying about feeding himself and began looking for the other people in the house.

He went up toward the front of the building through a hush like a palpable thickness of the air around him. There was no sound, no sign of anybody. In the stage-door corridor he stopped and looked down toward Mammy's room.

The door stood slightly open. Every hair on his head rose on

end. Now he was sure that something was wrong. He took one
step that way, turned, and went into the saloon.

The dawn light filled it. The smell of stale whiskey and old
sawdust tainted the air. For a moment, standing by the stage, he
thought with a rising panic that this place too was empty; then he
saw Laban, over by the doorway, painting.

A rush of relief broke over him. The world that had been tilting
steeply away from him swung back firm under his feet. He went
over toward the door. Laban was working along the right edge of
it; he had begun on the left side, and now he had come full circle,
all the way around the room, every inch of the walls covered with
his work.

Gil asked, "What's going on, Laban?"

The young man was painting in red. He did not look away from
his work. "Vigilantes come and take Mammy," he said.

Gil blurted, "Jesus."

Laban said, "Josh and everybody else went away." His voice
quivered over the last words. "They took all they could carry and
ran. Mammy, I don't know where she is."

"Mit. Where is he?"

"I don't know. Josh looked for him. I ain't seen him in a while,
days, maybe."

"He could be hanging out somewhere up in Chinatown. He has
a girl up there."

Laban lifted his head, his eyes widening; he had thought of
something. "Unless — maybe he's up in the back. You know —
where he hides?"

Gil said, "That place is still there?"

Laban stood up, wiping the brush clean. "Come on."

They went back to the bar and behind it, where the wall had
once opened into the hull of the ship. Now the ship was buried in
new building, and heavy vertical planks covered the hole. When
Gil hesitated before this blank wall, Laban bent down and pulled
at a plank, and a little door opened.

"He's got secret doors and tunnels all through this place,"

Laban said, dropping down on all fours. "Like a rabbit warren. I'll go look."

"I'm coming with you," Gil said. He lowered himself to hands and knees and crept through the little door to the darkness beyond.

There Laban was lighting a match. The yellow glow jumped and spread for a moment and then began to die, and Laban dropped it. A moment later he struck another. This time he had a lantern, found in the light of the first, and he started the wick burning and cranked the chimney down where it belonged.

Gil stood looking around him. The dull light of the lantern showed him the old gutted hull of the ship, with its curved timbers and the long track of the keel. He kicked a broken crate out of his way and stepped deeper into this wooden cave. In heaps toward the stern, in piles along the side of the ship, lay stacks of broken wood, piles of old clothes, a tangle of chairs like some primeval spider. He remembered buying up lots of goods in the early days of the city; whatever they could not use in the Shining Light they had stored in here, and here those goods still were.

He took another step back toward the stern. Off there in the edge of the lantern light was a big metal press with a lever handle. His heart jumped. He remembered, back in '49, buying an old printing press.

Laban said, "This way."

He turned and followed Laban up along the keel, the breastbone of the ship, toward the bow. Once half the people in the Shining Light had made their homes in this space, but as they moved out, their makeshift rooms had moved out with them, leaving behind jagged holes in the wood and crooked nails that stuck out like claws. He climbed up into the bow behind Laban, toward another blank wall, this one of canvas, tucked under the deck where the sides of the ship came together to form the bow.

Laban pushed the canvas aside. "Mitya," he said, and raised the lantern.

Gil pushed up beside him. The little pyramidal space inside the canvas was just big enough for the body of a man, his knees drawn up, his arms coiled around his head. Gil's stomach lurched. It was Mitya, passed out with drink. The reek of the enclosed space drove Gil a few steps backward down the keel.

Laban moved in beside Mitya, talking to him, and tried to rouse him, with no success. Gil climbed down and went along the keel, into the deepening gloom, to the printing press.

It was small, the kind of press traveling printers used, and every metal part was caked with rust. He pulled on the lever. For a moment the plate resisted, heavy as the earth itself, before it slowly gave way, rose up off the bed of the press, locked at the top of its frame. The inside of the bed looked cleaner than the outside. It smelled of ink.

Laban called, "Gil? Help me."

"Let him sleep it off," Gil said. He squatted down and rummaged around the feet of the press and found a wooden box, too heavy to move. He hoped that was the type. His nerves were singing, from lack of sleep, from new resolve. Suddenly he felt a giddy rush of triumph

Laban was coming toward him. "We ought to move him. In case the Vigilantes come back."

"Why? They won't find him there. I'm not leaving. Are you?" He took the lantern from Laban's hand and held it over the press. "Help me get this somewhere where I can use it."

Laban said, "What are you going to do?"

"Tell the truth," Gil said. "That's always very tonic. Help me."

"There's a door into the kitchen. Behind the stairs." Laban gripped the press on the other side and heaved. "This is heavy."

"We've got it," Gil said. "Let's go."

Frances was curled up in a little box, so small she could not lift her head off her knees, her knees pressed to her chest, her back bent. Around her was only darkness. A huge roaring voice filled her ears. Now, with a lurch, the box around her grew smaller yet, pushing on all sides of her, pressing her down toward nothing.

She woke. She was lying on the floor of the tiny attic room where Tierney Rudd had put her; she lay with her thighs drawn up to her chest, her head bent down against her knees. At first the dream gripped her so tightly she could not escape from this knot.

She pried one arm free, and then the other, and lifted her head. She was alone in the room, which was no more than a corner of space under the roof, walled off from the rest of the attic by stacks of heavy boxes. From floor to ceiling was so short a distance that she could barely stand upright. There was no furniture. Dust lay thick and gray on the floor except where she had swept it aside with her hand to make a place to lie down on. A narrow window let in the only light; the door was a trap in the floor. She had slept on it so that no one could get in without her knowing.

Probably no one knew she was here except Tierney Rudd. He had brought her in wrapped in a coat, late at night, through confusion and noise. Hiding her even from the other Vigilantes. Pushed her up through the trap door into the dark, and then slammed the trap behind her. Since then she had been alone.

She crept to the window and looked out through the panes of glass. Down below her was the front of the Vigilante stronghold, with its wall of gunnysacks, its cannon, its rows of white men with rifles. Pigstickers on the rifles. She wondered who they thought they would have to fight. To her right was the painted Eye, which she had glimpsed through the cloak folded over her face when Tierney Rudd dragged her in through the barricade. She could not see the Eye now, only the edge of the board it was painted on. The wind rocked it, clattering it against the bricks of the building.

Below her something was going on. The men with their rifles were running forward, and the gate in the gunnysack wall was opening. She pressed her nose to the glass, trying to see.

A carriage was rolling down Sacramento Street toward the gate. Rows of men with rifles marched alongside it. She looked for Tierney Rudd but did not see him. Looked for other men she knew to be among the Vigilantes and saw none of them either.

She would get no help from them. She was alone and helpless. For a moment a feathery panic shivered through all her veins, her blood turning to dust. She forced it down. She had come all this way on her own; she could face whatever happened. If this was the end, still she had come far on her own path. Below her the carriage wheeled slowly into the yard of the warehouse, and the doors opened, and the Vigilantes pulled out a man who struggled and shouted, to no use. They dragged him into the building. The carriage rolled off again.

She turned away from the window, her fists clenched in her shawl. She refused to be afraid.

After a little while the trap in the floor rattled. She backed away as far as she could and watched Tierney Rudd climb up through the opening. She squatted on the floor, staring at him. He could not stand upright in the small space and hunkered down on his heels, facing her. Their eyes met, and she did not look away; she fixed him with her look, and finally, nervously, he laughed.

"Well, Mammy. Things are a little different, aren't they. I used to bow and beg and kowtow to you, and now you're going to have to beg me."

She said nothing. She gathered all her hatred up into a stone below her heart.

He said, "Did you really think you could keep it up, Mammy? You must have known eventually I'd get the upper hand."

She snorted at him. "You ain't got the upper hand."

That nettled him. His head jerked toward her. "You stupid niggerwoman. I've got you right where I want you."

"You got me," she said, "but the reason you got me is that I got you first. The reason you hate me is because you needed me so much." She drilled him with her stare, the weight of her hatred and contempt in every word. "I made you. You can't change that, Tierney Rudd. Everything you are is because of me. You were just a hungry, proud, crooked little white boy, and without me that's what you'd be even now."

He lurched toward her, his hand cocked up; she sat still, rigid, waiting for the blow, her eyes still fixed on his.

She said, "You gonna kill me, Tierney, but you can't change what happened. That's why you got to kill me. You got to blot out the truth. And the more mean you are to me, the more that shows how much you needed me. But it won't work. You can't escape what is."

He lowered his hand. The effort of controlling himself showed in the bulging of his neck, the flare of his jaw, the slow flush of his cheeks. He said, "I'm not going to kill you, Mammy."

She stared at him, unspeaking. He thrust his face into hers, nose to nose.

"I have a friend with a ship in the harbor, a ship bound for New Orleans. He's going to take you along with him, and when he gets to the South, he'll turn you over to a slave dealer. And they'll strip you naked, Mammy, and sell you to the highest bidder, and you'll spend the rest of your life scrubbing floors. Or worse. Because you're nothing but a nigger slave, Mammy."

She let him talk, the words blowing by her like spume, and then she smiled into his face. "I may be nothing but a nigger," she said, "but I made you, Tierney Rudd. So what are you, then? Nothing but a nigger's thing."

This time he did hit her, across the face, open-handed. It hurt. She kept still, not caring that it hurt, not taking her gaze from him for an instant, not even blinking. He backed off, his face clouded, baffled, twisted with temper, and he wheeled, yanked the trap up, and dropped out of the room. The trap fit back in its hole with a clunk.

She shut her eyes; her cheek was numb. Exhausted, she sat there a long while before she could arouse the strength and will to get up again and go to the window. She leaned her face against the glass and rested her mind, thinking nothing.

The carriage came back, and the Vigilantes led out another man, who did not struggle but walked with a certain pride in the midst of the rifles and pigstickers. She guessed that was Charley Cora, who had a reputation for staying cool-headed. The gate closed.

She pushed her cheek against the glass of the window. She could break the glass with the chair and jump; that would free her, and kill her. The glass was cool and smelled sour. She shut her eyes.

✢   ✢   ✢

Isaac Bluxome tapped his fingers on the table. "Look, Twenty-two, this is a bit sticky."

"Where's the list?" Tierney said. "We have to begin making arrests and gathering evidence." Through the door behind him came half a dozen of the other Vigilantes, their boots loud on the floor, their voices booming.

"Any word yet about Jim King?"

"Still alive," Tierney said.

The man who had asked was a big redheaded Southerner with a gap-toothed grin punctuated by a cold, much-chewed segar. He said, "Kinda tough, since we just convicted Jim Casey of murdering him."

"He'll die," Tierney said. "Just a question of time. King's a tough little bird, but he got shot through the chest, and he'll die."

Over by the wall, a tall, thin man asked, "What about Cora?"

Isaac Bluxome stood up. "That's a little sticky," he said again.

His fingers played over his neckcloth; he looked around at these men with some distaste. Some of the other Vigilantes offended Isaac Bluxome's sense of class.

Tierney clapped him on the shoulder. "You're too nice, Thirty-eight."

Isaac said, "We tried Cora ourselves, and our own jury couldn't convict him of murder. I don't see that leaves us anywhere with him." He took his coat from the back of the chair where he had been sitting and put it on.

"We're going to hang him," Tierney said. "We're cleaning up San Francisco and he's a bad apple."

The redheaded man growled in agreement. His eyes glittered, looking from Tierney to Bluxome and back. "You fellahs see this?" He pulled a ragged piece of paper out of the pocket of his coat.

Tierney took it from him, his attention still fixed on Bluxome. "If we admit we can't do any better than the crook law, Thirty-eight, we might as well not try at all." He lowered his eyes to the paper in his hand.

Words jumped at him. This was a makeshift newspaper. Inch-tall type across the top read VIGILANTES SUBVERT JUSTICE.

"What is this?" He spun toward the redheaded man. "Where'd you get this?"

"They's up all over town," said the tall, thin man, coming away from the wall. "We tore down about twenty that was nailed up to buildings."

Bluxome said, "What is that?" and took the paper.

Tierney said, "It doesn't matter. We know we're right. We're going to hang Casey and Cora, just as soon as Jim King dies, and then we're going to round up every crook and every crooked judge and lawman in San Francisco and hang them too!"

The room was crowded now, with men spilling in from the hall beyond, where the Vigilantes drilled; the sound of his voice had brought in all within earshot, and they let up a thundering cheer. Bluxome looked up from the paper, glanced around, and said, "You know, this could be serious."

"It's meaningless. Forget about it." Tierney snatched the paper from him.

Bluxome was staring at him. "That's a pretty sordid accusation, Rudd."

Tierney read quickly through the smaller type below the head-line. What it said raised the hackles on his neck. "This is a pack of lies."

"You haven't made any moves of your own, under cover of the Committee? It says there you've made arrests of your own."

Tierney crumpled the paper up in his fist. "Nothing of the sort. Look, Thirty-eight, our enemies are going to mount a consider-able effort against us. They'll lie, they'll spread lies, they say anything they can to turn us against each other." He swelled his voice to reach the other men in the room and in the hall beyond. "We have to stick together. Keep our minds on what we're doing. We're saving San Francisco, damn it! Are you going to listen to the crooks?"

The answering bellow shook the room. The redheaded man grinned around his cold cigar. Isaac Bluxome frowned, his fore-head creased; but he did not know, nobody knew, about the little room under the roof and who was in there. Tierney kept his eyes level, his indignation righteous. He would get rid of her as soon as he could, and then nobody would ever know.

He said, "Are you with us, Thirty-eight, or are you backing out?"

"I'm with you," Bluxome said, looking surprised. "As long as you deny it, Tierney."

"I deny it," Tierney said. He stuffed the balled-up paper into his coat pocket. "Right now, I'm going out — I'll need some men to come with me." His gaze swept the pack around him, lit on the redheaded man, on the tall, thin man, two others. "You and you and you. You too. Come with me."

"Where are you going?" Bluxome asked.

"I'm going to find out who's printing this libel against me," Tierney said. "I'll be back. We can't do much until King dies, anyway."

He strode off, not letting Bluxome say or think anything more, and the men he had chosen fell into step after him. In the wide, dim hall beyond, he stopped and sent them for weapons. His gut felt tight. He had not been home in sixty hours; when this was done today, he would go to Daisy, bathe himself in her attentions. First he had to take care of this other, unexpected problem. It should be quick and easy. He knew where this paper was coming from; he could even guess who was writing it. When his men were armed and ready, he led them out of Fort Vigilance and off toward Pacific Street.

30

GIL LEANED OVER THE OPEN BED of the little printing press, trying to read the lines of type he had just set into the frame. He had run out of *w*'s, and what he was trying to say seemed to use a multitude of them; he had to recompose the story to avoid *who* and *what* and *which*, and the effort of reading backward was tangling his mind.

The press was set up in the middle of the empty saloon. The front door was still locked. Perched up on a ladder, Laban was painting the only blank space left on the wall, the area between the top of the door and the ceiling. He never said anything, but Gil was grateful for his presence, for the small sounds of his brush and his breathing, the occasional creak of the ladder. The emptiness of the vast building around them seemed like a dead weight pressing down, a weight that only their living bodies supported.

Gil went back to his work. He was trying to write a diatribe against the Vigilantes, wishing he had more concrete information; he wondered how many people had actually read the first one, of which he had been able to print only fifty copies. He had skulked around the city during the night tacking them up to the walls of buildings, hoping to get some readers that way, but it seemed to him a mere puff of smoke against the storm.

He had to do this, however minor its effect. If he stopped, he might as well join the rest of San Francisco, standing by the road to salute as the Vigilantes strutted by.

Laban said, "Hold on," and leapt down off his ladder.

Gil swiveled around, his mouth open to ask what he was doing, and the first blow sounded on the outside of the door.

He jumped like a rabbit; his hands clutched the sides of the press. A second blow crashed against the door. Somebody was breaking in. Laban bounded away toward the stage, trailing a dribble of yellow paint along the floor. Hastily Gil cranked down the top of the press; the lever stuck with the top plate halfway down. As he struggled with it, another heavy blow struck the door. Laban vanished into the corridor.

The door shattered from top to bottom. An arm reached through, pulling out chunks of broken wood. Gil fought desperately with the press, which would not close, flung a look back over his shoulder, and saw several men clawing their way in through the opening. He yelled. Seizing the half-open press, he dragged it off toward the bar.

Tierney Rudd led the attackers into the saloon. He wore his perfectly tailored coat, polished shoes, a banker's white shirt, but in either hand he carried a pistol.

Gil kept hauling the press toward the bar, knowing this was what they were after, knowing he could not escape, and then wheeled around and stood in front of the press, his arms spread to defend it. "What do you think you're doing?"

Tierney advanced into the middle of the room. "You're spreading lies about me, Marcus, and I'll have your hide for it. You're under arrest." He waved one of the guns casually at Gil. "All right, boys, we're going to burn this place down."

"No," Gil cried.

Tierney smiled at him. "What, do you think you can stop me?" He gave a leisurely look around the room while his men fanned out through it, curious, drawn toward the great picture. "This place is a sty. It's a favor to San Francisco to level it."

One of the other men said, "Hey, lookee here — I know that fellah." He bent over to peer at a face in the vast tangle of the picture.

Another of them, a big redheaded man, sauntered toward the bar. "Any whiskey in this place?"

Gil said, "I'm not going with you."

Tierney shrugged, the smile still pleating his cheeks. "Well then," he said, "your funeral," and he lifted the gun in his hand.

As suddenly as if the threat to the Shining Light had summoned him forth, Mitya bounded through the stage door into the room. His pistol crashed, and the big redheaded man, who was closest to him, gulped and sagged at the knees and slumped down to the ground.

Tierney sprang backward. One of his guns went off, but the bullet sang away into the ceiling. Gil turned and dove headlong over the bar. As he hit the floor on the far side an overlapping volley of shots went off behind him. On hands and knees he scrambled toward Mitya's hidden door in the bottom of the wall. The shooting stopped.

"What was that? What was that?" a breathless voice cried.

"That damned Indian," Tierney yelled. "Kill him! Kill him! He went that way, damn it."

Their feet pounded toward the stage. Gil was remembering that Mitya's gun was a two-shooter, while there were eight or ten guns out against him, and it would take him long moments to reload. His fingers finally located the hidden door but he did not know the trick to opening it, and then another shot rang out and somebody howled in pain.

Tierney swore. "Get him!"

Gil sank back. He could not pry the door out, but Tierney and his men were rushing off down the corridor toward Mammy's room and the clerestory. He leaned against the back of the bar and caught his breath. Maybe now he could rescue the press. He stood, and, to his amazement, there was Mitya, standing calmly in the middle of the room, reloading his gun. At his feet was a body, and another dead man sprawled along the floor below the stage.

The Indian saw Gil and smiled and nodded and beckoned to him, and went toward the stage door. Gil vaulted back over the bar and followed him. Mitya did not go through the door into the corridor. Instead he climbed up onto the stage and pulled back the curtain and slipped by it, and Gil, on his heels, found him in a narrow, dark space no bigger than a closet. A line of boards nailed up to the wall made footholds up to the ceiling. Mitya went up this ladder like a monkey, and Gil climbed after him.

"They're going to burn the building down," he whispered, at the top. In front of them was the narrow opening between the ceiling of the corridor and the roof.

"No," Mitya said. He turned to Gil again, still smiling. He stank of stale whiskey and sweat. "Go find Laban." Crawling up into the space under the roof he vanished into the darkness, his broad bare feet the last of him to disappear. Gil went down the ladder, his heart throbbing.

On the stage he looked around, wondering where to look for Laban. He could hear nothing. The hair on the backs of his hands prickled up. He tiptoed over to the stage door and opened it a crack and peered through into the corridor beyond.

It was empty, except for shadows. He sidled into it, dashed toward the next door, and eased that open enough to see into the clerestory corridor, filled with ghostly gray light.

Nobody here either. He wondered where Laban could have gone, thought of the warren of bedrooms upstairs, and went as quietly as he could down to the cookhouse.

From just outside this door he could hear voices in the room beyond. He recognized Tierney's voice. He stepped back, holding his breath, and stumbled and fell over.

The noise he made was like a crash of thunder. He scrambled up onto his feet again as the cookhouse door flew open, and Tierney and his remaining two men poured through. Tierney shouted, "I've got you, Marcus, stand where you are," and lifted his gun.

Gil backed up in a rush, trying to get out of pistol range. The other two men loitered in the doorway, peering fearfully all around them. "Where's that Indian?" Clearly they had taken notice of Mitya's ability to spring up out of nowhere. Gil wheeled and ran for the door, zigzagging with each step, and a pistol boomed and something pinked his sleeve and thwacked into the wall just ahead of him. He dodged through the door and ran for Mammy's room.

He could hear them shouting in the clerestory corridor, but nobody chased him. Tierney was shouting the loudest. There was a door from Mammy's room to the outside, and Gil went through it, into the damp, foggy air.

Find Laban. He ran along the outside wall of the clerestory corridor; Mitya was planning some new work here and the ground was leveled and the wood stacked, and Gil bounded over the lumber in his path like a steeplechaser. Out of breath, he reached the cookhouse and stopped and leaned against the wall and panted. His legs hurt. A warm, wet trickle ran down his arm, and his palm was already smeared with blood.

He eased his way along to the window, and looked in, and saw the three men bent around the fireplace, building up the fire. Tierney got the coal scuttle and scooped a load of red embers out of the hearth. He swung around, looking here and there, and abruptly he saw Gil in the window.

He yelled and waved his arm, but he did not shoot; his pistols lay on the counter by the sink. Maybe he was out of bullets. But the other men still held their guns. Gil ducked, and a slug crashed through the glass above him, showering him with the splinters. He shook himself all over to dislodge them. A man bellowed, almost in his ear, and smashed out the rest of the window and leaned out.

Seeing Gil, he thrust his arm out, pointing a gun at him, and then, in the cookhouse, another shot cracked.

Gil cowered down, the pistol above him looking like a cannon aimed at his face. The man holding it widened his eyes. Straightened slowly. Pitched forward halfway through the window and lay there, the blood spurting from a hole in the back of his neck. Gil recoiled, his stomach rolling.

Inside the cookhouse, somebody yelled, "I'm getting out of here."

"Damn you," Tierney cried. "Wait. Wait — " And then another shot split the air, and somebody, not Tierney, screamed.

"Damn you," Tierney shouted again, his voice high and wild. Gil stood up, trying to see past the body draped over the windowsill, and the outer door of the cookhouse blew open and Tierney Rudd came rushing through it. Knees high, arms pumping, he wheeled toward the alley and raced off.

Gil sobbed a sort of laughter. He slumped against the wall next to the window, wiped his hand over his face, and said, "Mitya?"

"Here." The Indian came out the door, popping the used caps off the nipples of his gun. He said, "Fire burns, a little. Come help."

Gil went in past him. The fourth and last of Tierney's men lay doubled up on the floor by the end of the table. The scuttle had been dumped over and hot coals littered the floor; Gil could already smell wood burning, and quickly he went for the broom and swept the coals up into a heap. With a plate off the shelf he scooped them into the scuttle. Mitya came back into the cookhouse. He kicked the body.

"Four shots," he said, holding up the fingers of his right hand. "Four kills." He stuck the gun down into the waistband of his pants. Gil had last seen him dead drunk and passed out; now he was sober, or nearly so, standing solid as a redwood on widespread bare feet, the thin smile curving his lips. His eyes glittered. He said, "You do good, Gil." He clapped Gil's shoulder with one hand. "Pull them good." He went on to the little door that led up to the bedrooms, opened it, and shouted, "Laban!"

Gil dumped the dirty coals back into the fireplace. Mitya had used him as a decoy, bait, set him running to draw Tierney's men out, so that Mitya could take them unawares. Gil's stomach still surged. His arm hurt now, and blood soaked his sleeve. He went to the sink in the counter, poured water into it from the bucket, and leaned over to wash his face, but instead he vomited into the water.

Mitya came up behind him and stroked one hand down his back. "What happens? Why Tierney Rudd come here?" Laban wobbled down the stairs, his eyes white.

Gil said, "The Vigilantes have taken over San Francisco."

"Mammy?"

"In their fort. They arrested her. Rather, Tierney arrested her, he's getting rid of her, under cover of all the rest."

Laban said, "Can we get her out?"

"Nobody is getting out of Fort Gunnybags." Gil emptied the

foul water of the sink out the door, put the iron basin back into its well in the counter, and poured in more water. His arm twinged. Unbuttoning his cuff, he pulled his sleeve up; Laban came quietly over and helped him wash the nick in his upper arm.

"Why Tierney come in here?" Mitya asked.

"To get me. I've been — all the newspapers in town are supporting the Vigilantes. I've been trying to print the truth, and they don't like that. I could use some help."

Mitya grunted at him. "I no write." He touched the butt of his pistol. "Only shoot."

"You can shoot only one at a time," Gil said. "They'll get you, in the end. If I can put a thousand of my papers out and around — "

Laban yelped, "Watch out!" and dodged behind the table.

Gil wheeled toward the door; Mitya's gun leapt into his hand. Somebody was in the doorway, shrinking back out of sight even as Gil laid eyes on her, but Mitya had seen her. He put the gun down and said, "Theresa."

The girl crept into the doorway again. Her face was stiff with terror. She wore her favorite yellow dress, stained and rumpled, and her feet were bare. She said, "I heard shots. Oh, my God." Her hands rose to her cheeks; she stared goggle-eyed at the bodies.

"We'd better get rid of these," Gil said.

Mitya ignored that. He reached out and gripped Theresa's wrist and pulled her into the cookhouse and shut the door behind her. "Where you come from? Where the rest?"

"Josh sent me — we're all hiding out, up in Chinatown." The girl gave a gasp of terror, pulled out of his hold, and rubbed her wrist with her other hand. "I gotta go," she said, and turned abruptly.

Mitya leapt between her and the door. "You go. Go find Daisy."

"Daisy!" Theresa gaped at him.

Gil said, "Daisy's on their side, Mit."

"No." The Indian got Theresa by the arm and shook her. "Do what I say, girl. Go bring Daisy."

"She belongs to Tierney," Gil said.

Mitya shot him a look of pent fury, turned to Theresa again, and said, "Do this, then. Go to Josh. Tell Josh, sit there. Stay away from here, wait, take care of people."

Theresa nodded. "I will. Let go of me, Mit, you're hurting me."

"Then come back here," Mitya said.

The octaroon girl licked her lips; her big black eyes turned a moment toward Gil and then back to Mitya. "I'll tell Josh to sit tight and keep everybody together, then I'll come back here."

"Good." Mitya let her go and stepped aside, and she darted out the door into the fog.

Laban sighed. "What we gonna do about our little Mammy?"

Mitya shook his head. "I no know." He went around the kitchen opening cupboards, looking for something to eat; in the course of this prowling he found a bottle of whiskey and took a pull on it.

Gil said, "I don't think we can rescue Mammy, not directly. But maybe we can bring down the Vigilantes."

Laban said, "Writing words? Making papers?" One hand rose, long and limp, and fell again to his knee.

"I need help," Gil said. "By myself I can't print enough papers to have any impact. But if we could cover San Francisco with them — "

Laban said, "Just words, is all."

Mitya looked from him to Gil. "I help you."

Gil said, "I knew you would." He smiled wide at Mitya; the mere fact that he had convinced the Indian lifted his spirits. "Come on. For openers, you can help me get this press unstuck."

31

ISAAC BLUXOME SAID, "We don't need search warrants. We're the people of San Francisco, that gives us any rights we want." He held out a long strip of paper with a list of names on it. "Go find these men and arrest them and bring them here."

"Yes, sir." The young man in front of his desk lifted one hand in a kind of salute, took the list, and went away, trailed by six or seven others. They all carried rifles, the bayonets sharpened to white along the edges; Tierney stood back to let them pass.

"Twenty-two!" Bluxome called. "Where have you been? We've brought in fifty prisoners already."

Tierney went up to the desk, which was carpeted over with lists like the one Bluxome had just given out. The younger man was reveling in his work; he reminded Tierney of something he had read once about Robespierre, that he was born in 1758 but really came alive only with the Revolution. A fire blazed in Bluxome now.

Tierney said, "Any word yet about Jim King?" He was hoping Bluxome wouldn't notice that he had returned alone.

Bluxome nodded. "He's rallying. He may not die after all."

"Jesus." Tierney stroked his hand back over his hair. "Wouldn't that be a mess. What about McGowan?"

"We can't find McGowan. He's taken to his heels like the cur he is. Cora wants to see you."

"Cora. What does he want?"

"I don't know." Bluxome raised his voice. "Three hundred twelve? Come in here."

"I'll go see Cora," Tierney said, glad that Bluxome wasn't more curious, and went out, past the eager young man rushing in to get his list of names.

The wide, open room beyond, where the Vigilantes drilled,

thronged with men. They had thrown up rifle racks along the walls, but only a few arms remained in them. The place was filthy, the air thick with dust, the floor littered with crumpled newspapers, hats and jackets thrown into corners; on a table under one of the front windows a man sat loading guns, the surface before him spread with a dozen pistols, a scale, a sack of gunpowder, a heap of lead balls. Tierney went across the room to the door at the far end and let himself through into the stairwell.

He thought they should put a sentry on the door, but probably it was needless, with a hundred Vigilantes always in the drill room. He climbed the steep, narrow stairs to the second floor, where they were keeping prisoners.

Cora was in a room almost directly under the trap door, beyond which Mammy Hardheart waited. Tierney paused, looking up at the square outline in the ceiling. He had wanted to tell her that the Shining Light was burnt, and he considered doing that anyway, but the corridor was always busy now, and he did not want to risk being seen going up there.

She would be hungry and thirsty by now. Let her suffer. He turned to the room where Charley Cora was.

What had happened at the Shining Light still played on his nerves. He had thought he was master of this, but one damned Indian had jumped into the middle of his plans and kicked them into pieces. Now he felt around him the presence of other unforeseen enemies, eyes on his back, guns aimed at him from the shadows. He stood in front of the door for a long time, getting up the courage to open it.

Cora was alone. He sat at a little table, his coat draped neatly over the back of his chair, a deck of cards in his hand. When Tierney came in, the gambler looked up and set the deck of cards on the table before him.

"Thank you for coming," he said.

"What do you want?" Tierney asked.

"I know you're going to hang me," Cora said. His voice was even, his hands steady, his eyes direct. "I want you to bring Belle here, and a priest, so that I can marry her before I die. I've promised her that for years, and I mean to keep my word to her.''

Tierney took a deep breath; it rattled him to see Cora so calm. He said, ''Jim King hasn't died yet.''

''I didn't shoot King,'' Cora said. ''Mine did die.'' His mouth warped into a smile that vanished as fast as it had appeared. ''Will you respect my request?''

Tierney licked his lips. It occurred to him that he had never married Daisy. When this was over they would get married, quietly, so that no one would remember they had lived for years in sin. He said, ''I'll do it. Of course. Tomorrow?''

''Whenever convenient for you.''

Tierney said, ''Very well then.'' He stood there a moment, awkward, unsure. Cora picked up the deck of cards and began to deal out a set-up for Idiot's Delight. There was nothing else to say. Tierney went out of the room. On the way down the stairs, he met a man hurrying up to find him and tell him that Jim King had finally died.

Frances stood at the window, looking out. It was night, but she was afraid to sleep because of the dream of the box, which came as soon as she shut her eyes, and went away only when she wakened. She had paced around the room until her feet hurt.

Anyway, even though it was the middle of the night, they were doing something out there, and obligingly enough they were even doing it on her level. Men carrying rifles and torches swarmed over the flat roof. Two little platforms jutted out from the edge, one on either side of the board that hung down over the wall.

The street below was packed with a great crowd, picked out with lantern light and torches. Their noise penetrated the glass window like the buzz of honeybees. They were all looking up at the roof. She pressed her cheek against the sour-smelling glass, trying to see more of what was going on there.

A man stepped out onto the farther platform, a tall, slim man in a white shirt, his hands behind him. He stood there as if he were ready to give a speech. Behind the nearer platform there was a struggle going on; she could not see it clearly because of the angle.

She knew what was happening. She could see the rope tied around the neck of the man in the white shirt.

Several men wrestled at the edge of the roof; finally one of them stepped onto that platform, against his will, leaning back, trying to get his feet onto the safety of the roof. Hands on his shoulders pushed him forward. He wobbled; with his hands tied behind him, he lost his balance and almost fell. The crowd in the street below let out a screech.

He caught himself. He straightened, his shoulders hunched, and his face turned toward Frances, and for a moment she thought he saw her. Then his mouth opened, a round O in his face, and the platform below him gave way.

It must have been on hinges; it did not fall, it simply dropped flat against the wall. The man dropped, but not far. Heavy as a sack of stones he pitched ten feet through the air and hit the end of the rope with a thud she could hear and a jerk that spun his body around. The crowd screamed, their arms waving like a thousand little feelers. A moment later the man in the white shirt fell too.

He had not fought, the other man had fought, but it made no difference; they hung side by side against the wall of the building, their heads cocked over at crazy angles. Frances lay down again on the floor and closed her eyes. She could sleep now, she thought. There were worse things in her mind now than little boxes.

32

THERE WAS NOTHING TO EAT at the Shining Light except some
cornmeal, salt and sugar, a lump of lard. Gil mixed the cornmeal
with water and fried it in the lard, making little cakes like the ones
his mother had called hoecakes, and he and Mitya ate them while
they worked the printing press.

Of course the Indian knew nothing of writing, but he was a
steady, tireless worker; with him to lay on paper and work the
crank while Gil inked the press and removed the finished work, the
broadsides flew off the press like falling leaves. By midnight they
had five hundred copies, and they were down to the last hoecake.

Gil broke it in half and held out one piece to Mitya, who
grunted at it and shook his head. Gil said, "They aren't very good,
are they. I'm sorry."

"Not so bad," Mitya said. "But not kasha." He reached for his
bottle of whiskey, now nearly gone. He drank more than he ate,
but he seemed almost sober. Gil remembered seeing him passed
out blind drunk and took his mind hastily off that subject.

"Kasha. What's that?"

"Undersea people food. They make good food always, like
mother food."

"The undersea people. What a strange name. Why do you call
them that?"

"They say Russians. Aleuts. You know Aleut?"

"Not really. Were they maybe some tribe of Esquimaux?"

Mitya shrugged off that word. He sipped again at the whiskey
and held the bottle out to Gil, who shook his head at it. "Aleut.
Fish eaters. They come with the Russians, when they build Fort
Ross. From the north, where the sea smokes." His voice softened
with pride, or memory, or regret, and he looked away, shielding
something from Gil. "I am part Aleut."

"Why did they leave your country?"

Mitya faced him again, shrugging. "No more otter. When the Russians go, Aleuts go. You know Sitka?"

"I've heard of Sitka. I've heard Sitka is as wild as San Francisco."

"More wild. More north, more cold, more wind. But not so many people."

"When were you there?"

The Indian's gaze slid away from his again. Protecting something, as before. "My grandfather tell me. My grandfather Aleut."

"But he left. Why didn't you go with him?"

Before him the Indian swelled, drawing in breath, and his lips parted; he seemed about to call someone. Then he shrank again, looked down, impassive, dark, closed over the old wound. "No want me," he said. He stooped, flicking one finger along the edge of the stack of paper. "What now?"

"We have to take them out and put them up on walls all around San Francisco, so everybody can see them."

Mitya made a sound in his chest. "You go. Not me."

"Mit! You said you'd help me."

Mitya pushed at the papers. "You do this. I help you plenty. I do other thing. You go."

Gil was silent. He felt betrayed, abandoned in the middle of the battle. Mitya lifted the whiskey bottle again, the glass covering his face. Stooping, the white man gathered up the papers and looked around for something to carry them in. There was a sack in the corner, and he stuffed them into it.

"Well," he said, "I'll be back."

"Watch around," Mitya said. He cradled the bottle in his hands. "Vigilante patrol all night, all over."

"Yes, I know." Gil pressed his lips together. He wanted to shout at Mitya, blast him for giving up now, with the task only half done, but he guessed that the Indian was loath to leave the Shining Light unguarded, and maybe he was right. There had to be some place to come home to. He said, loud, "Well, I'm going," and hoisted the papers onto his shoulder, and trudged alone to the door and into the cold, foggy night.

Theresa came back, later, and Mitya left her with his gun, to stand watch over the Shining Light. He went out across the dark town to the Saint Francis Hotel, where Tierney Rudd kept his rooms and his woman.

In the bottom floor of the hotel, at the back, was a place for servants. A narrow stair went up from it to the floors above. Mitya went up the stair to the top floor.

Mitya had been there once, to move heavy things, and he stood remembering it in the dark room where the stair came up. The sleeping place was away on the front of the building, and he went carefully through the space between, over a floor as soft as sheep's wool, past objects smooth as water under his hands. The place smelled like nothing he knew, no scent of earth or rain or people, only a dry cleanness. Before he opened the door to the last room he knew Daisy was inside.

She was alone. He waited by the threshold a moment, listening to her even breathing. This room smelled like crushed flowers. Through the cloth hangings over them he could see the shapes of the windows, letting in the light from the front of the hotel; he could see much of the room with that light. The floor was deep as redwood duff, the bed lay between uprights like trees. He went to the bed and sat down on the edge of it, next to her, and when she startled, awakening, he put one hand on her shoulder and held her fast and laid the other hand over her mouth.

She struggled, frightened, screaming against his palm, her body bucking under his grip. He lay down on top of her and said her name, over and over, while she thrashed, and at last she heard him and lay still.

"Mitya," she said, out of breath.

He straightened, letting her go. On a little wooden table by the bed, a candle stood, and he snapped a lucifer to flame and lit it. Daisy sat up in the bed, into the spreading yellow candle glow.

"Mitya," she said. "What are you doing here? You have to leave, you can't be here."

He said, "You come back now. No time anymore. You come now."

The dim candlelight washed her face clear. She laughed as if he had told a joke, and looked around at the darkness, and then pulled the cover over herself. "What?" She looked up at him, still laughing. "Whatever do you mean? I can't leave. Now, you really must go; if you're found here it won't be good."

"You come back," he said. "Now."

"Mitya! I can't go anywhere. Tierney has my carriage. It's the middle of the night." She pushed at her hair with one hand, her gaze drifting around her again, searching the darkness.

"Where Tierney?" Mitya asked.

"Tierney is at Fort Vigilance." Her face swung toward him, bright and clear as a bowl of water. "He's saving San Francisco. He says I should stay here and wait for him. When he comes back we're going to Oakland, to see how they're coming with our new house." She pulled a smile across her face like some new dress to put on. "I'm to have a wonderful new house, Mit."

He said, "Tierney no save San Francisco. Tierney take Mammy. Tierney break the Shining Light. You come now, no more time left, you no come now, then never, you lost."

The smile stayed a moment longer, a wall against his words, but then the words got through, and the smile broke. The face it left behind seemed to shrivel. Suddenly she looked old. The woman she would be if he did not reach her now looked out at him through that face. She said, "I can't." Her voice quavered. Her gaze tore away from his and traveled around her again, looking for something to hold on to. She said, "Tierney took Frances?"

"Yes."

"Well then, she's safe. They're business partners, you know, Frances and Tierney." She said this not to him. To the dark.

He reached out and took her face in his hand and turned her back to him. "You no think that. No lie, girl. Know truth, at least."

She blinked; she swallowed once. Her eyes were wide and glossy in the candlelight. She said, low, "The others — they're all right? Josh and Laban — Phineas?"

"Safe. Scared. Hiding."

She swallowed again. "I can't do anything, you know. I can't stop him." She tried to move her head, to turn away from him, but he held her, his hand along her jaw, he made her face him, and she shut her eyes instead. "He'd just hunt me down. I can't get away. And anyhow, I'm not sure I want to. I have my new house. All my clothes. Jewels, I have so many jewels. My maid." Then she opened her eyes and said, "Where's Gil?" In her eyes the tears shone like diamonds.

He sat back, drawing his hand away from her. "Shining Light."

"He's still there? Isn't he — isn't it dangerous?"

"He fight. He no run." Mitya stood up beside the bed and reached out his hand to her. "You come now. One more chance. Daisy, come now, or never have anything."

"Never have anything." She gaped at him. "I have everything now! I told you! I have everything!" She flung one arm around her. "Look! And you want me to give it up!"

"No," he said. "None of this yours. Tierney has. You, nothing. Once, yes, you great woman. Now, like this." He smacked the bed with his hand. "Just a pretty thing like this." Batted at the bedcovers. "All Tierney's. Nothing yours."

She stared at him, wide-eyed, and the tears rolled down her cheeks, and she made no answer. He held out his hand again, and this time she took it.

She said, "Gil won't take me back. He thinks I'm a whore."

"Maybe. Maybe no. Better try."

"I have to get dressed," she said. "Go in the next room."

He went into the next room; his blood sang. But when she came out there again, all dressed, the candle in her hand, he saw at once she was losing heart.

She wore a long skirt and shirt, with a cloak around her shoulders, and strong shoes, but her face was taut across the cheekbones, and she licked her lips. Still, she went toward the way out, a door that had its own little room, with a looking glass on the wall and a small table with a lamp.

There she stopped. She said, "Maybe I should leave a note."

Mitya folded his arms over his chest. "Why? You want him come?"

"I should leave him a note." She went to the little table and pulled the underside out partway and took a piece of paper out. "He might worry," she said. "He might think I was kidnapped." She groped around on the top of the table and in the drawer, not finding what she was looking for; she was crying again. He waited. He meant to carry her off by force if he had to. That would bring other people down on them; that would make trouble, he saw a bad end coming of that. She was still searching around the table, and now she took the whole drawer out.

"I know there's a pen in here somewhere!" She turned the drawer over, and the bottom fell to the floor. Not the real bottom. The drawer was still whole in her hands. A piece of paper floated down from the space between the two bottoms of the drawer.

Mitya stood there and did nothing, more interested in the drawer with two bottoms than in the paper, but she stooped and picked it up.

"Holy God," she said, in an undertone.

He moved a step closer, looking over her shoulder. The paper had a fancy picture on the top, two animals holding up an oblong shape between them. It was a shield; he had seen something like it, at Fort Ross. One of the animals was a horse with a horn on its head, the other looked like nothing he had ever seen.

Daisy said again, "Holy God."

"What?"

She swung toward him. "This is from the British consul. They're offering him and the Vigilantes everything they can carry to turn San Francisco over to the British Empire." Her fist clenched above the paper. "Damn you, Tierney — "

Mitya said, "Show Gil." He moved toward the door, reaching for the latch.

"Oh, yes," she said. "Gil has to see this. Let's go, hurry, before

Tierney comes back." She pulled the cloak around her and hurried out the door and down the stairs, so fast he had to leap to keep up.

33

GIL WAS TIRED; his arms hurt from lugging the sack of paper, from holding papers up against walls, from banging in the tacks. He had more than two hundred of his broadsides left and he could not go home, not yet. He trudged down Stockton Street, the sack over his shoulder, the hammer in his hand, keeping a watch out for the Vigilante patrols.

They had passed him twice already, a man on horseback carrying a lantern on a pole, two men on foot. Nothing else moved through the night streets. Here and there a lamp burned, in the window of a house, on a sconce above a door, but even the stray cats were staying out of sight. The fog drifted by the rooftops, pooled in alleyways, smelling of the harbor. To Gil, his own footsteps sounded loud as drums.

He trudged along Market Street, past dark shops and wagon yards, stopping every few strides to nail up another of the broadsides. The sameness of it sawed on his nerves, set his teeth on edge; suddenly he hated it all, he wanted to throw down the sack and run and keep running until around him there was nothing he knew, nothing familiar. He turned into Dupont Street, tacking up papers.

Ahead, he saw something moving. He drew back into the shadows of a doorway, thinking it was the Vigilante patrol. Then a voice called his name.

The hair on his neck stood up. He pressed himself against the doorway; he must have misheard.

"Gil? Is that you?"

His knees quivered. The sack of papers dropped from his hand, and he went out to the street and said, "Daisy."

She came up the street toward him, only a shape in the dark, her shoes tapping on the planks. "Gil. I found something, you have to see it. It's important." She came straight to him, holding something out in one hand.

He said again, "Daisy." His hands reached out and closed on her arms, holding her fast. "What are you doing here?"

"Gil," she said, breathless. "I came to . . . to bring you this." Her voice faltered. In the dark he could see only the shape of her face. She said, low, tremulous, "Gil, I was a fool. Please give me another chance."

"Daisy," he said, and his arms went around her, and he gathered her in against him. "Oh, God, Daisy." She tipped her face up toward his, and he kissed her.

"Gil." Her mouth was soft and sweet against his. Her hair smelled of perfume. She was crying. "Gil, I love you, I knew it when I saw you at the opera, when somebody said your name, I knew. I was just too much of an idiot to admit I'd been wrong."

"My dear one," he said. "My dear."

Gradually he realized they were standing in the middle of Dupont Street, in the dark, with dangers all around them, and he straightened, still holding her. "We have to get out of here," he said. "Where did you come from?" Then, by the side of the street, he saw Mitya.

His arms opened; he gripped Daisy by the hand and took a step toward the Indian. "Mit," he said. "So this is what you had to do."

"Go home now," Mitya said, coming toward them. In the dark he seemed to be smiling.

Gil pulled Daisy's arm in through the crook of his elbow. "I still have a lot of papers to put up."

"I do," Mitya said. "You go back. Theresa alone."

Daisy said, "Thanks, Mit." Her weight leaned against Gil. He slid his arm around her.

"You sure?" Gil said. But he was already going down the street, Daisy warm and quick beside him. "You be careful?"

"Go," Mitya said. He went into the doorway and emerged with the sack of papers and the hammer. He was definitely smiling. Gil led Daisy away down Dupont Street; after only a few steps, he had forgotten, again, all about the papers and the Vigilantes.

Mitya was still thinking about Gil and Daisy when he started home toward Pacific Street, just after daybreak. He had run out of whiskey and needed a drink. Maybe that was why he paid too little attention as he walked across the Plaza, and let the Vigilante patrol come up behind him.

"Hold it right there!"

He jumped, spinning around to face the voice. A man on a horse was trotting toward him, a gun in his hand. Mitya whirled and raced toward the alley beside the Bella Union.

Behind him a whoop rang out. "Catch him!" Hoofs pounded after him. The Plaza was empty, stark in the first daylight, but there were new trees planted at the far end, and the ground was all loose and dug up. Mitya stumbled on the soft dirt, and the man on the horse galloped around ahead of him. Mitya swerved, trying to dodge by, and the rider shrieked and spurred his horse, cutting him off from the alley, turning him back into the middle of the Plaza.

There the other two Vigilantes waited, their arms out, herding him like a rabbit. He stopped, panting. One of the men on foot shouted, "It's an Indian!"

"I'll show you how we handle Indians," cried the horseman.

Mitya started running again, dodging back and forth; he glanced over his shoulder and saw the rider hurtling down on him, and in one hand he was swinging a riata. Mitya's breath caught in his throat. He ran straight at the nearer of the men on foot, who backed up fast like a crab running and pulled out a gun. Mitya shrank from the gun. He spun around and headed toward the post office, and through the air a whistling sounded, closer, over his head, and the loop of the riata settled around his shoulders.

He yelled as the rope tightened around him. He got his hands up, caught the twisted hemp line just above the slip knot, and was jerked off his feet. He landed on his back. He clutched the rope with both hands, trying to flip onto his belly, to get a footing on the ground and enough slack in the rope to free himself. The rider let out a screech and spurred his horse away, and at the end of the rope Mitya bounced and slid across the rough ground.

Sand clogged his eyes, his nose, his mouth. He skidded along on his forearms and belly, burning the skin off; the rope ripped his hands and he let go and a rock gouged his chest and a terrible stab of pain shot through his groin and his thighs. He thrashed out with his legs, trying to turn over onto his back, and the rope slackened and he lay still a moment, gasping, blind with pain and dust. The horse thundered toward him, blowing soft snorts through its nostrils. The rider whooped and whistled, almost on top of him, and the hoofs pounded by him within reach of his flayed hands, and the rope snapped taut and dragged him off again, banging and rolling across the ground.

He shut his eyes, bit his lips together, ducked his head down to keep the sand out of his nose. His elbow hit something and his arm went numb, and the rope wrenched him over onto his back. He sobbed and choked on a mouthful of dust. The horse was slowing again.

He doubled his legs up, coughing, his arms fiery with hurt, and fought the hurt, forced his arms out, to seize hold of the rope again, to gather up some slack while the horse turned and raced back toward him. The rider bent and swiped at him with his rifle butt and Mitya flinched from the blow, but as the horse went past he got his feet under him and ran after it, clutching the slack of the rope in his bloody hands. The horse was galloping straight across the Plaza toward the Bella Union. Through the bleary pink haze of his vision he could barely make out the white flagpole in front of the government office. He swerved toward the white stripe of the pole. His knees hurt and he stumbled, but he kept running, his lungs full of dust and blood. The rope was tightening, whipping the slack out of his hands, and he darted around and around the flagpole, carrying the rope with him. The rope snapped taut; it bit his arms like a blade, jerked him up fast against the flagpole, and held. At the far end, the rider let out a surprised yell and sailed backward off his horse.

Mitya staggered up, fighting with the rope. A shot rang out. The other Vigilantes were running toward him, yelling and shooting. He fought his way out of the loop of the rope and ran away from them. The horse, saddleless, riderless, was galloping around the end of the Plaza; its rider sat on the ground, his feet still in the stirrups, and jerked his rifle up to his shoulder. Mitya's chest hurt, every breath a flame searing his lungs, his throat. He heard shots but felt no blows of bullets. His feet went on running. His eyes saw nothing but a red blur, but his feet knew where to take him. He stumbled down the alley past the Bella Union and ran headfirst into the fence there, and dropped to the ground and crawled under the fence. After lurching to his feet, he shambled on toward the next street.

No more shots. The fence had stopped them. They would circle around. He kept running. As he ran he clawed at his eyes with both hands, scraping gouts of mud out of the sockets, until he could see the shapes of the buildings ahead of him, see the color of the sky. He staggered down between two buildings, hit a mound of trash and waded through it, coughing and spitting out sand and blood. Ahead of him somewhere was Pacific Street. Ahead of him somewhere, the Shining Light. His legs were dead. His knees locked. He sagged to the ground.

"Mitya."

He struggled up onto all fours. "Here." He tried to shout but his voice croaked, feeble as a baby's. He crawled a little way and slumped to the ground again. Lying there he hacked the dust from his throat.

"Mitya! Mitya — "

"Here," he tried again, louder this time. He rolled onto his back and raised his arms, like a child, toward that voice, toward his friend, who had come back for him. A moment later Gil was bending over him.

"Oh, Jesus."

"Help me."

"Yes, hurry, they're coming." Gil hovered over him, trying to pick him up. "God, where can I touch you and not hurt you?" Mitya stretched one arm up and caught Gil by the shoulder. The white man heaved him to his feet. They stumbled away down the alley, away from the pounding feet and raw voices calling behind them.

Josh waited in the street outside Fort Gunnybags until he saw Tierney Rudd leave. Then he picked up his willow broom and went to the gate through the wall of sand-filled sacks.

A man with a rifle stepped into his way. Josh kept his gaze on the ground, his head bowed; he knew how to look like a slave. "Mr. Rudd send me to clean up," he said.

"Rudd's not here," said the sentry.

"Let him in," someone else called, from the steps of the building. "The place is a mess. Rudd knows what he's doing."

"Thank you, sir." Josh bobbed his head to the sentry and shuffled into the building. He kept himself low-headed, round-shouldered. The place was full of white men, and they all carried guns. His back tingled. It was hard to breathe deep, bent over like this. He remembered that from his days in Louisiana: being a slave meant you never breathed deep, you never looked up, you never strode out. Big as you got, you were always small.

In the big, filthy room beyond the first door, he put his broom to use, pushing the dust into a heap. Half a dozen men were marching up and down the room, performing military salutes with their rifles. He stayed out of their way. Coming on an empty gunnysack in a corner, he gathered garbage and papers and stuffed them into it. In this manner, cleaning and stooping and picking up trash, he made his way into Fort Gunnybags.

After a while, softly at first but then louder, he began to sing.

Frances walked around and around the tiny attic space, her teeth clenched. Her throat was dry with thirst, and hunger had clamped her belly against her backbone. She had not seen Tierney Rudd in two days, since he had promised to sell her into slavery.

Maybe he was too busy to care about her. All the Vigilantes were busy, busy with their work. When he had dragged her in here this place had been all but empty. Now people filled it. Through the floor below her she could hear the rustle and pound of their comings and goings, hear voices in the hall and in other rooms. Now and then men screamed or cursed or prayed; things hit the walls, doors slammed.

No one came near her. She thought of banging on the floor, but she was afraid of who would come to find her. She dragged herself around the little room, her feet scraping on the floor. She had to get her nerve up. She meant to break the glass in the window and throw herself down. Before she went back to slavery she would die, she would die free. But she could not force herself to the act.

If she waited too long — if she waited too long —

Her brain boiled, so loud with her thoughts that it took her a while for her mind to recognize what her ears had long been picking up. When she did hear it, she caught her breath fast and dropped to the floor by the trap, put her ear against it, and listened. Far away, through walls, through the constant undertone of all those other people, she heard a deep, mellow voice, singing.

Her knees trembled. Her hands clutched each other. She thought: This is a dream.

The voice was coming closer. She lay down flat on the trap, she pressed her ear to the wood. Now she could make out the words, and they reached into her like hands and seized her by the soul.

"O my sister sittin' on de tree of Life, and she yearde when Jordan roll."

All over her body the skin sizzled, electric. Dark and sweet, that voice, rising from the deeps, from the heart still quick after the whip and the chains and the long journey, from the undefeated memory. She whispered the words along with that voice.

"Roll, Jordan, roll. Roll, Jordan, roll."

Trembling with relief, she lay against the trap, her eyes shut, and waited for him to come near enough that she could tell him where she was.

"O my soul arise to Heaven, O Lord, for to yearde when Jordan roll."

"Any sign of McGowan?"

Bluxome shook his head. "No, no. He's gone south. We've gotten rid of him, which is what matters." He leaned his elbows on the desk, which was covered with stacks of papers. "Are you going to be around now for a while? There's a lot to be done. We have to have some trials. The place is full of prisoners now, and we have some confessions."

"All in due time." Tierney sat down on the only chair. Out the half-open door he could see men drilling in the main room. He was hungry, and he had to get home soon and see to Daisy, but first he meant to dispose of Mammy Hardheart. He had gone to the harbor that day and found the sea captain to take her to New Orleans; all he had to do now was to sneak her out of here.

Bluxome spoke briskly, his raised hands a tent before his lips. "I think we ought to get to work on it. I've called in Post and Dow and a couple of the other Executives, and I think we can run three or four trials tonight." He flipped at the papers before him. "The governor's sent us another letter."

"What did he say?"

"It's right there in front of you; take a look."

The letter lay at the edge of the desk. Tierney picked it up and began to read it; he was up on his feet again, without realizing it, walking around the room; he could not sit still anymore. The governor's letter was a bleat of terror, a plea that the Vigilantes "remember the cherished rights of Americans" and "uphold the ideals of law and order that our traditions are based on, back to Magna Carta." He laughed.

"We ought to answer him," Bluxome said.

"Oh, don't bother. He's just covering his back."

Bluxome's mouth kinked into a grimace. "You take this thing so lightly. I wish you were here more — doing more of the work. Then you'd see that it's a serious business."

Tierney's head snapped up. "I assure you, I understand the seriousness of the business."

"Now, calm down," said Bluxome. "It's just — whenever I need you, whenever anybody wants to talk over major issues, you're gone somewhere. Frankly, some of the other men are getting cold feet."

Tierney snorted in contempt. "Let them put their socks on. Or go home to their fireplaces." He lowered his gaze to the letter.

Bluxome said, "We need to get rid of some of these prisoners. We're out of room, and the men are bringing in more all the time."

"Then hold a few trials, damn it." Tierney tossed down the governor's letter. Between his teeth he said, "I'm doing my part, Thirty-eight. If you don't like it, I can leave."

"Nobody wants you to leave." Bluxome's voice grated with annoyance. "You're too important." He lowered his hands flat to the top of the desk, and his voice smoothed out to a soothing murmur. "You get things done. Like having the place cleaned up. The dirt was unbearable. It's hard to maintain our dignity when we're knee-deep in grime."

Tierney had noticed that the drill room was swept, but he had given it no more attention than that. He lifted his head, startled, and stared at Bluxome, who was fiddling with the papers on his desk.

"Maybe you could get in a few more of those colored. The one did a good job, but he did only the downstairs and the upstairs hall." Bluxome was sorting his papers neatly into stacks. "See if he'll come back tomorrow. I'd like this room swept."

Tierney almost said, "What colored man?"

Bluxome was scribbling on a list. Suddenly cold, Tierney stared at him, his mind working through this. A colored man had walked into Fort Vigilance. A colored man had cleaned up. And all the colored men in San Francisco sprang from the same foul hole.

His legs twitched, wanting to run out, race up the stairs and down the hall to the trap door into the attic, to make sure she was still there. In his ears there was a dull pound like a hammer.

Bluxome said, "We could put on some trials tonight. Maybe we could do them in batches." He lifted his head, frowning, his eyes keen. "What's wrong, Twenty-two? Are you listening to me?"

"Yes," Tierney said. "I'm sorry, I was just . . . it's nothing. It's not important. You're right, we should put on some trials. Let me see the evidence you've got." He leaned toward the desk full of papers, his gaze lowered, unwilling to meet Bluxome's suspicious stare. "You said there were some confessions?"

34

MITYA WAS SCRAPED and bruised and bloody, but all he wanted was whiskey; when he had the bottle in his hands, he lay down in the warmth of the cookhouse and went to sleep. Gil slept also, most of the day, leaving Daisy and Theresa to keep watch for the Vigilantes.

Daisy had given him the letter from the British consul, and in the afternoon he got up and spent the rest of the daylight setting the text into his printing press. He ran only a few copies of it at first; he had an idea he might not need any more than that. At sundown he went up onto the roof.

Mitya was there, sitting on the strip of old ship's deck that formed the balcony across the front of the Shining Light, from which he could see all over Pacific Street and most of San Francisco. When Gil sat down next to him, he held out his bottle, and Gil took a sip from it and handed it back, his belly on fire.

"How can you drink so much of that stuff?"

Mitya laughed. He lifted the bottle to his lips. His hands were thick with scabs. He wore a clean shirt, covering the rest of his wounds.

Gil said, "How do you feel?"

"Not enough drunk."

The raw edge in the Indian's voice, as much as his words, sent a shudder down Gil's spine. He aimed his gaze out over the rooftops of the city, spreading away from him in wooden waves toward the horizon. The night was taking it in, roof by roof, like soft velvet folds. There was no fog. The moon stood above the far edge of the world, a silver seal.

Gil said, "It's hard to believe that seven years ago this was nothing but sand."

Mitya grunted. The bottle rose again and poured liquid down his throat. He settled it down again, both hands on it, stared out across the city, and said, "Damn San Francisco."

Gil smeared his hands up over his face and dropped them in his lap again. "What happened — that was bad, Mit, but it was just a few men. This is our place, that's what we're fighting for, isn't it? To save San Francisco?"

"You do that," Mitya said. "I just hate white men."

"This city belongs to you as much as anybody. You helped build it." Gil leaned toward him, trying to read his face in the twilight. "God, Mit, where else would you have been what you are?"

Mitya gave a shake of his head. "The men drag me, they no know me. No care. All they see is Indian. What I am — " He thrust the scarred palm of his hand up into Gil's face. "This. Just this."

Gil blurted out, "It isn't that bad," and was at once ashamed. He lowered his eyes. The Indian's voice ground on, taut with old rage.

"I build Shining Light. No place else. No white man hire me build his house. I make wonderful thing, but no one sees. I no go into white store or white saloon. I fight — no difference. They look by me like nothing. They never know me. Nobody know me."

"What about Mammy's war?" Gil asked. "You told me once she knew how to fight back."

"Mammy lose." Mitya reached for his bottle and took another long slug of the whiskey. "Mammy good."

"No," Gil said.

"Yes. Yes. Mammy good, in here." Mitya touched his head and his chest, over his heart. "No come out. Only bad come out. All good lost." He lifted the bottle again.

Gil said, "Easy. I need you."

Mitya slammed the bottle down. "Nobody need me."

A dozen arguments bubbled into Gil's mind, and he almost said them, but did not. What Mitya said was truer than anything Gil could say, even if the Indian could not master the language.

Like a flash of light through the dark, the realization came to Gil that Mitya was mastering the language in the only honorable way he could. He used it, because he had to, but he dismembered it, tore it apart from its grammar, bent it and broke it until it was his, and not the other way around.

But the language rolled right over him, as San Francisco rolled right over him, took what he gave, let him fight until he was exhausted, swept on without even noticing that he was there. Like Mammy, all the good was lost.

"Mit, where are your people now?"

The Indian shrugged. "Maybe dead."

"You should go back."

"No back. No place."

"The place must be there, at least."

"No whiskey," Mitya said.

That silenced Gil. He turned his gaze back toward San Francisco, seeing it all differently now, not a booming glory but a stacked deck, where a man like Tierney Rudd got rich and a man like Mitya, in some way a genius, rotted and was ruined.

He sat silent, separated from the other man by a hundred years of guilt. He saw what had been done to Mitya as if it had been done to him; as he got used to that he saw that it had been done to him: he was as much a prisoner of his color as Mitya was. Suddenly he longed to touch the other man, skin to skin. His courage failed him. He knew it would do no good. So he sat there, cold air between them, and stared out across San Francisco, and Mitya sat there, and drank.

The north wind was blowing clouds across the sky like frightened sheep before a wolf; it lifted the great Eye on the front of Fort Gunnybags and clattered it against the bricks. Along the barricade of sandbags stood men with rifles, the bayonets jutting past their shoulders. In the middle of Sacramento Street Gil was trying to work up the will to go in there, among the Vigilantes.

He was alone. There was no use bringing Mitya, even if the Indian had been willing. The letter from the British consul and the copies he had printed were in his coat pocket. He had thought this all out ahead of time, he knew the best course was to go straight ahead, and yet now that he had to do it, his rabbit heart failed.

He thought about Daisy. He had not made love to her, wanting to marry her first, but he had held her in his arms half the night, talking, sharing with her his torments over Mitya, his fears and hopes, his dreams for the future. She had held him tenderly all the while. She seemed happier than he had ever seen her, in spite of everything.

Now he was risking his life, risking her happiness, their common future and their budding dreams, and he had forgotten why. The vast building stood like a tomb before him. Mammy was in there somewhere. That drowned his mood still deeper, thinking of Mammy buried alive. If she could not manage the Vigilantes, she who understood power so well, he had no hope.

"I love you," Daisy had said. "Be careful."

If he did not do this, he might as well be Tierney Rudd.

That cleared his head. He remembered what he hated about the Vigilantes, and what he was doing, and why he was doing it. His feet began to move. He walked toward the gap in the sandbag wall, toward the bayonets and the huge painted Eye.

The sentry stopped him. "Who're you?"

"My name's Gil Marcus. I have to see somebody inside."

The sentry was a boy in his teens, with the fanatic look of one committed. Like most of the ordinary soldiers of the Vigilantes he was a working man, not rich, not Tierney Rudd. He held his rifle crosswise between them and said, "Nobody goes in. They's holdin' trials."

"I have to see Tierney Rudd," Gil said. Several of the other men were listening with attention, and he raised his voice. "Send somebody, tell him I'm here, he'll let me in."

"Not today," the sentry said. "They's holdin' trials, I tole you." But behind him one of the other men turned and walked up the steps toward the door.

Gil asked, "Who are they trying?"

"Crooks," said the young sentry. His cheeks glowed. "Murderers and thieves and crooks, every last one of them. Time we get through, San Francisco will be holy as Jerusalem."

"Are you going to hang them?"

"Hanged them others." The boy shrugged one shoulder, careless: not his neck. "They doin' themselves in now, though, 'fore we even get to 'em." His mouth split into a grin. He was missing two top front teeth. "One of 'em killed hisself, last night."

"Killed himself." Gil stared up at the great Eye, the stone face of the building wall, feeling a thread of panic like a worm in his heart. "You're sure it was a man?"

"Was Yankee Sullivan. Stabbed hisself in the heart, 'cause he was guilty as hell and scared as sin." The boy spat.

Gil lowered his gaze to meet the boy's. "You mean, a prisoner in your jail here got hold of a knife to kill himself with? How could that happen?"

The boy shrugged again. His face was bland as butter. Set fast in his certainties, he had no need for reason. "Guilty as hell and scared as sin," he said again, a litany, and broke into his gapped smirk.

Behind him the man who had gone into the building came out again. "Let him in. We're gonna arrest him."

The sentry barked a laugh. "You too, hunh?" His gaze moved up and down over Gil, surveying him. "Turnin' yourself in? Go on." He stepped aside.

Gil went up the stairs; his feet felt like lumps, his legs barely controllable, his chest a seething cauldron. The man waiting for him swung back to let him pass and then fell in behind him. He walked through a big, open hall full of armed men. Every eye turned on him. His nose itched. He was sweating and he smelled himself and knew he stank of fear. Of guilt; of sin. A sudden panic seized him, he was an idiot, here they controlled even the meanings of words, and what he was doing was treason to them.

He stopped. The man behind him said, "Get going," and something hard and pointed poked him in the back.

"Where?" he said, helplessly. "Where do I go?"

"In there." The Vigilante pointed toward a door in the side wall of the vast main room. "Got to write you in first."

He had trouble getting his legs moving again. The bayonet jabbed him between the shoulderblades, helping him along. Almost on his toes he propelled himself across the room to the door.

The room he went into was smaller than the one he left, and jammed with people. In two rows of chairs along the back wall sat a dozen men, all in coats and hats, their faces solemn as Dutch burghers. He knew most of them, merchants and bankers, leading citizens, the heart of the Vigilance Committee. He knew better than to nod and wave.

In front of them, at a cluttered table, a younger man sat, a pen in one hand; this, he guessed, was Isaac Bluxome, the secretary of the Committee. Beside him, stiff as a starched collar, was Tierney Rudd.

Bluxome said, "Well, you're Gil Marcus?"

"Yes, I am." Gil went forward, into the middle of the room; for the first time he noticed the five prisoners lined up against the side wall, their hands manacled together. These men had no starch left in them at all; they drooped as if they were already hung, their eyes hollow, their unshaven faces sickly pale. He turned away from them. Fixed his gaze on Tierney Rudd.

He said, "I have —" and Bluxome cut him off.

"I'll ask the questions. You're Gil Marcus, and you've been

printing and putting abroad seditious and libelous papers against our work?"

"It isn't — "

"Just answer the question yes or no," Tierney said. His voice was rough as ripped wood.

Gil said, "It isn't libel."

"Yes or no," Bluxome said, writing. "Did you print those papers?"

"Yes," Gil said. "I — "

"You're under arrest." Bluxome stood up, nodding to the Vigilante with the rifle who still stood beside Gil. "Take him up and find a cell for him. Bring me back the number."

"No," Gil said. "Listen, I — "

"If you have anything to say in your behalf you can say it when your time comes," Bluxome said. "Right now we are supremely busy men, doing the necessary work of law and order, and we haven't got time to listen to craven drivel. Take him."

The Vigilante's hand gripped Gil by the elbow, pulling. Gil snatched the paper out of his coat.

"I have another one right here, if you'd care to read it."

"Evidence?" Bluxome's eyebrows climbed up toward his hairline. "That's obliging of you. Twenty-two, if you will."

Tierney got up from the table and strode forward. His face was set like a mask, except for the rapid blinking of his eyes. He said, "This is foolish even for you, Marcus," and took the paper. He nodded to the Vigilante. "Get him out of here."

Gil cried, "Read that. Read that." The hand on his elbow was hauling him back toward the door. With a surge of despair he realized Tierney was winning. Gil had walked into this like a fool, handed over everything, would disappear now, maybe forever, neatly tucked away like Yankee Sullivan. Bluxome had turned back to his writing. The Vigilante was wrestling Gil toward the door. Tierney looked down at the sheet of paper in his hand.

He gave a bleat, like a cat stepped on. His head jerked up, shot a look of fury at Gil. Two steps carried him across the room to the lamp on the wall, and he thrust the paper into the flame.

Bluxome looked up. The twelve men against the back wall stirred, murmuring.

Gil shouted, "Why didn't you burn it when you got it, Tierney?"

Bluxome said, "What is that?"

Nothing now, thought Gil. The ashes of the paper fluttered to the floor. Tierney stood there with his hands at his sides, his face the color of a gravestone. Bluxome stood up.

"What was that?" He shook his head at the Vigilante holding Gil. "Let him stay a moment."

"It's a lie," Tierney said, hoarse. "I never responded, I gave them no encouragement, I never agreed to anything."

Bluxome was staring at him, his mouth slightly open; the men in the second row of chairs were leaning forward to watch.

Gil said, "I have another copy. This one's printed, as you see." He reached into his coat for a second paper. His voice was quavering like a leaky organ pipe. "I have it set up in my press, and unless I get some satisfaction from you, my confederates will have it posted all over San Francisco by tomorrow morning." He held out a printed copy of the letter. His hand shook so hard the paper crackled. Bluxome came forward and took it from him.

Tierney wheeled toward him. "I'm not responsible for that — I didn't solicit it, I agreed to nothing."

One of the twelve men against the wall stood up. "What the hell is this?"

Bluxome was reading; at first he was silent, but then suddenly he burst out, " 'And when your Committee has destroyed the local government, the arrival of a British man-of-war in San Francisco Bay could quickly insure that the city becomes subject to Her Britannic Majesty, Queen Victoria.' "

His voice went on, but an avalanche of other voices overwhelmed and buried it. All the men in the twelve chairs were on their feet, all shouting, to one another, to Tierney Rudd, to Bluxome. Gil pressed his palms together. The paper in Bluxome's hand was only a copy. The real letter was gone now, the only hard evidence lost forever; frantically he conjured up arguments in his own support.

Tierney Rudd was his best witness. The tall man stood staring at the floor, his hands clenched at his sides. Every line of his body testified to the truth of the letter. Maybe he had not responded, as he claimed. But he had not destroyed the letter, either. Gil swallowed, his muscles loose, his stomach quivering. Tierney lifted his head, and their eyes met.

"How did you get that?"

Gil did not answer. Tierney looked ten years older than he had ten minutes before. One clenched fist rose, the arm cocked, the blow ready. Gil braced himself. Bluxome walked up to Tierney and seized his arm and tried to turn him, shouting at him, and Tierney shook his hand violently off, flung a wild glare at him, and walked long-striding out the door.

Gil backed up a step. Bluxome threw him a quick, oblique look as full of venom as a serpent's tooth, and then turned toward the other Vigilantes. They were arguing. Red-faced, one of the bankers walked out of the room, his arms swinging, and another man followed him, this one a commission merchant with six warehouses on the waterfront. Bluxome took two steps after them, his mouth open, trying to call them back. They left. The ones who remained were snarling and yelling and shaking their heads. Bluxome went into their midst, gripping one man by the arm, whispering into another man's ear. Gradually they quieted. Gil took his handkerchief out of his pocket and wiped his face. The Vigilante with the rifle scowled at him. "You son of a bitch."

Gil gave a shaky laugh. "What — I'm ending your fun?"

"Just you're a son of a bitch." The Vigilante turned and walked out of the room. The door slammed.

Bluxome turned, in the midst of the other men. He said, "Marcus. Do you realize what you're doing?"

Gil nodded. "Yes. I'm going to put this paper out on the street tomorrow. Unless you stop this rebellion." His gaze widened, taking in the others, who were going back to the row of chairs.

"Because if it goes on much longer, you know, the British won't really even need your cooperation. You'll destroy the city. They'll raise the Union Jack over the Plaza without any help at all."

They glowered at him. Hating him for this, as the common soldier did. One by one they took their seats again.

Bluxome slid onto his chair. His coat was rumpled. His hair hung in his eyes and he tossed it back. With both hands on his lapels he made the coat straight too. He coughed, cleared his throat, and spoke in a loud, clear, calm voice.

"We have, in fact, achieved our work. The hold of the Democratic machine on San Francisco has been broken forever. The murderers have been hanged who otherwise would have gone free. Other wicked men will see this and know to steer clear of San Francisco."

"Oh, yes," Gil said. "You can bet on that. And anyhow, if they do come, who'll know the difference?"

"Shut up," Bluxome said. "You've served the cause of the crooks, as far as I can see. All you newspapermen, you think because you write things down you make them happen." He thumped his fist on the table. "We will disband the Committee, our work having been accomplished, by midnight tomorrow. After that, if you dare attack us with this filthy libel, you'll be subject to the civil law."

Gil said, "That's good enough."

There was a growl from the watching men. Another of them heaved his bulk up off his chair and tramped out, slapping on his hat as he went out the door. As the door swung closed Gil saw a swarm of men waiting outside, peering in through the narrowing gap.

He nodded to Bluxome. "Is that all?"

"Get out," Bluxome said.

Gil said, "Thank you." He glanced once more at the ranks of angry faces behind Bluxome, swung around, and left.

Tierney sat in his carriage in Sacramento Street, staring straight ahead. He felt as if his skin were missing, as if he had no defense at all against the cold world around him.

"Where to, sir?" the driver asked.

Tierney opened his mouth to give orders, but nothing came out. The street was quiet; all the Vigilantes had gone inside as word of what was happening there reached them. Even the sentry was gone. A few curious people loitered on the opposite sidewalk. He felt their looks like pins stuck in his flesh.

"Sir?" the driver said.

Soon everybody would know. He was disgraced again, and once again, not his fault.

He would go home. Maybe Daisy was still there. He would explain to her. But he shrank from the thought of it. She would know too, she would despise him, as all the world would despise him. Not his fault. She would never believe that. No one would believe him.

"Sir?" The driver twisted in the high perch before him, looking back, puzzled. Tierney cleared his throat.

"Take me to the Jackson Street wharf. I'm going to Oakland." And never coming back, he thought. I'm never coming back.

"Yes, sir."

The lurch of the carriage slung him deep against the seat. He put his hat on, tugged the brim down low so that no one would recognize him, and shut his eyes.

35

GIL OPENED THE DOOR into the little room at the end of the corridor. Daisy was there, sitting in the stuffed chair, her face turned toward him. Gil started forward, and then his stomach clenched, tight as a fist.

Mammy Hardheart was there too.

Small and fierce, she sat in the middle of the room, a pistol in her lap. She said, "Thank you, Gilbert. Now get out."

He braced himself. A quick look at Daisy saw her white and still as a piece of ice, her hands in her lap. The sweetness and happiness of the night before had been wiped from her like old paint. Gil brought his gaze back to Mammy.

He said, "I broke the Vigilance Committee. I and Mitya."

"Yes," she said. "You did what you had to do. Now get out."

"I'm not leaving without Daisy."

Mammy lifted the gun. "Then I'll kill you."

"Damn you," Gil cried. "She loves me. She wants to go with me — Daisy, tell her."

Daisy's face seemed to buckle, like something under pressure; she lowered her head. She said, "Gil, I have told her. That's why she wants to kill you." She turned her haunted face toward him, her eyes sunk deep into her skull, all her beauty gone. "I made a promise to her. I'll stay and do as she wants, and she'll let you go."

Mammy cocked the pistol. "Take the deal, Gilbert. This is your only chance. Get out of San Francisco."

Gil flung out one hand toward Daisy, beseeching, desperate. "You gave her to Tierney."

"She didn't love Tierney," Mammy said. She leaned forward; her teeth showed. "I couldn't lose her to Tierney. She was always mine, she will always be mine." She raised the pistol in both hands. "Go now, Gilbert Marcus, before I shoot you."

Her gaze was perfectly steady; she did not blink. In her hands the gun muzzle looked at him like a third eye. He stood square on his feet and said, "Shoot me, then, because I'm not leaving Daisy."

Daisy moaned, "Oh, no." She slid down off the chair and knelt at Mammy's feet. "Please — I'll do whatever you say. Only let him go. Frances, please. Don't hurt him, not over me. I couldn't bear it."

Gil stepped toward her, his hands out; to see her begging for his life was like a knife ripping him in half. Mammy recoiled like a snake. One hand swung out to push Daisy down and away; the other raised the gun.

She said, "Too late, then, Gilbert. Good-bye."

From the room behind her Mitya stepped. He moved so fast, so silently that she had no warning, even though Daisy gasped and Gil jumped back a foot. The Indian's arm reached down over Mammy's shoulder and caught her hand with the gun, and the gun went off. Gil ducked down, hearing the thin zing of the bullet shearing past his head. Helpless, Mammy struggled against the Indian's grip.

"Damn you! Let me go! I'll kill you too."

Daisy leapt to her feet. Her eyes turned toward Gil and she plunged across the room, shielding him with her body. Gil wheeled, his arm around her, urging her ahead of him through the door. On the threshold, he glanced back.

Mitya held Mammy fast, one arm wrapped around her, lifting her off the floor as she fought. Frances Hardhardt screamed. Writhing and twisting in Mitya's arms she spat another curse at Gil and sobbed. Gil turned and ran out the door and down the corridor after Daisy.

The door swung idly half open. Mitya let Mammy go. He backed off, staring into her eyes, making space between them.

The gun lay at her feet. She stooped and snatched it up and aimed it at his chest. Slowly he backed toward the door, pushing at her with his stare. She raised the gun and cocked it and pulled the trigger. Unloaded, it made only a little click, but he jerked, anyway, as if a bullet struck him. He backed another step toward the door. She cocked the gun again and triggered it again; another click. And again. Shooting him even without bullets. Shooting him with her eyes like black stones driving him out. Riddled with her hate, he reached the door and went out.

He walked out at his own pace. He went on toward the saloon, and Josh came into the corridor and stopped.

"What's going on? I heard a shot."

Mitya jerked his head in the direction of the little room. "Mammy."

"Mammy." Josh started that way. Stopped, looking sharply at Mitya. "She all right?"

"All right. Mad. Hateful."

"At you. You goin'?"

Mitya nodded. "Me, Daisy, Gil. Not come back, Josh." He put out one hand, and the big man gripped it, hard, and held him.

"Never? Not gonna see you no more? Not any of you?"

"No more."

Josh stared at him, unblinking, taking this in. Finally, he said, "We'll keep the Shining Light. Laban, Phineas, Theresa — all of us. The way you did, true-built, Mitya."

"Good," he said. His voice gave way. He could say no more. He pulled his hand out of Josh's. "Good-bye."

"So long, Mit." Josh lifted his hand up toward his hat, making a kind of salute, and his gaze swung down toward the little room at the end of the corridor. "I'll see to Mammy." Heavily he walked away. Mitya went on out to the saloon.

Laban sat there on his ladder, working on the space over the door, his brush in one hand, a pot of paint in the other. Mitya slowed, thinking of saying good-bye to Laban, too. But Laban was painting; there was no talking to him when he was painting. Mitya looked around the room, seeing himself everywhere on the many-colored wall.

For Laban, maybe, Mitya would never leave this place. In his own mind, he was already gone. He circled around the ladder and went out to the street.

For a moment, standing on the sidewalk, he saw no sign of Gil and Daisy and he thought they had already left. The air was cold and raw, as if rain was coming. Then Daisy stepped out of the alley across the street, and she rushed to him and embraced him.

"Thank you." She pressed herself against him, her mouth against his cheek. "Thank you, Mitya."

He had never held her before. He knew he would never hold her again. He kissed her face, all wet with tears. "Go," he said. "Go fast."

"Yes." She drew back, her hands slipping down his chest. "Take care of youself, Mit. Be happy."

He knew he would never be happy. He looked past her at the man walking across the street after her.

Gil reached his hand out. "Mitya," he said, and then he was coming closer, following his hand. He put his arms out, and Mitya took him in like a brother, chest to chest. He clutched him tight, because he would never see Gil again either, because all this was gone now.

Gil stepped away, his face working, his eyes watery. "You told me once, Mitya, to go home. Now I'm telling you."

Mitya said, "Yes." It was the only word he could force past the heaviness in his throat. They were already walking away. Daisy was already turning her back, one hand out to Gil, and Gil had hold of her hand and they were walking away from him, down Pacific Street, away into a place where he could not follow.

He stood there in front of the Shining Light and watched them rush away down the street, hand in hand. He stood there a long while, long after he had stopped seeing them.

The night was falling thick and gray around him, the air moist on his face, smelling of old smoke. He lifted one foot and set it down. Lifted the other and put it past the first. Going nowhere. Just away. Keeping his back to the Shining Light, to see it never again.

36

IN THE DARK, THAT NIGHT, in the Plaza, Mitya knocked a man down and stole his money. Then when morning came he crossed the bay on a steamer ferry to Sausalito, bought a horse and three bottles of whiskey, and started north.

He told himself he was going up to the gold mines on the Trinity. But after two days' riding and one of the bottles of

whiskey he followed an old trail over a ridge covered with redwoods and looked down at the ocean, at Metini.

When his gaze first fell on it his heart quaked as if it would crack
in half. The long sweep of slope ran away from him down toward
the ocean; the spring grass was still green and the wind bent it
down in long ripples and waves, as if something unseen ran here
and there through it. Down by the shore the clump of black
cypress rose that had shaded his childhood, his growing up, his
marriage and the murder that ended his life here. To the south of
the cypress was the remnant of the old Russian fort: a few posts, a
collapsing house, the chapel with its round peaks. Beyond that,
the limitless blue ocean.

North of the cypress was the village where his people lived. He
rode down toward it, watching for white men — for any men; he
steered well away from the ruined fort, picked up the crease in the
land that led down between the fort and the village, and followed
this gulch as it turned wide and deep and choked with brush.
When he could see the meadow he stopped.

His belly went cold as a stone. The meadow was empty. The
village was gone.

After a while he turned and rode north, keeping to the high
ground. He would go to the mining camps on the Trinity. He
would live there. He would build another Shining Light. He
thought that over and over, like putting down planks over a hole
in the road.

He rode through the old fields of the undersea people, now
buried in berry brambles as high as his head. The winter cold had
turned the old growth purple and black, but new green shoots
arched up and over the dead vines. Deer trails wound through the
brambles. He spooked a doe champing on the crunchy leaves, and
she bounded away, her tail high. Underfoot, sometimes, he could
still make out the rippled marks left by the Russian plows.

Everything he saw struck his eyes like a lash on an old wound.
Everything he saw he knew. There was the rock called Tilted
Baskets, the old snag like a great broken hand sticking up, which

he and his brother had once climbed, and then Vanya had been afraid to come down. The flat rock poking out of the sea cliff, where they had gone to watch for the undersea people coming back.

They had not come back. Nobody came back to Metini. He was the only one.

At sundown he found a sink at the edge of the forest, a hole in the ground where the wind had torn a redwood out by the roots. He stopped and made camp, hobbling the horse, building a little fire. He had bought a loaf of bread and a chunk of cheese on his way, and he opened the second bottle of whiskey. The sink was full of ferns. Around the hole's edge young redwoods had sprouted, like a fence, giving shelter from the wind.

He had to save the whiskey. He sipped it, just a little at a time, staring at the fire. Not thinking of Metini. Not thinking of those people. The whiskey made him numb. He drank more of it than he should have. He was starting to fall asleep when suddenly he felt someone watching him.

He twisted, looking over his shoulder; his hand fell to the gun lying beside him. Above him on the rim of the sink a woman stood.

A low cry left him. He started up, and she was gone.

"Anna," he said. He staggered up, drunk, his blood surging, and went after her, scrambling up out of the redwood hole, down toward the meadow.

She was walking off across the meadow. The moon was rising and the long grass was silver and she was a black form walking through it. Surely she was a ghost, walking on the moonlight, in the wind. He called, "Anna!"

She turned and faced him, and he went after her, his breath short, his chest painfully tight. With the moon above her he could not see her face. She was a black shadow, an emptiness.

She said, "So you have come back."

"Anna," he said. He still thought she might be a ghost. "I thought you were gone."

"We had to leave Metini," she said. "The white men drove us out. But we are here still, we always will be." Her voice was cool as the moonlight. She seemed utterly unsurprised that he was there.

He said, "I came to see you."

"You cannot see us," she said.

"Anna, please."

She said, "You stink, my brother Mitya. You stink of whiskey and blood and white men." She turned and walked away from him.

He stayed where he was, watching her go. He felt wrapped around and around with iron ropes, weighted down with things that were not his. Finally he went back to the sink and drank most of the rest of the whiskey.

In the morning he saddled the horse and rode on, his head pounding, following the trail north. He knew it; this was the way to Sacred Mountain, to Clear Lake. The wind drove in off the ocean and he was cold. He had nothing left to eat and would have to kill something soon, and he rode with one hand on his gun. His head hurt.

He passed the copse of cypress where he had rested with his father once, hunting deer. The air felt like a weightless wing against his cheek. The smell of the air penetrated him with its astonishing sweetness. He thought over and over of his sister, cradling the pain, nourishing it.

Around noon he stopped, the gun still clutched in his hand. He had come to the bank of a creek running down to the sea; the trail had been flooded out and the bank broken, and he could make out no way to cross it. The wind was rising, carrying bright, hard beads of moisture in it. Out to sea a storm had come up, a bundle of clouds dragging dark sheets of rain along beneath. Its first winds struck him, and the horse snorted, moved, danced on its feet, wanting to find a shelter.

He held fast where he was, not for a reason, but only leaning back against the push. The rain swept down on him, hard, cold, plastered his hair down and soaked his clothes. The horse turned its rump to it, and so Mitya's back to it. The cold shocked him and he began to shiver.

The rain stopped. Trembling all over, he stared out over the sea cliff, where low clumps of trees grew, windworn and twisted. Down by the edge of the cliff was a bulge of gray rock his people called Whale Watching Place.

He was shuddering still. The wind flattened his sodden clothes against his chest. The land held him like a fist. He felt his father here, his mother, their souls in the long grass, their eyes in the wildflowers.

If he went much farther north he would come to the river; beyond that was land he did not know, where no one knew him.

The horse snorted and pulled at the bit, wanting to move on. The sun was coming out, a brief, fierce blaze that dazzled on every slick wet leaf, on the flat blade of the sea. He felt something in his hand and looked down and saw the gun.

He had to have something to eat soon. He had to have the gun to shoot something to eat. But he was shaking so much he knew he would never shoot straight enough to kill anything. The sun faded. Night was falling. He opened his hand and let the gun drop. Pulling the horse around, he went back the way he had come.

He did not know how to find her again except to go back to the sink where he had camped the night before. The rain returned, driving him on, a wet scourge on his back. When he reached the sink, he let the horse go without even taking the saddle off and crawled into the shelter of the hole and opened the last bottle of whiskey.

She came late in the night, when the rain had stopped. She said, "You should have made a fire."

He sat with the bottle in both hands, staring at her, while she gathered dry wood from under the bank of the sink, cleared space, dug a little hole, set wood in.

She said, "Where are your fire-making sticks?"

He grunted at her. From his pants pocket he took a tin of lucifers and lit the fire.

"See," he said. "I can do some things better."

"Oh, yes," she said. "That's why you are here now, isn't it. Mitya!" She leaned toward him, and when he lifted his head, she struck him in the face.

He bridled, but even his temper was dead now. She stared at him across the little garden of the flames.

"You can come back," she said. "You can come home. But you must clean yourself."

"I can't," he said.

"We will help you," she said. She reached out toward the bottle of whiskey.

He snatched it back from her. He knew she would throw it away. He clutched it against his chest and glared at her, and she stood up.

"Good-bye, Mitya." She walked off through the brush, into the darkness. He sat there staring at the fire, his fingers tight around the bottle.

After a while he lifted it up to drink from it. His lips touched the cold glass and he tipped it up and the whiskey came burning down into his mouth, and he felt it wiggle itself down into him, creep and crawl out through all his body, replacing him with itself. Eating him alive. He lowered the bottle, and at once he wanted another drink.

He put his feet on the ground and dragged himself upright. She had gone out there, somewhere. He could find them. He fell, going up the bank of the hole, and dropped the bottle, and scrabbled desperately around for a long moment before he found it again. Pulling himself up by the bendy trunks of young redwoods he reached his feet and went out to the meadow. She was out there somewhere. He trudged across the meadow, tripped, and fell again.

Falling knocked his insides loose. He vomited. The stench gagged him and he heaved over and over, braced up on his arms and legs, into a pool of steaming whiskey. Empty, exhausted, he swayed over it, his head hanging. The rain beat lightly on his back. He straightened onto his knees. He needed another drink.

He saw himself as a tool the whiskey used to drink itself, a foul sewer.

He said, "Anna." The rain washed him. From his mouth to his backside his gut felt raw and parched and hot. He reached toward the bottle and took hold of it, but when he lifted it, the smell reached him through the rain, sour and harsh for the smell of the rain around it.

He drew in his breath and let it out, a long sigh, while the rain streamed down over his skin and through his clothes to the ground. Slowly he lifted the bottle in his hand and turned it over and watched the whiskey run out. The smell made his belly roll again. He stumbled away from it and fell again and crawled, this time, all the way back to the sink and the fire.

"Here," she said. "Eat this."

He lifted his head; he had known she was here, but he could not remember when she had come. He was shaking all over. His teeth rattled. When he tried to lift the cup to drink he could not hold it, and he dropped the hot mush all over himself.

"Ah — ah — "

"Oh, Mitya," she said, and cleaned it off him, and made him more, and this time she fed it to him with a spoon. He lay there quaking. When the spoon came toward him it looked gigantic and he was afraid of it. She pushed the mush down into him and he vomited again and she cleaned it and him up again.

Other people came. He did not know if he had slept or not. His skin was burning and itching, and all he could think of was whiskey. He lifted his head and moved it around, to bring everything under his eyes, and saw he was not in the sinkhole anymore. He was in a lodge made of redwood slabs, and Vanya sat across from him.

Other people came, his kindred. They stayed there with him and Anna. When his legs jerked and his skin crawled they walked with him around and around the meadow, and they covered him with blankets when he was cold and pulled them off again when he was hot.

They built a sweathouse and sat in it with him and talked. They told him who had lived and who had died since he went away, they told him about what had happened when the Americans came and said they could no longer live at Metini. They told him how the white men shot at them sometimes, for sport, as if they were deer.

Mostly they told him old stories, tales of his father and his grandfather, of the undersea people, and of the time before the undersea people came. As the whiskey dried up out of him they filled the space it left behind with stories. Slowly he grew steadier. Slowly he stopped thinking all the time of whiskey.

They did not ask him where he had been. He began to forget that. San Francisco grew old and small in his mind. He forgot what Gil Marcus looked like, what Daisy looked like. He forgot Mammy Hardheart. He forgot the Shining Light.

He began to remember stories also. One night as they sat in the sweathouse, a little silence fell, the men around him tired and empty, and suddenly he was speaking of the time when the undersea people left Metini, when he was a boy, when the Russians sold Fort Ross, and the Russians and the Aleuts walked down the path in the sea cliff, down to their ships. Many of them wailing and crying, they carried their lives away in bundles, they took their wives and children, even those who belonged to Metini, and they got into their ships and sailed away under the sea again.

When he said this, from around the sweathouse came low voices saying, "Hai, hai," because they remembered, too; it was their story, too.

Then the next day they took him away from the meadow, down toward the sea, to a place where a young redwood stood. They put him into the lower branches of the tree, and then they set to work to chop it down. He sat in the branches of the redwood and watched them hack at the tree with axes. They used white men's axes, with metal heads, but they talked to the tree as they cut it. When it fell over, Mitya fell with it, unhurt.

Then they trimmed off the top of the tree, leaving a trunk twice as tall as Mitya, and they set one end into the ground. Anna took him and stood him up against the tree and wrapped a rope around him, tying him to the tree.

"Here," she said. "Hold this." She gave him the ends of the rope.

Quietly the other people gathered around him. Not only the men were here now but the women also. No one spoke to him. They brought slabs of redwood and set them in the ground in a ring around the tree, like a fence. They brought more redwood and laid it across the space between the fence and the center tree, to make a roof. Mitya stood in the middle of this, clutching the rope that bound him. He was afraid, like a baby being born. When they had made the house around him, they came into it one by one, and some sat down with drums and pipes and made music.

Then, one by one, the dancers came. He did not know them now. His brother was not there, but a Big Head was there, with a round headdress spiked and thorned all over. His cousin was not there, but a Bear Man was there, covered in skins. They danced around him in circles, stamping their feet in rhythm. Their voices sounded, low and steady, like the thumping of their hearts. Mitya's legs quivered, but he could not lift his feet. His muscles strained and jerked, but he was bound still to the centerpost. Anna stood before him. She held out her hands to him and began to dance.

He said, "I can't."

"You can," she said.

"I can't," he said. "I'm tied to this tree."

She said, "All you have to do is let go," and then she danced away. He stood there shaking a little, longing for his freedom. His hands were clenched tight. The others whirled around him, dancing. His feet began to move. His chest swelled with the first deep breath of his life. The ropes still bound him, as his will had always bound him, to change everything, to make everything himself.

He felt the rhythm of the drums and knew himself the drummer. He felt the movement of the dance and knew he was a dancer.

He felt the redwood tree against his back and knew he grew here, like the tree, and nowhere else.

He saw that she was right. He had fought all his life, struggled all his life to destroy himself, when the true way lay before him, and he had only to enter into it. Then he opened his hands. The rope fell away from him. The weight of his will lifted from him. He gave himself up to the truth. He stepped away from the tree, in among his people, and joined them in the dance.

Two days after Gil and Daisy left, the Vigilantes marched through San Francisco, thousands strong. They turned their guns in at Fort Vigilance, gave the city to the government again, and went back to being ordinary men.

Frances Hardhardt did not go to see this. She saw it anyway, because Laban painted it into the last space left to him, onto the wall above the door of the Shining Light.

She sat there on a stool and looked at the painting. Slowly people were coming back to the saloon, to drink, to sing, to dance, to gamble, to pour money into her hands. She was rich already; she would be richer still. But she knew it would not be the same, and being rich was a poor substitute for what she wanted to be. She had forgotten, somehow, what that was.

No matter. The moment was past. The city at the edge of time was gone now, time had caught up with it, swept on by toward the next horizon. San Francisco was locked in place, with its bricks and mortar, its laws and outlaws, its certainty of itself; it could only grow older, it would not change. The fulminating turbulence that had made everything possible had settled into an even pattern of straight lines and right angles, of expected things. She would go on, but whatever she did now would be only a repetition of something she had done before. There was no newness left for her. Laban had closed the ring. She wondered if she would ever again leave the Shining Light.